THE GOOD TURN

DERVLA McTIERNAN

THE GOOD TURN

Published in 2021 by Blackstone Publishing
Cover design by HarperCollins Design Studio
Cover images: Jetty by Paul O' Hanlon/Getty Images;
sunrise by Robert Canis/robertharding/Getty Images;
all other images by shutterstock.com

Printed in the United States of America

ISBN 979-8-200-69634-5
Fiction / Mystery & Detective / Police Procedural

1 3 5 7 9 10 8 6 4 2

CIP data for this book is available
from the Library of Congress

Blackstone Publishing
31 Mistletoe Rd.
Ashland, OR 97520

www.BlackstonePublishing.com

For Freya and Oisín,
(with apologies that this is neither the Wren & Robin book, nor the one about the witches and Volcano Mountain).

Tuesday, September 1, 2015

ANNA

Dublin, Ireland

The waiting room was ugly and neglected. It had been cleaned recently—the overpowering smell of disinfectant was testament to that—but in a desultory way that did nothing to brighten the grubby walls or lift years of ingrained dirt. The disinfectant failed to completely mask the smell of body odor and Anna sat with one hand in her daughter's and the other to her mouth and nose. The room was half-full. Mostly addicts waiting for their methadone appointment, from the look of them. There was an old man in the corner, coughing and coughing with his mouth wide open. A wet, porridgy, stomach-churning cough. He choked, then coughed again, harder, and something splattered on the tiles in front of him. *Jesus.* Anna looked away, squeezed Tilly's hand for comfort. The little girl didn't react. She was distracted, absorbed in reading the posters stuck to the noticeboard on the opposite wall. One poster dominated the board. It had a white background and jolly red letters, was a bit Christmassy-looking.

> *Do you use snow blow? People who take snow blow may take more risks. People who inject snow blow are likely to inject more often, therefore increasing the risk*

of sharing injecting equipment. Using snow blow may also enhance your sex drive, increasing the risk of unprotected sex.

God. Anna gave Tilly's hand a little pull, drawing her attention away from the poster. "Won't be long now, love," she said. "We'll be in and out, and then I'll bring you to school, all right?"

Tilly's gray eyes darkened at the mention of school, and Anna tried to smile reassurance at her, felt the smile fail on her lips. Tilly did have a few friends at school. Some of them were right little bitches, always ready with a game—as long as that game involved hurting someone. But at nine you just want to belong, don't you? To be part of something.

"Will we do something nice this weekend, do you think?"

A young fella sitting across from them and a few seats down looked at Anna as if the invitation had been meant for him. He'd been sitting there just like they had for the last hour and a half, his right hand picking and picking at his track pants. Pick-pick-scratch, pick-pick-scratch. Anna gave him her best you-must-be-fucking-joking look and turned back to her daughter.

"We could go to the library," she said. "Get you a few new books." Tilly smiled, but there was no spark to it. They went to the library every Saturday. "Or we could go to the zoo. What would you think about that?" Anna wanted to bite the words back as soon as they left her mouth. The bus trip alone would be at least ten, tickets another twenty or thirty euros. But Tilly's smile widened into something almost convincing and Anna forced herself to smile back.

"Matilda Collins?"

Anna stood. The receptionist nodded in the direction of an open door.

"He's ready for you."

Anna went in, Tilly following so closely on her heels that they almost tripped over each other. The doctor didn't look up when they entered just kept tapping away, head bent over his keyboard. He was youngish, red-haired, freckled. The beginnings of a bald patch.

"What can I do for you today . . . Anna, is it?" His eyes were kind. Anna sat. Tilly hovered beside her.

"It's Tilly," Anna said. "Her teacher said I should come and see you." Had demanded it actually. Had picked up the phone and threatened to call in the social worker if Anna didn't do as she was told.

"Yes?"

"Because Tilly hasn't been speaking," Anna said.

The doctor's eyes flicked to the little girl. He gave her a little encouraging smile. "Right. And how long has this been going on?"

"About a month," said Anna.

"A month?" He frowned.

Anna swallowed. It had been three months. Three months of silence. "Yes," she said.

The doctor was more concerned now; Anna could see it. Could see the beginnings of mistrust hidden behind a veneer of warmth.

"Any other symptoms?"

Anna shook her head. The doctor wheeled back on his chair and drew Tilly toward him. Massaged her throat, then had her open her mouth so he could look inside with the help of the little flashlight thing and a popsicle stick. Tilly stared up at him, eyes wide, body weight shifting. She looked like a fawn that might take flight at any moment.

"Are you sore here?" he asked, pressing on her throat.

Tilly shook her head.

"Nothing hurts," Anna said. "I'd know if something was hurting her. She's just decided not to speak. That's her choice, isn't it?"

"I don't see any signs of physical trauma. Nothing to suggest a t— . . . a lump of any kind." He'd been about to say tumor. Cancer. Jesus. The idea had never occurred to her.

"Which means this may be psychological," the doctor continued. "Can you think of anything that might have triggered Matilda to react in this way? A stressful event? Something upsetting?"

Anna shook her head.

He cleared his throat, lowered his voice. Didn't quite meet her eye. "It will be difficult to help Tilly, you know, Anna, if I don't know everything there is to know. I do understand that some things are hard to talk about . . ."

Anna said nothing, pressed her lips tightly closed.

"What are your living arrangements at home?" He looked at her bare left hand. Her fingernails were bitten bloody. She clenched her fist, too late. "Is Tilly's dad in the picture? Or another man?"

Anna lifted her chin. "What's that got to do with anything?" she said.

"I'm just . . . I'll refer Tilly on to an ENT specialist, in case there's something physical going on here that I can't see. But if there isn't, if Tilly is simply choosing not to talk, that's something called selective mutism. It can happen in children after they've experienced a trauma of some kind. And I wondered, I need to ask you if Tilly has ever seen violence in your home. If perhaps your partner . . .?"

Anna could see what he thought of her. A single mother, too young, probably on gear or something. The kind of woman who would put some violent, bastard of a man before her daughter.

"I've no partner," Anna said. "And I'd never let anyone hurt Tilly. Or me either," she said, firmly.

He nodded slowly.

"And you can't think of anything Tilly might have seen or experienced that might have upset her?"

"No," Anna said, and nearly choked on the lie. She tried to hold his gaze, but the weight of the sham was too much and she looked away.

He sighed. "I'll need to refer Tilly to a pediatric psychologist, for assessment. But in the meantime, I have a duty to ensure that Tilly is in a safe environment. That her home is a safe place. Do you understand?"

Anna swallowed. Fear clutched at the base of her stomach. "Of course I understand. I'm not stupid. And everything's fine at home. It's just me and Tilly. We live by ourselves." Lies, lies, more lies.

"Good," he said. "That's good." He turned back to his computer, found her address and read it out, waited for her to confirm it. Then he spoke to Tilly, his expression very kind, his voice very gentle.

"Tilly, if there's anything at all you'd like to tell me about, I'd really like to hear it. If you're afraid, or you need help with something. If you don't want to talk, you can write it down if you like."

He offered her a piece of paper and a pen. Tilly looked at them like they were foreign things, like she'd never seen them before. Then she turned into Anna, folded herself into her mother and hid her face in Anna's neck, as if she were much younger than her nine years.

"Tilly's fine," Anna said, her voice thick with unshed tears. She couldn't cry. "We're fine."

A long, painful moment passed. Anna stayed perfectly still, watched the doctor, watched as his expression dissolved into something that looked like disappointment, then she breathed an inward sigh of relief.

"Very well," he said. He turned back to his computer, started typing. "I'm going to refer you to Doctor Williams, Andrea Williams, for an urgent appointment. She specializes in these kinds of cases." His printer sputtered into life beside him. He waited, then pulled the letter from the tray, signed it, then handed it to her. "Call this number, today, please. I'll call Doctor Williams's office myself, to let them know to expect to hear from you."

Anna took the letter. "That will be fine," she said. What kind of cases?

They made their way out of the clinic. Outside, in the cool sunshine of a September day in Dublin, Anna took a deep, deep breath, and let it out again. She looked down at the upturned, worried face of her daughter, and wondered what the hell she was going to do next.

PART ONE

Saturday, October 31, 2015

CHAPTER ONE

Galway, Ireland

Peter Fisher was woken by movement in his bed. The room was dark, only a sliver of early morning light making its way through the curtains. He blinked, tasted last night's beer on his tongue, sour and tacky. More movement. He turned in time to see a woman's dark head disappear under the covers. He lifted the duvet, looked down at her.

"What are you doing?" His voice was on the rough side. He cleared his throat.

She stilled. "Looking for my knickers." A laugh in her voice, a hint of embarrassment.

He thought about it. "I think they're on the floor on your side."

She emerged from under the blankets, looked at him. "Right. Close your eyes."

Smiling, Peter dropped his head back on his pillow, closed his eyes, and took a moment to replay the previous night's activities. When he opened them again she was standing at the end of the bed. Her knickers were white cotton, her bra black lace. God, but she was in great shape.

"Sneaking out, were you?"

She pulled on her jeans, looked around for her T-shirt.

"I've got training," she said. "And I'm late, late, late."

She played camogie. Her team had a semifinal coming up. Which was why she hadn't been drinking the night before, and he had.

Peter let out a heavy sigh. "I knew if I let you take advantage of me you wouldn't respect me in the morning."

She grinned at him, pulled her T-shirt over her head, and looked around for her boots.

"You're a hard woman."

She sat on the end of the bed, started to lace up her boots, gave him a sideways look. "I'd say you'll recover," she said.

She was ferociously cute. Even first thing in the morning. He wanted to pull her back into bed and kiss her, but would be better to keep his distance until he found toothpaste and half a gallon of mouthwash. She might have had the same concern—when she came close to say goodbye, she kissed him briefly on the cheek before headed for the door.

"I'll see ya," she said.

"Hey, Niamh," he said. She turned.

"D'you want to meet for lunch?"

She looked surprised. "I'm meeting my sister," she said. "But . . . maybe later?"

He nodded. "I'll give you a shout."

One last smile, warmer this time, and she was gone.

Peter considered going in search of water, thought better of it, rolled over, and went back to sleep. When he woke for the second time there was more light coming through between the curtains, and his headache had receded a bit. This time he made straight for the shower and his toothbrush, came back to his room to dress and straighten the bedclothes. He pulled back the curtains and opened a window to let out the stale air of the night before. Cold, fresh October air streamed in. He headed for the kitchen.

The apartment was a two-bedroom on the second floor of a

three-story building on St. Mary's Road. His roommate, Aoife, had found the place for them, had actually signed for it and paid the deposit before he'd even seen it. Which was just as well—you had to move fast to find someplace that was both decent and affordable in Galway. In his price bracket there was a lot of competition from students. Aoife was a doctor at the hospital. She could probably have stretched to a fancy one-bedroom, somewhere with new carpets and fully functional plumbing, but they liked to live together, and she never made a thing out of the fact that his crappy salary narrowed their options considerably. Besides, their place was two minutes' walk from the hospital, which worked well for her.

Aoife was stretched out on the couch in the living room. She was wearing jeans, socks with a hole on the right heel, and a navy sweater that looked suspiciously big for her. The Saturday papers with their glossy magazine supplements were spread all around her. There was an empty coffee cup from the place on the corner sitting on the small table at her knee, a plate with a few lonely croissant crumbs keeping it company. She raised bright eyes to him.

"You've emerged. You do realize it's nearly lunchtime?"

Peter gave her a grin that was half a grimace, went into the little kitchen, and came back with a glass of water, drank it down.

"That bad?" Aoife asked.

Peter shook his head. "Is that my sweater?" he asked.

She looked down at the jumper in mock surprise. "Is it?" she said. "Did I hear the lovely Niamh commence the walk of shame a few hours ago? Did you kick her out?"

Peter laughed, dropped into the armchair. He felt buoyant, despite the hangover. First day off in two weeks, and so far it was pretty close to perfect.

"She had training. We're meeting for dinner, maybe."

Aoife raised an eyebrow. "Jesus," she said. "Commitment."

Peter shrugged. He liked Niamh and he knew Aoife did too—she'd introduced them in the pub a few weeks before. They'd kissed that first night. Then again another night, or was it two? Last night they'd taken it further. He did like her. She was bright and funny. She always seemed happy, too, and that was nice to be around when so much of his work meant being knee-deep in human misery.

"Not working?" Aoife asked, reading his mind.

He looked at his phone. "Not so far, anyway." First day off in two weeks, but that didn't mean he'd get to keep it.

Aoife stretched, knocking half the papers onto the floor in the process. "Any plans for the day?"

"Haven't thought about it." He should go to the gym, or for a run maybe. The annual physical was coming up. Peter poked a dubious finger into his stomach, thought about shuttle runs and the previous night's beers. Nah. "Do you want to go to the cinema?" There was a new Bond film—*Spectre*. He'd heard good things about it.

Aoife looked wary. "Maybe," she said. "Which movie?"

Peter's phone rang before he could answer her. Aoife rolled her eyes and let out a sigh of exasperation. Peter checked his screen before answering. It was a blocked number, probably the station. He pressed the button.

"Fisher."

"Reilly wants to know if you can come in for the afternoon." Peter recognized the voice. It was Deirdre Russell. A colleague.

Peter looked at his watch. "I'm off today," he said, unnecessarily.

"I know," she said. "I told him. But he said to ask you anyway. We're very short."

Nothing new about that, not lately anyway.

"Who else is in?" Peter asked. He locked eyes with Aoife, who stood and started to gather up her newspapers. Peter stayed where he was, listening, not yet willing to accept that his day off had just been canceled.

"Basically me, Reilly, and Mulcair," Deirdre was saying. "The entire task force is out on surveillance—they left hours ago. They think there's stuff coming in by boat this evening."

Peter stood up, looked out of the window, felt a flicker of irritation. "Yeah," he said. "It's mad how they always get a tip-off when it's a sunny day, isn't it?"

Deirdre paused. "They seemed sure this time," she said.

Peter snorted. "I'll be there in a half-hour," he said. Silence on the other end of the phone. "What?"

"Can you stop off on the way in? It's Reilly who's asking, not me," Deirdre added hurriedly. "A call came in on 999. An eleven-year-old boy in Knocknacarra. He says he saw a girl his age abducted from in front of his house, about fifteen minutes ago." Deirdre's tone wasn't right for the news she was delivering. There was tension in her voice, but only a hint of it, not enough to suggest a major operation was about to kick off.

"All right," Peter said. "What are you leaving out?" He went to the kitchen. Leaned against the wall. Aoife was pouring cornflakes into a bowl. He mouthed a *sorry* in her direction—she responded with another eye-roll. Peter went into his bedroom, phone still pressed to his ear, and shut the door.

"Well, he says he saw Slender Man do it," Deirdre said.

Peter paused in the act of pushing off his shoes. He'd need to change out of his jeans if he was going to the station. "What?"

"You know, the internet thing. Slender Man," Deirdre was saying. "Look, I didn't talk to him myself, so . . ."

"Right. So it's a prank or a crank." He looked at his watch.

It was early enough that the traffic on the road to Knocknacarra wouldn't be too bad. "Anything else?"

"The boy's name is Fred Fletcher. Address is Number One, The Rise," Deirdre said in a rush, maybe relieved he wasn't making a big deal out of it.

They hung up, and Peter started to strip off his jeans and T-shirt. At least he didn't have to go looking for a uniform. He was plainclothes now, had been ever since his transfer to the Special Detective Unit had been approved. SDU headquarters was in Harcourt Square, in Dublin, but these days the unit had personnel spread throughout the regions. Which meant he'd been able to transfer to detectives and stay in Galway.

Peter pulled a clean T-shirt out of his wardrobe. The dress code of a detective depended on the nature of the work. On a standard day, he aimed for respectability. That meant slacks rather than jeans, and a shirt with a collar on it. Being SDU meant that he also now carried a gun, something he still wasn't used to. A Walther P99c to be precise. It was compact, as semiautomatic pistols go, but the weight of it felt strange, in the holster and in his hands. He would get used to it, no doubt, in time.

Peter wouldn't admit it to anyone, but even though his day off had gone down the drain and there was a good chance he wouldn't now get to meet Niamh for the promised dinner, he still felt a flicker of pleasure as he made his way to his car. His job was difficult, sometimes dangerous, and god knows it left him with little money in his pocket, but the truth was there was nothing in the world that he'd rather be doing.

CHAPTER TWO

Peter didn't bother with lights or the siren, other than giving them a brief flick to get through the tailback at the top of Threadneedle Road. He was in no great hurry to get into the station, where he would likely spend the day glued to a chair, dealing with stacks of neglected paperwork. This call-out to Knocknacarra was a reprieve and he had every intention of taking his time on the drive there and back. He wondered if the dispatcher had asked to speak to the boy's parents. The Slender Man reference had to have had her thinking she was dealing with a crank.

Fifteen minutes later Peter pulled in outside a mock-Tudor semidetached. The house was painted a brisk white. A flowerbed planted with a random-seeming selection of clashing orange and pink flowers formed a border around a square of neat lawn. All the houses on the street were identical, some better maintained than others. Peter got out of the car, looked around. The Rise was not a particularly apt name for the little cul-de-sac, which had no hill at all, and no view. The front door of number one opened, and a woman who looked to be in her late forties stared out at him anxiously. Peter reached for his badge, introduced himself.

"I'm looking for a Fred Fletcher," he said. The woman nodded a yes and gestured impatiently for him to come inside.

"He's upstairs. I made him get into bed. Look, he's not very well. You'll go easy on him, won't you?" She led the way up narrow, carpeted stairs. The house smelled of baking, and Peter was suddenly starving.

"Fred is your son, Mrs. . . .?" She obviously knew why he was there, knew that her son had called the police.

"It's Angela," she said. She reached the landing and opened a door into a small bedroom, very tidily arranged, furnished with a single bed made up with crisp white linen and occupied by a boy, small for eleven. He had a tablet clutched in one hand, and was wearing a pair of Harry Potter–style glasses pushed back on his nose. He looked flushed and unwell.

"Fred?" Peter asked.

The boy nodded. "Yes," he said, his voice not much more than a whisper. He coughed.

"You've been sick, Fred?"

A shrug. "First bronchitis, then tonsillitis, now bronchitis again. No school for two weeks. Mum's had to stay home from work to mind me." The boy managed to look pleased and worried at the same time.

"All right," Peter said. "Look, Fred, I'm here because you called 999, and told the dispatcher that you'd witnessed an abduction."

A vigorous nod, no signs of embarrassment. Peter felt the first stirrings of concern in his gut.

"You told the dispatcher that you saw Slender Man abduct a girl . . . Is that right?"

Confusion passed over Fred's small face. "No," he said. For the first time, his eyes went to his mother's face, but it wasn't the guilty glance of a little boy caught out in a lie.

"You didn't say anything about Slender Man?" Peter asked. "Do you know what Slender Man is?" If the boy denied it, Peter didn't relish the task of explaining. His own knowledge was limited to what he'd picked up from a few newspaper reports about a stabbing in North America. Slender Man was a sort-of digital urban legend, as best as he'd been able to make out. Something born in a photoshop challenge run on a message board that morphed into an entire mythology, given fresh impetus when two teenage girls stabbed a third to within the brink of death, then claimed that Slender Man made them do it.

But Fred was nodding. He half-lifted his tablet toward Peter. "I was playing *Slender Man's Forest*," he said. "The app. That's what I told the dispatcher. I was playing the app before I looked out the window and saw what happened."

Oh, Christ. "And what did you see, Fred? Tell me exactly." Peter kept his voice very calm. He could almost feel the thrum of Angela's anxiety from the doorway behind him.

Fred glanced toward the window. "I saw a girl, walking her dog. Then a car came and parked a bit down the street." Fred made a vague gesture toward the window. He was struggling to get the words out, his voice a rasping whisper. "A man got out and walked toward her. I thought he was going to go into the house next door. But then . . ." Fred aimed another glance at his mum.

"It's all right, Fred," Angela said from behind Peter.

"He punched her in the stomach. Really, really hard. She fell and let her dog's lead go. The dog just yapped and yapped until the man kicked it and it sort of crouched down and backed off. Then he picked the girl up from the ground, and he put her into the trunk of his car, and he drove away. The dog ran after the car. I don't know where it is now." Fred sat back on his pillow, gasped in a deep breath.

There was absolutely no doubt in Peter's mind that the boy was telling the truth. The dispatcher had screwed up, she'd misheard the boy, which, given the state of his voice, might be understandable. Why the hell had his mother let him make the call himself? Peter cringed inwardly at the thought of his leisurely drive in the sunshine. How much time had passed since the call came through? At least half an hour.

"What kind of car was the man driving?" Peter asked.

A shrug. "I don't really know cars," Fred said. His voice broke on the last word and he coughed, a nasty-sounding rattle. He pushed his tablet across the bed toward Peter. "It was black," he said. He gestured at the tablet.

Peter's mouth went dry. "Did you get a picture?" he asked.

Fred seemed to feel the futility of trying to speak. He woke the screen of his tablet, tapped on an app, tapped again, and turned the screen to face Peter. Peter watched as a short video played out and looped. Fred had taken it from his bedroom window. The glass through which he'd shot the video was grubby and the video itself was innocuous enough. It showed a black Volkswagen Passat, parked about fifty feet down the street, pulling away from the curb and driving off, leaving a barking little white terrier in its wake. Peter couldn't make out anything of the driver, but he could make out at least part of the registration.

Peter looked at Fred, and two red-rimmed blue eyes looked back at him.

Peter stood. "You did brilliantly, all right? And don't worry, we're going to find her." The boy held the tablet out to him, and he took it. "I'll get this back to you as soon as I can," he said. Fred shrugged.

"Did you know the girl?" Peter asked. "Did you recognize her, or the man?"

A shake of the head. No.

"Could you describe him to me, Fred?"

In his strained whisper, every second word lost, Fred described the man as tall and thin, dark hair, a beard. He'd been wearing slacks, and a navy puffer jacket, just like Fred's dad wore sometimes.

"What about his age?"

The boy hesitated, unsure.

"Older or younger than your dad?"

"About the same, I think," said Fred.

"And the girl?"

Fred shrugged. "She never turned around. She had long dark hair. A blue coat down to her knees."

Peter turned to Angela, gave her the nod, and she followed him out to the landing.

"What age is your husband?" Peter asked.

"Ex-husband," she said. "He's forty-two. What was all that about a slender man?"

"Just a misunderstanding," Peter said. "The dispatcher couldn't quite make out what Fred was saying . . ."

"He called you lot before he even told me what had happened. Then he came and found me in the kitchen, bawling his eyes out. Poor kid. He's a really good boy, you know? A really good boy." She hesitated. "Don't go getting any crazy ideas about his dad either, right? It wasn't him. Fred's dad lives in London, he's blond, and only a few inches taller than I am."

"All right," Peter said. "Can you give me a minute? I need to make a call, but I have a few more questions for you."

Peter took the stairs, went outside, and dialed Cormac Reilly directly on his mobile.

"Reilly."

"It's Fisher. I'm in Knocknacarra. I responded to that call." Peter wanted to sound cool, professional, in control but he could hear the fear and excitement in his voice. He took a breath, tried to slow himself down.

"Okay." Reilly sounded distracted.

"Uh . . . the reported abduction," Peter said. "A young boy—Fred Fletcher—called it in. He spoke to control in Dublin and there was a mix-up. Some confusion. His call wasn't taken seriously but I think this is the real deal. He has video of the car driving away. I've got his tablet here with the recording on it. The recording isn't perfect, but I can read a partial."

"Tell me the story from the beginning."

Quickly, Peter ran Reilly through everything he knew. His report was briefly interrupted when Reilly took a few seconds to repeat the partial plate and issue instructions to the officers in the squad room.

"I'll be with you soon," Reilly said. He sounded tense, urgent. "They'll get to work on the partial but see if you can email the video directly to tech. When you get that done, start on the door-to-door. We'll be with you in twenty minutes."

Reilly hung up, and Peter turned to see Angela Fletcher watching him from her front door. Peter held up the iPad.

"Can I use your Wi-Fi?" he asked. "I need to email the video to the station."

"Of course," she stepped back, made room for him to enter the house.

It only took Peter a minute to log into his own email account, attach the video, and send it off marked urgent, and for most of that minute, he was mentally berating himself for not having done so before he called Reilly. He'd been worked up, maybe not thinking straight. Well, that was the last mistake he was going to make. From now on, he was keeping his head. He waited for the confirmation that the email was received, then turned to Angela.

"Thanks. I'll need to keep the tablet, I'm afraid, but we'll get it back to you as soon as possible."

She nodded.

"What can you tell me about the neighbors?" he asked, already moving toward the door. She followed.

"I don't think you'll get much out of them," she said.

Peter reached the open front door. He stepped outside. There were twelve semidetached houses in total in the little cul-de-sac, six on one side of the street, six on the other. Signs of life were minimal. Angela stood in the doorway, arms crossed.

"Mrs. McCluskey across the road will have been at home. She never goes anywhere but she's as blind as a bat and sleeps half the day. You might get a few others. But if anyone saw it they would have called you, wouldn't they? It's not the kind of thing you ignore."

"Okay, thank you." Peter was halfway down the driveway by now, still looking back toward Angela. Movement from the bedroom window above caught his eye. He looked and saw Fred standing there, staring down at him, looking half afraid and wholly sick. He was so pale, with great dark circles under his eyes. Peter thought of Reilly mobilizing the few officers they had left. Thought of the video, which, after all, had shown nothing much.

"Angela, what are the chances that Fred made this up?" Peter asked. "In a bid for attention, maybe?" Fred's dad lived in London. How often did they see each other?

"Jesus," she rolled her eyes. "I've been hovering over him for the last two weeks. How much more attention do you think he might need? No, I'm telling you, he's not the type. My son's a smart, capable boy who does well in school and is well-liked by his friends. There's no way he would do something like that." She paused, glanced up at the boy's window.

Angela didn't seem to be the rose-tinted glasses type. On the other hand . . .

"That video game . . . the app that Fred was playing. It's definitely not suitable for an eleven-year-old."

Angela Fletcher looked surprised, then gave him a hard look. "Jesus. Everyone's a parent, aren't they? Haven't you got bigger problems right now?"

Peter flushed, nodded, and got on with it.

CHAPTER THREE

"I need a team. I need experienced officers, on the phones and out on the ground. We're talking about a child here."

Brian Murphy, safely ensconced behind his desk, frowned and looked down at the pen he held in his right hand. Cormac wanted to pick him up and shake him.

"The task force—"

"The task force is sucking up resources we badly need. Things have gone too far there."

A flash of anger in Murphy's eyes, quickly muted. Cormac took a breath. He needed to go more slowly at this, step more carefully. But there was no time. And he'd tried diplomatic methods. Had pushed for months to get some resources and gotten nowhere.

"Sir, virtually every experienced officer we have has been out on surveillance for months now, spread halfway across the county, from Westport to Clifden and we don't have anything to show for it. In the meantime, things are going to hell here in Galway. Street assaults are up—we've no one in the Square on Saturday nights. At best we can put together a skeleton crew but that pulls our last few officers out of the station. And it might not be showing up in your stats yet, but I'm telling you, another couple of months like this and your ratio of detected versus recorded crime is going to plummet. The Assistant Commissioner will be on the phone asking questions."

"*My* ratio?" Murphy said, one eyebrow raised, a stain of red appearing high on each cheekbone.

"I meant the station. The station's ratio."

"All I'm hearing from you are excuses, Reilly. When it operates in Dublin the task force asks for and gets exactly this level of support."

"With respect, sir, Dublin's a completely different story. When the task force is in Dublin they lean on local stations for support, yes, but they take up what? Ten percent, maybe twenty percent, worst-case scenario, of local resources. Here we've had nights where fully sixty or seventy percent of our officers are off on surveillance. And I have to say again, we have nothing to show for all of this. Not a single arrest or a useful piece of information in six months. Morale is down. We are inundated with complaints from local people because of all the minor offenses that are going uninvestigated."

"We are all working in a constrained environment, Reilly. That's just part of modern policing. Good officers adapt. They innovate. They don't waste time moaning about the efforts made by others to make our world a safer place."

A safer place? Christ almighty. There was a knock on the door behind him. Trevor Murphy, garda sergeant, second-in-command of the task force that was the subject under discussion, and Brian Murphy's first-born son, put his head around the door.

"Am I interrupting?" Trevor said. "If you have a moment, I need to run you through a few details about tonight's surveillance before we head out."

Brian Murphy waved his son into the room and Cormac shrugged back a flare of irritation. Trevor Murphy shouldn't even be in Galway. It was against garda regulations for son to report to father. Under normal circumstances Trevor would be stationed as far from his father's command as was reasonably practicable. They only got away with the current arrangement because, technically, the drugs task force reported through the Assistant Commissioner, Special Crime Operations, whereas Superintendent Brian Murphy reported up through the Assistant Commissioner, Western Region. Two different reporting structures meant that, officially at least, Trevor Murphy was not in his father's chain of command. The reality, however, was that Trevor had been working out of Mill Street Garda Station for nearly six months, and his father did not hesitate to provide him with everything he asked for and more.

"We're not finished, sir," Cormac said to Brian Murphy. "I need an experienced team, and I need them right now." He turned to Trevor. "You'll need to release some of my officers, Sergeant Murphy."

Trevor Murphy leaned back against the wall, drummed his fingers on the plaster, adopted a faux-serious expression.

"No can do, I'm afraid. Pivotal point in our operation."

"A child has been abducted," Cormac said, articulating each word clearly and firmly, determined to break through the bull-shit. "Over an hour ago. I need people, right now."

Trevor Murphy's eyes flicked briefly to his father's then he shook his head. "Sorry. Can't be done."

"That's not your decision to make," Cormac said. The jumped-up little bastard. That he was even a sergeant was a bloody travesty. He should never have been promoted.

Trevor Murphy smirked at him.

Brian Murphy cleared his throat. "The discussion *is* over, actually, Reilly," he said. "Resource allocations have already been made. You can't expect other operations to accommodate this kind of last-minute ad hoc request."

It took Cormac a second to realize he was being dismissed. He didn't move. Fury sparked and ignited deep in his stomach. This was unbelievable.

"Sir, you can't be serious about this. This is a little girl, shoved into the trunk of a car, and you know the clock is ticking. I need people. I need a team."

"You need to do your job. You're an experienced sergeant. You should be able to handle a missing-persons inquiry."

Cormac stood up. "This is not a teenager who's run away with her boyfriend."

He tried to read Murphy's expression, but the older man avoided eye contact. None of this made sense. Trevor was a useless piece of shit. He cut corners and he took favors and he might be doing a hell of a lot worse than that. But Brian Murphy was a totally different creature. His strengths might lie more in administration and politics than frontline policing, but Cormac had come to regard him as an honest broker. And he'd been a police officer for thirty years. He had to know that press would be all over this in a matter of hours if they weren't already on the trail. Questions would be asked by people who couldn't be ignored.

"I can't do my job," Cormac said stiffly. "You're making that impossible."

Murphy cleared his throat. "I'll call Salthill and Oranmore. See if they can spare a couple of bodies. In the meantime, you need to work with what you've got."

Calling on other stations did not guarantee resources. Everyone was understaffed these days. The five-year hiring freeze had come to an end, but the few hundred new recruits were yet to make it through training college. Mill Street was struggling more than most, given the burden of the task force, but it was really a question of degree.

In desperation Cormac turned to Trevor. "This is a kid we're talking about. Whatever you're doing tonight . . ." Another pointless wander around the bogs and fishing villages of north Galway. "Whatever it is you're doing can surely wait for a few days, or a week."

Trevor shrugged. "Need my people."

"They're not your people," Cormac snapped.

"They're not yours either," Brian Murphy said, and now his voice was cold and controlled. "If your job is beyond your abilities, Reilly, maybe it's time you looked at other options. I want you to make an appointment with one of the independent counselors. Discuss your options."

"Excuse me?"

Murphy's gaze was ice. "Maybe it's time you took a step back. Or down. You're not the first to burn out. You won't be the last. We have support for that sort of thing now."

Blood rushed to Cormac's face as he felt a rush of fury so intense that the edges of his vision blacked out. He tried one more time.

"Sir . . . a child . . ."

"The door, Sergeant," Murphy said.

"You'll leave me no choice but to make a formal complaint," Cormac said.

"You do that, Sergeant Reilly. Let's see how far it gets you," Murphy said, and he pointed again to the door.

CHAPTER FOUR

The door-to-door was going exactly as Angela Fletcher predicted. Peter had started at the house opposite the Fletchers, which was occupied by the aforementioned Mrs. McCluskey. She was, as he'd been warned, half-blind, and she was half-deaf into the bargain. He'd had to explain the situation three times before she confirmed that she'd seen and heard nothing. At the next two houses, he'd found no one at home, at the three after that his inquiries were met with shaken heads and bemused looks. If the abduction had happened, it had happened too fast for anyone but Fred to see anything. Peter was knocking at the seventh door and waiting for an answer that did not appear to be coming when the sound of an approaching police siren alerted him to Reilly's impending arrival. Peter turned and went back down the drive, waited as two squad cars pulled up in quick succession. Reilly was first out of the lead car.

"Fisher. Anything more for me?"

"Nothing from the neighbors. I've tried these." Peter indicated the side of the street he'd already doorknocked. "Nothing useful so far. No obvious cameras in any of the neighboring houses. Our witness, Fred Fletcher, is sick. He's lost his voice, is running a temperature. His mother's put him to bed, but I don't think he has anything more to give us in any case."

"Nothing more from his description of the suspect?"

Fisher shook his head, feeling inadequate. "Just what I called in. A tall, thin man with dark hair and a beard. Aged about forty, wearing slacks and a puffer jacket."

"And he didn't know the girl?"

"He only ever saw her from behind, but she didn't seem familiar. She had long dark hair, a blue knee-length coat." Peter was distracted. He'd expected Reilly to bring a full team with him. Instead it looked like he'd driven himself, and only one officer climbed out of the second car. Rory Mulcair, who was young and inexperienced.

"You've got the video there?" Reilly asked, indicating the tablet still in Peter's hands. Peter handed it over. They watched it together and Peter felt a twinge of anxiety. Not so much that he'd misread the situation—on balance he believed that Fred Fletcher was telling the truth—but that without the benefit of speaking with the boy Reilly might not see what he saw. By itself, the video didn't seem like much. He needn't have worried. Reilly handed the tablet back to him.

"Bring that into tech right now," he said. "I got a call on the way here. They couldn't do anything with the emailed version you sent them. Resolution was too low, or it got corrupted or something. I want you to hand-deliver that. Call me the minute they have anything." Cormac looked around, grimaced. "We should be looking for that dog too," he said. "It might be the fastest way to identify her."

Peter hesitated, unsure whether Cormac meant him to stay and help, until the older man snapped, "Go, Peter."

Peter made for his car. By the time he pulled away from the scene, Rory Mulcair was taping off the section of footpath where the black car had pulled in, and Reilly was at Angela Fletcher's door. Peter's adrenaline was now well and truly pumping, but the fear was there too, curling its way into his stomach. Because this was about a child, a little girl, and the outcome on a case like this could be as bad as it gets.

When Peter reached the station, he dropped the tablet to the technical team and made his way upstairs to the squad room. Deirdre Russell was alone, sitting at a desk in an open-plan area meant for twenty-five.

“Right,” Peter said. He looked around again at all the empty desks. “So it’s just us then.”

Deirdre shrugged. “Looks like it,” she said. She had bruising around her mouth, a few painful-looking stitches. The injury was a week old now, had turned brown and yellow where it had been shades of purple and green the week before. Deirdre was tough—she’d taken an elbow to the mouth when she’d jumped in on some gurrier beating his girlfriend—but Peter found the bruising hard to look at.

“I’ve run a search on the family of the boy who called it in,” Deirdre said. “The father has had a few speeding tickets, but that’s it. No criminal record for him, none for the mum.”

“And no one’s reported a girl missing?” Peter asked.

“Not yet.”

There wasn’t a whole hell of a lot they could do without more information. Peter logged in at the computer beside Deirdre’s. It wasn’t where he usually sat, but it would have felt weird and purposeless working fifty feet away from her under the circumstances.

She gave him a sideways look. “This feels wrong, doesn’t it? It’s like a ghost town in here. Gives me the creeps.”

“Yeah,” Peter said with a grimace. He didn’t want to say anything else, didn’t want to get dragged into a discussion about something that had already been talked to death.

“I think Reilly’s had another run-in with the boss. He went

straight to Murphy's office after your call and came back fuming. I've never seen him lose his cool before."

Peter kept his mouth shut. Reilly had been on a collision course with Brian Murphy for months. It wasn't that Peter couldn't see his point, but sometimes it seemed like Reilly poured fuel on a fire when he could have just damped it down. Lately, the conflict between Reilly and Murphy had been getting worse. If things kept on the way they were, Peter might look for a transfer out of Galway altogether. In the meantime, he was going to keep his head down.

"Reilly said we're not to take any other jobs. The call center's already been warned. Everything is going to be diverted until we've a few more back on board."

"That's good." Peter was looking at the PULSE home screen. He logged in, then paused with his hands hovering over the keyboard. Suddenly he couldn't think of a single thing to do.

Deirdre leaned back in her seat. "I've been thinking. Whoever this guy is, wherever he was going, he would have had to drive through Knocknacarra Park, then Shangort Road. No cameras on Shangort Road. And from that point on there are more options, but if he went east toward the city and stuck to the main route, he would have passed a camera at the junction at Taylor's Hill. If he went west toward the coast and didn't turn off on any of the minor roads, he would have passed one at Barna."

"Can we get the camera footage?" Peter asked.

Deirdre shook her head. "I asked the technical team, but they said there's not much point until we have the numberplate."

"Okay, well, they've got the video now. Hopefully they'll be able to enhance it and match the number against the ANPR."

There weren't many cameras in Galway capable of automatic numberplate recognition and they were mostly on the outskirts of the city, on the motorways and national routes, but he thought there might be one on Taylor's Hill. Possibly one at Barna.

"And in the meantime . . ." Peter turned to his computer, ran a quick search for the partial plate on PULSE. "There," he said. He turned his screen a little so she could see. "I've got twelve hits for black Volkswagen Passats for the partial."

Deirdre looked at the list on his screen. "Exclude women," she said.

Peter filtered the search. "Seven left," he said. "But if I exclude men aged under thirty and over sixty, I can get it down to two." He felt uneasy. Fred was young. He'd seen the man through a dirty window from the first floor and only for a few seconds. Excluding everyone over sixty was one thing, but the under-thirties might be a risk. Still. They had to start somewhere. "Why don't we take one name each and have a look? See if anything interesting comes up?"

Deirdre nodded briskly "It's as good an idea as any." She leaned forward to get a closer look at his screen. "I'll take the first one . . . uh . . . Michael Foxford. You take Jason Kelly."

They ran their searches. Peter found very little initially. There was nothing on PULSE—Jason Kelly had not previously come to the attention of the gardaí—and he had no social media presence, kept himself private. Except no one really kept themselves private in this internet age. Not without concerted effort and a degree of expertise. Peter kept searching. His first search, *Jason Kelly Galway*, yielded an unworkable two million hits. There was a plastic surgeon by that name, it seemed, and a student with an active social life and an apparent addiction to social media. Peter tried a couple more searches; one for the name combined with Jason Kelly's date of birth, and another for the name combined with Kelly's known address. Still nothing useful. Finally he ran an image search using the photograph scanned into the system from Kelly's driver's license application. In the photo, Kelly had a tight, almost military haircut, a beard, deep-set eyes, and a full mouth that would have looked better on a woman. Peter didn't hold out much hope—the photograph was blurry, poor quality—so he was mildly surprised when the computer threw up more than one hit.

Peter clicked on the links and saw that Jason Kelly appeared in a number of group photographs posted to social media, personal blogs, and once to a website for angling holidays in the West of Ireland. He was named in the captions on some of the photos. Jason Kelly was, it seemed, a fisherman. Based on the photographs and posts, he liked to go angling with friends in and around north county Galway, where he enjoyed a reasonable level of success if the photographs of glassy-eyed fish were any indication.

Deirdre had already finished her search. She was sitting quietly, watching over his shoulder, waiting for him to finish. Peter took his hands from his keyboard and looked at her.

"Michael Foxford," she said, turning her screen so that he could see it. "No criminal record, never come to our attention for anything other than a couple of speeding tickets ten years apart. There's nothing else on PULSE about this guy. Social media tells me he's married with two children. Lives in Oranmore. He works for Lidl, but I can't tell where or in what capacity."

Foxford looked unexceptional. Dark-haired, he had a high forehead, a receding hairline. He looked like someone's dad.

"What have you got?" Deirdre asked.

"Jason Kelly," Peter said. "Nothing on PULSE. Very little online. I think he's something of a fisherman, an angler by the looks of it. Thirty-five, nothing online about a partner or kids."

"Where does he work?"

Peter shrugged. "I don't know. Though he has been tagged in a comment . . . Something about him being handy with his tools and could he help out a friend. So maybe he's a carpenter of sorts. But really, there's very little to go on. He keeps his life off the internet."

"Address?"

"Headford Road." Peter said. "A small housing estate there. Ashfort."

They looked at each other. There was disappointingly little to go on.

"We should probably let Reilly know. Let him make the call whether or not we should take it further," Deirdre said.

"Right," Peter said.

"You do it," she said.

He didn't argue. There was no time for a back and forth. He made the call, delivered the news.

"I'm on the way back in," Reilly said. "It's thin, but if tech has nothing for us yet you might as well keep going with it. One of you needs to stay put. Fisher, you go to the Headford Road, see if you can track Kelly down. Deirdre can get on to Lidl, see if she can confirm if Foxford was at work today."

Peter relayed the orders to Deirdre, took one last glance at the photos of Foxford and Kelly as he pulled on his jacket. They'd only been up on screen for a couple of minutes, and already the images had taken on a malevolence that hadn't been there a few moments ago. Suddenly Kelly didn't look like a fisherman nor Foxford like someone's dad. Instead they both looked like the kind of men who would be capable of walking up to a young girl on the street and punching her full in the stomach. And a man who could do that could do anything.

CHAPTER FIVE

Peter headed first for the bank of squad cars, then changed his mind and took an unmarked. On the off chance that Jason Kelly was their man, he didn't want to spook him into doing something drastic. The car was equipped with lights and a siren, and Peter used them to bully his way through city traffic and out the other side. He didn't like what he was feeling. This was different from other cases, different even from murder cases. For those, morbidly, there had always been a sense of excitement, a feeling of being on the hunt. Now, he felt only a sense of dread, a sense that the outcome of this case was a foregone conclusion. It was sick-making.

Peter turned off the lights and siren as he drove up Headford Road and took the turn into Ashfort. It was a small estate, sixteen semidetached houses laid out around a little cul-de-sac. Here there were no flowers planted in borders, no neatly maintained lawns. The houses were smaller, lawns were scrubby and overly long. Most of these houses were probably rentals. They had that lonely, unloved look about them. Jason Kelly's place was quiet. No car in the driveway, curtains drawn. There wasn't a garage. Wherever the girl was, and whether or not Kelly had taken her, he wouldn't find her here.

Peter got out of the car and knocked on the door. No answer.

He peered through a window, saw a glimpse of a well-ordered living room through a gap in the curtains. No signs of life. A door opened across the street. Peter turned and watched as a woman ushered two little girls, one dressed like a Disney princess, the other as a witch, down the drive. Both children carried plastic pumpkins. Of course. It was Halloween. The woman opened the car door and the children climbed inside. She was bringing them somewhere else for their trick-or-treating.

"Can I help you?"

Peter turned. The voice was that of a neighbor, an older man wearing workman's boots and paint-spattered trousers.

"I'm looking for Jason," Peter said. "Have you seen him today?"

"I haven't," the other man said. He glanced toward the unmarked car, then back at Peter. "Is everything all right?"

"I'd like to speak to him. It's urgent. Would you have a number for him, Mr. . . .?"

"Loughnane. It's Francis Loughnane." He offered his hand but looked at Peter as if he had twigged that this wasn't a social call. Was it that obvious? Did he give off a garda vibe? Maybe it was the haircut. It couldn't be the unmarked car. The powers that be had finally figured out that a fleet of Ford Mondeos with Dublin registration numbers and double antennae was just a bit of a giveaway. These days the reg numbers were a mixed bag, the cars were more varied, and the technology was tucked away out of sight. "I don't have his number," Loughnane said. "Sorry about that. But I don't really know him well. I suppose we're both out and about most of the day. We mostly bump into each other when we're taking the bins out for collection."

"Right," Peter said. He looked up and down the road, conscious that any pointed questions now would confirm

Loughnane's evident suspicion that something was indeed up, but not wanting to leave empty-handed. "Do you know if Mr. Kelly is in a relationship? If he has a partner I could call? I really do want to get hold of him today, if possible."

Loughnane shook his head, and his face was impassive now. Perhaps he had decided that Peter wasn't a cop after all. Maybe a debt collector.

"Sorry," he said. "Can't help you." And with a nod of farewell, he retreated.

Peter made it back to the station at the same time as Cormac Reilly and Rory Mulcair. He walked with them up the stairs, filled Reilly in on the wasted trip. They entered the squad room to the sound of Deirdre Russell's raised voice, arguing on the telephone.

"I'm calling you about the abduction of a young girl. You do realize that, right? You're obstructing our investigation. You're slowing us down." She turned to look at Peter and Reilly as they entered the room, her face a picture of frustration. She put one hand over the receiver, turned her head away from the phone. "Lidl," she said. "Giving me chapter and verse about company policy, privacy, and data protection legislation."

Reilly's face darkened. "They won't give you anything?" he said. At her shaken head, he held his hand out for the phone.

"This is Detective Sergeant Cormac Reilly," Reilly said, the receiver pressed to his ear. "My badge number is G82 and I work out of Mill Street Station. Do you have that down?" He waited for a moment before continuing. "When all of this is done, if you want someone to make a formal complaint about, I'm your man. But right now, we are trying to find a little girl. We are trying to find her alive. A half-hour now means the difference between us finding her raped and battered body abandoned in a ditch, and bringing that child back safely to her family, so don't give me any bollocks about privacy policies or warrants, or so help me god I will make it my business to ensure that every gurrier in this town knows that Lidl is a free mark. That they can rob you to their heart's content and not a garda in this county, in this whole fucking country, will lift a finger to stop them." Reilly's face was thunderous, but he wasn't shouting. His voice was low and intense and ice-cold, and Peter believed in that moment that he meant every word he'd said.

"We will roll out the red carpet for them," Reilly continued, biting off every word. "And when your bosses in Berlin or Switzerland or wherever the fuck they are, when they come looking for answers as to why their profit is walking out of the back of every warehouse in the land, I'll be happy to tell them it's because an officious little prick like you decided to exercise his wee bit of authority, and lost a little girl her life."

A pause. He was letting it sink in.

"If you don't want that to happen, you will tell Garda Russell here everything you know about Michael Foxford and every other employee she should see fit to ask you about. And later, if you're still worried about covering your arse, we'll get you your warrant."

Reilly waited a beat, a moment. He got the response he wanted, said, "Right," and handed the phone back to Deirdre. "Get what we need," he said. And he walked out of the room.

After Reilly's scolding, Lidl became remarkably cooperative. It took only a few minutes for Deirdre to confirm that Foxford worked at the supermarket in Oranmore, that he'd clocked in at three minutes to nine that morning and was rostered to work until five. They gave her the name of the manager and a number to call. She put the phone on speaker when she called the manager, who told her that he could see Foxford from where he was standing, and that the man had been working a till all morning. Job done. She hung up and turned back to Peter and Rory, eyes wide.

"That was out of character, wasn't it?" she said.

"What was?" Peter said.

She gave him a look. "Come on. Reilly's Mr. Calm and Collected. Have you ever seen him go off like that before?"

"He's very snappish," Rory chipped in. "He's angry about something."

"A girl's been taken," Peter said. "We're all a bit wound up. And maybe we should be." He shook his head. "Regardless, it worked." He turned to Rory. "How did you do at the scene? Did you get anything else?"

Rory shook his head. "Nothing much. No one saw anything, except the kid. Well, there was no one there to see anything. It's a ghost town during the day, it seems. Everyone but the kid's mother and the old lady next door were out."

"Shite."

Peter took a seat at a desk, logged in, and returned to his Jason Kelly research. He found more photographs of fishing trips. Started trying to link them to specific locations. Where did Jason Kelly like to spend his time? Reilly returned to the room before he'd made much progress.

"How did you do?" Reilly asked.

"Foxford is off the list," Deirdre said, and quickly updated him.

Reilly nodded. "The task force is out in Westport for the night," he said grimly. "We won't see any resources back with us until tomorrow at the earliest. It will be Monday before we're up to full complement, best-case scenario, and I can't tell how long we'll have people for before they're pulled out again. General operations for our district has been officially transferred to Salthill until then. We're handling the reported abduction, but all other calls will continue to be diverted." He turned to Fisher. "Call the lads downstairs. See where they are."

Peter made the call to the technical team, was told that they'd been unable to enhance the plate, and had sent the tablet off to the team in Dublin to see what they could do with it. They assured him that they'd done their best and had now turned to running the partial plate through the ANPR. Peter passed the message along to Reilly who shook his head and didn't look up. Peter went back to his Jason Kelly searches, found little else of interest. His feeling of discomfort was growing. He'd done precisely nothing to help this case along. He'd taken his time responding to the call in the first place, dawdled along with his window down, enjoying the sunshine. His trip to Ashfort had been a waste of time, and Reilly was behaving in a way that was completely out of character. The way he'd dealt with the Lidl guy, for example. It might have been satisfying to hear, and it had certainly worked, but Reilly was usually effective without resorting to that kind of intimidation.

The phone on Deirdre's desk rang. She picked it up, listened for a moment, then transferred the call to Reilly. Peter couldn't help but listen in. Moments later he gave up any pretense of doing anything else. Reilly put down the phone after a terse conversation, then stood up, already reaching for his jacket.

"We've had a missing person's report. Girl's name is Peggah Abbassi. She's twelve years old. She was at home with her father, Amir, all day. Her mother was at work in town. Peggah went out to walk her dog, a white west highland terrier named Jester, and she hasn't come back." When he mentioned the dog, Reilly nodded in Peter's direction, an acknowledgment, Peter supposed, that Fred's statement had been straight down the line of every detail so far.

"I'm going out to meet with the family," Reilly said. "Keep

doing what you're doing, and keep me posted." Fisher expected to be asked along for the interview, almost rose out of his chair, but Reilly sent the nod to Mulcair. Peter subsided back into his chair, sure he'd made his thoughts obvious, feeling stupid and frustrated.

CHAPTER SIX

Cormac nearly brought Deirdre Russell with him for the family interview. She was a good officer, committed, experienced, and, when her face wasn't bruised and battered, she looked more like a kindergarten teacher than a policewoman. There was a warmth about her too that people responded to, and that was the message he wanted to send to the family from the moment they stepped inside the door. Here are friends. Here are allies. We are not here to examine you, to accuse you, to peer inside your every relationship, and to pry apart your every secret. Deirdre Russell's pretty face and her natural charm would have broadcast that reassurance every moment she was in the house, which would have freed him up to get what he needed. But the stitches in her lip and the bruising around her mouth made it impossible. He couldn't take Fisher either. Of the three officers he had to work with, Fisher was the one he trusted most. Fisher had more experience than Deirdre, but more than that, he had excellent judgment and he wasn't afraid to use his initiative. If they were to have any chance at all of a good outcome they would need both in spades. Which left him with Rory Mulcair. Rory was all right, but he was too young, too self-conscious, and too self-critical to be of much use in the upcoming interview.

Cormac tried to swallow back the burning anger, to take a breath and calm down. He couldn't allow himself to go into a family interview like this. He clenched his fists. There was a shake in his hands from the adrenaline and fury that he'd managed—just—to contain in Murphy's office. None of this made sense. Brian Murphy was a politician. He protected himself and his own interests first and foremost, yes, but he wasn't stupid, and he wasn't a monster. This was a child abduction. Murphy should be throwing every resource under his command at a case like this. He should be working the phones, pulling in support from other districts, shining a great big light on every area of this city and as much of the surrounding countryside as they could cover. Instead, he was trying to bury it. Ignore it. Why? What the hell was Murphy playing at?

"Jesus." Rory Mulcair braked suddenly and swore under his breath as a BMW, slow to move out of the way despite the siren and lights, blocked their progress through a set of lights. Rory pushed the squad car up close, too close, touched the bumper, all but nudging the other car out of the way.

"Easy, Mulcair," Cormac said. He braced himself in his seat as Rory pulled away from the lights and used his phone to run a search on the family. He found nothing at all on Peggah Abbassi, but then she was too young for social media. Nothing much for her father either. There was a LinkedIn profile that might be the same Amir Abbassi, listing him as a senior project manager for Medtronic.

They pulled in outside the house—it was unremarkable, a nice-looking detached two-story in a row of similar houses—and Cormac was out and moving almost before Rory had brought the car to a complete stop. Rory had to jog a few steps to catch him as they approached the front door, which opened as soon as Cormac's finger made contact with the doorbell. A woman opened it. She was attractive, elegantly dressed in tailored trousers, her hair hidden behind a patterned headscarf. Her worried eyes flicked to his face, to Rory, then back again.

"Are you police? Have you found her? Have you found my daughter?"

"We haven't found her yet, Mrs. Abbassi, but we're working quickly." Cormac held out his hand, shook hers, introduced himself and Rory. "We'd like to talk to you, inside would be better."

She led the way into the house, through a tidy hall, and into the living room beyond where a man was waiting.

"My husband, Amir," she said, by way of introduction.

Amir Abbassi looked at them, but Cormac wasn't sure if he saw them. He had never seen a man look more terrified. Amir was sitting on the couch utterly still, as if any movement would set off a catastrophe from which he would never recover.

"Would you mind if we sit for a minute, Mrs. Abbassi?" Cormac asked. "We need to run through some questions with you. I know you want to find Peggah as quickly as possible and we want to do that for you. But we'll need your help. I know how difficult this is, but . . ."

Mrs. Abbassi held up a hand to silence him. "My name is Lena. Call me Lena, please. And ask your questions. Ask any question. We will do everything, anything, to get her back."

CHAPTER SEVEN

Peter dug back into his work on Jason Kelly, clicked through his angling pals' social media accounts, trying to find references to Kelly, to anywhere he might work. His phone rang—caller ID showed it was Mark from the tech team.

"This is Fisher."

"We've had a hit on the ANPR for a black Volkswagen Passat with the partial you gave us, heading out on the Clifden Road about forty minutes ago."

The Clifden Road was on the other side of the city from Fred Fletcher's house. Peter looked at his watch. It had been more than five hours since the reported abduction. Plenty of time.

"So it passed through camera SG23 at exactly four twenty-two p.m., just past Glenlo Abbey," Mark said. "The full reg number is 12 G 456."

Peter took the number down. "Hang on a second." He swung around in his chair, looking for Deirdre. "Can you call Oughterard station?" Peter asked. "See if they can get a roadblock up on the Clifden Road immediately. They're looking for a black Volkswagen Passat with this reg."

Deirdre nodded, and Peter turned back to his phone call.

"The next camera's at Oughterard," Mark was saying. "We think we've got half an hour before he reaches Oughterard, assuming he stays on the main road. But I've got the map open here in front of me. He's got a lot of options. I'm counting . . . I see at least sixteen side roads he could take between where our camera picked him up and Oughterard. He could take any one of them."

Peter had the phone tucked under one ear, his hands working the keyboard. He brought up an online map of the area and could see what Mark was talking about. Any of the left turns off the Clifden Road would bring the Volkswagen into hilly farmland, plenty of houses. A right turn would bring him through wetter, boggier, and less populated land for a little while, then onward ultimately to Lough Corrib.

"What can we do?" Peter said. "How do we track him if he turns off?"

"We don't have any magic satellite answers, if that's what you're asking me," Mark said. "If he turns off, our best chance is getting the chopper down to search for him. After that our only option is men on the ground, I suppose."

Except that they didn't have any. Peter thanked Mark and hung up, just as Deirdre finished her conversation with Oughterard station.

"They're going to set up the roadblock. There are only two of them there, but they're going to shut down the station to do it."

"That's good," he said. His hands were busy on his keyboard, pulling up Jason Kelly's registration number.

"They wanted to know if there was backup on the way. I didn't want to say no. It makes us sound . . . I don't know . . ."

"Incompetent?" Peter said.

"I don't know," she said again.

Peter's screen finally served up Kelly's reg number. He leaned forward, tapped the screen.

"It's him. It's Jason Kelly in that car."

They stared at the map in silence. It was after five o'clock now. It was getting dark outside, and away from the lights of the city would be darker still. Peter imagined the twists and turns. In his mind's eye, he could see that black Volkswagen, snaking through the silent backroads, swallowed up by the landscape.

"He's going to turn off," Peter said abruptly. "Kelly's a fisherman. He must know the area. He's going to the lake. Maybe he has a place he can bring her."

Deirdre shook her head. "I don't know. I'm not saying you're wrong, but we don't have any evidence that Kelly has the girl. We only have a partial match from the video. It might have been someone else's car. And Peter, even if he does have her, what can we do about it?" She gestured around the empty room. "There's no one here but us."

Peter picked up the phone, dialed Reilly's mobile number, listened to the ringtone as the call rang out.

"Shite."

"He's not answering?"

Peter shook his head. He tried Rory's number, got the same result.

"They're tied up with the family," Deirdre said. "Phones on mute."

"We need to get a helicopter out there, right now."

"You could ask the super," Deirdre said.

Neither of them said anything for a long moment. Peter stood up, hesitated.

"We have to try," Deirdre said. "Do you want me to . . .?"

"No, I'll do it."

Peter moved quickly down the corridor. He knocked briskly on the door to Brian Murphy's office, waited, but there was no answer. He tried the door, but it was locked. There was an office next door with civilian admin staff. He tried there next. Knocked and opened the door, leaned in.

"I'm looking for the boss," he said. "Is he about?"

The sole occupant of the room, a very thin woman with frizzy over-dyed red hair, was typing from dictation at her desk. She removed her headphones and looked at him inquiringly.

"Is the boss about?" Peter asked again. He couldn't remember her name. Was it Fran? Something like that.

"He's gone for the day," she said. "Can I help at all?"

"He won't be back?"

She shook her head. "Not on a Saturday night. Is it urgent?"

"I . . . yeah. It is. Can you call him?"

"You don't have his number?"

Peter shrugged. He didn't want to say it—she looked nervous and he didn't want to make her worse—but Brian Murphy didn't give out his mobile number to the rank and file.

She hesitated.

"It's very important," Peter said. "You won't get into any trouble."

"I'm not worried about that," she said with a toss of her head, suddenly snippy. She pressed a few buttons, dialed a number.

"It's out of service," she said. "Turned off, I suppose."

"Turned off? Is that normal?"

"Well, I'm sure it is. Everyone needs downtime, don't they?"

"Can you try it again?"

She did, with the same result. "There's his home number . . ."

"Try it," Peter said. "Please."

She dialed the number, pressed the phone to her ear again. "It's ringing out," she said.

Peter thanked her and retreated. He was running out of options. A station the size of Mill Street should have at least three sergeants, but Carrie O'Halloran had taken a transfer for Oranmore Station, and Melanie Hackett had been on stress leave for the last six months. Which left only Cormac Reilly to keep the show on the road. Peter made his way back to the squad room.

"No luck?" Deirdre asked.

He shook his head.

"Try Rory one more time," Deirdre said.

He picked up the phone, dialed, listened to it ring once, then twice, then finally, an answer.

"Uh . . . it's Mulcair here."

"Can you put me on to DS Reilly?"

"He's with the family right now. It's not the best time to interrupt them," Rory said. He sounded nervous. There were raised voices in the background.

Peter filled him in on developments, on the sighting of Jason Kelly's car, on his fear that Kelly would turn off on one of the side roads to Lough Corrib, his theory that as a fisherman he'd know the lake, maybe park the car under cover and be lost to them. "We need to get the chopper out looking for the car, but it'll take thirty minutes to get to Galway from Dublin, so I need to talk to him now."

"You can't," Rory said. The voices in the background were louder. There was an argument, maybe crying. "He's right in the middle of it. He's just, uh, calming everything down, getting it settled. I can't interrupt him, all right? But I'll get him to call you back as soon as possible, okay?" Rory hung up.

Peter took the phone away from his ear and stared down at it.

"What is it?" Deirdre asked.

He shook his head, unable to bring himself to explain the situation. His sense of impending doom returned with a vengeance. Deirdre was still watching him.

"Can't we call the flight crew anyway? Explain that the boss is tied up and he'll send through authorization as soon as he's available."

Peter tried. But he knew before he started that he didn't have a snowball's chance in hell. No way in hell the air support unit was going to release a helicopter on his say-so. He tried anyway, pitched it hard, heard the sympathy in the voice of the officer on the other end of the line, but ultimately got nowhere.

"Look, we can be with you in thirty minutes once we get the go-ahead. Get your sergeant on the line and we'll be in the air."

Peter hung up.

"We'll just have to wait a few minutes," Deirdre said. "Reilly will call us back and we can get things moving."

"Yeah," Peter said. "I think he's going to turn off. I think he'll turn off the main road and by the time we get the chopper it will be too late."

"You don't know that."

Peter shook his head, swiveled his computer screen in her direction.

"Look at these." The screen displayed the photographs of Jason Kelly that he gathered through his earlier social media search. Peter clicked on and enlarged the center picture, a photograph that had captured Kelly in the background, looking pissed off, while another man, grinning widely, held a fish to the camera. It was a wide-angled shot, taken at dusk. Clouds gathered on the horizon so that the water of the nearby lake was dark and murky. In the far-right corner of the photograph, there was a low stone building with one small window and an aging red tin roof. A boathouse, it looked like. Other than the men, their boat, and the boathouse, there were no signs of development in the photograph. It looked like a lonely place.

Deirdre leaned forward. "Where is it? Lough Corrib?"

"According to the post it was taken at Ross Lake. That's

only about a mile off Clifden Road. Ross Lake is small, not as popular, and nowhere near as busy as Lough Corrib. At this time of year, in this weather, I would think it would be fairly deserted."

Deirdre tilted her head sideways, considering.

Peter clicked back to the map, zoomed in a bit closer. "I think the boathouse would be somewhere around here," he said. "I had a look at some satellite images online earlier and they weren't clear, but it looked like there was a structure around here that might match up. We know that the ANPR caught him on his way out on the Clifden Road. If I'm right about this there are at least two routes he could take from where the camera picked him up to get to Ross Lake, and neither would take him much more than twenty minutes."

They stared at the map together. An old stone building like that, in the middle of nowhere. It would be cold and damp inside, with a stone or dirt floor. No other buildings around for miles, and it was already dark. The place would be deserted. If Kelly took Peggah there, he could be sure that no one would see him, no one would hear her. And if he wanted to dispose of her, wasn't the lake right there?

"We could be wrong," Deirdre said abruptly.

"What?"

"About all of it. We don't know for sure that it's Kelly we're looking for. And we don't know where he is headed. We're chasing a lot of possibles and maybes."

"I know," he said. "We need the full plate number from the video. It really shouldn't be taking this long."

"I'll call Dublin," Deirdre said. "Try to hurry them along."

While she made the call, Peter studied the map of the Clifden Road and the side roads coming off it. Looked at the satellite images. Ross Lake was small. His best guess had it no more than two or three miles long, maybe a mile wide. There was a smattering of buildings close to the lake, but not many. It must have been twilight when the satellite images were taken. In the images the water was dark, the surrounding land a green so dark it was almost black. Peter zoomed the screen in again, tried to follow the two possible routes closely, to understand how they linked up with where he thought the boathouse was located.

He couldn't get an image out of his head: Peggah Abbassi pulled from the trunk of a car on the shores of a dark lake, dragged into that boathouse. Five minutes, ten minutes. Surely they couldn't afford to wait even one.

"I'm going out there," he said abruptly, straightening up. He glanced around for his car keys.

"What?"

"I'll drive out there, you keep trying Reilly," he said. "We'll stay in touch over the phone or the radio. Keep me posted."

"But shouldn't you wait for the boss? What about the helicopter?"

Peter was already shrugging his jacket over his shoulders. "I'm not achieving anything here," he said. "Reilly will finish with the family soon, and he'll call in. You fill him in on the ANPR information, and he'll get the chopper moving. In the meantime, I'll get out there, see what I can see."

"We haven't even confirmed the plate," Deirdre said. "Don't you . . . wouldn't it be better to wait? Make sure?"

Peter couldn't have borne it. Not another minute sitting in that seat. He needed to move.

He was very aware that he was crossing a line. Reilly expected him to stay in the squad room. But Reilly wasn't there to see how things had developed and Peter couldn't sit there and do nothing. Not when he was sure that he was right. If Kelly had abducted Peggah Abbassi, he'd done it using his own car. That suggested a lack of planning, that Kelly was running on instinct. Which meant he would have to bring her to somewhere he already knew well. Somewhere he wasn't likely to be seen or overheard. Somewhere like a lonely boathouse on the shores of a lake.

"Call me when you speak to Reilly," he said, and left.

Fisher turned on his siren and lights and took off from Mill Street Garda Station at speed. He was going to break every record that had ever been set in a police car.

CHAPTER EIGHT

The meeting with the family went more or less as Cormac had expected, right up until Lena's sister arrived, and started shouting at Amir for letting Peggah out to walk the dog alone. That had caused Amir to collapse into himself completely. Up until that moment, he had been just about hanging in there, responding to questions with monosyllables. With the attack from Lena's sister he had started sobbing uncontrollably, which prompted Lena to step in and defend her husband and the whole thing escalated until nothing could be heard but the two women shouting at each other and Amir moaning in the background. It took precious time to calm everyone down, get them quiet and listening. And Rory Mulcair was no help. He stood there uselessly, then disappeared into the hall to take a call. Cormac drew Lena to one side.

"We don't know anything," she said, wringing her hands.

"You know more than you think," he said. "You know more than we do. We need to understand Peggah's day-to-day life. The people she spends time with, the places she goes. You can give us all that and more. But I know it's very difficult. It's a big ask, to put aside all of your emotion and your fear and concentrate on the questions we need to ask you. Can you do that? Can you sit down with me for half an hour and answer every question I can throw at you, as fully and honestly as you can? Can you do that for Peggah?"

Lena's response was to give him a look of contempt, as if to say that he could not begin to imagine what she could do for her daughter. She took a seat on the couch, tucked her hands under her legs, and looked at him expectantly. After a moment, her sister joined her. The family's day unfolded itself.

Lena had left the house for work at eight-thirty that morning—she worked as a dispensing pharmacist in the city. Amir worked Monday to Friday at Boston Scientific. He was home on the weekends. He said he had slept in, that Peggah had made her own breakfast. They'd talked a little when he got up, but Peggah had been distracted, playing a computer game.

"I let her play," Amir said. "For longer than I should have. She was cross with me when I told her to stop. She went to her room. I tidied the kitchen and I . . . I think I read the newspaper. Then the dog wanted to go out." He started to cry again. He didn't seem to notice the tears, just let them roll down his face unheeded. "I called Peggah down from her room. I made her take the dog out."

"What time was that?" Cormac asked.

Amir looked helplessly at his wife. "I don't know. I wasn't paying attention."

"Does Peggah have a phone?" Cormac asked.

"She has a very basic phone," Lena said. "No internet. For calls only, to me or her father. But the phone is here." She pointed toward the hall. "It is on the hall table."

"All right," Cormac said. "And you mentioned Peggah was using a computer game this morning. What sort of device was she using? What I mean is, does it have internet access? Could she have been in contact with someone through the game or device?"

Lena shook her head firmly. "No," she said. "We do not allow that. No tablet, no internet. We have a console for playing games. Peggah's auntie bought it for Christmas. But no internet."

Cormac let his eyes slide to Lena's sister and she nodded her head in confirmation.

"Right," Cormac said. "Let's talk about Peggah's friends."

It took time to work through the pivotal questions. Rory hovered in the background, saying nothing, but checking his watch intermittently and looking increasingly anxious as time wore on. Cormac extricated himself as quickly as possible from a family who didn't want him to leave. It was a very normal response to extraordinary circumstances. Logically, of course, they should want him gone, want him out working the case. But with him in the room, asking questions, they had something to focus on. When the interview was over, they would be left with nothing but the gaping hole of Peggah's absence. Cormac stood finally, assured them that a family liaison officer would be in touch with them as soon as possible, hoping that it was true, and left, nodding to Rory to follow.

"What was the call about?" Cormac asked as they walked to the car.

"I . . . wasn't sure if I should interrupt," Rory said. "Peter Fisher called to let you know that a camera caught a Volkswagen Passat with a reg number that matched the partial from the video, heading toward Clifden just after four o'clock. Peter wants to call out the helicopter, but he needs your okay."

Cormac stopped in his tracks.

"Are you serious? Why didn't you tell me?"

Rory took a step back. "I wasn't sure . . . the family was very upset, I didn't think it was the time to . . ."

"Christ," Cormac said, cutting across the excuses. "Come on."

Cormac called the station from the car, reached Deirdre Russell.

Stumbling over her words, Deirdre Russell recapped what Mulcair had already told him.

"There's no one else there to approve this? You didn't speak to the superintendent?"

"He's left for the day. And there's no one else. I've been thinking maybe I should call Salthill station, but—"

"I'll call the flight squad now," Cormac interrupted.

"There's a roadblock at Oughterard. And Fisher has driven out ahead. He's sure that Jason Kelly has got the girl. He has a theory that Kelly may be going to a boathouse on Ross Lake. Fisher found a photograph online—Kelly's been there before, and it would be on the route the Volkswagen's taking. Fisher's going to try to find the boathouse—he has a couple of possible locations based on what we can see on Google Earth."

"Right. Good work." Inwardly Cormac felt like screaming. A child had been abducted and they were cobbling this operation together. "I'll get the air crew moving. I'm going to get some more cars from Salthill, Oranmore, wherever. I'll send them out to Fisher's general location. Stand by to coordinate."

"Yes, sir."

Cormac hung up, got in the car, and made his calls, calling in favors while Mulcair drove for the station.

CHAPTER NINE

The drive deteriorated quickly once Peter left the main road. The road was narrow, barely wide enough for two cars, and heavily pockmarked with potholes. He passed a few houses on either side of the road, mostly new, with unfinished driveways and gardens, remnants of an economic boom that had felt, for a little while, like it would last forever. A few minutes more and he'd left the houses behind. The road narrowed further. It was too tight for a second car now; if he met someone coming the other way, one of them would have to reverse until they reached a passing bay. Peter slowed down and hugged the left-hand side of the road. The hedgerow was thick on either side, and a good six feet high. Branches scraped the side of the car. He glanced intermittently at the map on his phone. He was getting closer.

The road widened suddenly. There was a gravel clearing on the left, with plenty of space for parking. Peter pulled in, then hesitated, confused. On the map this had looked like the best access point to reach the lakeside. The navigation app showed a narrow road leading down to the lake. He'd found the clearing and the parking area, but no access road to the lake. Peter nudged the car forward, allowing the lights from his headlights to spill across the trees and hedges. There. An entrance to a slender laneway, half-hidden behind overgrown hedges and blocked by a steel boom gate. It didn't look promising.

Peter turned off the ignition and got out of the car. It was very quiet, the only sound he could heard was the crunch of his boots on the gravel. The air was damp, he could nearly taste the lake. It must be very close. He went to the barrier, tried to lift it. It moved easily. The chain that was intended to secure it hung loose. Peter stood there for a moment, turned and looked in the direction he'd come from, then back toward the lake. It was so quiet. The laneway beyond the gate was narrow, steep, and in poor condition. Standing there in the darkness, his theory that Jason Kelly had come this way seemed very unlikely. But the laneway was wide enough for a car—just. And if Kelly had come here before, maybe multiple times in daylight and good weather, he might have driven the route more than once. The path would be less intimidating to someone who knew it already, and, after all, he would be motivated. The quieter, the more deserted, the better.

Peter lifted the boom gate high, leaving it open before returning to the car, starting it and heading for the narrow path. He thought about calling the station, filling them in, but his confidence in the decision he'd made was waning. He had visions of a chopper arriving, the few cars that Reilly would be able to scrape from somewhere, all racing out to Ross Lake on a wild goose chase he'd set them on. No, he wanted something, some little bit of validation, first.

The incline was getting steeper now, and the engine of the car complained with the climb. The squad car he was driving was a Hyundai i30 Estate, part of a batch bought for the force in 2014 and rapidly reaching the point at which it would need to be taken out of service. The car had no special modifications. With the exception of the livery and lights, it was exactly the same model sold off car lots across Ireland. Peter cursed the shortsightedness of the pen pushers who continuously underfunded the gardaí while expecting more and more as his tires slipped on the gravel and mud and his engine whined. If Kelly was somewhere up ahead, he would surely hear Peter coming. Brambles and tree branches scraped the sides of the car. He kept going.

The top of the rise was there before he knew it and then he was up and over, his foot clamping down on the brake as his headlights picked out twenty yards of steep rock-strewn descent and nothing but darkness beyond. His imagination presented him with an image of a path that ended in a twenty-foot cliff over dark water. The car bounced and slid down the hill for what felt like minutes but must only have been seconds. Peter turned his steering wheel, released the brake, then braked again and finally regained control and could breathe again. Jesus. He might have gone back. If it had been an option. But there was nowhere to turn, and even if there had been, he wasn't confident that the car would make it. There was no choice now but to go on, to allow the car to creep and slide until the slope finally started to level off, and he felt it was safe enough to stop the car and park it.

Peter got out, made for the trunk of the car, and found the powerful flashlight that was part of the standard kit. He flicked it on and shone it around him. The light picked out reeds and scrub, the bank of the lake uncomfortably close, just a few short yards ahead, but no sign of anyone else, no sign of Jason Kelly. Peter took a minute to zip up his coat. It was freezing, so cold that he was already shivering. He made his way forward, closer to the water. He'd been right about the cliff, though the drop was only a few yards. It was nearly all granite underfoot here, but the surface was uneven, interrupted by clumps of weeds and frozen puddles. Peter shone the flashlight over the water. It was deep, or so it seemed to him, standing on the shore in the darkness. The water was black and choppy. Hostile. Far in the distance, on the other side of the lake, he could see the glimmer of lights, but here there was nothing but silent trees and the lap of the water.

He shone the flashlight beam first to the left, but that way there was no path at all, only trees and heavy undergrowth. He turned it to the right where the undergrowth was lighter, started to walk, and quickly saw something that made his heart beat faster. Two clear tire tracks leading onward.

Peter took his gun from its holster, moved forward. The weight of it felt unfamiliar, awkward. He shone the flashlight in a semicircle ahead of him, picking up nothing but more trees and the occasional insect attracted to the light. He was conscious that if Kelly was ahead of him, the flashlight did an excellent job of alerting the other man to his exact location. He considered turning it off, then thought about stumbling through the darkness, and dismissed the idea. He kept walking and moments later the flashlight dimmed suddenly, then came back strongly. Bloody hell. The batteries. That was the last thing he needed. Peter sped up, following the tire tracks which hugged the lake's edge. He heard something and stopped. The sound—if he hadn't been imagining it—had been that of a car door being closed, very gently. Peter switched off the flashlight, crept forward, feeling his way in the darkness. The clouds parted, and moonlight slipped through. It took a minute for his eyes to adjust and then he could see, a little. There was a jetty now, to his left, and there in the distance, low-slung and hulking, was the boathouse.

He'd found it. And someone else was here. If he hadn't known it from the tire tracks and the sound he'd heard, he would have felt it. An itch between his shoulder blades, a cold hand on the back of his neck. Peter kept moving forward, focused on the boathouse. The doorway was dark and cavernous—from this distance he couldn't tell if there was a door there, or if it gaped open. There was a single window, too small for even a child to crawl through. The sound . . . he had been sure that it was a car door. But now . . . Had he heard it? Imagined it? As the seconds slipped by, the memory of whatever he'd heard lost its clarity, became muffled by the recollection of other noises he'd called forward in an effort to compare and identify. Perhaps it had been nothing. Still. Peter chambered a round, the metallic click echoing in the quiet.

He was nearly at the boathouse. There was a door. Its paint was peeling but it was heavy and solid-looking and there was a keyhole. Peter reached out a hand to try the handle, and that was when the silence was broken by the roar of a car engine coming to life, then being revved and revved again. Peter stepped back, turning toward the direction of the sound and bringing his gun up. He blinked against the sudden light of powerful headlamps and the engine roared again. He willed his eyes to adjust to the brightness. Peter felt trapped against the boathouse. He tried the door, it was locked. He took four steps backward in rapid succession, gun still raised, horribly aware of the cliff's edge somewhere behind him, and the dark water below.

"Armed garda," he shouted. He kept his gun trained on the car. "Turn it off. Turn the lights off."

But the engine revved one final time and then the car was hurtling toward him and there was nowhere left for him to go. Peter didn't think. Instinct and training tightened his trigger finger and the gun fired. Once. Twice. Three times. With the engine noise and the adrenaline pounding through him and his heart thudding in his ears, he barely heard the sound of the gunshots, but the kickback jerked the gun in his hands and he saw the windshield shatter. The roar of the engine quieted, and the car slowed but it kept coming and he should move, he knew he should move but his feet were so firmly planted and his body wouldn't obey him.

"Armed garda," Peter shouted again, unnecessarily. "Stop the car."

But it kept rolling forward, forcing him backward toward the cliff as his body, mercifully, woke up, and then, finally, the car slowed to a stop. The driver was a dark shape behind the wheel. Peter moved forward. His gun was up, it tracked the driver who was still as Peter moved to the door and pulled it open.

"Turn off the engine and get out of the car," he shouted.

It was so dark, too dark to make out details, but the man behind the wheel was gasping for breath. It was Kelly. Jason Kelly, blood bubbling at the corner of his mouth and a spreading stain on his chest where at least one bullet had entered his body. "Where is she?" Peter said. His voice was shaking. "Where's the little girl? Where is Peggah?"

Confusion in Kelly's eyes. He tried to speak and failed. Tried to draw a breath and his failure brought panic. He reached out a hand, grabbed on to Peter's jacket. "Where is she?" Peter said again. "Tell me where she is. Is she in the boathouse?"

Kelly shook his head. He opened his mouth and blood spilled out. Peter pulled Kelly's hand off his shoulder, and the other man slumped forward. Peter made for the trunk of the car, pulled it open. It was empty. No sign of Peggah Abbassi. Peter turned back to the boathouse, tried the door again, but it was solid, a good hundred pounds of oak that no little girl could ever take down. Peter went to Jason, searched his pockets roughly, found a key. The man was choking, struggling to breathe. Peter left him there. He tried the key in the lock. The door swung open. Peter remembered the flashlight, flicked it on. The light picked out the details easily. There was a steep boat ramp that ran down into the water. A concrete platform that ran around the ramp. There were shelves, empty but for a few tins of oil, a couple of tools that Peter didn't recognize, some coils of rope. The ramp was empty, no boat. He ran the flashlight around the shed again.

"Peggah?" he shouted. His voice echoed. "Peggah?" He said it more quietly the second time. She wasn't here. There was nowhere here to hide her. He walked all the way around the platform, just in case, shone the light down into the water, but she wasn't here. Peter half-ran, half-stumbled back to the car, suddenly afraid that Kelly would have disappeared, but he was still there, slumped behind the wheel. His eyes were closed. Was he breathing? Peter felt for a pulse and found one, though it seemed weak and thready. He shook Kelly's shoulder.

"Wake up," he said. "Wake up, Jason. Is she here? Did you put her somewhere? You have to tell me where you put her."

But Kelly didn't wake up, didn't react at all. Instead, Peter started a frantic search of the nearby area. He stumbled over the rocky ground and into the heavy undergrowth, searching and searching until the flashlight battery started to give out. He turned back then, made for the car, and reached it just as he heard the first rumblings of an approaching helicopter. He'd left the car door open. Peter reached in again, touched Kelly's neck. This time his skin was cold.

CHAPTER TEN

The helicopter circled the area, its powerful searchlights sweeping the trees and the lakeside. Peter found that he was holding his breath—would they see something he had missed? Another building? Where else could Kelly have stashed the girl? It was so cold now. He was vaguely aware that he'd started to shiver again. How long would it take the others to arrive? He should call in. He searched his pockets for his phone, didn't find it. An image of the phone propped up on the central console of the police car presented itself to him. He'd left it there. Oh Christ. Peter swallowed against a wave of nausea. He wasn't going to puke here, not at the scene, where the contents of his stomach could be later dissected in a forensics report. The helicopter made another pass but showed no signs of coming in to land. He needed to call in. He should get his phone. Peter turned and looked back into Kelly's car. What if he'd been wrong? What if he'd missed a weak pulse? Peter leaned into the car, placed his fingers at Kelly's neck, then his wrist. Nothing. Nothing but cold, inert flesh, and fingers that came away sticky with blood.

Peter wiped his hand on his trousers. The helicopter was overhead again, hovering and blinding him with the searchlight. Useless bastards. What good were they there? Peter waved his arms over his head, made a sweeping gesture to try to encourage a search, then gave up and started to pick his way back along the shore to his car and his waiting phone.

He told Reilly everything.

"I can't find her," Peter said, and he felt the beginnings of panic clawing at his stomach as he spoke. "She has to be here somewhere, but it's so dark, and the undergrowth is very thick. It's not an easy area to search. We're going to need a lot of bodies, but access is a challenge. We'll need to get our hands on some four-wheel drives to access the lakeside."

It was noisy, wherever Reilly was. Peter could hear muffled voices, a flurry of activity. It helped a bit, made him feel a little less alone.

"I'm going back to search again," Peter said. "I have a flashlight, though the battery is a bit shaky. How far out is everyone else?"

"Stay with your vehicle," Reilly said. "No more searching until help arrives."

Peter looked back in the direction of the boathouse. The helicopter had pulled back, he could hear the sound of its retreating engines. Without the searchlights everything melded again in the muddled, indistinct shadow. He couldn't see the boathouse.

"It's very cold," Peter said. "If she's tied up somewhere, in this weather, we need to find her quickly."

Reilly's voice was firm and chilly with formality. "Stay with your car. You are not to search the scene further. Do you understand me, Fisher? Stay with your car, turn on the heat. No further searching."

Reilly only waited long enough to hear Peter's confirmation that he had heard and understood, and then he rang off.

Help was a long time coming. First to arrive were the paramedics. They came in by air, the helicopter taking its time, hovering for what felt like too long, but setting down gently in the end as if it was no big deal. Two paramedics spilled from the chopper, heads low, and medical bags in hand as they ran toward Kelly's car. Peter followed them there, watched them at work, saw the urgency go out of them as they confirmed what he already knew.

"You're the cop?" The older of them stepped back from the car, looked Peter's way.

"I didn't mean to kill him," Peter said. "It all happened so fast."

The paramedic made a sound that could have meant anything.

"No one else here yet?"

"They're on the way," Peter said.

The paramedic nodded. His colleague was repacking his bag, shaking his head. Without looking up he said, "Three times. You shot him three times. Was once not enough for you?"

Peter took one half-step backward. "He was driving straight at me. He would have hit me, gone into the water. I thought . . . look, I didn't have any other option."

"Could you not have stepped to the side?"

"He would have gone into the water," Peter said.

"In the water is better than three bullets in the chest."

Peter clenched his jaw. "He took a twelve-year-old girl. Punched her in the stomach and threw her in the boot of his car. I thought she was still in there. He would have taken her with him. He was driving straight at me, at speed."

The older paramedic put a hand on his colleague's arm. "It's been a long day," he said. "This is our third call-out. First two were car crashes and they weren't good either." It was an attempt at defusing the situation, but it didn't work.

"So where is she then?" the younger paramedic asked, chin up. "Where's the girl?"

The older man gave him a warning look, stepped between

them. "That's enough of that," he said. "Come on, back to the chopper. There's nothing we can do here."

"You need to stay," Peter said. "Help will be here soon. A search party. We need to search the woods, and when we find her, she might need your help."

The younger man snorted in obvious disgust and stalked off toward the helicopter. The older man followed, offering Peter only a shake of his head and a muttered "That's not what we do" in his wake.

Peter stood there, looking after them, trying to make sense of what had just happened and wondering what he was missing.

It was four hours before Peter got an answer to that question. Eventually he was bundled away from the scene, left to cool his heels in an otherwise empty squad car, then driven back to Mill Street by a civilian driver who knew less than he did. The station car park was empty, dark. Detective Sergeant Carrie O'Halloran stood alone on the steps of the station, waiting for him. Carrie used to work out of Mill Street but had taken a transfer to a smaller station on the outskirts of Galway six months ago. He'd barely seen her since.

"Are you all right?" she asked.

"I'm fine," Peter said. It came out sounding defensive, and he tried again. "I'm all right," he said. "I just . . . I want to help find her."

"You know there's a process we have to go through after a shooting. I've been asked to act as your support officer. You've already handed in your gun?"

Peter nodded. "At the scene."

"No injuries? You're physically all right?"

"I'm fine."

"What about food? When was the last time you ate something?"

Peter thought about it. "I don't think I have. The day got away from me."

A car pulled into the car park, then another.

"Okay," Carrie said. "We'll sort out food first, then you'll need to give your initial statement. That's just a basic run-through of the facts, as you see them, leading up to the shooting. After that, if you want to, you can go home and get some rest."

A third car pulled in. Officers climbed out of the cars, talking, laughing. There was a lot of backslapping.

"What's that about?" Peter asked.

"The word is that the task force had a big win tonight," Carrie said. "They raided a yacht off the coast, got a big score."

"That's good," Peter said. But he felt a dull sinking inside him, a sense of distance and isolation from the celebration in which he would take no part.

Carrie started up the stairs.

"You've got seven days in which to give your detailed statement," she said. "In addition to me you can have a solicitor or a member of the union with you through that process."

Peter followed. "I can't go home until we find Peggah," he said. "Not until we find her."

Carrie glanced at him over her shoulder, but her eyes gave nothing away. "Let's get started," she said.

He wasn't allowed back to the squad room, couldn't be part of the investigation now, or anywhere near the evidence. So Carrie led him to one of the interview rooms, then disappeared for long enough to find a coffee and a plastic-wrapped sandwich from somewhere. Sat opposite him while he wolfed it down. It felt obscene, somehow, to have an appetite in these circumstances, but he was starving. He finished the last bite, scrunched the plastic in his hand. Carrie had a notebook and pen. She flipped the notebook open to the first page.

"Are you ready?" she asked. "Let's get the debrief done."

"I thought you were my support officer," he said.

She shrugged. "There's no one else. At least not until tomorrow. Let's keep it high-level. Just the facts as you saw them. When the post-incident investigator is appointed, she can take your full statement."

It didn't take long to run through things. Carrie made no comment, just prompted him here or there where she felt something needed clarification, or when he left something out.

"You should go home," she said, closing her notebook. "Get some sleep. This process, it isn't easy. Better to go into it with a clear mind and a rested brain."

"I can't," he said. "Not until I know."

Carrie stood up, glanced around the room. It was a standard interview room. Lino floor, white painted walls, table and chairs screwed to the floor. "You'd be better off waiting at home," she said.

She was right. Peter knew she was right, but he found himself just shaking his head. She came close enough to put a hand on his shoulder.

"Hang in there," she said.

An hour passed very slowly. It was two a.m. before Cormac Reilly came to find him. He opened the door, took a seat opposite Peter.

"How are you?" he asked.

"Did you find her?" Peter said. "She's dead, isn't she? I was too late." He'd been thinking about the deep water in the boathouse. There were tools, things Kelly could have used to weigh down her body.

"She's fine," Cormac said. "Peggah's fine. She's in the hospital, but it's just a precaution. Her parents are with her now."

Peter felt a rush of energy that left him giddy and off-balance. "Where? Where did you find her? I searched . . ."

"She was never at the lake," Cormac said.

"What?"

Reilly's eyes were very steady. "She was never at the lake, Peter. She was taken, just as the Fletcher boy said, but whoever took her just let her out on the side of the road. It was down a rural back road, near Allanspark, in the dark. She was afraid, so she ran and she hid, and it took her quite a while to find a house, and then more time to build up the courage to go and knock on the door. I've just come from the hospital. She's a bit shaken up, but the doctors say there are no significant physical injuries. Other than that first punch to the stomach, Peggah says he never touched her."

Peter let his head sink into his hands. "Thank god. Seriously. Thank god. She's alive and she's all right."

"Yes."

"But I don't understand. Why would Kelly take her only to let her go?"

"I don't have an answer for that. Not yet anyway," Reilly said. There was something in his eyes. Caution, maybe. Or worry.

"What?" Peter asked.

"I showed Peggah a photo array. She didn't recognize Kelly. She says she didn't get a good look at the man who took her. She never really looked at him before he punched her. She was focused on her dog and it happened before she had a chance to think."

"Right. I see." Peter's stomach sank.

"We've got a bit of help now. A couple of extra bodies from Salthill finally showed up. And forensics are at the scene. We'll take the car in for testing and we'll expedite testing on DNA from the trunk. I feel confident that Kelly is the one that took her, and I'm sure we'll be able to prove that. It might just take a little time."

Fisher nodded rapidly, blinking. "Yeah. It might just take a little time."

They sat in silence for a long moment. Peter swallowed. "So, what happens from here? To me, I mean?"

"There'll be an investigation. The superintendent wants you to take some paid leave for the next week or two, until we can clear a few things up," Cormac said.

"That's it?" Hope briefly fought the dread in Peter's stomach. Dread won. "Kelly's dead. He wasn't armed, and Peggah wasn't in any danger when I shot him. I fucked up."

"You thought she was in danger and that was a reasonable assumption. We're going to prove that it was his car in the abduction video, and obviously he was driving it as he was in it when you found him. Forensics will prove that she was in the trunk of the car earlier in the day. My theory is that he let her go because he was tipped off. You and Deirdre Russell, you did good work in identifying him as a suspect quickly. And Fisher," Reilly leaned forward across the desk, "he was driving straight for you when you shot him. He did have a weapon. He had two tons of metal under his control and he was aiming it at you. Don't forget that."

It took a minute before Peter could be sure that his voice was steady enough to ask his question. "Will I have a job at the end of this?" he said in the end.

"You did your job. You did it well," Reilly said. "That girl is safe with her family today because of the work you and the team did today. Hold your head up. You will be back on the team, moaning about overtime again, before Christmas."

Tuesday, September 1, 2015

ANNA

Dublin, Ireland

Anna was ready at two o'clock, but school didn't finish until three. It was freezing cold, and dark gray clouds hung low in the sky. The clouds unleashed a scatter of sleety rain every now and again, but you could tell that those were just rehearsals for the upcoming main event. There was a coffee shop opposite the school. It was a place she'd passed many times. Nothing fancy, not much more than a greasy spoon with a few wrapped-up muffins near the till. But when you can't afford even a cup of coffee, a place takes on a certain sheen. She stood outside for a moment, looking in the window, then told herself to move on. This was the start of a new life. Everything was going to be different from now on, which meant she had to be different too. She pushed the door open, maneuvered her suitcase and bags inside. A young fella came in on her heels, stood too close behind, crowding her. The girl inside the counter was flipping through a magazine. She didn't look up.

"I'll have a coffee and one of them muffins," Anna said.

"Six-fifty," the girl said. She didn't move until Anna put her tenner on the counter. "Take a seat and I'll bring it over."

Anna pushed her suitcase and her plastic bags as far under the table as she could get them. The table was small and round and had a slight wobble. There was a sticky patina on the surface, the residue of a thousand spills half-wiped with a dirty cloth. Anna kept her hands in her lap, looked around. It was dead in here. There was an old couple in the corner, slowly making their way through their meatballs and fries. They didn't talk to each other, just stared into space and chewed. There was a young one at a table near the window, an empty cup at her elbow, jabbing away at a laptop. The fella who'd come in after her sat at a table at the opposite wall. He caught her eye and scowled. Anna looked away, felt that his eyes were still on her.

The girl behind the counter brought over the coffee and the muffin, still wrapped in its plastic. She ate the muffin, drank the coffee. The coffee was all right. The muffin was dry as shite. It reminded her of the cakes her grandmother made at Christmas. She'd let them have a bite, her and Niall, if there were visitors over to see her do it. It had lined her mouth in just the same way. She drank more coffee, washed it down. When she had her own place and her own job she would learn to bake properly. She would make cakes and muffins and cookies and all the kids would want to come home with Tilly every day for a play, and to see what Tilly's mother had for them. Anna risked a look at the young fella across the room. He was picking at his fingernails. Not watching her then. Just bored.

Anna made her coffee last the hour. The girl behind the counter couldn't have cared less. She just brought a plate of fries and sausages to the young fella, then returned to her post behind the counter where her magazine was waiting. Anna watched the clock. The next bus left for Galway at three-thirty. They would have to get a taxi if they were going to make it. The money didn't matter. Not for this. She called the cab at three o'clock on the dot. The young fella gave her a dirty when she was on the phone, but he was gone by the time she finished. The cab company promised it would just be a couple of minutes.

Tilly was one of the first kids out.

Anna called her name. "Matilda. Tilly!" She waved. Kids were coming out in gaggles and clumps, talking and shoving and laughing and messing. Only Tilly was alone, back bowed under the weight of her schoolbag. Tilly looked up when she heard her name, stopped walking when she saw Anna, took in the suitcase. But she saw . . . something . . . in Anna's face and her face lit up and she hurried forward, a question in her eyes.

Anna reached down and hugged her, hard. "We're going on a trip, Tils," she said.

Tilly looked mystified, but not unhappy. She leaned down and picked up one of the black plastic bags, looked back at Anna.

"Thanks, love," Anna said. She felt almost giddy now. A car horn beeped from somewhere behind them. The cab. Anna grabbed the other bags. More than one person was looking now. The bags had drawn a bit of attention, the cab would draw a bit more. She ignored them all. "Come on, Tils."

Sleet came again as they made their way to the car, the cab driver didn't bother getting out to help. Anna put Tilly in the back seat, loaded up the trunk herself, and got in.

"Aston Quay," she said.

The cab driver nodded wordlessly, and they set off.

Aston Quay was right by the Liffey, just around the corner from Temple Bar. They would have to pass the flat. Anna took Tilly's hand, gave it a squeeze.

"We're moving, Tils. We're leaving Dublin. It's no good for us anymore. We're going to live in Galway. I told you my mother used to bring us there on holidays when we were kids. We used to stay in a flat by the sea. It's different there. Not so many people." She was thinking about the drugs which she knew would be in Galway too but also of that trapped awful feeling of being watched and being part of something you had never chosen, which wouldn't. "We'd go swimming in the bay and it was bleeding freezing, Tils, but it was lovely too. And then Mam would get us fish and chips and we would sit on the rocks by the sea and eat them and they were the best days." Nerves always made her talkative.

Tilly's eyes were bright, and Anna felt a surge of happiness.

"I'm going to get us a new flat, and you'll have a new school. I'm going to get a job just for your school hours, and I'm going to collect you every day and it's going to be great."

They were just coming up to Thomas Street and Tilly's face tightened. She turned to look out of the window as they passed the flat, then looked at Anna with a question in her eyes. Anna could have ignored it, could have pretended that she didn't see it, but she wouldn't do that to her daughter.

"Uncle Niall will be all right. Maybe he'll come and visit us when we're all settled."

Tilly didn't look very sure, but she settled back into the seat and looked forward. She was just a child, after all. Anna wished she could lie to herself as easily.

Earlier that morning, after the appointment at the doctor's office, Anna had walked Tilly to school. She had been in panic mode, could feel it in the flutter of breath in her lungs, in the tightness she felt in her chest. She'd kissed Tilly's head as she left her at the gate, watched her little girl walk across the concrete courtyard with a pain in her heart. Anna hated that school, hated the ugliness of the brushed concrete walls, stained with years of heavy weather, the fact that there wasn't a blade of grass to be seen from one iron gate to another. Every time she let Tilly walk in the doors, she felt like the school was swallowing her up, abrading her, stealing another little bit of her future.

Afterward, she'd hurried back to the flat, taken the stairs to the fourth floor, unlocked the door. She went inside, closed the door behind her, and leaned back on it with her eyes closed. She could smell it. Not the heroin, because that had no smell at all, but what he smelled like when he was using. Unwashed, unhappy. She hated this place now almost as much as the school. It hurt to remember how happy she'd been when she'd first been given the flat. A place of her own, a safe place to raise her daughter.

She had to wait for twenty minutes before she could wake him enough to talk to him. Twenty minutes during which she sat on the armchair and looked at him, sleeping on her couch. His face was still dear to her. Despite everything, when she looked at him, at his dark sandy hair that reminded her so much of Tilly's, at the hand that was curled in sleep that had held hers so many times when she'd needed him most, all she felt was love. He was her whole family, her whole life really.

She shook him awake in the end. He blinked at her slowly.

"I need to talk to you," she said.

He smiled at her, but it wasn't his real smile. It was that dopey smile that made her skin crawl and her stomach churn.

"Wake up, Niall. This is important."

"Yeah, I'm up. Of course." He sat up on the couch, wiped his mouth with the back of his hand, all his movements slow, like he was under water.

"I . . . I need to . . . you have to leave."

He blinked. "What?"

"I brought Tilly to the doctor. The school was insisting. The doctor said she must have had some trauma, something must have scared her or hurt her so that she stopped talking. He's going to send social workers out to check on the flat. If they find you here, they'll kick us all out. We'll be homeless."

He shook his head, looked around at his blankets on the couch, his jacket on the back of the chair, the few bits of things that indicated he lived there. "We'll put everything away, so that they can't prove I'm living here. It'll be grand." He reached out and patted her gently on the knee. His hands and nails were clean.

"No," she said. "No, Niall. It's not going to be grand. It's more than just the social. It's Tilly. She's not all right. I don't know how to help her. I don't know how to make it better." Her voice was shaking with fear and emotion, but it didn't reach him. He was nodding off, losing track of the conversation. "Niall," she said. Then again, louder, "Niall."

"Sorry, Anna," he said. "Sorry." But it was too much for him. He didn't try to stay with her. She watched him as he allowed himself to sink back into it. A minute passed. Niall allowed his head to fall back against the couch. His mouth was half-open. Then he was asleep. Like this, he didn't look like her brother. Like this, he looked like a stranger.

In the end, she made the decision quickly. She'd been carrying around the dream of getting free from all this for so long, and somehow, that morning, it started to feel like something that could be real. She left Niall asleep on the couch and started to pack. She had one battered old suitcase, so she started with that, packed their best and warmest clothes, Tilly's few old teddies, their shampoo, and toothbrushes. The suitcase was already overflowing. She sat on it to close it, looked around. There was no way she'd be able to replace everything in Galway, she would need to bring as much as she could carry.

Anna did her sums as she packed. On Tuesdays, she got her social welfare payment straight into her bank account. That was nearly two hundred euros a week, and tomorrow would be the first Tuesday of the month, which meant she would get an extra hundred and forty for child benefit. She had exactly three hundred and thirty euros in savings, left over from the cleaning job. It had taken her two years year to get that money together. She had six hundred and seventy euros to her name. It was enough. It would have to be.

Anna found a roll of black plastic bin liners, doubled them, and used those for the few sheets and towels she had. It took an hour to pack, and in the end, she left everything that wouldn't fit into the suitcase or two double-bagged bin liners. When everything was ready, she brought the bags to the door. When she turned around, Niall was awake again. Watching her.

"I dreamed this," he said.

"What?"

"That you were gone. That you took her and left."

"I'm sorry," she said.

He shook his head. "No," he said. Shook it again. "No. It's a good thing. Maybe if you go, you'll find somewhere better. Tils will get better. You can be happy."

Anna felt the tears coming but the fear and the need for something better was stronger than the love. She went to him in quick, quick strides and hugged him hard, held on to him for as long as she could. She wanted to give him money, but she wouldn't, not now. She was letting him go. She told herself they would find each other again someday and knew that it was almost certainly a lie. Without her, he would sink.

"Love you," she said.

"Love you too."

She'd left without a backward glance. Left him on the couch, knowing that he would use again as soon as he could. That he would block it all out.

Anna and Tilly made it to the bus with ten minutes to spare. Two tickets to Galway cost her twenty-nine euros. That was all right. She'd planned for it. She bought them both sandwiches from the SuperValu on the Quay and a bottle of water and another muffin for sharing. That was fifteen euros. Which left . . . about five hundred and ninety euros. That would be all right. She would make it work. They boarded the bus. Anna put her arm around Tilly and they stared out of the window, watched the streets of Dublin pass by. It was all going to be fine. Better than fine. She wasn't a kid anymore, she didn't need to sit back and let things happen to her. In Galway she would be a different person. She'd always tried, always worked hard, but she'd been stupid. Now she knew how the world worked. It was survival of the fittest, just like in nature. And she would be the strongest of them all, for Tilly's sake.

PART TWO

Monday, November 2, 2015

CHAPTER ELEVEN

Galway, Ireland

With the death of Jason Kelly and the recovery of Peggah Abbassi, some of the immediate urgency went out of the case. Cormac stayed in the station until the early hours of Sunday morning, then went home and slept for a few hours. When he woke up, he went to the hospital to see Peggah, where she was being held for observation, then he went home again and did what work he could from the house. There was no point in going to the station. Now that Peggah was safe, the technical work would have to take its place in the queue. They wouldn't hear anything from the team in Dublin until Monday or Tuesday at the earliest. Deirdre Russell was taking a badly needed day off, and he wouldn't get anyone back from the task force until the following day. He might as well stay at home and do some thinking while he was at it.

Cormac arrived at the station at eight a.m. on Monday morning. Deirdre Russell and Rory Mulcair arrived shortly after.

"Case conference at nine," Cormac said. "Upstairs. I've got an action list ready to go but any suggestions you've got, I want to hear them."

Deirdre Russell looked pale, as if she'd missed sleep. "You mean about Jason Kelly?" she asked.

"Kelly is part of it, but let's start from the beginning. We need to start with the abduction, follow the evidence and see where it leads us."

"And it's just going to be us?" Deirdre asked. "Working the inquiry, I mean."

"I'll clarify that shortly," Cormac said.

Deirdre gestured around the squad room, which was already half full. Officers returning from the task force with the telltale energy of a successful operation. The contrast with their own subdued corner could not have been starker. "They're all here," she said. "We could do with the help."

"I'll confirm who we have by this afternoon. Meanwhile I want the action list tied down and I want to get moving on it, all right? Let's not hang around on this one."

Cormac went back to his desk, focused his attention again on mapping out the lines of inquiry where he saw the most potential. This was going to be a time-sensitive operation. He wanted to get ahead of rumor.

At ten minutes to nine, Dave McCarthy appeared beside his desk.

"Do you have a minute?" Dave asked. Dave was a fixture at the station. He had a good ten or fifteen years on Cormac. One of those officers who knew his job well, had carved out a space for himself, and wasn't particularly interested in promotion. Dave could be an asset when he was interested in the job, if you were willing to accept the boundaries he created for himself. Cormac had found that Dave was worth a bit of flexibility. He had the experience, and he could be very effective.

"I do," Cormac said.

"In private," Dave said.

Cormac followed Dave into one of the small meeting

rooms, pushed the door closed behind him. Dave had a folded newspaper in one hand. He spread it open on the table. The headline took up two-thirds of the page: GARDA SHOOTING: ONE DEAD. The subhead was smaller: A CASE OF MISTAKEN IDENTITY?

Cormac picked up the newspaper and started to read. The piece was short and decidedly one-sided. The journalist had already spoken to Jason Kelly's family. They claimed that Kelly had been fixing up the old boathouse, that he worked there during his free time, often at weekends and late into the evening. According to the piece, Kelly was a carpenter and handyman, unmarried but close to his older brother and younger sister, and a beloved uncle to his nieces and nephews. He had no criminal history whatsoever. It was unthinkable that he would have been involved in the abduction of a young girl, who had, after all, been found entirely unharmed miles from the scene. The piece claimed that little was known about the detective who had fired the shots, except that he was young and inexperienced. The garda press office had declined to comment when contacted by the journalist.

Cormac put the paper down.

"Christ," he said.

McCarthy nodded. He reached out and took the paper, folded it up again, with the headline on the inside.

"They got there awfully quickly," Cormac said.

"That's what I was thinking."

Cormac tried to read his expression. McCarthy was better connected in Galway than he was.

"Am I missing something, Dave?"

A slow shrug. "I don't know," Dave said. "But it struck me as odd that the press office had nothing to say."

"It hasn't even been forty-eight hours," Cormac said. "I

doubt if Peggah's family is speaking to the press." He'd seen them at the hospital.

They'd been happy, if a little confused and worried. They'd feared their daughter dead and she'd been handed back to them unharmed, at least physically. But they'd had no chance to process their own distress and trauma, and had been given no explanation for her abduction. Peggah had been shy, overwhelmed, and mostly concerned about her dog, who was still missing. No one had said anything about journalists.

"Someone's been speaking to the press," McCarthy said. "They didn't get the bit about Peggah being found unharmed from out of thin air."

"No."

There was silence in the small room. They could hear the chatter from the squad room, a sudden burst of laughter.

"You were out with the task force," Cormac said. "On Saturday night."

"Yes."

"Congratulations," Cormac said. "It's a win."

"Plenty of pats on the back to share around there," McCarthy said dryly.

"Right," Cormac said. "So what's the story now? You're still assigned to the task force or are you back with general operations?"

"I'd have thought you'd know more than I do about all that," he said.

Cormac opened his hands in a helpless gesture.

"Well, no one's said anything officially," McCarthy said. "Not yet, at least. But I wasn't exactly an integrated member of the team. None of us were. They just wanted bodies out there, along the coast, watching the access routes. Now they've got their arrests, they've got the drugs. I heard they interviewed the suspects yesterday but the only people in the room were Healy and Murphy Junior. They're using a couple of uniforms they brought with them from Dublin for support."

Cormac nodded. "Well, if you're free I want you back on my team," he said. He gestured to the newspaper still in McCarthy's hand. "We need to establish some facts. Get ahead of that."

"Fine," McCarthy said.

"Right. I've got Russell and Mulcair already. Grab a couple of extra bodies and meet us upstairs in five minutes, all right?"

McCarthy gave a wry smile. "So I'm your number two on this?"

"If you want it," Cormac said.

"Until we sort all of this out, and Peter comes back, and then I'm on the back burner again, right?"

Cormac let out a breath in frustration. "Jesus, Dave, what . . ."

"Forget it," McCarthy said. He moved toward the door.

"No, look, wait. What are you saying to me?" McCarthy gave him a look that said it shouldn't need explaining. It didn't. "You're telling me you want more responsibility. That's not a problem. I'll be honest with you, Dave, I didn't think you wanted it."

"I don't have a problem with the way you run things. I'm just saying. I have seniority, that's all. But when Fisher's here, he's your number two, whether I'm on the team or not. People notice. It gets awkward."

"Right," Cormac said. He was tempted to ask the other man to clarify if it was more responsibility he wanted, or the appearance of more responsibility. "I hear you. You're number two on this operation all the way to the end, whether or not we get Fisher back. After that, if all's gone well, I'll make sure you get a fair go."

"Can't ask for more than that," McCarthy said.

Ten minutes later, Cormac's team, such as it was, had assembled in the case room. Greetings had been exchanged and they were settling in. Cormac plugged his laptop into the whiteboard, pulled up his notes. It wasn't so much a presentation as a bullet-point list of the open questions in the case, the items he felt needed immediate attention.

"I want to start with forensics," Cormac said. "We're waiting on fiber reports from the trunk of Kelly's car, but unless we get very lucky, I'm not expecting to get anything there. I spoke with Peggah Abbassi last night. She told me that the trunk was lined with a tarp when she was in it. There was no tarp in the car when it was examined at the boathouse. I expect that Kelly dumped it after he let Peggah go."

"Assuming she was in there in the first place," McCarthy said.

"What?" Deirdre Russell turned on McCarthy, face tight with disapproval.

"I'm just saying, we shouldn't assume anything. The girl doesn't know whose car she was in."

"Jesus." Deirdre shook her head in obvious disgust. It was out of character for her. If anything, she was usually the peacemaker in the room.

"We're not assuming anything here," Cormac said. "We'll be building this investigation from the ground up, going back over every decision, and pursuing every line of inquiry, wherever it takes us. But this *is* time sensitive. If there was a tarp, and if Kelly did dump it . . ." Cormac leaned over and clicked on his laptop mouse. A map of the area around Ross Lake came up on the whiteboard. "This is the area we need to search to try to find the tarp. I estimate it's at least fifteen square miles. If we have to walk every inch of that it'll take us months, but I think Kelly was under pressure. There's a good chance he dumped it in a ditch at the side of a road."

Cormac took a red marker and drew an "X" at a point on the whiteboard. "This is where Peggah Abbassi was found, or at least it's the house she made her way to after her release." He drew a red meandering line from the X to the laneway that led to Ross Lake. "Assuming Kelly was the one who took her, he could have let her go here, at Allanspark, and then continued on to the lake."

"That's a lot of ground to cover," McCarthy said. "It's what . . . six miles?"

"Give or take," Cormac said. "We—"

"Excuse me."

Cormac was interrupted by a voice from the doorway. He turned to see a man he didn't recognize, wearing the uniform of a garda inspector.

"Can I help you?" Cormac asked. The inspector was in his forties, with the haircut of an older man.

"It would be better if we spoke outside." Cormac followed the man into the corridor. "Inspector Reynolds," the man said, by way of introduction. "GSOC. I'm taking over this investigation as of now."

"Sorry, you're doing what?" Cormac said.

A group of four uniformed officers trouped up the stairs toward them. Reynolds nodded them toward the open door of the case room.

"In there, boys," he said. Cormac opened his mouth to

protest and Reynolds cut him off. "Your super should have spoken to you. If he hasn't, I suggest you speak to him now. But you're off this case, Sergeant Reilly, as of now."

When Cormac reached Brian Murphy's office, he found Peter Fisher waiting outside, looking very ill at ease.

"What are you doing here?" Cormac asked. It came out like an accusation.

"I . . . I got a phone call. Telling me to come in."

"Right."

Murphy's aide was there. Cormac ignored her. He knocked once on the office door and entered, leaving Peter in the corridor. Murphy was alone, sitting behind his desk, a file open in front of him. He looked up briefly, gestured to the seat opposite him.

"Reilly," he said.

"Sir, my case room has just been taken over by an Inspector Reynolds from the Garda Ombudsman's office. I'm assuming that you know why."

Murphy was cool. "Inspector Reynolds is here at my invitation. And if I hadn't invited him, he would have come anyway."

"Sir, I—"

"Please," Murphy said, holding up one hand. "Let's not pretend we have anything here other than a screw-up of epic proportions, all right?" He gestured toward the paperwork on his desk. Cormac glanced at it—loose pages spilling from a thin file. It looked like a statement transcript, maybe a scene report.

"A girl disappears for an afternoon and is found hours later unharmed. She claims to have been abducted—"

"We have a witness." Cormac interrupted.

"Yes. A sick child who witnessed the alleged abduction from a distance after he'd spent hours playing highly suggestive video games. You can imagine what a lawyer would do with that. Regardless of whether the girl left voluntarily or was in fact taken, it is not in dispute that she was found completely unharmed a few hours later."

"There's video footage of a black Volkswagen Passat car at the scene of the abduction. Our witness saw a man matching Kelly's description assault Peggah Abbassi and bundle her into the trunk of that car. The fact that he let her go does not—"

"No," Murphy said.

"Sir . . ."

"No," Murphy said again. "Peter Fisher *claims* that there was video footage which showed a black Volkswagen Passat with a partial registration number that matched Jason Kelly's. And every action he took after that flowed from that piece of evidence, which, and let me emphasize this for you, Sergeant, *no one else has seen.* As you know, the email he sent with the video attached was corrupted."

"The tablet?" Cormac said.

"Has been lost," Murphy said crisply. "It was sent to Dublin for review by the technical team and we cannot locate it. Until such time as the tablet is found, we have only Peter Fisher's word that the partial registration number he was able to make out is as he reported it. No one else has seen it."

"*I* saw it," Cormac said. "I watched the video at the scene before the tablet went into the station. I saw the reg number. And I don't understand how the video could have been lost completely. Even if it was lost in transit, surely the technical team here would have copied it before it was sent for transport."

"You saw it?" Murphy said flatly.

"Yes."

"Convenient."

Cormac paused. "It's just a matter of fact, sir."

"What is also a matter of fact is that a Section 91

investigation has been opened into the fatal shooting of Jason Kelly by Detective Garda Peter Fisher. What remains to be determined is whether or not that investigation will, in turn, result in a Section 98 investigation."

Cormac took a breath, a sudden involuntary inhalation. He felt as if the solid ground beneath his feet had been removed, as if he was standing, swaying, at the top of a cliff and the wind was at his back.

"I don't understand," he said.

Murphy, irritated, made a clicking sound with his tongue. "You should understand. None of this should be a surprise to you."

"It was a good shooting," Cormac said. "Fisher was in fear for his life. The driver of the car, Kelly, he drove at Fisher at speed. If Fisher hadn't shot him, he'd be dead now himself, or seriously injured."

"We only have Peter Fisher's word for that. There were no other witnesses, and the forensic evidence is inconclusive. What we do know is that on the thinnest of evidence—a partial plate number that we can't even substantiate—Peter Fisher came up with a suspect, virtually on his own, and he pursued that suspect, without the consent or approval of his superior officer, and shot that man dead."

"Fisher was under immense pressure. We were ridiculously understaffed for the operation, which he couldn't help but be aware of. He tried to contact me, on more than one occasion. He made the best decisions he could in the circumstances," Cormac said. "A criminal investigation into his actions, even if it doesn't result in a prosecution, will destroy his career. He doesn't deserve that. And it's premature. If we prove that Kelly did take the girl—"

"And that is precisely why this is no longer your investigation," Murphy said. He leaned across the table. "If it was left with you, you would bend the investigation to back Fisher up, wouldn't you, Reilly? Suddenly everything would point to Jason Kelly, and Peter Fisher—and you yourself, of course—would come out smelling of roses."

"That is . . . I would never do that," Cormac said. "My investigation would have been entirely above board. My record . . ." Cormac let his voice trail off. He'd wanted to point to a spotless disciplinary record, argue that there'd never been the smallest suggestion that he ran things any way other than straight down the line. But he couldn't claim that, could he? Not anymore.

"I can't and won't cover for you, Reilly," Murphy said. "You left Fisher, an inexperienced officer, unsupervised. You could not be contacted for a prolonged period of time at a key point in the investigation. Peter Fisher has serious questions to answer, and so do you."

"What are you going to do?" Cormac asked.

"As of now, you're suspended pending the outcome of this investigation," Murphy said.

"And Fisher?" Cormac said.

Murphy paused. "It depends on the outcome of the Section 91 investigation. But the suggestion has been made that Peter Fisher was . . . led astray. With another superior officer, the outcome might have been very different."

For the three years Cormac had known Murphy, he'd known him to be a politician, a mediocre officer, and an occasional clown. Lately, he'd been something worse. But Murphy had never been one to give much away. His inner thoughts had always been well concealed behind a distant, professional mask. Now, as Cormac looked at him across the desk, he saw an unmissable *fuck you* in Murphy's eyes.

"Fisher will be offered a chance," Murphy said. "It's up to him whether he wants to take it."

CHAPTER TWELVE

Peter went home after the meeting with Murphy. He stopped at the liquor store on the way, picked up a six-pack of beer and a bottle of whiskey. The flat was empty and cold. He poured a beer into a pint glass, sat on his bed, and stared into space while the beer in his hand went flat. Time went by. Time during which he thought about everything he had done and everything he hadn't. Eventually, Aoife came home. He heard her footsteps outside the flat, her keys in the door. He thought about getting up and shutting his door but couldn't seem to muster the energy, and then it was too late. She was in his doorway, leaning against the door jam, arms crossed.

"Well?" she said.

He told her everything.

"Explain it to me again," she said.

"God, Aoife, what else is there to say? I killed a man. If they think that I crossed the line, that the shooting was criminal, I can be prosecuted the same way as anyone else. Go to prison."

Peter was mildly surprised that he could deliver the words with no shake to his voice. When Murphy had delivered the news, that he was staring down the barrel of a possible criminal prosecution, it had been all he could do not to cry like a baby.

"For fuck's sake. That's ridiculous. You were trying to save a little girl."

"Except that she was miles away at the time. And there's no proof he took her in the first place."

"Well, he was going to kill you. He was driving his car straight at you."

"No proof of that either, it seems," Peter said. "The tire markings are inconclusive."

"You were there? Isn't your word enough?"

Peter rolled his eyes. "Come on, Aoife. If it was anyone but me, you wouldn't accept that for an instant. You'd be the first one kicking up, calling for an investigation."

That quieted her. She stood there and looked at him until it got uncomfortable. He got up, headed into the kitchen where he emptied the stale beer down the sink. She followed.

"We should get you a lawyer," she said. "Someone good. Someone really vicious."

Peter grimaced. He opened the fridge, contemplated the remaining beers. No. He took two clean glasses down from the kitchen cupboard, poured a generous measure of whiskey into each, and offered one to Aoife. She took it.

"You haven't told me everything, have you?" she asked.

He shook his head slowly, gazed into his whiskey, then knocked half of it back.

"Nope."

"Well then?"

"Murphy offered me a choice. He said I could go on suspension pending the outcome of the investigation, or I could take a transfer until everything is resolved."

"That sounds promising," Aoife said, though she had

obviously picked up something in his tone. Her eyes were serious, focused on him, trying to read his expression.

"It seems that a garda sergeant in good standing is willing to take me under his wing, supervise me closely, teach me everything Reilly failed to teach me."

The sarcasm silenced her. She waited for him to fill her in.

"Roundstone. They want to send me to Roundstone. To Dad."

"Jesus," Aoife said. "Des."

"Yep. According to Murphy he got in touch. Vouched for me. Claimed I was led astray, and a bit of redirection and *appropriate* supervision would get me back on track."

"You said no," Aoife said.

Peter knocked back the rest of the whiskey.

"You didn't agree, Peter. Tell me you didn't say yes."

"He shouldn't even have been able to manage it. He's my father. It's clearly against regulations, me reporting to him. But that's Des for you. He's always got some friend willing to look the other way."

Peter reached for the whiskey bottle, poured another measure. Aoife watched him fill his glass. She knocked back her own drink, made a face at the harshness of the liquor, then held out her own glass for a refill.

"There was a murder, a few months back. The investigation was taken over by a Dublin team, but there's a mountain of paperwork that needs to be cleaned up, and Des thinks I'd be just perfect for that."

"Tell me you said no."

"I didn't have a choice," Peter said. "Murphy made it very clear. I go to Roundstone, and he'll keep the wolves at bay. Assuming they can prove that Kelly was the man who took her, Murphy will use whatever influence he has to make sure that the Section 91 is the end of it. But if I said no, kicked up a fuss, I'm on suspension and he washes his hands of me. The investigation becomes a criminal one and I could go to prison."

"He said all that?"

"He made it very clear."

"But you don't want the bloody job if it means working with your father, I know that as well as you do."

"It's not just about the job," Peter said.

"Well, you're not going to Ballygobackwards to work beside that prick, that's for sure."

Peter laughed, he couldn't help it. His eyes and head ached from the effort of not crying like a child, but Aoife was so outraged, so furious, that it helped a little. She was always on his side. Since they were children, she'd always been brave. A fighter.

"I don't know what I'm going to do," he said.

Aoife put her glass down. "Do you honestly think you killed an innocent man?" she asked.

It took him a moment to gather himself enough to answer. "I don't know," he said at last. Aoife, irritated, opened her mouth to speak, but Peter held up a hand to forestall her. "I believe that Jason Kelly took Peggah Abbassi that night. But there's no proof, Aoife. There's nothing to prove Peggah was ever in his car except the word of an eleven-year-old boy who saw Kelly, if he saw him at all, from fifty feet away through a dirty window. And a possible partial numberplate. That's not enough. I shot the man dead. His family is out for blood."

"He would have killed you. You came home that night and you told me he drove straight at you."

"He did."

"Well then."

"I told you. There's no proof of that either, it seems. Nothing at the scene."

Aoife threw her hands up in the air. "What happened to

cops sticking up for each other no matter what? Where's the benefit of the doubt?"

"It's not that simple."

"Why? Why isn't it that simple?"

"Because I'm . . . the perception in the station is that I'm with Reilly, I'm on his side, and Reilly isn't liked. Not widely and not by the right people."

Aoife pressed her lips together and shook her head. She took another drink, was silent for a long moment.

"What is Des playing at?" she asked.

Fisher shrugged.

"You have to call him," Aoife said.

"Who? My father?"

"Reilly. You need to call Reilly. If it's his fault you're in this mess, then he needs to pull whatever strings he can to get you out of it."

"Thing is, Aoife, I'm not sure he has any strings left."

Peter didn't call Reilly that night. Instead, he sat up with Aoife, drinking beer and eventually more whiskey, talking the situation over until they'd talked it to death, then going over old memories, spending the last half-hour or so laughing at Aoife's efforts to suggest alternative careers for him. That degenerated fairly quickly, when the tears that he'd forced down all day finally won through. He drank a pint of water, went to bed, and fell asleep straight away.

Peter woke to the sound of voices outside his bedroom door. He recognized Aoife's immediately. Reilly's, out of context, took a moment longer. Peter stumbled out of bed, made for the door then realized he was only wearing his boxers. He hopped clumsily into his jeans, pulled a T-shirt over his head, and opened the door.

"Aoife," he said.

She had her back to him, was still wearing the shorts and tank top she'd worn to bed, the one that said *Riots not Diets* across the front. She'd opened the door to Reilly—Peter could just make out his face through the half-open door—but hadn't invited him in.

"It's all right, Aoife," Peter said. He stepped forward, held the door over Aoife's head.

"Fine," she said. He knew by the look of her that she had a raging hangover. He was feeling the effects himself. His head was aching worse than the day before, and his mouth tasted like he'd eaten garlic and cheese chips and not brushed his teeth.

Aoife gave Reilly a final unimpressed look and disappeared into her bedroom.

Reilly gave Peter a wry look. "Your sister?" he asked.

"Almost," Peter said. It said a lot about Reilly, that question. First of all, that he was perceptive enough to recognize that Aoife wasn't his girlfriend, which was what most people thought when they first met them. And second, that for all that they'd worked together closely for three years now, Reilly knew fuck-all about Peter's personal life.

Peter had met Aoife at the boarding school his father had shipped him off to at the age of eight. When eight-year-old Aoife arrived six months later, she hadn't been able to stop wetting the bed for the first month. Peter had helped her to hide it. He already knew how to hide the dirty linen under the bed until lunchtime, when you could sneak upstairs and change your sheets without any of the other kids noticing. By the time she found her feet, they were fast friends. They needed each other. The school wasn't a bad place. It was small, due to the fact that there wasn't much demand for a boarding school for primary-aged children in the country. The principal had founded the place with his wife, and they provided a kind of casual, all-purpose love, spread thinly across the forty or so students. This was augmented by the kindness and general decency of the small staff, so that there was just enough for the kids to manage, if not exactly thrive. It was the kind of environment that forged deep and lasting friendships between the children, who turned to each other for what no one else in their lives was willing or able to provide. Aoife was his sister in every way that it counted.

"She's a friend," Peter said. "We've known each other since we were kids."

Reilly was nodding but was obviously intent on discussing other things. "Have you got a few minutes?"

Peter hesitated, then held the door open. He wasn't sure what he felt about Reilly showing up at his front door early in the morning. He wasn't sure how he felt about any of it.

Peter led Reilly into the living room. He expected to see the detritus of the night before—empty cans and whiskey glasses—but Aoife must have cleared it up. The air smelled stale though, and he opened the windows, let in the chilly morning air. They sat opposite each other, Reilly on the armchair near the empty fireplace, Peter on the arm of the couch. Reilly kept his coat on. He clearly wasn't expecting to stay for long. He leaned forward, forearms on his thighs and hands loosely clasped together. His eyes held Peter's.

"I wanted to see how you were. Where things were with you."

"I presume Murphy told you," Peter said. Murphy had called Peter into his office as Reilly had left. There'd been no time for conversation, but Reilly surely knew the story.

"Most of it, I think, but Murphy said something about giving you a chance. He didn't elaborate."

Peter folded his arms. He felt a childish urge to keep the information to himself, fought with it, and won. "He said I had a chance if I took a transfer to Roundstone. My father's a sergeant there. It seems he made some promises to Murphy, said he'd keep me on the straight and narrow. Murphy wants me to take the transfer. He gave me the impression that he'd do what he could to prevent a Section 98 if I go to Roundstone. If I don't, I'm on suspension and I'm on my own."

Cormac was silent for a long moment. "You should take it," he said in the end. "Take the transfer, wait it out."

Peter felt a surge of fury. "I don't have much choice, do I?" he said. "If my choices are prison or a uniform in a two-man-band station, it's not much of a choice, is it?"

Cormac's face stilled. Whatever he was feeling disappeared behind a professional veneer.

"I want you to know that I believe that Jason Kelly abducted Peggah Abbassi. You did not shoot an innocent man."

"There's no way to be sure of that, is there?" Peter said. "Based on the evidence." Peter couldn't keep the anger or the fear from his voice.

"It's true that Peggah couldn't ID him," Reilly said. He was so calm, the way he was with suspects, with emotional witnesses. It made Peter want to punch him.

"When he grabbed her from the street, she had been watching her dog," Reilly continued. "She was trying to teach him not to jump up on strangers, so when Kelly approached her, she didn't look at him—she was looking down at her dog, feeding him treats, trying to keep the dog's attention on her. Kelly hit her hard, bundled her into the trunk, and took off. When he let her go on the side of the road it was very dark, and she was very frightened. He told her to keep her eyes closed if she wanted to live, and she did what she was told."

"Well then," Peter said.

"On the other hand," Cormac said. "I'm told that Fred

Fletcher gave a very clear identification. He said he was one hundred percent sure that Kelly was the man he saw."

"What happened to the video?" Peter asked. "The video Fred took, the one I dropped into tech. I don't understand why they haven't managed to enhance the license plate by now."

"They lost it," Reilly said.

"What?"

"Tech say they sent it with the usual courier to Dublin. Tech in Dublin say they never got it. It's disappeared."

Peter stared at Reilly, fighting rising panic. Evidence was lost sometimes, it happened, but not like this.

"It's not my investigation anymore. I only know what I managed to learn working at home yesterday and in an hour at the station this morning. But I'm told the team searched Kelly's house today. They found porn. Some downloads, subscriptions to online video sites. Kelly was smart enough to stay just this side of legal, but his preference was for young Middle Eastern or Asian girls. Sweet sixteen. Barely legal. That sort of thing, but the girls look quite a bit younger."

Peter sat forward.

"Kelly was a carpenter. He worked from time to time for different building companies around Galway. It seems he wasn't well-liked. He had a reputation for being difficult, argumentative. Which is probably why he didn't have a steady job with any of the companies he worked for. They just called on him when they hit a particularly busy period. The rest of the time Kelly advertised on an online labor-hire website as a handyman and carpenter."

It was getting cold in the living room now. Peter got up and shut the windows. He could hear the sound of running water—Aoife having a shower.

"I spoke to Peggah's mother yesterday. Peggah is a gymnast,"

Reilly was saying. "She's a member of the local gym club in Knocknacarra. I called the owner of the gym. She confirmed that Kelly carried out some carpentry work for her. She found him online and he was cheaper than the other quotes. Quite a bit cheaper. She claims, very forcefully, that Kelly was never on the premises when the kids were there. But I think she's lying. She knows she can't have anyone without a police check on the premises when kids are around, and I suspect she didn't want to let a bit of red tape get in the way of the cheap quote."

Peter took a deep breath. Steadied himself mentally. "You're saying he chose her. That he knew who she was, followed her, planned the abduction."

"Yes."

"Then I don't understand. The super seemed to think . . . he made it very clear that he thinks I fucked up."

Reilly stood, went to the windows, and looked out. It was a cold, crisp day outside. Peter's watch and phone were still in his bedroom. What time was it? Given how bright it was outside, it must be after nine a.m. Reilly should be at the station. He should be chasing down evidence, not sitting here in Peter's living room. Soon he would have to go. Unlike Peter, he had work to do.

"When you shot Kelly, he was unarmed. Peggah wasn't in danger. You say that he drove the car at you, that you acted in self-defense when you pulled the trigger, but we haven't been able to prove that. The tire markings at the scene aren't conclusive. Still, your word as a police officer, combined with the circumstantial evidence we've been able to gather so far, should, in my view, have resulted in complete exoneration."

Reilly fell silent. The running water in the bathroom next door stopped. The sound of the traffic outside seemed louder suddenly. "What are you saying?" Peter asked.

Reilly said nothing. He seemed to be reaching for a response, discarding it, and reaching again. He was obviously holding something back. Peter's fear and frustration spilled over.

"This is because of you, isn't it, Reilly? You've pissed Murphy off because that's how you are. You think you're better than everyone else. Nobody likes that and you can't blame them for it. I'm in this situation because you are out in the cold, and now I'm swinging out here with you. I'm a target because, like a fool, I've supported you."

Peter fell silent, waited for a response that didn't come. Reilly stood up.

"I can't help you right now, Fisher. I can't pull you out of this hole. You should take the transfer. It's a good option. I might . . . I don't know. Maybe I can fix this, maybe not."

"Christ," Peter said, as he half-closed his eyes, rubbed his forehead with his right hand. "Please don't. You'll only make things worse."

Reilly made for the door. Spoke one more time before he left.

"Don't give up. You're a good detective. If you can, take this job with your father, stick it out for a few months. Give it a bit of time. All right? Just give it a bit of time."

CHAPTER THIRTEEN

Peter was angry, and he let that anger fuel him as he bundled his clothes and a few toiletries into a bag. He shoveled some cereal into his mouth, deflected Aoife's attempts to draw him into conversation, and drove out of Galway at eleven a.m. on Tuesday morning. He couldn't wait, couldn't stay in Galway for a minute longer than he needed to, or his nerve might fail him and he'd never leave at all. But his hangover was brutal. It was painfully bright, one of those brisk sunny days November occasionally offered up. A reminder that winter wouldn't last forever, though the worst of it lay ahead. The sun was high in the sky when he set off, and the roads were dry enough that he didn't have to contend with ice, at least. Just the headache, and the nausea, and the occasional stray sheep. The N59 from Galway to Clifden was narrow, winding, and scarred by the occasional deep pothole. A dangerous drive if he didn't keep his wits about him. The road curled itself around craggy hills and turloughs, so clear that they perfectly reflected the blue sky above. As he drove out of Oughterard and the landscape opened up around him, Peter shifted in his seat, turned up the heat and the music, and kept his eyes firmly on the road. Connemara was undeniably beautiful, but it held too many bad memories.

How could this have happened? A few days ago he'd been waking up with Niamh beside him, a date on the cards, and all was right in the world. Now all of that was gone. He'd canceled their dinner with the shortest of texts when he'd been in the midst of the case and hadn't even considered calling her since. What could he say? They'd been at the flirty fun stage. Not the *I just killed a man and I'm not sure how I feel about it and by the way I might be prosecuted and also I hate my father because he fucked every woman who had the bad luck to pass through his eyeline while my mother was dying of cancer and how was your day* stage.

Peter reached the village at around lunchtime. Roundstone hadn't changed. It was exceptionally pretty, all terraced houses overlooking the sea. There was a church, a couple of pubs, one convenience store, and a hotel that served the tourist trade. It didn't have a hell of a lot else to offer, besides the boat ramp and, about a mile away, the beach at Gurteen Bay.

Peter drove first to Horan's shop, pulled in outside. There were half a dozen ragged bouquets of flowers out front in a stand. He chose the best of them, went inside. The shop took its name from Simon Horan, who'd been gray and stooped even when Peter was a child, and he still half-expected to see the old man behind the counter. Instead, it was staffed by a bored-looking teenage girl, seated on a stool, and watching a small TV which was behind the counter. She looked up when he came in.

"Close the door, would you? Don't let the heat out."

He pulled it closed behind him, looked around at the overstocked shelves, the buckets and spades, and colorful kids' fishing nets left over from summer. "Have you tins of biscuits?" he asked.

"Back there," she said, pointing to the back of the shop. "We've the Christmas stock in so you've a choice."

"Thanks."

He made his way through the narrow aisle, picked the biggest box of chocolate cookies he could see, and returned to the counter. He put the flowers and the cookie tin in front of the girl, waited for the inevitable comments and questions—the first thing you generally sacrificed in Roundstone was any expectation of privacy—but she was pleasantly disinterested in his purchases, rang them up without saying a thing, and Peter felt one tiny knot of tension release. He swiped his card, typed in his pin. The shop bell dinged as the door opened behind him, letting in a blast of cold air.

"I'll take twenty Benson, Sharon," said a familiar voice from behind him.

Peter turned and saw at his father. Des was off duty and out of uniform. He didn't look well. He'd been a handsome man in his youth, but you'd have to search hard to find a trace of it now. His beer gut strained his shirt, and he'd had taken to belting his pants under his belly fat. That was a new development. How long had it been since he'd last seen his father? Two years? Three? Des was clean-shaven, but his skin looked painful, had that red flaky look that sometimes comes with heavy drinking.

"Des," Peter said. He picked up his biscuits and flowers and made to leave. Des nodded at his purchases.

"A girlfriend in town? Already? Fast mover. Like father, like son." Des winked at the girl behind the counter as he paid for his cigarettes.

Revulsion and hatred swept over Peter, but he made damn sure that nothing showed on his face but blank disinterest. "These are for Maggie," he said.

Des snorted. "It'll take a bit more than a few biscuits to please her up. When was the last time you bothered your arse coming out to see her? You make her drive in to Galway, don't you? An old woman like that. I'd call that selfish, wouldn't you, Sharon?"

Sharon was looking back and forth between them with sudden interest. She had an appetite for gossip after all, it seemed. Fucking Des. It could hardly be a coincidence that he'd walked into the shop a minute after Peter's arrival. Some crony had spotted Peter's arrival and alerted him. Or maybe Des had been keeping an eye out himself. That was more likely. How else could he have gotten there so quickly?

Sharon put the packet of cigarettes on the counter and Des reached into his pants pocket and pulled out a roll of cash, peeled off a twenty.

"Where are you staying?" Des asked. He flicked one finger at the flowers. "If you're thinking of old Mags, that's not an option. She already has a guest." He looked Peter up and down, took his time about it. "I've a spare bedroom. You're welcome to it."

No fucking way.

"If Maggie can't have me, I'll stay in the hotel," Peter said. "I'll see you at the station tomorrow morning." He left, feeling his father's eyes on his back all the way to the car.

Maggie Robinson was Peter's grandmother. His mother's mother. She lived in a stone dormer cottage at the top of a steep hill a short drive from Horan's. The cottage had two bedrooms, a comfortable kitchen and living room, and a breathtaking view over the village and the sea beyond. Maggie had lived there alone for as long as Peter could remember, except for the few months before his mother's death. When Peter's mother's cancer had been deemed incurable, she had finally left Des and returned home to Maggie, bringing Peter with her. Des had had no objection. Peter remembered those last months as peaceful, mostly, with moments of happiness, even as the ax of her illness hung over their heads. When she'd died, Des had insisted on organizing the funeral, and he'd adopted the role of chief mourner. Peter had been eight, and the hypocrisy had been more than he could stomach, but there was nothing at all he could do about it. Three weeks after his mother's death, Des had shown up at Maggie's house and informed Peter that he would be attending boarding school. Maggie had argued against it as best she could but of course she had no power to prevent his removal. And so Des had dragged Peter off, dumped him in the school, and that was that. Des paid the fees and considered the box of fatherhood and responsibility well and truly ticked.

Peter drove up the hill, then turned into the cottage, pulling in over the cattle grid. Everything looked the same. The cottage had a bit of land around it, but it would have been generous to call it a garden. Maggie's skills and interest didn't lie in that direction, so there wasn't much in it but a bit of grass, usually in need of a cut, and a few hardy shrubs and bushes. Today everything looked more or less as he'd expected. The grass was a bit neater than usual, but still scrubby, the way it got out here with the heavy rain and the high, salt-laden winds. The whitewash on the cottage was clean and bright, and—here was something new—Maggie had window boxes now, planted with trailing ivies and some sort of purple-and-white flower that could obviously handle a Roundstone winter. Peter got out of the car, gathered up the cookie tin and flowers. He went to the back door, knocked.

"Mags, you home?"

No answer, so he tried the handle. It was unlocked. He pushed the door open and it stuck a little, the frame warped from years of bad weather.

"Mags?" he called again. He found her in the kitchen, sleeping in an armchair that had been pushed in close to the Aga cooker, a blanket tucked across her lap. It was a most un-Maggie-like position. Maggie was a bustler. She liked to keep busy.

Peter put the biscuits and flowers on the counter, then gently touched her arm.

"Mags," he said. "Maggie?" He'd never called her granny, not even when he was a little boy. She was slow to wake, blinking at him in obvious confusion.

"Mags. Sorry to just arrive like this. Maybe I shouldn't have woken you?"

"Peter?" Her voice was weak, querulous, and Peter felt the first stirrings of alarm. She was very pale, and her skin looked paper-thin.

"Have you been sick? I'm sorry I haven't been by for a visit." How long since he had seen her in person? Could it have been a year? But they'd spoken on the phone, just last month. Or maybe it had been the month before.

"I've been . . . under the weather."

"Has the doctor been to see you?"

Her brow furrowed, and when she spoke again it was with a reassuring trace of Maggie-like impatience. "He comes twice a week. It's too much. I'm not on my deathbed yet, and if I were, there's little enough he could do about it."

Peter laughed, a little shakily.

"Make tea, Peter, will you? I haven't had a thing since Anna left this morning."

Peter filled the kettle, went in search of the teapot and tea leaves. Everything was where he'd expected to find it, and the cupboards and fridge were well stocked. There were a few children's yogurts in the fridge, which was odd.

"What are you doing here, anyway?" she asked.

"Well, that's a warm welcome home," he said in the lightest tone he could manage. He'd planned on telling her everything as soon as he arrived, had looked forward to her support and her counsel, but suddenly he realized that he couldn't. He couldn't tell her that he'd killed a man, that he might be prosecuted for it, and that his only possible way out was to work for a man they both despised. He couldn't dump all of that on her. She was too old and too tired. He should be the one looking after her.

Maggie's eyes went to the flowers and the biscuits. "Are you just here for a visit?" she asked.

"I'm here for a while," he said. "A month or two." The kettle boiled, and he scooped a few spoonfuls of tea leaves into the pot and filled it. He rummaged in the cupboard for a couple of coffee mugs, then found sugar and milk.

"Open the biscuits," she said.

"Right." He brought everything to the kitchen table, but she didn't move. There was an awkward pause.

"I'm so warm here, I think I'll stay where I am," she said. "Can you bring over the little table?" She gestured to a small coffee table that had been placed off to the side in the room. Peter picked it up, carried it over. Was it new? He couldn't remember having seen it before. He poured the tea, opened the cookies, and brought Maggie her cup, a small plate. He brought over a chair for himself so he could be a bit closer to her, offered her the tin. She chose a cookie with seeming enthusiasm, but set it aside on the plate. He wolfed two down straight away.

"You never change," she said.

"Don't know about that," he mumbled, through a mouth full of cookie, and immediately felt about eight years old again.

Maggie took a sip from her tea, put the mug back down. She made no move to eat; the cookie sat untouched on her plate. Her hands were thinner than he remembered, and her cheekbones were more prominent. Was she eating enough?

"Have you seen your father?" she asked.

"I bumped into him at Horan's," Peter said.

She sniffed, unimpressed.

"He said you have a guest staying at the moment. Is that the Anna you mentioned?"

"Anna's not a guest," Maggie said. "She's a home help. A live-in."

"Really?"

"You needn't look like that, Peter. I'm getting older, you know. And I'm not some batty old woman too stubborn to admit that she needs a bit of help. I'd much rather have a nice girl live in than go to some old folks' home that smells of cabbage and nappies."

Peter held his hands up in mock defensiveness. "Okay, okay. I didn't say it was a bad idea."

He was thrown. Maggie seemed like she'd aged ten years. She had been a million miles away from considering a home help when he'd last seen her. She'd been talking about taking a trip to West Cork with a friend, if he remembered correctly. And now she was tucked up in an armchair by the stove, too tired to move to the kitchen table for a cup of tea.

Peter took another biscuit, sipped his tea. "So, tell me about Anna," he said. "What's she like? Where did you find her?"

"Desmond brought her over, with Tilly," Maggie said.

Peter looked at her. "Des? Since when do you take advice from Des?"

"It wasn't advice. It was practicality. Anna needed a place to stay. She and Tilly both. And I needed a hand around the place. It was just going to be for a week or two, until I was back on my feet. But, well . . . we suit each other."

"Right," Peter said. "That makes sense."

Except that it didn't. Maggie and Des didn't even *speak* to each other. Maggie had managed to maintain the barest civility toward Des until Peter had turned eighteen. Then she'd felt free enough of the threat of Peter's complete removal from her orbit, so she'd waited for the anniversary of her daughter's death, and then she'd confronted Des, publicly, at the seat of his power. Gilmartin's pub. She'd torn strips off him, loudly—and creatively. She'd called him pathetic. An aging, delusional playboy who'd failed her daughter again and again and then profoundly failed her when she'd needed him most. He'd been too busy chasing tourist women, who were happy to take a night's entertainment from his slight charm, to go home to his child and his dying wife. Right there, in front of all his cronies, standing her ground and refusing to budge, she'd declaimed his many failures as a father, as a husband, *and* as a garda. In the end, Des had physically bundled her out of the place, and as far as Peter knew, they had never spoken again. Knowing his father, Des would have taken some sort of revenge, except that Maggie was well-liked in the village and the whole thing had been too public. So he'd been obliged to let it go and they'd avoided each other as much as possible since.

"I'm just surprised you'd take someone Des recommended," Peter said, carefully.

"I do make my own decisions, you know," Maggie said. "Desmond brought her to this house, but he didn't know her. She wasn't a *friend* of his, if that's what you're thinking. She came to the pub, looking for a room for the night. They were booked out and so he brought her here. And I liked her."

Peter was suddenly convinced that this Anna was exactly what Maggie thought she wasn't—one of Des's women. An hour ago, if someone had suggested that Des would have been able to fool

Maggie in that way, Peter would have laughed in their face. But despite her upbeat, confident words there was a trace of anxiety in Maggie's face when she spoke about Anna and this Tilly—who the fuck was Tilly?—and his heart twisted at the idea that Des would be so cruel as to set up one of his flings in Maggie's house, and that Maggie should be so vulnerable as to allow it.

"I can get you somebody," Peter said. "I'm going to be here for a month or two, Mags. I can move back in, if you'll have me. Keep you company and give you a hand around the place, and when I head back to Galway, I can help you find someone you like. You don't have to have someone live in, either, if you don't want that, you know? That's your call. We could have someone who just comes in every day . . ."

"You're here for a month or two? Why?" Maggie asked. She wasn't her usual self, he'd noticed. She seemed a little breathless. She was resting back in her chair again, the tea and biscuit forgotten.

"It's just a work thing, Mags. Nothing to worry about."

"Working with Desmond?" she asked.

He nodded, reluctantly.

"It's just temporary." One way or the other, he was going to make sure of that.

With a level of effort that distressed him, Maggie sat forward and took his hand.

"I don't want you moving here, Peter. The only young people you'll see will be seasonal workers and tourists. There's no life for you in the village. What were you thinking? Working with Des is a terrible idea. You and he . . ." She shook her head. "Promise me that you'll go back to Galway, straight away."

Peter laughed unsteadily, tried to draw his hand from hers, but she held on.

"Promise me," she said.

He was shocked to see tears in her eyes. He squeezed her hand.

"Yes, Mags. I'll go back. It might not be straight away, but soon."

He got her a tissue and she wiped her eyes, and the intense emotion seemed to blow out of her as quickly as it had arrived, leaving her wilted.

"Will you be working on the murder?" she asked. Of course she knew about it. Everyone would.

"Did you know them?" Peter asked. "The victims, I mean?"

"A little," Maggie said sadly. "I played cards with Miles sometimes." She was quiet for a long moment, then she smiled at him tiredly.

"It's nice of you to visit, Peter. Why don't you make some tea?"

Not long after that, Maggie drifted off to sleep. Peter sat with her for another hour, half-hoping she would wake again, half-relieved when she didn't. He didn't know what to do about this Maggie, who so clearly needed help. How could he have missed this? Peter desperately wanted the mysterious Anna to put in an appearance—he needed to row with somebody, and she seemed a likely candidate—but she never showed. She was probably in the pub with her mate Tilly, knocking back the pints and laughing at Des's jokes. Eventually, Peter stood up, quietly tidied away the tea, and let himself out.

Peter drove to the little boutique hotel in the village, mentally calculating how far he could push his budget. That was a very real problem. He was still paying rent for the flat in Galway and a garda's salary did not stretch too much beyond basic subsistence, these days. His credit card limit could handle a few nights at the hotel, but after that, he'd have to make other plans. Peter parked in the parking lot, shouldered his bag, and made his way inside to a faint smell of a turf fire and fresh flowers. He made himself known to the girl at reception, asked for a room for two nights, and was all but laughed out of the place.

"We've a wedding," she said. "Fully booked."

"But it's Tuesday," Peter said.

She shrugged. "Saturday weddings are booked up for two years. Sundays too. People are branching out."

"In winter?"

She nodded in the direction of the front windows, which looked out over the little dock and the water beyond. "Pictures," she said, eloquently. "You can get pictures by the dock, by the fishing boats, in between the rain, and then a few behind the bar pulling pints. That's what people like."

"You've no rooms at all?"

Her hands flew across the keyboard. "I've three rooms free tomorrow, but I need them back on Thursday. That any good to you?"

Peter retreated to his car, took out his phone. He thought about a B&B, groaned at the thought of the interest, the inquiries, the watching of his comings and goings. He wanted anonymity, what little he could get here in Roundstone, where the main occupation of every inhabitant aged forty and older was minding each other's business. Still, he called them. They were all booked for the wedding. The only other obvious option was Gilmartin's pub on the main street. They used to have a few rooms upstairs. Shabby, but liveable. Peter couldn't do it. The pub was his father's fiefdom. His little domain, the regular drinkers a mix of those who genuinely seemed to enjoy Des Fisher's company, and those who might not like him but wouldn't cross him for fear of making themselves his target. The end result would be the same. Every move Peter made would be reported to Des within moments.

Peter shook himself. He needed somewhere that would

work longer term anyway. Reilly had said he should give it at least a few months, but Peter knew his limits. He had already promised himself that he would give it eight weeks and not a day longer. If he hadn't found a way back to Galway at the end of the two months, he would hand in his notice and find another way to earn a living. Still, two months was two months. He needed somewhere semipermanent to lay his head. He tried a private holiday rentals website, scrolled through the listings, and winced at the prices. There was one place—a one-bedroom flat, much cheaper than everywhere else. He squinted at the photographs, which were suspiciously blurry. Fuck it. Beggars can't be choosers. He took a breath, sent a message. A few minutes later he'd made a deal for one month's rental at a reduced price, a price that made his shoulders tighten and which would decimate his limited savings, his credit card limit, and basically every bit of cash he had. He'd have to borrow a few quid from Aoife. She would say yes without a thought, and she could afford it. Her parents didn't want a lesbian for a daughter. They had managed their guilt by giving her a generous lump sum on her twenty-first birthday and then encouraging her to not bother visiting. She had that money sitting in a bank account somewhere, and her doctor's salary, neither of which she had time to spend with the hours she worked. It didn't make it all right, though. He would have done almost anything to avoid borrowing money from her, anything but live with his father. He called Aoife, asked her for the bare minimum he needed to survive. She said she would transfer double and then hung up before he could argue.

Twenty minutes later he met the owner—a taciturn German—at the flat and took possession of the keys. The flat was one of four built cheaply during the Celtic Tiger, probably with the benefit of a tax break of some description. The plaster was gray and crumbling, struggling already with the onslaught of the weather and the proximity to the Atlantic. The German disappeared quickly. A quick look around told Peter why. There were no sheets on the bed and none in the linen closet. Just a thinning duvet, a lumpy pillow, and a smallish threadbare towel. The place smelled of damp and neglect. It was very cold. Peter dumped his bags in the corner of the living room. He'd make it work. Figure out the heat, and if that couldn't be made to work, there was a fireplace. There was a fridge, an oven, a toaster and kettle, and a washing machine, and the electricity was on. He felt a small sense of relief, of satisfaction. As long as he had a space of his own, he could get through these next weeks and get out. Maybe it wouldn't be as bad as he had feared.

CHAPTER FOURTEEN

Galway, Ireland

Cormac heard the broadcast on Tuesday evening. He was at home, about to sit down to, for lack of anything else to do, a fairly elaborate dinner by his normal standards. The radio was playing in the background:

> *"The garda press office has confirmed that gardaí made a major heroin seizure off the coast of the West of Ireland on Saturday evening, amidst a worrying increase in the supply of the killer drug across Europe this year. A thirty-five-year-old man and a thirty-two-year-old woman, both Irish nationals, were arrested and are being held for questioning about the haul. Gardaí are yet to confirm quantities seized, but it is understood at least seventy pounds of heroin, worth six-point-five million euros, were discovered."*

Cormac looked at his lamb, his untouched potato gratin. He stood and dumped the lot in the bin, went upstairs to change into shorts and a T-shirt. He grabbed his runners, his jacket, and headed out the door. He needed to run. It was already dark, coming up on seven-thirty p.m., and the city traffic was quieting down. He turned his back to it, ran out toward the water. The setting sun cast a gray and pallid light over the ocean. It was a cold night but there were still walkers and other runners about. He recognized a few faces and upped his speed. He was in no mood for conversation, and pace was as good an isolator as a pair of headphones.

Cormac pushed on, running hard, taking little pleasure in the fact that the pace was comfortable. The first four months after Emma had left he'd taken to going to the pub once or twice a week for a couple of pints, and that had slowly become his routine. One evening he found himself heading for the pub after work on a Tuesday evening, and knew that it was more likely than not that he'd be there every night until Saturday. It was boredom that drove him there, and a loneliness he wouldn't admit to, rather than any particular yen for the drink, but the motivation didn't matter when the outcome was the same. He'd knocked it on the head that night, packed a bag for the gym the following morning, and exercise had become his alternative method of passing the time. Now, as he ran, he had to acknowledge that though the gym was a healthier choice, it was no more satisfying. Oh, he was pleased enough that his burgeoning beer belly was a thing of the past, that despite long hours at the station, he was leaner and stronger than he had been in years. But after a month or two, an hour spent running or in the gym felt as empty as sinking pints in the pub. More so, maybe. He'd thought about finding a rugby team. A team of old farts like himself, men who were carrying enough old injuries that they had no urge to beat each other to a pulp just to prove a point. He'd been thinking about it for months but had done nothing. The truth was that with Emma away he'd been in a holding pattern. Waiting for her. Waiting for change.

The run did what it was meant to do. By the time he got

back to the house the clear night sky had given way to clouds, and there was a smattering of cold rain that he welcomed. He had a long shower, dressed, and came downstairs. He stood for a minute in the doorway of the kitchen, letting his eyes drift around the room. With Emma away, he lived small. Laundry once a week, meals for one. He was naturally disciplined so he tidied up after himself. His life had become almost military in its routine. He wished now it hadn't. If the place were a tip, he'd have something to do at least. Could make some sort of project out of fixing things up. But the place was clean, everything more or less as it should be. Cormac snorted to himself. Who was he kidding—without Emma, his life had been more monastic than military. Cormac turned and grabbed his keys. He didn't want to be here anymore.

He went to the pub. To The Front Door, specifically. The task force was having drinks, a celebration of the record-breaking raid they'd just pulled off. He had no intention of missing it.

The place was heaving when he got there, and it wasn't just the task force. Every cop in Galway wanted to get in on this, be a part of it, and some of them looked like they'd been at it all day. Everyone, that is, except for his own little team. There was no sign of Dave McCarthy, Deirdre Russell, or Rory Mulcair. Reynolds must be working them hard. Anthony Healy was there, in position at the back bar. He was red-faced and sweaty, held a pint in one hand, gesticulated with the other. No sign at first glance of Trevor Murphy. Cormac moved among the crowd, had a few words with some of the lads. Conversations quieted, at first, when he drew near, but they were still on a high and they wanted to talk. How many of them knew about his suspension? All of them, surely. Cormac took his time, worked hard at giving off a relaxed vibe, gave them a bit of encouragement. Soon enough he was hearing stories about cold nights sitting on one rocky shore or another, or out on a boat, chasing what felt like wisps of rumors. Stories about Saturday night, when it seemed that everything had changed. Operating on a tip-off from one of Trevor Murphy's informants, they'd gone out with the coastguard, followed a small pleasure yacht coming in at a distance, and managed to take down both supplier and receiver. Cormac made all the right noises. He listened, nodded, smiled, and bought a few pints. He spotted Carrie O'Halloran, momentarily alone at a corner table. He made his way over and joined her there. Her dark eyes assessed him.

"Well," he said.

"Well yourself."

"Enjoying the party?"

She shrugged. "It's a big win. You have to celebrate the wins. We don't get enough of them."

He nodded. "Not lately, anyway."

"I heard about the suspension," she said.

Cormac grimaced. "I didn't see it coming."

Carrie gave a tired sigh. "You need to get better at making friends, Cormac. Murphy's not the worst. I know he's not your kind of cop, but he does what he must to survive."

"What he's done over the last few months is rip the guts out of the station. Poured resources into his son's pet project."

Carrie gestured to the crowd in the pub. "Yeah. And look at the outcome. You might not like it, but you have to give credit where it's due."

Cormac nodded slowly, took a sip from his pint. He'd been nursing one since he arrived, was less than halfway through it.

"I was hoping I'd bump into you this evening," he said.

"You want to ask me about Peter."

"That too."

She laughed ruefully, shook her head. "You probably know more about it than I do. I just sat in on his debrief. I haven't seen him since Saturday night."

"He's been offered a transfer, to the sticks. Murphy intimated that if he went quietly, he might come out of this thing reasonably intact."

"That's good," she said. She paused. "It might be better than he deserves."

Cormac felt that. He put his pint down.

"You know, Cormac, what happened with Fisher wasn't their fault." Carrie gestured toward the crowded pub. "No one sent him out there after that car but himself. He was always too eager to please you."

"You're saying he shot Kelly to *please* me?"

"You know what I'm saying. He should have waited. Yes, you were short-staffed. And yes, he was worried for the girl, but he needs to be able to handle that sort of pressure, still make good decisions. You can't blame Murphy for what Peter did."

"I never said I did," Cormac said, deliberately mildly.

That irritated her. He'd noticed that about Carrie. The more even-tempered he appeared, the more exasperated she seemed to get. She leaned forward across the table. "Then stop pissing people off," she hissed. "Make some friends and you might even be able to bring Fisher in from the cold. Keep it up and maybe you'll end up in Siberia with him."

He smiled at her, couldn't help it, even though part of him knew it would probably annoy her even more. She was just so bloody decent, she was such a fighter. He liked that about her so much.

She scowled back at him, then sat back and took a sip from her wine. "How's Emma?" she asked.

"She's grand. Working hard."

"Still in Brussels?"

He nodded.

"See much of her?"

"I booked a flight. I'm going tomorrow."

"That's probably a good idea," she said, but after a moment she narrowed her eyes, leaned forward. "It's not like you to run away, Cormac."

They were interrupted before anything more was said.

"So this is where you're hiding." Anthony Healy's voice was loud, full of false bonhomie. He put a moist hand on Cormac's shoulder, swaying a little on his feet. His eyes went from Carrie to Cormac and back again. "Did you hear about our little raid, Reilly?" he asked.

"Congratulations," Cormac said, his tone very dry. "It was quite a win."

Healy pulled a stool out from under their table, sat down unsteadily. He put his pint down in front of him, lined it up carefully.

"How's your little protégé?" he asked.

Cormac took a drink from his own pint, then pushed it away. "I'm not sure who you mean," he said.

"I mean that young fella. Fisher. The guy with the heavy trigger finger. I hear he's been banished."

"I haven't spoken to him recently," Cormac said evenly. "I'm sure he's fine."

Healy was looking at him intently. Carrie had withdrawn a little and it seemed as if Healy had forgotten her presence. He leaned forward, bloodshot eyes oozing sincerity.

"You're a good detective, Reilly. I know we haven't been the best of friends, but you're a good detective, I've never denied it. But you've got one problem, you know that?"

"I'm sure you'll tell me," Cormac said.

Healy waved a hand expansively as if Cormac had just made his point for him. "You think you're better than everyone else." He smiled widely, let the silence fall, and waited for Cormac to respond. When Cormac said nothing, he took it as an invitation to continue.

"Look, what happened to Fisher could have happened to any of us. That's my point. That's why we need to stick together. Brotherhood." A clumsy gesture toward Carrie. "Sisterhood, if you want. It's about trust. It's about belief. You want to have friends you can call on when things go wrong? They need to know that you'll be there for them too, that you've got their backs."

It was so close to what Carrie had said just a few minutes before that for a second Cormac thought that they'd discussed it beforehand. Conspired. That this was some sort of clumsy intervention. Well-intentioned, at least on Carrie's part, but if she'd thrown in her lot with Healy, that was a colossal misjudgment, and he'd thought more of her. He tried to catch her eye, but she was looking at Healy and there was dislike in her eyes.

"How's the wife, Healy?" she asked.

Healy's face contorted in sudden anger. "That bitch," he said. "She's sitting on her fat ass in my house in Spain, did you know that? She's never worked a day in her life, but somehow I'm expected to keep her in style now that she's left me. Fucking women." His eyes wandered from Carrie's face to her breasts and back. "You'd never do that, O'Halloran," he said. "I'll give you this much. You're a hard worker."

Carrie finished her wine. "Oh, I'm a bitch in my own little way," she said. She stood, picked up her jacket from the back of her chair. "I'm off," she said. "Early night."

Cormac followed her lead. He'd gotten what he'd come here

for. He stood. Nodded to Healy. "Congratulations again," he said. "Great outcome."

But Healy said nothing. He watched Cormac and Carrie leave, a curl to his lip. As soon as the door had closed behind them, he returned to the bar, and made sure to point out to anyone who'd listen that Carrie O'Halloran and Cormac Reilly had left the pub together.

CHAPTER FIFTEEN

Roundstone, Ireland

Peter's first night in the flat was a cold one. Fixing the boiler had proved beyond his limited abilities and Horan's was closed when he went out in search of firewood. He was helped a little bit by the fact that the apartment he was renting was on the second floor. The ground floor unit below his was occupied, and some small amount of heat must have penetrated upward from the rooms below. But he felt it. The cold that had seemed bearable when he climbed fully clothed under the duvet at ten o'clock was bitter when he woke at three a.m., and again at five. His breath condensed in the air. He couldn't stop shivering.

By seven a.m. he gave up, got up, and searched through the cupboards in the little kitchenette. He filled the kettle and found some teabags, presumably abandoned by a previous tenant. There was no milk or sugar, but the comfort of hot tea was still welcome. At eight he left the apartment in search of food and warmth. Horan's was open. Sharon was there, well wrapped in a puffer jacket and hat, her gloved hands curled around a cup of coffee.

"Christ but it takes ages for this place to heat up in the mornings," she said. She yawned widely, making no effort to cover her mouth. She nodded toward the back of the shop. "There's a coffee machine back there. And if you're looking for food, I can nuke one of those sausage rolls for you."

"Thanks—I'll take two, please," Peter said. He got his coffee, returned to the counter.

"So Sergeant Fisher's your father?" she asked, as she swiped his card.

"Technically, yes," he said.

"Like that, is it?"

"Yes," he said. He didn't want to encourage conversation about this particular topic, but neither did he want anyone getting the impression that he and Des were close.

"Same," she said. She didn't say anything else, just bagged his sausage rolls and returned her gaze to her TV.

"See ya, Sharon," he said.

"Mm-hmm." She didn't look up, and Peter smiled to himself as he left the shop.

Peter drove to the garda station, but the building was dark, still locked up. He sat in the car and ate his food and drank his coffee, with the heater on full blast. Nine a.m. came and went with no sign of Des. Nine-thirty. What a surprise. Peter yawned and blinked for what felt like the fortieth time. The heat in the car was knocking him out. Fuck it. He put his seat back, folded his arms, and closed his eyes. He fell asleep in moments, was woken, disoriented, by a knock on his car window. A man who was not his father was leaning over, grinning in at him.

"You must be Peter," the man said, raising his voice and putting his face right up to the glass, squinting a little. "Come in and I'll make the tea." He stepped back then stood, waiting, grin intact. Peter pulled himself together and climbed out of the car. The other man offered his hand and Peter shook it.

"James Brennan. Jim. Your dad probably mentioned me."

Peter, still half asleep, shook his head.

"You haven't seen Des yet today?" Jim asked.

"Not yet."

"He'll be out in the community," Jim said. "He's great at the relationship building. Always keeps a finger on the pulse. But you'll know that yourself."

Peter stared at Jim Brennan. He must be taking the piss, surely? But Jim's smiling face radiated sincerity.

"You haven't been working with Des for very long, then?" said Peter.

"Five years now," Jim said cheerily, and he turned and led the way into the station.

Peter was familiar with Roundstone Garda Station. Des had brought him there once or twice when he was a child, on the rare occasions when he hadn't managed to completely avoid his parental responsibilities. The building was a small converted cottage. Peter remembered a tiny reception area just inside the front door, and behind it one large office with a few desks and shelving units, a small bathroom at the very back. By the bathroom was a second small room with bars on the window and a reinforced door—used as a short-term holding cell. The main office had always smelled damp and musty and had been stuffed with stacks of paper files. The bathroom at the back was always freezing, even in summer, and had smelled faintly of wee. Jim unlocked the door to the station and ushered him inside. Peter was relieved to see there had been a few small improvements.

"Welcome, anyway," Jim said. "I'll make the tea. I have a few muffins too, left over from yesterday, if you've a bit of a sweet tooth like myself."

Some things were the same. There was paper everywhere and the shelves along the walls were filled to overflowing with hanging files. But the smell of damp was gone, replaced by the smell of coffee—Peter didn't miss a new-looking coffee machine installed on a small table in the corner. It was warmer too. They must have replaced the insulation, or the heat, or both.

"You've upgraded a few bits," Peter said.

"Not really," Jim said. "We only get what's left over, you know yourself. Have you been in the new station in Galway city yet?"

Peter shook his head. The room was so bloody small. He would be sitting cheek to jowl or face to face with his father, with nowhere to hide, every day for months.

"Where do I sit?" Peter asked.

"That's Des there," Jim said, pointing to the desk to Peter's left, the one nearest the door. "I'm opposite." Jim pointed to the desk on the right. "You can take this one, if you like. It's all set up." It was the desk to Des's left, near the coffee machine.

Peter took off his coat and sat. He hit a few keys on the keyboard. The familiar garda logo and the log-in prompt for the PULSE system came up, and he was unexpectedly comforted by it. He shifted some of the files to make a bit of space, and logged in. Jim made coffee and delivered one to Peter's desk.

"Thanks."

Jim nodded.

"It's good you're here," Jim said. "I'm three days a week in Clifden, and with this murder, Des has too much work on his plate. Your being here will make a difference."

"Right," he said. "Busy, is he?"

"It's the paperwork," Jim said chattily. "Your dad has always been a more hands-on kind of man. He'd rather be out and about, meeting people, building relationships, not filing three versions of this and four of the other."

"He's not one for computers then, no?"

Jim grinned. "He'll use the system all right," he said. "He's as good as any cop at getting it to spit out the information we need, better than most. But he doesn't like to feed it, as it were." Who was this guy? He was almost a caricature of a jolly police officer—he had the same round, happy face as Mr. Plod in the *Noddy* cartoons Peter had watched as a little boy. It was unsettling.

"That's where you come in," Jim continued.

"Oh?"

"You've worked a murder. More than one, I'm told. We thought you could get on top of whatever procedural stuff we haven't quite managed ourselves. Dot the i's and cross the t's."

"I see."

"Don't worry," Jim said. "It's just a bit of tidying up on this end, that's all. The SDU in Dublin took over the formal investigation. It's not closed, but they know who did it. One of those Dublin gangs. They came down, looking to rip off a pensioner, and things got out of hand. So all the hard slog is being done elsewhere. We're just needing someone to keep on top of the paperwork."

"Right."

Jim was looking puzzled now, picking up on Peter's lack of enthusiasm. "You're probably like your dad, are you? You'd rather be out and about? I'm sure Des will bring you on some of his rounds, teach you a bit about community policing. There's no better man for it."

"Ah no, Jimmy," a voice came from the door, and it dripped sarcasm. "Peter's above all that. He's a *detective* garda. He wants to be solving real crimes, the tough stuff, not dealing with petty misdemeanors in our little village."

Jim laughed as if the comment was a bit of good-natured teasing.

Des Fisher made his way comfortably over to the coffee machine and set about making himself a cup. The room already felt smaller.

"I was just filling Peter here in on the murder," Jim said. "Or at least, I was about to."

Des nodded and continued with the coffee machine, without looking up.

"It was about four weeks ago," Jim continued. "On a Saturday."

"Saturday, third of October," Des put in. He found the pod he wanted, inserted it in the machine, and chose a cup.

Jim nodded. "That's right. The victims were Miles Lynch and his nephew, Carl. Miles had a bit of a farm, and Carl worked it with him. They lived together in the farmhouse, and that's where they were killed."

"How?" Peter asked.

"They were beaten to death," Des said flatly. "Someone picked up the poker where it lay in the grate and beat the living shite out of them. Miles was in his late seventies. Carl was a young man. Thirty-two."

"What makes you think it was a Dublin gang?" Peter asked.

Des laughed. "Why? Who do you think it was, Peter? Sharon down the shop?"

Jim Brennan chuckled. "It wasn't much of a mystery," he said. "There was a spate of robberies in the area at the time, from Oughterard to Maam Cross. They lifted a LandCruiser from south county Dublin and went on a bit of a spree down west, then dumped and burned out the car near Mullingar. There were Cruiser tire tracks at the scene—not too many of those around here, you know."

It didn't sound like much to base a theory on to Peter. "Who inherits the farm?" he asked.

Des laughed again, sounding genuinely amused. He turned around, leaned back against the coffee table, cup in hand. "Aren't we in luck, Jimmy? Peter's here, all the way from Galway, ready to solve this great big mystery we have on our hands. We're only poor country gardaí, only fit to manage a few lost heifers. Thank god we have Peter here to set us straight."

"I'm not trying to set anyone straight," Peter said. "I'm just asking the obvious questions." God, but he couldn't stand his father. Couldn't stand his slick little gibes or his grinning face. Peter aimed his remarks at Jim Brennan. "You've already been through all of this. But I'm just catching up. So these are new questions to me."

Des took a sip from his coffee, his eyes on his son, measuring. "Tell him about the farm, Jimmy."

"Well. You know yourself. It's not the best farming country. Miles had fifty acres or so, another nine of commonage. He'd a bit of road frontage, some nice views over Dog's Bay. Back in the boom, someone might have gone for planning permission. But these days it wouldn't be worth a lot. Maybe two hundred thousand. Three hundred at the outside."

"And the 'heir'?" Des used his hands to draw imaginary quote marks in the air.

"That would be Carl's sister, Miles's niece. Naoise. She's a bright girl, Naoise. She studied computer science at the GMIT. She lives in California."

"She's a software engineer," said Des. "Married to a heart surgeon. Two children. Lives in a six-bedroom mansion in Orange County. Hasn't visited Ireland in twelve years. She's president of her PTA. Based on the pictures on her Facebook page, I'd say she's five feet two inches, weighs about a hundred pounds. What do you think, Peter? Do you think she took a secret trip to Ireland to beat her uncle and brother to death with a poker?"

Peter shook his head. "No. I'd say it doesn't sound likely at all."

"No," Des said.

Silence fell.

"Was anything taken?" Peter asked.

"For fuck's sake." Des rolled his eyes, went to his desk and picked up a file, started to leaf through it. It was clear he wasn't willing to engage on the subject, but Jim was happy to talk.

"It's hard to know. The place was messed about. Books thrown around, a few bits of ornaments smashed. We found a bit of cash, but there might have been more. You know the way these old fellas are. They don't trust the banks."

"Can't blame them for that," Peter said.

Jim laughed appreciatively. "You can't. That's right, Peter. So it's hard to know. Miles and Carl kept to themselves mostly. Carl had been doing a line for a time with a woman from Recess, but that had broken up about six months earlier, and she'd never been to the farm. The gang might have taken something, and there'd be no way for us to tell, really."

Peter nodded. "Tricky," he said.

"There's nothing tricky about it," Des said. "A gang of gougers came down from Dublin. They target vulnerable people living alone on remote farms. That's what they do, and that's what they did here. Miles was tough. He was old but he wasn't a pushover. He told them where to go and they didn't like it. They killed him for it. That's what happened." Des's eyes were hard.

Peter stared back at him, unable to hide his hostility. Des clenched his jaw.

"The paperwork is there," Des said. "You know what to do. Get on with it."

Peter looked through the files on his desk, found one marked Lynch, logged in to PULSE, and got to work.

Peter took his time with the file. He started by orienting himself geographically. The Lynch farm was located about halfway between Roundstone and Errisbeg. He ran a Google Maps search, switched to Street View, scrolled, and clicked for a while, but couldn't find the farm. He searched through the file again for a map but found nothing.

"Jim?" he said.

The other man looked up.

"Could you give me a hand? I'm just trying to figure out where the farm is, exactly."

Jim Brennan stood up and wandered over.

"Having a bit of trouble?" He leaned over Peter's screen, squinting. He put his hand on Peter's mouse, zoomed out a bit. "You're nearly there." He pointed one thick finger at the screen. "It's about there, I think," he said. He sounded uncertain.

"You're sure?" Peter asked.

"It's around there," he said.

Des shifted in his seat, and Jim returned to his desk.

"Thanks," Peter said. He'd have to go out and find the place. That was the only way to be sure. The farm was definitely off the beaten track.

He went back to the paperwork, started with the forensics reports. He read through them slowly, taking note of anything that stood out as unusual. The first nugget came from the fingerprints report. The farmhouse had been comprehensively dusted. Not just the living room, where the murders had taken place, but the kitchen, bedrooms, and even the bathroom. Five separate sets of fingerprints had been found in the house. Two sets belonged to the victims. The other three had not been traced. Peter couldn't find anything in the file to indicate that the prints had even been run through the system, though they surely must have been. He thought about asking Des, decided against it. Anything that could be interpreted as criticism would provoke a snarky response, and he just wanted to get through the day. He sent off a request to run the prints himself. It would take a day to get the results. He wasn't expecting a gotcha moment to result from the exercise, but at least the file would be a little more in order and that was, after all, what he was there for.

Only three sets of prints other than their own. Clearly Miles Lynch hadn't had any little grandchildren running around, touching surfaces with sticky fingers. No circle of friends coming over for cards and a glass of something in front of the fire. Peter flicked to the witness statements, which were sparse. No one had seen or heard anything, it seemed. The closest neighbor, who was half a mile away, said that the Lynches lived a quiet life. They hadn't been social. Not hermits, exactly, but . . . isolated. By choice. Which was sad, but interesting. According to the statements, Miles Lynch had worked his farm his entire life, and Carl had grown up just outside Roundstone, had attended primary school in the village. Was it odd that they had been so lacking in connections? Maybe not. It happened. With farmers, in particular those who didn't marry. They worked their own land, could choose, if they wished, to interact little with the wider world.

The fingerprint report indicated that the first set of unidentified prints had been found in multiple locations throughout the kitchen—inside and outside cupboards, on the table, on the outside of the fridge. That was interesting. It suggested someone familiar, someone who felt comfortable moving around the kitchen, looking after themselves. So perhaps there had been at least one friend, or maybe a housekeeper. The other two sets had left far fewer prints. One set had shown up in three places—one perfect fingerprint on the doorbell button, and the same print and a thumbprint on the antique dresser that stood in the hall of the farmhouse. The final set had been found in four locations in the living room—on the mantelpiece, on a coffee table, and twice on the arm of a chair.

Peter moved on. The bodies had been discovered by the local GP, who'd been treating Miles Lynch for diabetes. According to the doctor's statement, Miles had a history of managing his disease poorly. As a result, he had developed peripheral vascular disease and was prone to foot ulcers. He also suffered from peripheral neuropathy—a numbness in his hands and feet—that increased the risk of injury. When Miles Lynch had missed an appointment and the practice nurse failed to reach him by telephone over the following days, the doctor decided to call over to the Lynch house after his clinic the following week. The front door had been open and blowing in the wind. He'd found the bodies of Miles and Carl Lynch in their living room, Carl on the floor in front of the fireplace, Miles still sitting up in an armchair. According to the doctor's statement, he'd gone to both bodies, confirmed that they were dead, and then withdrawn straight away. He'd called the station and Des and Jim Brennan had both attended. They'd taken photographs, then taped off the scene and immediately called in the big guns. Forensics arrived first, about three hours after the call. Two detectives from the SDU in Dublin arrived the following morning. By then the bodies had been removed to the morgue in Galway.

Peter turned to the photographs. Miles and Carl had been dead for a week by the time they'd been found. They'd died in September, the weather had been warmer, and the door to the house had been left open. It was clear from the photographs that putrefaction had begun. The bodies were swollen. There was clear evidence of insect activity. Christ. It was stomach churning, even looking at the photographs. How much worse would it have been in real life, with the smell, and knowing the men personally? It would have been traumatic for the doctor to stumble across the body of a patient in circumstances like that. Peter made a mental note that he should talk to him as soon as the opportunity presented itself. People talked to their doctors—even lonely, isolated men like Miles Lynch. If the Lynch murder hadn't been a random act of violence, the doctor might have some insight into circumstances in Lynch's life that might have exposed him to the murderer.

Peter sat back in his chair. He was supposed to be cleaning up the paperwork, not re-investigating a murder. Des wanted to put him in a tight little box of bullshit nothingness. But if he was going to be stuck in this place for a month, or even two . . . he wouldn't last if he didn't have something to occupy his brain. As long as he was there, he might as well do the job right.

CHAPTER SIXTEEN

Dublin, Ireland

Cormac drove to Dublin on Wednesday afternoon, left his car in long-term parking at the airport, and boarded the plane to Belgium. It was a journey he knew well. He'd made the trip at least once a fortnight for the past eight months, ever since Emma had decided to walk away from her work in Galway. He'd agreed with her decision—they'd both felt that she'd had no choice. The ethical compromises she would have had to make to stay working in the lab in Galway would have been too profound, too fundamental, but resigning from the project before it was completed had triggered a penalty clause in her contract. The company she had been working for had taken ownership of the intellectual property rights to a design that Emma had created, and which was now proving to be extremely valuable. Worse than the loss of the money was the fact that the project was now moving forward without her. They didn't talk about it anymore, but he knew it was hurting her. She'd always been driven. Now she was angry, more determined to make her mark and control her own destiny. The opportunity in Brussels came up unexpectedly, when a former colleague had had a family crisis that forced a return from Brussels to the United States, leaving his project without a lead. They'd discussed it, briefly, and the following day Emma had agreed to take on the project for the six months that her colleague expected to be away. The six months had since become eight months, and there was no end in sight.

The plane landed on time. Cormac got the train to Central Station, a tram to the Châtelain district, and walked the rest of the way. Evenings in the Châtelain district were usually busy, the bars and restaurants popular with Bruxellois and tourists alike. Cormac moved quickly down the street, zipping his jacket to his chin, and shifting his bag to a more comfortable position on his shoulder. Music spilled out of the restaurants he passed. He could smell good food and hear the buzz of lively conversation. His spirits lifted. He reached the apartment building, swiped his way inside, and nodded hello to the concierge. The lift required a key card and a six-digit number before it started its climb to the penthouse. The lift opened to a private hall and a second locked door that required a second key card. Cormac fumbled in his wallet, found it. He swiped, then knocked and opened.

"Emma?" It always felt weird to enter unannounced. It would be different, maybe, if he'd ever lived here with her, but in Brussels he always felt like a visitor. He dropped his bag in the hall, pushed the door closed behind him.

A moment's silence, then, "Cormac?" Emma appeared in the hallway, wearing a pair of silk pajama bottoms and one of his old sweaters, hair soft and loose, a pair of socks on her feet. She had papers in one hand, a pen in the other. The sight of her was so welcome, such a comfort, that he stepped forward and hugged her, wrapped her in his arms, and lifted her a little off the ground. He kissed her and put her back down, and she smiled up at him.

"Well, there's a nice surprise," she said.

"I haven't disturbed you?" he asked. "Did you have plans?"

She glanced at her watch. "Well, Giovanni left half an hour ago, and Luc won't be here until ten, so you've just caught me between boyfriends."

"Great," he said. "We've a bit of time."

She laughed and hugged him back, led him into the living room.

His eyes wandered the apartment, taking in the changes. It was beautiful, if very different from their cozy place in Galway. The building was a renovated 1830s mansion, but the style was modern, all concrete floors and bare walls. When Emma had rented the place, it had come fully furnished, but the furniture had always seemed too small, lost in the vast open-plan living space. But now the rented furniture was gone. In its place was a new couch and a large modular sofa that looked soft and inviting, with a thick-pile rug in muted colors covering the floor. An expensive-looking glass coffee table hosted a stack of printouts and Emma's laptop, as well as a half-empty glass of wine.

"You've made some changes," he said.

She avoided his eye. "Roisín came over for the weekend. You know what she's like. She said it was depressing. Like a hotel room. So we went shopping."

"It looks good," Cormac said.

She flashed a smile at him, went to the kitchen, and came back with a second glass and the bottle.

"What will you do for bookshelves?" he asked. The white melamine bookshelves that had lined one wall were gone, and little stacks of books sat on the floor awaiting a new home.

"Oh," she said. "I haven't decided. Maybe built-ins." She drew him down to sit on the couch. She sat cross-legged, tucked her feet underneath her. "I've been reading about Peter Fisher," she said. "It's all over the papers, online. Is he all right? How is he doing?"

Cormac took a sip from his wine glass, relaxed into the couch. He reached out and put one hand on her knee, and she immediately put her hand on his.

"He's okay, I think." Cormac shook his head. "Actually, I don't know, really. He's shell-shocked. He killed someone. It's a hard thing to wrap your head around."

"I know that," Emma said, an edge to her voice.

"Yes," Cormac said. "Sorry. I know."

"But it wasn't his fault," she said. "He was trying to save that little girl. The way those articles are written you would think Peter was a loose cannon. That can't be the real story?"

"No," Cormac said. "But . . . Peter's exposed. The child wasn't there when he shot Kelly. If Kelly was the one who took her—and we haven't proven that yet—then he'd already released her by the time Peter shot him."

Emma shook her head. "I don't believe Peter shot him without good reason."

"Kelly was in his car. He drove it straight at Peter. That's when Peter shot him."

"Well, for god's sake. Then it's clearly self-defense. And he's a garda, too. It all happened in the line of duty. But there's nothing in the media from the garda press office. Nothing to put Peter's side of things forward." Emma drank from her glass, a long swallow, finishing the wine. She reached for the bottle, topped it up. Her eyes went to his glass, but he'd barely started.

"Kelly's family is talking to the papers. Until the investigation proves that he was the one who took Peggah, it's probably better not to feed the machine."

"That's debatable," Emma said. "Sometimes it's a case of give them nothing and they'll fill the space with what they've got."

She would know, of course. She'd seen it from Peter's side of the fence.

Cormac just nodded. He felt a heaviness settle over him again, the good humor that had been lit by their spark, by the warmth between them, extinguished by the realities of the situation.

"I'm not sure that I'm going to be able to do much to help," he said. "I'm off the investigation. Suspended, actually, pending an investigation. The suggestion is that I fucked up. That Peter was off by himself, inexperienced and unsupervised by me."

Emma's lips parted. She drew in a slow breath, let it out again, and put her wine glass down on the coffee table with an unsteady hand.

"It's never going to stop, is it, Cormac? They're never going to leave you alone."

"It will be fine. This is just . . . it's just a blip. The whole situation was a disaster. I went to Murphy to ask for bodies as soon as I knew about the abduction. He wouldn't release anyone to me. I had a handful of inexperienced officers, no support staff."

"And Murphy'll back you up on that, will he? When the ombudsman comes calling, and you tell them that's what happened, Murphy's going to say, *Oh yes, sir, actually, it's my fault because I've had a target on Cormac Reilly's back for two years, so I've been setting him up to fail.*"

Cormac frowned and rubbed his hand across his jawline, hard enough that he could almost hear the rasp of his stubble.

"I don't know what he's going to say. But the facts are what they are. It's a matter of record that I've been asking for resources for months."

Emma was quiet for a long moment. She filled the space with another long drink from her glass. Cormac glanced at the bottle. She'd had at least two glasses before he arrived. It wasn't like her.

"I think you need to leave," she said.

"What?"

She reached out and took his hand, squeezed it. She leaned forward, eyes moist and intense. "Why stay? They don't want you, Cormac. Don't you think they've made that very clear? Let's say you're right. Let's say you get through this suspension and out the other side, what then? Are you just going to go back to working side by side with Murphy, as if nothing happened? I don't think anything will change; if anything, it will be worse. And I don't think he's ever going to be happy to let you be, do you?"

Cormac leaned back against the couch, let his head rest back, and stared up at the ceiling. He let out a long breath.

"I'll have to figure something out," he said. "I'll have to be smarter. Maybe I should have dealt with things differently. I misjudged the situation. Miscalculated."

She squeezed his hand. "Corm, I think . . . isn't it madness to stay? Do you really want to spend the next ten years watching your back? Waiting for whatever they come up with next? Look what they did to that guy, what was his name? You know, the garda whistleblower who tried to report incompetence and corner cutting. McCoy? McCabe? Look what they did to him. They just don't stop when they want someone gone. Next thing you know, you'll have some trumped-up charge of child abuse made against you, and then your life will just be over. Over."

She blinked back tears, wiped angrily at her face with the back of one hand.

"Emma, come on. That was a long time ago. We're not . . . I'm not in that situation. And I had friends. I have colleagues who support me."

She shook her head, swallowed, wiped her eyes with the back of her hand. "Sorry," she said. "Too much wine." She put her glass down. "You should come here," she said, in a stronger voice. "Come here and live with me and leave all of that behind you. It's not worth it, Cormac. It's just not worth it."

He looked into her eyes, searched for words and couldn't find them. He reached out, drew her near, and kissed her. She came closer, swung one leg across so that she straddled him, then wrapped her arms tightly around him and hugged him hard. She kissed him again, then deepened the kiss and molded her body to his like she would crawl inside his skin if she could. Suddenly, being with her was the only thing he wanted. A chance to hold her and love her and forget about everything else. They moved to the bedroom, and for a little while, all was well between them. She fell asleep afterward. Cormac lay awake and thought about all the things they hadn't said.

CHAPTER SEVENTEEN

Roundstone, Ireland

Peter worked until five, and he was the last to leave. Des had disappeared after lunch and never came back. Jim Brennan lasted until three-thirty, then departed with a suggestion that Peter give him a call if anything came in. Nothing did. Peter had only the Lynch file to keep him company for the rest of the day.

He drove past Horan's on the way back to the flat, picked up a bag of turf and some firelighters, a box of cereal, milk, some bacon, and a loaf of bread. That was about all the place offered. He'd have to go to Clifden soon, stock up, as much as his bank balance would allow. When he got back to the flat, he fried his bacon, made a sandwich. Ate without taking his jacket off. It was so bloody cold. He got the pillow and duvet from the bedroom, set them up on the couch. He'd light the fire and sleep out here. Peter was down on his hands and knees, clearing out the grate, when a knock came at the apartment door. He sat back on his haunches, looked at the door, then back at his hands—they were black with soot and ash. He gave them a quick wash at the sink and a second knock came before he had a chance to move toward the door. He opened it to his father. Des looked past him into the small apartment, clearly unimpressed.

"So this is where you've settled yourself," he said. "Must be costing you."

"I got a deal," Peter said. He was standing there in his socks and wished he wasn't.

"Not as cheap as free, though, is it?"

Peter stood there in silence. There was no way he was inviting him in.

"Will you come for a drink?" Des said gruffly.

"What?"

"The pub. A pint. You might have heard of the idea."

"I was having an early night," Peter said.

"Work very demanding at the moment, is it? Full of early starts and long hours?" Des asked. Another silence. Then, "Come for a pint, Peter. It won't kill you. I can almost guarantee it."

Oh Christ. Was this going to be part of the deal? Forced socializing? He wanted to say no. But . . . Des was his boss, at least for the foreseeable. It wouldn't help him to have open warfare.

"Fine," he said. Peter turned to the couch, sat, and started to pull on his boots. Des said nothing, but Peter could see him taking it in. The empty grate, the depressing kitchen, the couch set up like a bed with a single cheap paperback on the coffee table. Peter stood up, back very straight, and grabbed his coat.

"Are we going or aren't we?"

Des led the way into Gilmartin's with the kind of swagger that announced to all that he had arrived, he was at home, and he was in control. He gave a nod to the barman as he settled himself onto a bar stool. The barman reached for a pint glass.

"What'll you have?" Des asked Peter.

"A pint," Peter said. He didn't want to accept a drink from his father, but he might need alcohol to get through the next hour.

In Galway, there was a growing fashion for renovated super-pubs, all chrome and glass and gleaming maple countertops. There was none of that here. The bar had whitewashed stone walls, a slate floor, and a bar counter than had been in place for generations. There was an open fireplace with a turf fire, and a few round tables. The owner, Brian Gilmartin, had always said that the locals came for familiarity, and the tourists came for the traditional Irish pub experience. He therefore kept the place clean and well maintained but refused to change a thing. Looking around, it was obvious Gilmartin knew his trade. It was a Wednesday night, and the place was doing all right for numbers. There was a couple, probably American—they had that confident look about them—eating a meal at a front table with a bored-looking teenage daughter. A man with a laptop in the corner, finishing his meal. And a cabal of regular drinkers in the back bar.

"Séan Cummins," Des said.

"Sorry?" Peter said.

"Séan Cummins. He was an old schoolmate of yours, wasn't he?" Des asked. "Or he might have been a couple of years ahead of you."

Peter shook his head. "Do you mean the school in Roundstone?"

At Des's nod, Peter shook his head again. He could have pointed out that he hadn't gone to school in Roundstone since he was eight, so even if Cummins had gone to school with him, chances are he would have forgotten the name.

"Who is he?" Peter asked.

"He's a piece of shit," Des said. "Sexually assaulted his niece. We're bringing him in tomorrow for an interview."

"Right," Peter said. "You and Jim, you mean?"

"She's fourteen years old," Des said. "I'd say chances are he did it. He has a reputation. There were rumors a few years back that he managed to get his hands on some GHB. There was talk that he might have spiked a couple of drinks at a nightclub in

Clifden. But no one ever came forward to report him, so there wasn't anything we could do."

"What's the family dynamic like?" Peter asked.

Des shrugged. "We might have some trouble ahead. The mother wants his head on a platter, the father has his doubts that it happened. Cummins is his brother. He doesn't want to accept it."

"And the girl. The niece?" Peter said. He had an image in his head of Des—a serial womanizer—and Jim Brennan interviewing a fourteen-year-old girl, a victim of sexual abuse, and it wasn't good.

Des held up one hand, tilted it one way, then the other. "She's all right, under the circumstances. We'll have to see how it goes. If the father puts pressure on her, she might retract the allegation"

"That would be . . . bad," Peter said.

"He'll be a fucking eejit if he tries it. The wife won't have it. She'll leave him rather than risk Cummins having access to the girl again. Rightly so. Fucking prick needs a gun to the head. If I had my way that's how we'd deal with all of these bastards. Shoot them. Or take them out, string them up. Leave the rest for the birds."

Peter made a noncommittal sound, took a drink from his pint.

"You don't agree?" Des looked. His expression was unreadable. It was hard to tell if he was serious, or just letting off steam.

"There's a process," Peter said. "It's not perfect, but it's what we've got."

"It's far from perfect," Des said. "We'll work this case for months, Jim and I. Half the time we'll be glorified social workers, dealing with the family fallout. We'll put a case together for the prosecutor, and then, always assuming they think the case is strong enough for court, it's more likely than not that a jury of his peers will find him not guilty. And maybe by then the family will have managed to convince themselves that Jane was just looking for attention. And soon enough Cummins will be back at it again. Except maybe with the younger sister this time. She's ten, by the way. Name's Elaine. Great little dancer, I'm told."

"I thought you said the mother wouldn't have it."

"She won't," Des said. "I'm just making the point. A gun to the back of the head. A nice handy boghole. Save the state a lot of money and the family a lot of heartache."

Peter took another long pull of his pint, avoided eye contact. Where was Des going with this? It felt like a lecture with an agenda attached.

Des laughed. "You don't approve. You weren't always such a goody-two-shoes. You didn't get that from me. Is that the influence of your former boss? I'm told he's a bit of a box-ticker."

"You mean Reilly?" Peter asked. "What's your problem with him?"

"Who says I have a problem with him?" Des said. He was enjoying himself. Peter could see it in the gleam in his eye.

"You brought him up," Peter said. "And you clearly want to have a go.'"

"I don't even know the man," Des said. He picked up his glass, downed half his pint. There was a burst of laughter from the back bar. Peter looked at his watch. It was only eight o'clock. The place was getting busier, a little louder.

"What's the story with drunk driving in the village?" he asked. He nodded toward the back bar. "Will that lot go for their cars after this?"

"No, no," Des said. "There's a little minibus that picks them all up and drops them home. Collects them in the morning and brings them back for their cars."

"Oh, right," Peter said, nodding.

Des laughed. "Jesus, no. There's no minibus. They'll be driving. You know that."

"And you'll turn a blind eye?"

"I'll use my subjective judgment," Des said. "I police this community twelve months of the year. Most of the people who live here are good people. They work hard, raise their families. If they want to have a couple of pints in the local after a long day at work, I'm not going to be taking their keys off them. That's how you kill the heart of a place. Take away the pub and you take away the place where people meet, share a laugh, talk about their kids, their marriages, and go home a bit happier. This is where they build the friendships they can call on when things get rough."

"That's grand, yeah," Peter said. "Until one of them kills one of those kids on the way home. That's not likely to do much for community spirit."

Des gave him a pitying look. "On two pints?"

Peter wanted to point out that Des wasn't down in the back bar watching how much drink was being poured down throats, and he sure as hell wasn't out on the streets with the breathalizer, so how did he know if they were keeping to two pints or six? Peter finished his own drink. Surely his duty was now done. Before he could open his mouth to make his excuses, Des had given the nod to the barman, who started pulling another two pints. The barman was chattier this time.

"I'd heard we had another garda in town," he said, giving Peter a friendly nod. "It must be good to be back in the hometown, working with your da."

Des laughed. "Oh, he's too good for the likes for us, Mike. He wants to be up in the big smoke, dealing with all the murders."

"Is that right?" The barman smiled as he handed over the pints. Peter felt a surge of irritation.

"Actually, Mike, speaking of murder," Peter said. "I

wouldn't mind having a chat with you about Carl Lynch, if you have a moment."

The barman raised an eyebrow. His eyes flicked briefly to Des's face. "Sure," he said. "I'm not sure I can be much help, though."

"He wasn't a regular?"

Mike shook his head. "He'd come in from time to time, a couple of times a month. But he wasn't social. He came in for a meal, a pint. He'd sit by himself at the front."

"What about his uncle?"

"Miles hasn't been in for years. I think he wasn't in good health."

"Was there much talk, then, after the murders? How did the farming community react? They must have been worried that it might happen again."

"Well, I suppose there was a bit of worry, in the beginning. But then, the word went around that it was a Dublin gang, and . . ." He lowered his voice, his eyes again going to Des. "We heard it was a one-off, you know yourself."

"Sorry?" Peter asked.

"You know. That it was probably to do with Carl's gambling."

Peter looked back at him. This was the first he'd heard about gambling.

"Never mind it, Mike," Des said. "The young fellas are always a bit over-enthusiastic. They want the danger. They're devastated when they find out the job is all speed traps and passport applications, instead of drug dens and murder sprees."

Mike smiled a little and moved away.

"There's nothing about gambling in the file," Peter said.

"Isn't there?" Des said mildly. "Well, it was only one of several theories. Maybe it was never documented."

"He seems to think it was pretty much certain," Peter said, nodding in Mike's direction.

Des shrugged. "Some stories have a way of growing legs. People believe what they want to believe. Whatever makes it a bit easier to get through the week."

Peter looked at his father. There was a strong whiff of bullshit about what he'd just said. "You didn't encourage them a little? Give that story a gentle push?" he asked.

Des just smiled, sipped his pint, and Peter suppressed another flare of irritation.

"I'd better go," said Peter. "I didn't get much sleep last night. Want to make an early start."

"Stay where you are for a minute," Des said. "I want to talk to you about something."

Peter stayed. The American family had departed, but there was more noise coming from the back bar. The barman was busy with his regulars, pulling pints and exchanging banter.

"Cormac Reilly," Des said. "I've never met him, but I know the type."

"What do you mean, the type?"

"I've heard the stories. Two years ago, he shot a garda, a fellow officer." He held up a hand to forestall Peter's objection. "I know what you're about to say. I know all about the circumstances. But the shooting, that's just an indication of the kind of man he is. He's an outsider and he's a trouble maker."

Peter shook his head. "You've got him wrong."

"He's lost the run of himself, Peter. He builds bridges only to burn them down. Look, I grant you, he's been effective in the past. He's smart; when he's pushed to it, he can get things done. But men like that only last for so long. And he's on his way out."

Peter felt sick. The words were horribly close to what he'd

thrown at Reilly in their last argument. He turned to look at his father.

"You need to stay away from him if you want to keep your career." Des sounded as sincere as Peter had ever heard him.

"Reilly's been a good boss," Peter said. "I've learned a lot from him." Peter's discomfort was growing. It was true that he'd learned a lot from Reilly, but that didn't make him perfect. On the other hand, Des was a toxic, selfish, lying bastard, and Peter would treat every word out of his mouth with suspicion.

"I'm sure you have," Des said. "But Reilly's a black-and-white operator in a world that's all gray. And that just doesn't work." Des sighed. "Look, there's more to community policing than bashing people over the head with every minor little misdemeanor. I'm not here to make money for the government, fining working people the minute they put a toe halfway over the line. Do you get me? Maintaining a healthy community, that takes a bit of discretion. You have to leave room for people to be human. To make the odd mistake. You have to be able to tell the difference between someone destructive, or dangerous, and someone who's generally a contributor, and who just wanted to let off a bit of steam."

You couldn't argue with that, and Peter didn't want to. He just wanted to go. He gave a small nod, and Des leaned back, satisfied.

"But working in the gray, it can get messy. People make mistakes. Even the best of people. So we have to look out for each other. We're caught between a rock and a hard place. Government doesn't give a shit about us. We're a political football, given a kicking one day and held up as paragons of vote-winning virtue the next. And then there's the public, with their mobile phone recordings and their compo claims. Nobody gives a shit if a garda loses an eye to some scumbag glassing him on a Friday night. But god forbid little Johnny should get a bump when we arrest him for beating the shit out of his underage girlfriend. We are on the back foot, every day. You need to have friends in this job if you want to survive it."

"I don't disagree with you," Peter said. "But it's not . . ."

"You have to have complete confidence in the men—and the women—that you work with. You've got to have the trust. If you haven't got that, if you start looking over everyone else's shoulder, who's going to have your back when you need it?"

"Yeah," Peter said. "But there's a limit to everything."

Des snorted. "That goes without saying. I'm not suggesting that we go around beating up prisoners or covering up each other's misdeeds. But I'm talking about an attitude. A way of seeing the world."

Peter rubbed at his forehead. This was just . . . bizarre. It was like getting a lesson in ethics from Sepp Blatter. The worst bit was, Des wasn't saying much he could argue with.

"Do you know how close you came to a Section 98 investigation?" Des asked, conversationally.

Peter's breath caught inside his lungs and he went very still inside. He turned on the stool to look at his father, but Des kept his eyes forward. "What do you know about that?" Peter said.

"I know enough," Des said. "I'm wondering what you were told."

"I . . . met with the superintendent. He said that it wasn't going to go that way."

Des laughed. "Your super sent your case to the garda ombudsman with a recommendation that no further action be taken for one reason only—because he owes me a very big favor. He owes me such a big favor, because over the years I've done lots of little favors for him and his. And you needn't look at me like that, Peter. I'm not talking about anything illegal, though god knows we sailed close to the wind to pull *your* feet out of the fire. I'm talking about relationships. I'm talking about *trust*. I'm talking about what makes the world go around."

Peter opened his mouth, and all that came out was, "I didn't know . . ."

Des nodded, and there was satisfaction in his eyes. The look of a man who is getting long-overdue recognition. "You've been a garda for a few years now, Peter. We're not close, no point pretending otherwise, but I've always kept an eye out for you. I've been in the force a long time. I've made friends. You're my son, so my friends are also your friends. Up to a point."

"Up to a point . . ."

Another nod. "But you need to cut whatever ties you have left with Reilly. He doesn't belong, and he's on his way out."

It took Peter a second to respond. It was all coming at him too fast to fully process. "Are you telling me that someone's going after Reilly?"

Des rolled his eyes. "For a bright lad, you're slow on the uptake here. What I'm saying is that no one needs to go after him. He's doing it to himself. He's burned all his bridges and now he's looking for trouble where there's none to find. Maybe he used to do good work. I'm not saying he wasn't a good detective. But something's gone wrong in his head. Maybe he never recovered from that shooting. Whatever the cause, the man is paranoid."

"You're wrong," Peter said. "You're wrong about him."

"The man isn't a complete fool," Des said. "I'll give him that much. He's visiting friends overseas, angling for a nice desk job in Europe, I'd imagine."

That hit hard. Peter took a deep pull from his pint, thought of Emma Sweeney, working away in Brussels. It would make sense for Cormac to go after a job at Interpol. Better for him to do that than for Emma to move back to Galway, after everything she'd been through. But where did that leave him? This purgatory in Roundstone was only bearable because he had believed that Cormac was working on a solution in Galway. Working on getting him back. What if he wasn't?

Des drained the last of his pint. Peter looked down at his glass, realized that somewhere in the conversation he'd picked it up, and it was now all but finished.

"That's all I wanted to say to you, Peter. Just put a word in your ear that the sooner you pull away from Reilly, the better. Take a step back and do a bit of ordinary, decent police work for a while, and all will be forgiven." Des stood up, dropped a few notes on the bar. "Don't be late tomorrow," he said. "I've a few bits lined up for you." He left without a backward glance.

Peter looked down at his empty pint. He'd had two, that put him over the limit. Shite. He made for the bathroom, took a piss, and tried to make sense of the conversation he'd just had. Cormac Reilly, the bad guy, and Des, his guardian angel. Bullshit. And yet . . . he'd come close to prosecution, sickeningly close. And his father had stepped in to pull him out of it. By calling in a major, maybe once-in-a-lifetime favor. A price, it seemed, he'd been willing to pay. Whereas Reilly was off in Europe, trying to lay down an escape route.

Peter washed his hands, retrieved his jacket, and left the pub. It was dark now, and bloody freezing. He zipped up his jacket, wished he'd thought to bring his hat and gloves. He put his hands into his pockets, wrapped his right hand around his car keys. The car was just sitting there, waiting. Cursing his father, he started walking.

Thursday, November 5, 2015

CHAPTER EIGHTEEN

Brussels, Belgium

Cormac woke on Thursday morning to find Emma already dressed.

"Work?" he asked.

She came to sit on the end of the bed, held his hand. "Actually, I've already called to tell them I won't be in," she said. "I thought we could spend the day together."

They went out for breakfast, buried themselves in menus, food, and newspaper headlines. He hadn't missed her change in mood. She was sober, quieter than usual. Afterward, they walked in the Bois de la Cambre. The park was all but empty, on that cold November morning. No kids this early in the day, just dog walkers doing their laps, the older of them smiling and friendly, the younger ones headphoned, more often than not.

"You're not coming back," Cormac said into the silence.

Emma hesitated for so long that for a moment he thought she was going to deny it.

"To Galway, you mean?" she said.

He nodded.

She said nothing for the longest time, as if she couldn't quite bring herself to give the answer he knew was coming.

"No," she said.

He'd sensed it for a while, on some level, but it still came as a shock. Knocked the breath out of him. Over the past three years he'd built an image of his future in his mind and Emma was at the center of that. She was its foundation.

"Is Dublin an option?" he said. She was still holding his hand, her hand warm and dry in his.

Emma stopped walking, turned to him. "I want to stay here," she said. "Or if not here, somewhere in mainland Europe. Ireland is . . ." She shook her head. "It's just misery, Cormac. Bad memories and bad-minded people."

"Emma, come on . . ."

"Please," she said. "Please won't you come here and live with me? It's such a beautiful place. Really it is. You've only seen scraps of it. Just stay here with me now. Don't bother going back. We'll hire a lawyer to represent you in whatever disciplinary farce the gardaí come up with, make sure you come out of it with your name intact. They won't care anyway, once they know you're leaving. Just imagine, Cormac. You could be done with it all by the end of the day. Free of the lot of them."

He thought of their little house on the canal, how much he'd loved it there once, the loneliness of it without her.

"And then what, Em? I come here and do what?"

"There's no rush to figure that out," she said. "You know that."

"You mean that you'll pay the bills while I sit on my backside."

She stiffened. "Money isn't important," she said. Then, at his look, "We're lucky enough that we don't have to worry about it. If you let money come between us, I'll—"

"It's not about money, Emma. I'm thinking about later. When I've had my time to settle in and you're caught up in your work. What about then? What sort of work will there be for a forty-two-year-old former garda in Brussels, an ex-police officer who left his old job with a disciplinary action hot on his heels?"

She opened her mouth to object, but he kept talking.

"And after that. When I've got my job as a security man in some Belgian shopping mall, or personal security for some sociopathic CEO who went too far and made a few enemies, what then? Would you feel the same way about me then?"

"Of course I would," she said.

"I don't think you would, Emma, and I wouldn't blame you because the truth is I wouldn't be happy. That isn't what I want."

They were silent for a long moment, then Cormac spoke again.

"Do you want children? We've never much talked about it and I think I assumed that was down to me. But . . . do you, Emma? Do you want kids?"

She was so pale, so quiet. There were dark shadows under her gray eyes, and he thought now, looking at her, that she'd lost weight. Had she been happy at all, in all the years they'd been together? Had he ever made her happy?

Emma slowly shook her head. "I don't," she said. "I thought . . . maybe I just hoped, that you felt the same way. You never brought it up."

"I know. I should have, maybe."

"Is that what you want?" she asked. "Two point four children. The whole nine yards?"

He shook his head. "I don't even know, really. I think some part of me thought that that part of my life was ahead of me. But then one day I woke up and I was forty-two and the day still hadn't arrived. I'm still not sure . . . but it would give it all some meaning, wouldn't it? If I moved here so we could be together, maybe I wouldn't mind working a job I didn't care about if there was something else, something bigger to focus on."

"I'm not enough?" Her eyes were dry, the words were softly, sadly said.

He wanted to hug her, but there was a distance between them already, and he didn't know how to cross it.

"It's not that I don't love children," she said. "I just . . . I don't see myself that way. I don't get excited when I think about it. Not the way I get excited about my work. And I don't think that's a good starting point for making a family."

"No," he said.

They walked on. After a while she reached out and took his hand again. He wanted to ask her again if Dublin could ever be an option, but he didn't want to hear her say no. The inevitability of what would happen next was settling inside him like a lead weight, and he wasn't ready for it.

He looked away from her, across the ornamental lake. The air was crisp and cold, the sky a clear blue. He wanted to tell her that he knew her work was important to her, that he had no interest in holding her back from what she wanted to do. It was part of what he loved about her, her drive and her passion to create something greater than herself. The trouble was, he didn't have any solutions to offer. He was a police officer. He didn't speak Dutch or French, and even if he did, even if he was able by some miracle to get work in policing in Belgium, how long would she stay here? Her next project could just as easily be based in America, or the UK, or Germany. What would it do to him, to follow her like a puppy around the world? What would it do to them?

"What are you thinking?" she asked, looking up into his face. He'd been quiet too long.

"I had a phone call. This morning, when you were in the

shower. I need to get back to Dublin. I've been asked to come in for a meeting. Something about an old case they need a bit of background on."

She knew he was lying, but she went along with it. Maybe she wasn't ready to face things either.

"When will you be back?" she asked.

"As soon as I can," he said.

And they left it at that.

Cormac went back to the apartment just long enough to pick up his bag. Emma sat on the couch, waiting for him. He called a cab, slung his bag over his shoulder—he'd never had a chance to unpack it—and joined her in the living room.

"Don't come down," he said. She stood up, and he hugged her. She held on tight.

"Call me when you get there," she said.

"Right." He bent his head and kissed her hair. She hugged harder, for just a second, then let him go.

"I'll come to Ireland next time," she said. "Let me know when it works for you."

"I'll come back," he said. "I'm on suspension. So . . . all the time in the world." He gave her a crooked smile. He kissed her one more time. "I'll call you later."

The cab was waiting on the street. Cormac asked the driver to take him to the train station. He made a quick phone call at the station, then boarded a train. Lyon was less than four hours south. The train was no more than half full, which was a gift. He sat in silence, stared out of the window, and tried not to think about Emma. The train pulled into Lyon just after one o'clock. Cormac found a cab, asked the driver to bring him to a bar near Interpol headquarters, then ordered a pint and sent a text to Matt Staunton to let him know where he was.

Matt found him at the bar half an hour later, announcing his arrival with an enthusiastic pat on Cormac's back.

"Cormac, good to see you."

Cormac stood up. They hugged, backslapped.

"I thought we were meeting tomorrow?" Matt said.

"Change of plans," Cormac said. "I hope I didn't interrupt anything important."

Matt eyed his near-empty pint glass. "Are you finished with that? Are you hungry? This place doesn't do food, but there's a good spot around the corner."

"I could eat," Cormac said. "Lead the way." He smiled to himself. Matt was six foot five and a bear of a man. Red-headed in his youth, the red had faded to mostly gray, and now he wore a scraggly beard where he'd once been clean-shaven. The appetite, it seemed, remained the same.

The place around the corner turned out to be a steakhouse, cozy rather than fashionable, with quiet background music and little booths that offered a degree of privacy. Drinks came quickly. Matt eyed him while they waited for their food.

"Well?" he said. "What's the story?"

There was a tone to the question, and Cormac raised an eyebrow.

"You've obviously heard something," he said. Matt had left the Garda Síochána ten years ago, had been with Interpol ever since, but the garda grapevine still worked fine, even here.

"I've heard a lot. None of which I believe. So spit it out."

Cormac blew out a breath. "I think I fucked up," he said.

"No kidding."

Cormac looked at him.

"What?" Matt said. He took a drink from his pint. "Three years ago, you left Dublin with a halo firmly attached to your head. Now you're on unpaid suspension with a disciplinary noose tightening around your neck. What happened? Is there a drinking problem I don't know about? An interest in drugs you have never before exhibited? Women? Gambling?"

Cormac shook his head, half-laughing, despite the situation.

"Well?" Matt said.

"Politics."

"Ah." Matt grimaced. "Talk to me."

"I don't know where to start."

Matt shrugged. "The beginning. Where else?"

Cormac took a second before he began. He wanted to do this the right way.

"Two years ago, I asked you if you had heard any scuttlebutt about Anthony Healy, and you sent me a video of Healy standing beside an incinerator, bales and bales of plastic-wrapped drugs around him, about to be destroyed," Cormac said.

"I remember," Matt said.

"I figured you were trying to tell me something."

"I was."

"I asked you about Healy because his drug task force was in Galway at the time. I thought there might be a link between Healy and drugs and a case I was working. But that case . . . resolved itself, the drug task force went back to Dublin, and I got busy with other things."

"So you let it go."

"I was distracted," Cormac said. "I had other things on my plate last year. But in June, Anthony Healy came back to Galway, and I got an up-close and personal view of the task force's operations. I saw a force that was over-resourced with virtually no supervision. A raid here or there with occasional big scores, but the seizures never seemed to impact the price of drugs on the street. Healy's second-in-command is Trevor Murphy. He's a recent sergeant and his father is—"

"Superintendent Brian Murphy?" Matt interrupted. He was lounging back on his side of the booth, outwardly relaxed, but his eyes were very sharp.

Cormac nodded. "The task force started to suck up more and more resources, to the point where we were trying to run general operations on a skeleton crew. I objected, pushed back, but got nowhere. Then things started to get . . . difficult."

"You think you were targeted?" Matt asked.

Cormac shook his head. "It didn't seem targeted. I lost staff, resources to the task force, but so did a lot of other operations. Murphy—Brian Murphy, I mean—seemed to have blinkers on about that. His decision to pour everything we had into one drug task force seemed crazy to me, but I put it down to nepotism. Trevor Murphy is his son. I thought he was trying to get Trevor a big win, something that would get him more visibility. Promotion. You know the drill."

"But then?"

They'd been speaking quietly, but Cormac lowered his voice further. "Then, on Saturday, a little girl was abducted, bundled into the trunk of a car."

"I read about it," Matt said. "She was found, right?"

Cormac nodded. "But before she was found, I went to Brian Murphy looking for resources—and I mean I had no one, Matt. A handful of inexperienced officers, no support staff, nothing. Murphy blew me off. He made a token call to Salthill to pull in a couple of bodies, but he wasn't willing to borrow any of our own officers back in from the task force, even for a few hours."

"You think he was setting you up to fail?" Matt asked.

"I wondered about that," Cormac said slowly. "But no, I think that would have been too big a risk. He couldn't have known that the girl would be found. What if she'd been killed or just disappeared forever? Murphy would have been very vulnerable. Hard to cover up a fuck-up of that magnitude. No, I think he didn't give me resources because he couldn't. Hours after the conversation I had with Murphy, the task force scored a major win. They raided a boat off the coast and came home with thirty-two kilos of heroin."

Matt's brow furrowed. "I'm not following you. You think his decision was legitimate? He knew things were about to go down and he didn't want to risk blowing the operation?"

"It's possible," Cormac said. "But that's a pretty delicate balancing exercise, don't you think? The life of a young girl, which was absolutely, for sure, at risk, versus the *chance* of a successful drug raid? Would you make that call? Would you say, screw the kid, let's go after the drugs?"

Matt shook his head. "But I'm not Brian Murphy. He's always been a politician, like you said."

"Right. So why didn't he make more than a token effort?"

"I don't know," Matt said. "But I have a feeling you're about to tell me."

The waitress arrived with their food, took away the empty pint glasses, and brought back, at Matt's request, a bottle of red wine. She offered to pour for them. Matt smiled a thank you at her but took the bottle. They waited for her to leave.

Cormac cut into his steak, took a bite, chewed, and swallowed. "How much information crosses your desk about drug flows into Ireland?"

Matt shrugged. "A bit," he said. "A fair bit."

Cormac took a sip of coffee. "I'm told we seized about seven-hundred-million euros' worth of drugs last year, mostly cannabis, heroin, and cocaine."

"Sounds about right."

"That's up ten percent on the previous year. All right, drug seizures fluctuate, no big deal. But the big difference this year is what's driving the raids. Last year less than thirty percent of seizures came about because of internal garda operations. All the other seizures were as a result of international cooperation. Interpol or FBI tip-offs, in other words."

"Right," Matt nodded.

"This year, as I understand it, it looks like internal garda operations are over fifty percent of total seizures."

Matt's eyes narrowed. "That's a big change."

"It is," Cormac said. "You'll be aware that most of the drug activity in Ireland is driven by two gangs, the Killeens and the McGraths. And interestingly, we've been very successful at raiding the Killeen drug gang, in particular. Raids against the Killeens are way up. At the same time, seizures based on Interpol tips have decreased. Except if you look at the detail, you'll notice that seizures against the Killeens are holding steady. It's seizures against the McGraths that have decreased."

Matt was silent for a few months. They ate, drank, considered.

"Any evidence of any money changing hands?" Matt said.

"Anthony Healy," Cormac said. "He lives in a four-bedroom house in Howth, overlooking the water. His wife doesn't work. She's living in a villa in Alicante. Sea views there too, I'm told. I've wondered how he's paying for all of it."

"You're suggesting that the McGraths are paying off Anthony Healy and his friends to look the other way."

Cormac leaned forward. "I'm saying more than that, Matt, as I think you very well know. I think that Healy and Trevor Murphy are actively working with the McGraths. I think they are seizing drugs from the McGraths' rivals, and then diverting those drugs from evidence storage to the McGraths for resale. It would explain why seizures are up but the price of drugs on the street is dropping. It might explain that photograph you sent me. You know about it, don't you? You've known about it for a long time."

Matt didn't reply. He cut his steak, ate with his eyes on his plate. He was thinking, maybe deciding what he could share.

"I reported it," Cormac said.

Matt's eyes flew to his. "You did what?"

Cormac looked back at him steadily. "I gathered together what I knew, and I made a protected disclosure. I passed the information up the line."

Matt was looking at him in disbelief. "I can't believe you did that. You're lucky you still have a head. Who did you report it to? Internal Affairs?"

"IA is useless," Cormac said. "Worse than useless. They leak like a sieve at the best of times and the rest of the time they're ineffectual."

"Who? Who did you report to?"

"The Assistant Commissioner for the Western Region."

"How long ago?"

"Early September. Almost two months ago."

"And nothing's happened since? No action's been taken?"

"They would have to investigate before taking steps," Cormac said. "That could take time."

Matt snorted. "You seriously think that's the problem? That they've done nothing because they're diligently investigating the situation?"

There was a long silence.

"No," Cormac said.

"This diversion of your resources to the task force, did that get worse after you made the disclosure?"

"Yes," Cormac said.

"And now you're suspended."

"Yes."

"Jesus." Matt leaned forward. "You had to have known that it was a crazy move, making that disclosure. What the hell were you thinking?"

"It's supposed to be confidential. That's the whole point of a protected disclosure. And look, I had no idea . . . it didn't occur to me that this thing might be that widely spread. It still doesn't seem possible. The Assistant Commissioner? Come on, Matt."

Matt fell silent.

"Talk to me," Cormac said.

Matt said nothing.

"You've known, haven't you? You've known for a long time."

"We don't *know* anything. Or not much, anyway."

"Come on. You sent me that photograph of Healy at the incinerator. You sent me down this path because you knew there was something to find."

"We've been asking questions for a while," Matt said. "We've heard rumors."

"Who's 'we'?"

"Interpol. And we've been talking to someone in Internal Affairs. Someone we trust. Trying to build the picture. But you can't imagine how hard it is to make progress on this. We're an outside agency. You know that. We advise. We coordinate. We can't just jump in and run an operation on Irish soil. We need the police force on the ground to do the grunt work, and how the hell do you do that if it's the police force that needs investigating? We've had to go step by step, testing the ground."

"You talk as if the entire force is under suspicion."

Matt shook his head. "It's hard to know where it starts and

finishes. Who's in it up to their necks, and who's just doing a favor for a friend."

Cormac leaned forward. "The longer we sit back and do nothing, the wider that corruption will spread. It's time to take action, Matt. It's long past time."

CHAPTER NINETEEN

Roundstone, Ireland

On Thursday morning Peter dragged himself back into Roundstone Station and was pleasantly surprised to find the fingerprint report he'd requested for the Lynch case waiting for him in his inbox. Peter heaved a sigh of relief and got to work. The search had generated a match. The fingerprints that had been found sprinkled liberally throughout the Lynch kitchen belonged to a man named Stephen Kielty. Kielty had a record—a single prior arrest for drug possession and disorderly conduct. Peter took down the record number, ran a search on PULSE. The record was ten years old and Kielty had been nineteen at the time. According to the file, he'd been seen taking a leak down a side alley late at night by two gardaí. He would probably have gotten off with a warning, but when challenged he'd been drunk and belligerent. He'd been arrested and when they searched him, they'd found a gram of cocaine in his pocket. That little find had resulted in a conviction and a suspended sentence but, at least as far as the PULSE system was concerned, Kielty had stayed out of trouble since. It wasn't a lot, but it still needed to be checked out, a reason found for Kielty's presence in the Lynch household. Peter turned the pages of the file again. There was nothing on it to suggest that Kielty had already been interviewed. Peter was noting down Kielty's old address and telephone number when Jim Brennan arrived, greeting him with a cheerful nod.

"Hard at work, I see," Jim said. "Take after your dad."

"Hmm." Peter kept his head down. "Do you know if this is all of it?" Peter asked, indicating the slim folders on the desk in front of him. "For the Lynch file, I mean."

Jim nodded. "That's the lot," he said. "At least the bit of work we dealt with. Once the SDU took over they started their own file. That would be in Dublin, of course."

"Right," Peter said. He looked down at his notes. Maybe he should just call Dublin, find out if he was going over old ground.

"You haven't seen Des yet today?" Jim asked.

Peter shook his head. "Should I take it personally, do you think?"

"What's that now?" Jim was hanging his coat at the door. His cheeks were red from the cold. He reached into his pocket for a tissue and blew his nose loudly.

"The fact that he's not here much. Is that a recent thing?"

Jim looked mystified. "You mean Des? He'll be out meeting people. I think he's at the primary school today. Community policing. That's what it's all about in a small town like this."

Brennan seemed entirely sincere. There was nothing in his expression to suggest sarcasm. Which meant he was either an accomplished actor, or Des Fisher was a far more dedicated cop than Peter had ever known him to be. Jim hummed to himself as he made his way over to the coffee machine, started a hunt for cookies.

"Will you have a cup yourself?" Jim asked.

They had coffee at their desks, made small talk for a few minutes.

"Des mentioned you've an interview this evening?" Peter said.

Jim's face darkened. "You mean Cummins."

"Séan Cummins, I think he said."

"I'd like to string him up," Jim said. "Jane Cummins plays camogie with my daughter. Fourteen years old."

"You're fairly convinced, then. That he did it?"

Brennan looked up. "Not a doubt in my mind. Jane and her mother came to talk to me about it the other night, at the house. Jane couldn't stop crying, couldn't look at her mother, or me. He used to pick her up from training every week as a favor for her parents. Took her the long way home."

"Jesus." Peter shook his head. They were silent for a moment. Peter felt for the other man. "What time are you bringing him in?"

"Five o'clock."

Conversation died then, and they both got on with their work. It was after lunch before Des finally showed up. He didn't come in, just opened the door, leaned into reception, and crooked his finger at Peter.

"You're with me," he said. "Come on." He disappeared.

Peter looked at Brennan, who shrugged. "He's the boss," he said. "I wouldn't hang about, if I were you."

Peter got his coat and went outside. Des was already sitting in the driver's seat of the station's sole marked car. Peter opened the passenger door, climbed in. Des turned the key in the ignition, pulled out of the station.

"You're going to Galway this weekend, I take it?" he said.

"Yes."

"Make sure you bring your blues back with you next week."

Peter turned to look at his father. "I'm a detective," he said. "Detectives wear plain clothes."

"Not in Roundstone, they don't," Des said. "If you're going to be any use to me as anything more than a glorified paper shuffler, you need a uniform. I'll bring you out today, show you the ropes, but next week you and Jim will be doing the speed traps."

"Fine," Peter said. This was one of the reasons why being with his father had always been so bloody infuriating. He was good at putting you in situations you hated, but that you couldn't legitimately object to. A station the size of Roundstone didn't need a full-time detective. Peter would have to pull his weight with whatever work was available, and that included speed detection. He'd like to point out that he could do speed detection in plain clothes just as well, but it seemed a petty argument. Peter looked out of the window, swallowed his frustration.

They drove out. Des went to pedantic lengths on how best to select a safe location for a speed trap, his own personal favorites, and how often he used and rotated them. When they took up position on a raised parking bay off to the side of the R341, Des handed the speed gun to Fisher and picked up a newspaper.

"Off you go," he said.

"What's the point of this?" Peter asked, holding the gun loosely in one hand. "Even if I get someone, we've no one up the road to pull them in. They'll just keep driving." Unlike static speed traps, speed guns didn't have a camera. You needed two cars to use it. One garda stood out and took the readings, the other waited down the road for a radio call from the first, ready to pull a speeding driver in.

Des didn't look up from his newspaper. "It's a deterrent," he said. "If they're really pushing it, wave at them to slow down and pull in. We can always drive after them."

Peter gritted his teeth, switched the gun on, and got out of the car. He leaned against the hood and waited. The road was quiet, and their position was a poor one. Cars had to take a corner before they approached the straight and naturally slowed down to do so. By the time they took the corner and spotted the garda car on the ridge ahead, they were generally well under the speed limit. A few less attentive drivers sped up a bit before spotting him and hitting the brakes, but they were all within the margin of error. It was an hour before he caught someone with a reading worth shouting about.

Peter waved at the car to slow and pull in. It braked but continued on down the road. Peter climbed back into the marked car, gave his father a none-too-gentle shove on the arm.

"Come on," he said.

Des snorted himself awake and got the car moving. It was too slow. Peter was sure the speeding driver would be long gone, but when they got around the corner the car, a navy Mazda3, had pulled in on the side of the road. Des followed suit, took up his paper again. "Off you go," he said.

The driver was smoking, had his window rolled down to let the smoke out. He was wearing a high-vis jacket and had a heavy beard.

"Do you know why I pulled you over?" Peter asked.

The driver took a drag from his cigarette. "Peter," he said. "I heard you were back. How are things?"

It took Peter an uncomfortably long moment to place the man behind the wheel. "Conall," he said in the end. "Conall Harty."

Conall smiled. "Don't look so surprised, Pete. I might get offended. We've all changed a bit since the old days."

"I'm more surprised that you recognized me," Peter said. "It's been a while." More than a while. It must be ten years at least, longer, since they'd exchanged anything more than a nod from a distance.

"I probably wouldn't have," Conall admitted. "But it's all around town that you're back."

Peter glanced down the road. "Were you rushing somewhere?" he asked.

Conall shrugged. "I've to pick up my young one from school. I don't like to be late for her."

"Where are you coming from?" Peter asked.

"Work," Conall said shortly. "Over at Recess. I'm a fisheries officer."

Shite. This was bloody awkward.

"You know you were doing a hundred and twenty-three in a hundred zone," Peter said. He started to pull the ticket book from his back pocket.

Conall read the signals and tensed up. He looked away from Peter before he spoke.

"I work the early shift, finish at two-thirty. I pick her up from school at three. Every day since January, when her mother died."

Peter stilled "Her mother?"

"I married Maedbh Regan," he said. "You might remember her."

Peter thought he did, maybe. An image came to him of a girl with a crooked smile, freckles on her nose.

"Maedbh got breast cancer," Conall said. "We all thought it would be all right. It mostly is, with breast cancer. But she only had six months in the end."

He said it straight, no hint of self-pity. Peter's eyes wandered around the car. It was more than fifteen years old, had taken a fair amount of wear. Conall wouldn't be earning much as a fisheries officer. Peter thought about his own waning bank balance, about how a fine of eighty euros would affect him, and how much harder it might be to carry if you were a single father of one. He pushed the ticket book back into his pocket.

"I'm very sorry to hear that," he said. "I'm sorry for your loss."

Conall nodded. He took another drag of his cigarette. "I'll put this out before I go again," he said. "I don't smoke in the car, usually, and never around my young one."

"Right," Peter said. "Well, I'll see you around, I'm sure." With a final nod, he walked away.

"Have you the ticket?" Des asked, as Peter got back into the car.

"That was Conall Harty," Peter said. "His wife just died. He has a little girl."

Des paused. "You let him off, did you?"

"I gave him a warning," Peter said.

Des nodded soberly, turned the keys in the ignition. "I think that was the right call. He does his best, Harty." He looked left and right, getting ready to pull away.

Peter shook his head. "This was a set-up, wasn't it?"

"What are you talking about?"

"Conall comes this way every day from his job, to pick up his daughter from school. Finished in Recess at two-thirty and has to be at the school by three. To get there on time he'd have to speed, every time, wouldn't he? And you knew about it." Peter didn't miss the hint of a smile at the corner of his father's mouth. "What is this? Were you trying to make a point?"

"Gray areas, Peter," Des said. "Gray areas."

"Jesus." Peter didn't know whether to laugh or cry. He shook his head again. "What am I doing here, Des? What's all this about?"

"I don't know what you mean."

"Why did you drag me back to Roundstone? Is this some sort of belated attempt to be a father to me? If so, you're only about twenty years too late."

Des turned to him, and the car suddenly felt like far too close a space for this conversation. "Maybe I wasn't a great father," he said. "And maybe I wasn't the world's greatest husband.

Although I hope that as an adult you realize that relationships are complicated, and there was a lot you probably didn't understand when you were a boy."

Peter opened his mouth to object, but Des raised a hand to forestall him.

"Look, I'm not trying to justify myself. I have my . . . weaknesses. But I've always wanted the best for you, Peter."

Peter looked away. He thought about all those weeks, when his mother lay dying upstairs in Maggie's cottage, and Des was nowhere to be seen. He thought about the day he was sent away to school, only weeks after his mother's death. How he'd wrapped his arms around Maggie and held on for dear life, and how Des had unpeeled his fingers, pulled him off and stuffed him, crying, into the back seat of the car. He didn't have the words ready for this conversation.

"I'm not asking you to forgive me," Des said. "Frankly, Peter, I don't think I have much to ask for forgiveness for. I did my best. The best I knew how to do. And the past is the past. Neither one of us could change it, even if we wanted to."

Peter felt a rush of anger. If they wanted to? Of course he would change it. Change every bit of it, if he could.

"You need to make the best of the situation you're in," Des said. "In a year or two, if you want to move on, spread your wings, that's fine with me. In the meantime, do what's asked of you, keep your eyes and ears open, and see if you can learn a thing or two."

"I didn't ask you to bring me here," Peter said. "I didn't ask you to get involved in my life." He was conscious that he sounded like a whining ungrateful teenager and he hated it. It was a cold day, and Des had had the heater running in the car. It felt fuggy and uncomfortable. Peter cracked the window, looked through it, and away. "How did you manage it, anyway?" he asked. "It shouldn't have been possible. You're my father. Working together is against regulations."

Des snorted. "I heard my son was in trouble. I heard he'd bitten off far more than he could chew, and he was in the firing line. So yes, I called in a favor or two. And you can turn your nose up at that if you like, Peter, but if it wasn't for me you would be looking down the barrel at a criminal prosecution."

Peter shook his head.

"I'll take my thank you now, if you please," Des said.

"I didn't ask for your help," Peter said. "I didn't want your help. If you hadn't stuck your oar in, I would have been okay."

"Don't kid yourself. You think you have other friends, and maybe you do. But they're in no position to help you out of the situation you got yourself into, all by yourself."

Peter took a breath. "You got me here. You can let me go. Just let me go. Whatever point you wanted to make, you've made it."

Des took his time responding. "You're here to do a job. I suggest you get on with it."

Silence fell between them.

"I need to go to the scene," Peter said flatly.

"What scene?" Des asked.

"The Lynch farm," Peter said. "There are discrepancies in the file. Contradictions. Specifically, the distance between the blood splatter near where the poker was found. The file has two different measurements, taken by two different officers."

"That's forensics' problem," Des said. "It's Dublin's case to run."

"If you want me here to do a job, that's fine," Peter said. "Let me do it properly. Otherwise, I walk." In that moment, it wasn't even a bluff. He was ready to do it, he realized, even if it meant throwing in the towel on his career. Des seemed to read it in him. He heaved a sigh.

"It's a waste of time, but fine. If that's what you want." He signaled out.

"What, now?"

"No time like the present."

CHAPTER TWENTY

Des drove halfway to Errisbeg, then turned off the main road, went on for another five minutes down a rapidly narrowing secondary road, and finally pulled in at a farm gate. Through the gate was a steep, muddy lane.

"We're walking from here," he said.

"Up there?" Peter asked. There was no sign of the farmhouse. "How far?"

Des was already out of the car. "The exercise will do you good," he said. He went to the trunk, pulled out a pair of wellies, and changed into them. Peter looked down at his good leather shoes.

"You don't have another pair in there, do you?" Peter asked.

Des shook his head. "Not today."

Peter came around to the trunk of the car, searched through the gear stored there until he found a tape measure. Then they set off. The gate was far from secure. Just a standard farm gate tied closed with a bit of yellow string. Peter pulled it closed behind him, tied it again.

"You could have left it," Des said. "The stock's all been removed. Taken down and sold off."

Peter shrugged. They started the climb, Peter working to keep his shoes out of the muddier sections. The cold made it easier. The ground was almost frozen in places.

"I'm guessing the raiders didn't walk up," Peter said.

"I told you they had a four-wheel drive." Des stopped walking, indicated tire markings in the mud of the lane. "Tire markings were consistent with a LandCruiser. The same car was found burnt out outside Newbridge a couple of days later."

Peter nodded. As far as he could tell, they'd pinned the entire case on those tire markings.

They went on in silence. In other circumstances it might have been pleasant enough. A walk in the countryside. Nothing but the sound of birds. The temperature had dropped again, but there was no sign of rain and the air was crystal clear. They reached the top of the hill and the house was right there, but Peter was distracted by the view. Acres of farmland spread out in front of them, segmented into small fields by dry stone walls, and beyond that, the Atlantic Ocean with Inishlacken Island in the distance.

"Miles owned all that," Des said.

"Right down to the water?"

A nod.

Peter took in the small, rocky fields, the reedy grass. There was a loneliness about the place that made him want to shiver. It might be beautiful, but it was a harsh, unfriendly sort of beauty. The kind you could only appreciate when you had a warm fire to return to, a hot meal, and good company. He turned to the house. It was a small seventies bungalow, not a lot to say for itself. The paint was peeling. The house was so exposed to the elements here, it would probably need a fresh coat every year. There was a single farm shed, in reasonable condition. If there was any machinery it was tucked away inside, but Peter suspected there wouldn't be much. It felt like a place that was hanging on. A place where you could eke out survival on EU subsidies and a few sheep.

"That's a new roof," Peter said. The tiles were black and darkly shining, unmarred by mildew or bird shit. They stood out.

Des nodded. "Miles had it done a few months back. The old one was in bad shape. Leaks everywhere. He had a new kitchen put in at the same time. But the rest of the place is a mess. Two bachelor farmers."

Des unlocked the front door. The door was warped from the weather and he had to force it open with his hip. There was no police tape. Maybe it had been removed. Maybe it had just blown away. The murders were two months ago now and forensics was long finished with the crime scene.

Des led the way into the house. Peter rolled his shoulders against a sudden tightness between his shoulder blades. He'd seen the photographs, he knew what to expect, but there was something about entering a place where two people had violently lost their lives. It left something behind, apart from bodily fluids and the smell. A residue.

The front door opened onto a cluttered little hallway. To the left hung a mirror, and a few hooks holding up a plethora of coats and jackets. There were three pairs of muddy boots on the tiled floor, neatly lined up to the left of the door. So far the smell was more of mud and fertilizer than anything sinister. Then Des opened the door to the living room, and there it was, the faint scent of death, of old blood and decay, cloying and unmistakable. Des stood back as if to display the room.

Peter's eyes went from the fireplace to the armchair to the floor and back again. The stains were there, but they were dried out, rust-colored—meeker versions of the photographs in the file. There was no sign that anyone had made an attempt to clean up, but nature's cleaners had done their work. Flies had been here. Been and gone.

Peter set about his work with the tape measure. He crouched

down, measured the stains, the gaps between them, photographed them with his phone, noted the measurements. Des watched him in unimpressed silence.

Peter sat back on his haunches. "The poker was used to kill both of them," he said.

"Yes," Des said. His tone said, what of it?

"I'm just struggling to see it," Peter said. "So the theory is that raiders from Dublin did it. Part of an organized gang. Which means there should have been at least two of them—reports suggest they usually come in groups of four. But these murders were committed by one man, wielding a poker. Did the others just stand around?"

Des sniffed. "One or two of them might have held Miles down. Held him in his chair while the first one beat the shit out of Carl."

Peter nodded. "Might have happened that way," he said. "But doesn't it all seem wrong to you? First of all, how did they even know the house was here? It's not exactly visible from the main road. And why this place? It's clear there wasn't much money. And why kill them, in that way?" He thought about the photographs of Carl Lynch, the autopsy report. "It feels like it was done in a fury. Like it was . . . personal."

Des was silent for a long moment. Peter looked at him, saw from his face that something was brewing, and stood up.

"What?" he said.

"Don't borrow trouble," Des said.

"I don't know what you mean by that."

"You're not here to investigate this case. You're here to tidy up some paperwork, close the file, and move on."

"It's a murder case," Peter said. "We need to do the best we can with whatever we've got. The SDU has plenty of other cases. They might not be paying proper attention to this one."

"Jesus, Peter, have you been listening to a word I've been saying to you? This. Is. Not. Your. Case. And even if it was, that shite you were going on with. . . What are you, a psychologist? A fucking FBI profiler?" Des laughed, but he was angry, and he didn't try to hide it. "We're finished here. I've got an interview." He stalked from the room and out of the front door, which he let slam behind him.

Peter looked around the room carefully, absorbing all the details he could, then took out his phone again and took a video, capturing everything he thought might be relevant. Then he followed his father out of the house. Des hadn't waited for him. Peter followed down the muddy slope, hurrying now, half afraid that Des would drive off and leave him there. But the squad car was still there when Peter got to the bottom, engine running, heater blowing.

"The front door isn't locked," Peter said. "You've got the keys."

Des ignored him, drove back to the station the rest of the way in a surly silence. He pulled into the gravel drive, stopped the car.

"Don't come in," he said. "Jim and I have the interview. There's no room for a third. You can drive a patrol before you knock off for the evening. Make yourself useful."

CHAPTER TWENTY-ONE

Peter took the squad car and left the station. Des had said he should go on patrol, but he had no intention of driving aimlessly around Roundstone village. There was work to do—he was more determined than ever that he would work the Lynch case from every angle he could think of. Peter told himself that he was driven by the need to do the best work he could do, and not just a desire to prove his father wrong. The closer Des tried to get to him, the more Peter felt like he needed to pull back, to get the hell away. This role Des wanted to play, he was years too late for it, and the box he wanted to put Peter in was far too tight.

Peter pulled in on the side of the road and took out his notebook. He dialed the number he had for Stephen Kielty, the public urinator whose fingerprints had been found in the Lynch's kitchen. It was a landline. Peter reached Kielty's mother, who assumed he was a friend of her son's, and handed over Kielty's mobile number without an issue. Peter dialed again, and this time Kielty answered. When Peter explained who he was and why he was calling, Kielty was cautious, but not defensive. It took him only a minute to come up with an explanation.

"In Roundstone?" he asked. "Ah, that would have been

months ago. I put in a kitchen up there. That was the farmhouse, wasn't it? Way up on the hill?"

"That's the one," Peter said. "You're a carpenter then?"

"Cabinet-maker," Kielty said with obvious pride. He named the company he worked for, and Peter took a note with the intention of confirming the information later. "Yeah, I put in a kitchen for the old fella there . . . god, it would have been back in July? I'd have to check the invoice for the date. Do you need the date? I'll be in the office tomorrow."

"A date would be very useful," Peter said. He gave Kielty his number.

"So . . . something happened up there?" Kielty said. "A burglary, was it?"

"They were murdered," Peter said. "Both of them. Miles and Carl Lynch."

"Ah god, that's terrible. I did hear something about it on the news, to be honest. I'd wondered, but no . . ."

"Wondered what?" Peter asked, more sharply than he'd intended.

"I thought maybe the young fella had killed his uncle. That's a terrible thing to say, now. He was murdered himself, like."

"Why? What made you think that Carl might have hurt his uncle?"

"They used to argue, that's all. They didn't seem to like each other much. The younger one . . . Carl. He was very angry with his uncle. He'd have a go at him. But I just got on with job, you know?"

Peter murmured agreement. "You don't know what was behind the bad feeling?"

"I haven't a clue. But they lived alone, with just each other. Had done for years. I think you'd hate your own mother if you were cooped up in the middle of nowhere with her for years. Wouldn't anyone?"

Peter asked Kielty a few more questions. The man was more relaxed the longer the conversation went on, seemed happy to talk, but didn't have anything else useful to add. Peter rang off, made one more call, and Kielty's employers were happy to confirm that he'd installed a kitchen for the Lynches, back in late July.

Despite the fact that Kielty was looking like a dead-end, Peter felt the beginnings of confidence building, felt a bit of fire in the belly. There was more to the Lynch case than met the eye, he could feel it. He had two months in Roundstone, and he would spend them investigating this case as it should have been investigated in the first place. He would think of his father as he would any other difficult senior officer. Someone to be avoided, or managed. It was obvious that Des had no interest in investigating the Lynch murders himself, and Peter was fairly sure he knew what his father's reaction would be if he found out that Peter was out interviewing witnesses, following up on leads. Des wanted him to be a grateful little gofer, sitting in the corner, filing paperwork. Peter drove slowly down the main street. He didn't want to go back to the flat, was half afraid that Des would show up with another lecture ready to go. It was nearly four-thirty. He should go to Maggie's, see how she was doing. Meet this Anna, if he should be so lucky. There was one more phone call he needed to make in the meantime.

He drove up the hill to Maggie's cottage. There was a car already parked there, a new-looking red Nissan Patrol. Not Maggie's, that was for sure. And it didn't belong to a local farmer. It had a back seat, for starters, and it was too clean and shiny to be a farm vehicle. She must have a visitor. Peter pulled in alongside the Nissan Patrol. He could make his call from the car.

Carl Lynch's sister, Naoise, was living in California.

Four-thirty p.m. in Galway meant eight-thirty a.m. in California. That was a little early, maybe, but not outrageously so. Peter called the number and it was answered on the third ring.

"Hello?" A woman's voice. He heard heels on pavement, a shouted goodbye in the background.

"Am I speaking with Naoise Lynch?" he asked.

"Well, I'm O'Gorman now," she said. "But yes, this is Naoise." Her accent was almost American, which surprised him. The Irish accent wasn't an easy one to shed, and most people didn't try. More background noise on the call. He heard a car door open and shut, there was shuffling, the sound of an engine switching on, and then a change in the ambient noise that told him he was now on speaker.

"Is this a bad time, Mrs. O'Gorman?" he asked. "I'm Garda Peter Fisher, calling from Roundstone. I was hoping to speak to you about your brother and your uncle."

"Right. Oh, right. It's fine. I'm driving, but I've got you on hands-free. And I have a crazy day, so if you want to speak to me, now is as good a time as you're likely to get."

"Okay. Thank you." Peter hesitated, suddenly unsure of himself. "If you've already spoken to someone about this, then I apologize. We're just trying to fill in a few gaps."

"Well, I'm glad to hear from you, actually. I haven't heard from anyone since you notified me of the deaths. And obviously I'd like to hear what's going on. What sort of progress has been made in getting to the bottom of things."

"Right. Well, I'm just looking to fill in some background for now. To get a picture from you about the kind of people Miles and Carl were."

She let out a little huff of breath. "I'm not sure I'm the right person for that. I hadn't seen either of them for more than ten years."

"You and Carl weren't close?"

"Not really," she said. "We didn't have an awful lot in common. Our parents were very traditional. They were happy to have Carl. Someone to pass the farm on to. They were less interested in me, and if I'm honest, I resented it. The circumstances didn't exactly encourage a close relationship between me and Carl." She was matter-of-fact, like it was a story she had told many times.

"I see. Did you fall out with your parents? Is that why you went to America?"

"Nothing so dramatic," she said. "I went away to college—paid my own way, I'd just like to point out—and the gap that was already there widened. I came home on the holidays, at least for the first couple of years. But when I graduated, I applied for the green card lottery and got lucky."

"And you've never been back?"

"Nope."

"Your parents . . ."

"They passed on almost ten years ago now. My father first, my mother a few months later." Her voice was tight. "And no, I didn't go back for the funerals. My daughter wasn't well, and I was needed here. And, to be frank, I didn't want to play the dutiful daughter when we'd had no real relationship before they died. I said my goodbyes my own way, in my own home."

"Of course," Peter said. She thought he was judging her. He really wasn't.

"Look, is there anything else? Because I need to get to the office."

"What did happen with your parents' farm?" Peter asked. "I'm just asking because Carl had been farming with your uncle. I would have thought he wouldn't have needed to do that if he'd inherited from your parents."

"Oh god. It was mortgaged to the hilt. They weren't the best with money. I suppose they added to the mortgage over the years. In the end the place had to be sold and it just about covered what was owed. Carl was devastated." She paused. "I did feel sorry for him about that. Especially with what came later. He'd lived his whole life on other peoples' promises. And it all came to nothing in the end." There might have been sympathy in her voice, but there was a hint of judgment too. Naoise Lynch had relied on no one. She'd struck out on her own.

"What will you do with Miles's place?" Peter asked. "I assume you'll put it up for sale. Will you come and see it first?"

"Me?" The surprise in her voice seemed genuine.

"Well, you're the next of kin. I think the assumption was that you would inherit it."

"No. Look, Miles would never have left the place to me anyway, but . . . hadn't he agreed to sell it?"

Peter was silent.

"I mean, wasn't that what was the argument was about?"

"What argument?" Peter asked.

Naoise let out a sigh. "Look, hold on for a moment." He could hear more background noise, a car door opening and closing, heels again, clicking on a hard surface, then low voices in conversation followed by quiet, before her voice came back on the line.

"Carl called," she said. "We weren't close, but he called me, rarely, and usually when he had a problem."

"When?" Peter asked.

"He called me in July. He was very drunk, and very upset. You have to understand that he was devastated with what happened with our parents' farm. He'd built his entire life around his belief that he would inherit it. Then that fell apart. And Miles stepped in. According to Carl he made all sorts of promises. If Carl came to work with him on the farm, Miles would leave it to him in his will."

"And he didn't?"

"Carl told me he'd found out that Miles had signed a contract to sell the farm. Look, Carl wasn't making a lot of sense. He was rambling. But he said something about Miles's diabetes. Miles wasn't well, and he was getting worse. His doctor said if he kept going as he was, he would need a lot of support. Nursing care, that sort of thing. And if Miles couldn't afford that sort of care at home, he was going to have to go into a public nursing home."

Peter frowned, thinking through the implications. Then he caught movement out of the corner of his eye, turned his head, and saw a woman and a young girl, well wrapped in heavy coats, hats, and gloves, cycling up the driveway. They glanced his way but didn't stop, just propped their bikes up against the house and disappeared inside.

"Are you still there?" Naoise said, a trace of impatience in her voice.

"Yes, sorry."

"I'm really going to have to go. I have a meeting."

"Just one more minute, if you can. Just so I can be sure I understand. You're saying that Carl told you that Miles had agreed to sell the farm to someone, and that Carl was very upset about it."

"Yes. Well, most of the farm. He was going to keep the house and a bit of land around it."

"But Carl told you this back in July. So it looks like the sale never went ahead?"

"I suppose. I don't know."

"You didn't call him?" Frustration made the question sound like an accusation. "I mean, you didn't speak again?"

Naoise sighed. "I didn't call him, no. I felt sorry for him, but . . . Look, I told him he needed to get on with things. Go out, get a job, earn some money. Get some control back instead of being dependent on other people. That pissed him off. He hung up on me."

"And that was the last time you spoke to him?"

"Yes."

The word hung in the air. It was hard to see how the information could help him. There was fury in the murder scene. Fury in the injuries to Miles Lynch, who had been beaten about the head with the poker. It was one of the reasons Peter wasn't convinced by Des's theory about anonymous Dublin raiders. But clearly, Carl Lynch could not have first murdered his uncle, and then beaten himself to death with the poker. Still, Naoise had given him something. A thread that he would follow and see where it took him.

"Look, I really have to go," Naoise said.

"Yes, of course. Thank you for your time."

She hesitated. "If you find anything out, you'll call me?"

He assured her that he would.

"I feel badly that I didn't call him again. But there really wasn't anything I could have said that he would have wanted to hear. I didn't understand his choices. I got out the first chance I got. He stayed, and his life seemed to get narrower and narrower every year that passed. I just . . . talking to him made me feel panicky, you know? As if his choices might be catching. And he never listened to my advice anyway."

She wanted forgiveness. This phone call from an anonymous garda thousands of miles away was probably her only connection to Ireland.

"It sounds like you were very different people," Peter said, in the end.

"Yes," she said. "Exactly."

There was a moment's silence, and then she hung up.

CHAPTER TWENTY-TWO

Lyon, France

Cormac had thought about staying overnight in Lyon on Thursday night, but he and Matt had finished eating by four o'clock, and the conversation was not the sort that naturally led on to a night of pints and reminiscing. There was a flight to Dublin at seven. Matt had driven him to the airport, and they'd used the drive to talk through a plan and make phone calls, set a few things up. They shook hands in the car at the drop-off area.

"I'll see you tomorrow," Cormac said.

"You will. I hope this is the right call."

"Trust me, Matt," Cormac said. "There's nothing to be gained by standing still."

By the time Cormac landed in Dublin, it was after eight and he was beginning to feel the effects of a long and challenging day. He picked up his car and drove the two and a half hours west to Galway, listening to music and occasionally rolling the window down when he felt he needed the cold air to wake himself up. He pulled in outside the little house on Canal Road at eleven-fifteen, parked the car, and turned off the ignition. He sat there in the dark for a moment. There was a car parked across the road. It was very dark, and the light from the streetlamps was muted, but hadn't he seen movement, just as he pulled in?

Cormac shook himself. He was overtired and wound up. He needed sleep and a shower, some food. He got out of the car and was halfway to the house when he heard the other car door open. He turned to see a slight figure making its way toward him. Moments later, as she passed under a streetlamp, he recognized Deirdre Russell.

"How long have you been sitting out there?" he asked.

"Not long. I just came off shift. Sorry, I know it's late. Can you talk?"

He led the way to the house, unlocked the door, and invited her in. The place was freezing. She was wearing a uniform and a padded garda jacket, but he caught the shiver.

"Sorry," he said. "Heat's been off. I've been away for a couple of days."

They went into the living room and her eyes scanned the room, taking it in. Suddenly he saw the place as she might. It might not have the warmth of Emma's presence, but it was still his home. Those were his books on the table. The ashes in the grate were from a fire he'd lit the previous Friday, before everything had gone south. The painting on the wall was one he'd chosen, and those were his family photographs on the mantelpiece. Emma had taken hers with her to Brussels when she'd left.

"I'm sorry to come so late," Deirdre said. "I won't stay long, but I need to talk to you about Peter."

"What about him?"

"Well, not about Peter, exactly. It's about the Peggah Abbassi case. You know it's been reassigned?"

"Yes. To . . . Reynolds, wasn't it? The inspector from GSOC?"

She shook her head. "He left on Tuesday. We were told that that was only a temporary arrangement, intended to *facilitate a smooth transition.*" Deirdre held up her hands and made air quotes with her fingers.

"So who's running it now?" Cormac asked.

"Moira Hanley's been made acting sergeant. She's running it."

The words were so unexpected that Cormac simply sat for a moment in silence. Moira Hanley might be one of the longest-serving gardaí at Mill Street station, but she was not someone he would have chosen for promotion. And definitely not for a sensitive case like this. It was highly unusual, too, to appoint someone to an acting position in a city center station, when there were surely other sergeants available to transfer into the position.

"How are things going?" Cormac asked, when he'd processed the information.

Deirdre shook her head. "We're getting nowhere fast. And I don't understand what she's thinking. We spent half the day yesterday with the Abbassi family, grilling them on every member of their extended family as if they're all suspects."

Cormac felt like he was on a go-slow. He needed a cold shower or a cup of coffee, anything that would shock him into wakefulness. Deirdre was looking at him with an intent expression on her face. She hadn't come here lightly. She wasn't the type to bitch and moan about office politics. Quite the opposite. She was the kind of officer who liked to be active. Where she could, she spent her time out on patrol or following up on burglary inquiries, minor assaults, anything that would get her out and about and working. The bruising around her mouth was healing, fading to a dirty yellow. She looked very young, sitting there. She was young, only what? Twenty-four? Twenty-five?

"You know, that needs to be done sometimes," Cormac

said. "We may feel that the most likely suspect for the abduction is Jason Kelly, but the superintendent was keen to ensure that we didn't ignore other avenues of investigation. Everything needs to be done properly here. No stone unturned."

"Yeah, but that's the problem. Do you remember the tarp? The one that must have been in Kelly's boot when he took Peggah? On Monday, before you were taken off the case, you said finding that tarp was the first priority. Well, today's Thursday and we still haven't gone out to look for it and I don't think we ever will. Moira says it would be a wild-goose chase. Which it probably would be now, because even if we found it, it's been out in the weather for five days."

Cormac shook his head. That was . . . crazy. It was the obvious first step.

"Yeah," said Deirdre, warming to her theme. "And on top of that, we spent an hour this morning grilling poor Fred Fletcher, trying to get him to change his story about the video he took. She kept at him and at him, suggesting that he'd imagined seeing the abduction, that he'd taken the video of the car on another occasion, until finally Fred's mother lost the rag and kicked us out."

Cormac rubbed at his forehead, pushed his hand back through his hair. He couldn't make sense of this.

Deirdre spoke again, disrupting his train of thought. "I know this sounds paranoid, but I can't stop thinking about Fred's tablet going missing. I mean, what are the chances of that? It was delivered to the technical guys in Phoenix Park, signed in, and then suddenly it disappears. And it's all over the papers about Peter shooting Jason Kelly. And you know, they're hammering him. Suggesting that Kelly was a blameless bystander and Peter a trigger-happy eejit. Look, I'm not saying what Peter did was right. But if the papers are suggesting that the gardaí might be covering for him, what I'm seeing is the exact opposite. It's as if Moira wants to bury or ignore every bit of evidence that suggests Kelly's guilt. Every bit of evidence that would suggest that Kelly abducted Peggah Abbassi, she either tries to disprove or she just ignores it. And then we're chasing down random remote connections to distant family members in the Middle East, as if the mere mention of a Muslim-sounding name is enough to implicate them."

She stopped talking abruptly, looked at him as if she expected him to be able to hand her a solution, preferably wrapped up and tied with a bow.

"You know I'm on suspension," he said.

"I didn't know who else I could talk to," she said. "I didn't know who I could trust."

"I'm doing my best to resolve my own situation. Until I do, there's a limit on what I can do to help."

Her face fell.

"I'm not saying there are no options," he said. "Listen, the day that Peggah was abducted, and you and Peter were chasing down leads, who did you speak to about Jason Kelly? I mean, who did you speak to that knew him personally?"

"I don't know. That was all Peter. I was on the other suspect."

"Can you find out? Peter would have been debriefed, after the shooting. The information should be on the case file."

She nodded slowly, her eyes very serious. "I could," she said. "What are you looking for?"

"If Kelly abducted Peggah, then he let her go for a reason. I think he might have been tipped off. Maybe Peter spoke to someone who called Kelly, told him the gardaí were looking for him. It might have spooked him enough that he dumped her."

"I'll find out," she said. "And then what?"

"Leave that to me, all right?" Cormac said.

Deirdre stood up. She looked replenished, as if the little bit of hope he'd given her had had the same effect as twelve hours solid sleep and a good breakfast. Cormac suddenly felt every one of his forty-two years.

"I'll go," she said. "Let you get to bed." She was nearly at the door when she turned again. "Why are they doing it?" she asked. "It seems mad. All this, letting a child abductor off the hook, just to get at Peter? What did he ever do to anyone?"

"I don't think they see it that way," Cormac said. "Kelly's dead. There's no risk of him going after another child. And maybe they don't want Peter back in the station. They want him isolated."

Her brow was furrowed. "Who is *they?*" she asked.

Cormac had no answer to that question.

After Deirdre left, he took a quick shower and fell into bed. He saw his phone only when he went to plug it in to recharge, realized he'd missed two calls from Emma. It was much too late to call her back now. It would have to wait until the morning.

CHAPTER TWENTY-THREE

Roundstone, Ireland

The front door of Maggie's cottage was ajar when Peter reached it. He pushed it open and went inside, heard hushed voices coming from the living room. He knocked on the living room door and opened it. Maggie was half-sitting, half-lying on the couch. She looked flushed and disheveled. The young woman he'd seen arrive by bicycle sat by her side, holding her hand—this must surely be Anna. She didn't look at all as he had expected. She was slight, with an anxious little face and mousy hair tied back in a loose ponytail. She was pretty, certainly, but not in the generous, rounded way that Des liked, and she couldn't have been more than twenty-five. And the mysterious Tilly must be the little girl he'd seen arrive with her—a daughter, then, not a tag-along friend.

There was a man sitting in the armchair. He was in his forties, wearing neat slacks and an open-collared shirt, and had a medical bag at his feet. He was leaning forward in his chair, speaking in a low voice to Anna.

Peter cleared his throat. "Is everything all right?" he asked.

Anna and the doctor turned to look at him, but Maggie didn't seem to notice his arrival.

"Sorry. We haven't met. I'm Peter Fisher, Maggie's grandson." Maggie's eyes weren't quite focused. "Everything all right,

Mags?" he asked. He wanted to take her hand, but Anna was in the way.

The doctor stood, offered a hand. "Richard Barrett," he said. "Maggie's doctor. I called by to see her today, and I'm afraid she'd had a bit of a fall. I found her here, on the floor."

"What happened, Maggie? How did you manage to fall?" Anna asked. She spoke with a strong north-Dublin accent.

"It could have been one of a number of reasons," Barrett said. "Maggie's blood pressure is quite low, but there are a few other potential causes that we should talk about."

"I'm fine," Maggie said weakly. "I'm just fine. I don't like a fuss." She pulled her hand from Anna's.

"I think the best thing now would be for Maggie to take a rest, and ideally, have a good meal," said Barrett. "Not too much talk. She might be better off going to bed. A good night's sleep is the best thing for her. And I can come by and check on her again tomorrow."

"Thank you," Peter said.

"But you were fine when I left you," Anna said. "You were fine."

"It isn't anyone's fault, Anna," Doctor Barrett said gently. He put a hand on her shoulder but his eyes went to Peter. "These things happen to the best of us, don't they? And you're feeling better now, aren't you, Maggie? I'll see you tomorrow afternoon, all right?"

Barrett gave Peter a discreet nod, and Peter walked him out.

"Sorry," said the doctor, when they were outside. "These are difficult circumstances to meet for the first time."

"Yes," Peter said. He pushed his hands into his pockets. "I've never seen Maggie like that. I mean, she was a little confused, maybe, when we spoke the other day. But not like this."

Barrett nodded. "I've been worried about her for a little while. For a woman of her age, we might expect some confusion, but she's been losing weight lately too, and her blood pressure is consistently low."

"What does that mean?" Peter asked.

The doctor gave a small frown. "It's difficult to know, really. Sometimes people lose their appetite when they age, or they simply forget to eat. If she's not eating enough, if she's getting insufficient nutrition, that could cause her low blood pressure. These things, in the elderly, they can fall into something of a dangerous circle." Barrett hesitated. "I do feel that Anna's doing her best. She seems to genuinely care about Maggie. But of course, she can't be there all the time."

"Right," Peter said. He glanced back toward the house. "I'm sorry. I feel like I'm new to all this. I've just come back to Roundstone. It's a while since I've seen Maggie in person, but still . . . I can't get my head around how much things have changed. Are you saying that Maggie needs more help?"

"It's a lot to take in, and you don't need to make any immediate decisions. Take some time to think about things, and maybe we can discuss it again in a few days. I'll come and check on her again tomorrow, see how she's doing."

Barrett opened his car door, put his bag inside.

"Thanks," Peter said. "Thanks for everything."

"Most welcome." The doctor gave him a sober nod and departed.

Peter went back into the house. Maggie was drinking a glass of water, Anna hovering beside her. And there was the little girl, about nine years old, curled up on the couch beside Maggie and holding her hand. She had thick, sandy-colored hair, a bit paler than Anna's, tied in two long plaits, and brown eyes. She froze when Peter came into the room, looked for a moment like she might run, then curled herself closer to Maggie.

"Hi," Peter said.

"Hi yourself," Anna said. She barely glanced at him. He wasn't imagining the hostility there. For whatever reason, she didn't want him around. Maggie finished her drink and Anna took the glass from her. "Are you hungry, Maggie?" she asked.

Maggie shook her head. Her eyes were half-closed. She looked like she was drifting off.

"You must be Anna," Peter said. "Maggie told me all about you when I came to see her the other day."

"Did she?" Anna said. Her shoulders were tense.

"She told me you were living here, taking care of her."

"I think she needs to go to bed," Anna said. "Will you help me get her upstairs? If she sleeps for an hour, maybe she'll be hungry later."

"I . . . sure." Peter came forward, and Tilly scooted back along the couch as he approached. Peter slid an arm under Maggie's shoulders, tried to encourage her to stand, but it was clear very quickly that she had little to no power in her legs.

"I'm sorry. I don't think I can manage today," Maggie said politely. From the way she looked at him, he wasn't quite convinced that she knew who he was.

"That's all right, Mags," he said. "Why don't I just pick you up?"

Maggie considered, then agreed, and he scooped her up easily. Too easily. He carried her upstairs to her bedroom, Anna trailing in their wake. Anna flipped the quilt and top sheet out of the way. Peter laid Maggie gently down on the bed, then tucked the covers over her again. Anna stood at the end of the bed.

"Can you give us a minute?" Peter asked.

Anna gave him a sharp look. "Don't keep her awake," she said. "She needs her sleep." Then she retreated, closing the door firmly behind her.

Peter sat beside Maggie on her bed and took her hand. She smiled at him.

"Thank you, Peter. It's very good of you."

He felt a sudden, unexpected wave of guilt, and had to swallow hard to keep tears back.?

"How have you been getting on with your father?" she asked unexpectedly.

"Grand," he said. She gave him a measuring look that was suddenly all Maggie. "Fine, seriously, it's all fine."

"I hope so," she said. She let out a breath, closed her eyes. "Will you come and see me again?"

"Of course, of course I will." He stood up and kissed her forehead. Had to blink hard. "Do you need anything else?"

But she was already asleep

He found Anna in the kitchen. She was at the sink, peeling vegetables.

"Maggie's asleep," he said.

She turned to face him, carrot still in one hand, peeler in the other. "What did he say to you?" she said.

"Sorry?"

"The doctor. He said something to you, didn't he, when you walked him to the car?"

"He's worried about Maggie," Peter said slowly. "Her blood pressure is too low. He said there have been other problems. Has he not said anything to you about it?"

Anna's face was tight. "But she's fine, most of the time."

"Maybe it seems that way," Peter said. "But if she's falling, or fainting, then she's not fine. If she falls again and breaks something—"

"I won't let that happen," Anna said, cutting him off.

Peter shook his head. "Look, Anna. With the best will in the world you can't be here twenty-four hours a day. You weren't here today."

She took a step forward, the potato peeler still clutched in her right hand. "I had to work. I have a job, you know, outside of this place."

"Sure," he said. He didn't know the first thing about her. Where had Des picked her up anyway? And was she remotely qualified to be taking care of an elderly woman who clearly had medical needs? He could see that the cottage was clean and tidy. She obviously bought and prepared food, but if Maggie was losing weight, was she eating any of it? Christ, for all he knew Anna could be stealing every penny Maggie had. How could he find out? He didn't know the first thing about Maggie's financial arrangements. Anna was looking at him as if he was about to throw her out onto the street. Shite.

"Was that your little girl?" Peter asked. "Here, I mean, earlier."

Anna nodded. "That's Tilly," she said. "Matilda. Don't take it personally. She's afraid of cops."

Peter raised an eyebrow, and Anna flushed.

"How did she know that I'm a garda?" Peter asked.

"Maggie mentioned it," Anna said.

They stood in silence for a long moment.

"I'd better go," he said. "I'll be back tomorrow. To see how she's doing."

Anna nodded, a single jerk of her head.

He hesitated. "And you'll bring Maggie dinner later?"

Anger flashed in her eyes, but her voice was controlled when she responded. "Yes," she said.

"Right," Peter said. "See you tomorrow."

Peter was thoroughly depressed by the time he left Maggie's cottage. He was also starving. He desperately wanted something other than reheated sausage rolls from Horan's shop, but he still hadn't been into Clifden to buy groceries. That left only the pub. His bank balance would just about stretch to fish and chips, but the thought of seeing Des there put him off. He couldn't face another loaded conversation right now. So it was Horan's again, to see what he could glean from the little freezer in the back. For once it wasn't Sharon behind the counter, but an older man. He had greasy hair that hung into his eyes, and his T-shirt was stained. He watched Peter carefully as he browsed the aisles. He found a microwavable dinner in the freezer, picked up two bags of chips and a Wispa bar to go with it. It was going to be that kind of night. Peter nodded a greeting to the man, put his purchases up on the counter. His eyes fell on a small pile of newspapers stacked to the right of the till. The front cover had a stock photograph of a garda wearing a tactical vest. The headline screamed up at him: QUESTIONS ASKED ABOUT GARDA TACTICAL TRAINING IN WAKE OF FATAL SHOOTING.

Peter picked up the newspaper, unfolded it and his heart sank. A photograph of a smiling Jason Kelly stared up at him. The piece took up most of the front page of a national broadsheet. Sub-headings and quotes jumped out at him. Kelly was alternatively "well-liked," or he "kept himself to himself." He was a good neighbor, a hard worker, a volunteer, an avid fisherman. The only reference in the whole piece to Peggah Abbassi was a one-line reminder that the girl had been found, unharmed, some distance from Kelly, and as yet the gardaí had not reported any evidence linking Kelly to Peggah's abduction.

"Isn't that just more of it?"

Peter looked up. The man behind the counter was nodding at the paper.

"Bloody cops. They're useless when you need them for something, and trigger-happy the rest of the time." He leaned forward, across the counter. "You know, they're all corrupt, every man jack of them." He pointed with a dirty fingernail to a jagged scar at his left elbow. "See that? They gave me that. Broke my elbow, just because I was exercising my protest rights."

"Oh?"

He jabbed his finger at the photograph of Jason Kelly. "That poor fucker got on the wrong side of them, and this is what he gets. Wait 'til you see. It'll all come out in the end."

"You're wrong," Peter said. "You've got it wrong."

The man looked at him with mingled contempt and pity. "You're a believer, are you? You should open your eyes, man. The police force in this country is corrupt."

"That man, Kelly. He took a child," Peter said. He knew he shouldn't be having this discussion. Shouldn't engage with the other man at all, but he couldn't help it.

"That's their excuse all right. And it's not a very good one, is it? Not up to the standard of their usual lies. That girl was found miles away." He jabbed at the paper again, this time with satisfaction. "You mark my words. It'll all come out this time. The people of this country are sick of it all. They won't stand by this time."

Peter leaned forward on the counter. "You don't know what you're talking about. You haven't a clue."

The other man sniffed. "That'll be sixteen forty-six," he said, and he held out his hand for Peter's card.

Peter drove home to the flat. His hands were shaking. He'd wanted to punch the paranoid old fucker, but he couldn't help but wonder, who else was reading these articles and drawing their own conclusions? And would pressure start to build again on the ombudsman's office, to take things further? He'd thought being stuck in Roundstone with his father for company was the worst that could happen. Peter dropped his food on the kitchen counter and took the newspaper to the couch. He sat, read the front-page article, then the follow-up section in the back pages, then the opinion piece. Then he lay back on the couch and thought.

Anyone reading the article would be at least halfway convinced that Kelly was innocent, the victim of misidentification. But that wasn't what had happened. Fred Fletcher, at least, had identified him. So why hadn't the garda press office told journalists that there was an eyewitness? That Kelly had been seen? Were they trying to protect Fred? If so, fair enough, but that left Peter being hung out to dry in the papers. And Kelly's family were clearly falling over themselves to give interviews. About how Jason had loved to fish. That he'd loved the boathouse, had been working on it, upgrading and repairing it for months. Jason's mother claimed that was why he had been there late that evening. Despite himself, Peter felt the first doubts creeping into his head and nausea lurked at the bottom of his stomach. Could he have fucked it up that badly? Could he have killed an innocent man?

Peter rubbed at his forehead with both hands, forced himself to sit up. He looked at the empty grate of the fireplace, at his plastic bag of microwavable shite on the counter. Then he picked up his phone and called Aoife. She answered on the second ring.

"How are you?" she asked.

"Fine. How're things?" he asked. He listened for the sounds of hospital bustle in the background. If she was at work he'd ring off, let her get back to it. But it was quiet, wherever she was. He thought about their cozy little apartment and felt a wave of self-pity. Told himself to cop on.

"How are you really?" she asked. "I called you yesterday."

"Sorry, yeah," he said. "I meant to call you back."

"How's it going with Des? Have you talked to him? Properly, I mean? Has he told you why he dragged you out there?"

Peter sat forward on the couch. He had his phone pressed to his left ear, his right hand pressed to his forehead. How could he explain the situation with Des? He didn't understand it himself.

"He seems to think he's helping me," was the best he could manage. "He says he pulled me out of a bad spot. I'm getting a lot of lectures on how to be a good copper." He was trying to keep it light. The words didn't begin to capture his confusion about his father, about the situation generally.

"That's a bit rich, coming from him."

"I suppose, to give him some credit, he has at least acknowledged that. Sort of."

Aoife snorted, didn't comment. She seemed to know that he had something specific he wanted to discuss and was waiting for it.

"Did you see today's paper?" he asked.

She paused. "Yes," she said. "I saw today's and the one before that. It's all just noise, Peter. You can't pay any attention to it. Normal people know it's all bullshit. Clickbait."

"It's a national paper, Aoife. It feels like it's getting worse, not going away." Normal people, she'd said. He thought about Niamh. He'd called her, twice. The first time he'd left a message, apologizing for missing their dinner. The second time he didn't bother with the message. She never called back. She would have read all of this, have seen the TV coverage. Did she think he was a murderer?

He'd expected Aoife to brush off his concerns with a few reassuring words, but instead, she was silent.

"I'm in trouble, aren't I?" he said. "It's not going away."

"I don't know, Peter," she said in the end. "It could go away. All it would take is for something else newsworthy to blow up, and people will move on." She paused. "Have you spoken to Reilly?"

He shook his head. "No. But we left things badly. I don't know where I stand there, to be honest."

They fell silent.

"Aoife," he said quietly. "Part of me keeps thinking that maybe they're right. I had other options. I could have jumped to the side, or tried to. I could have waited for backup at the bottom of the lane. I could have pulled the trigger once, and not three times."

Aoife sighed. "It's always easy, looking back, to see how things might have been different. But you did what you did for the right reasons. It's the nature of your job to put you in situations where you have to make life and death decisions, sometimes with not enough sleep and no food and fuck-all support. It's not the same, exactly, but trust me when I say that I know what it's like. You have to learn to make a call in the moment, and then live with it, moving forward without destroying yourself with regrets. You did your best, Peter."

"Maybe," he said.

"How's Maggie?" Aoife asked after a beat, her tone a bit lighter, as if she wanted to cheer him up.

Peter let out a shaky laugh. "God, Aoife. Things aren't great there either." He filled her in on Maggie's condition, his conversation with the doctor.

"Maggie would hate it, living in a nursing home. And I think the next time I talk to the doctor, he's going to want to talk about that as an option. But I can't make her decisions for her, you know? And she has this woman living in. Helping her out. She's young, maybe early twenties, and she has a young daughter. I get the feeling that moving in with Maggie was a godsend for them. If Maggie goes to a nursing home, then they lose their place too, don't they? I feel like I'd be putting them out on the street."

"It sounds to me like things are moving a bit fast," Aoife said. "I think I'd bring Maggie into hospital, get her admitted for a few days. Have her monitored and get a medication review done. You might see a big difference. And maybe with the woman's help, and a bit of extra nursing, Maggie could stay at home longer." Aoife sounded sad. She'd always had a soft spot for Maggie.

"Yeah," Peter said. "I could do that."

"So where are you staying? If Maggie's place is full?"

He told her about the shit-hole flat. Made it seem funny rather than tragic.

"At least you'll be back in Galway for the weekend," Aoife said. "You need a bit of normalcy. A bit of craic."

"Yeah," he said. He didn't tell her that he was suddenly very unsure about it. If the press coverage got worse, there would be names named and pictures published. Ireland was a small country. Peter Fisher, killer cop. That's who he'd be for the rest of his life. "I'll think about it," he said.

Friday, November 6, 2015

CHAPTER TWENTY-FOUR

Outside Galway, Ireland

By ten o'clock on Friday morning, Cormac was in the car and on his way back to Dublin, his freshly packed bag on the back seat. The meeting with Matt and Internal Affairs was set up for two o'clock and he wanted to get to Dublin in plenty of time to check in to his hotel before the meeting. He called Emma on the hands-free as soon as he reached the motorway.

"Corm? Can you give me a second?" He could hear a murmur of voices in the background, then Emma came back on the line. "Sorry," she said. "How are you?"

"You're at work, I'm sure. Sorry . . . I meant to call you earlier. Forgot to set an alarm."

"It's fine. Not a problem. How was your flight?" She was distracted, her attention elsewhere.

"Emma, look, I'm sorry I chased off yesterday. I should have stayed."

"You had things to do," she said. "I understand."

"Yes, but I should have stayed."

More voices in the background. Someone speaking whose voice he couldn't distinguish, Emma responding, "Well, put it back 'til twelve, then." A pause. "So, call him and ask." Another pause. "Just try, okay?"

She came back on the line. "I'm really sorry. Can I call you later?"

"No problem."

Cormac hung up, and the phone rang again two minutes later. He accepted the call without taking his eyes off the road.

"Emma?"

A hesitation on the other end of the line. Then, "Sorry, no. This is Deirdre. Deirdre Russell. I've got the name you asked for."

"Deirdre. Right."

"You asked me to track down the people Peter spoke to on the day Peggah Abbassi disappeared. According to the file, he spoke to a guy called Francis Loughnane, a neighbor of Jason Kelly's, at around two o'clock."

"Okay," Cormac said. "That's great. Does Loughnane have a record?"

"Nothing," she said. "Nothing at all that I can see. But this has to be it, don't you think? He must have tipped Kelly off."

"Mmm," Cormac said.

"What do we do next?" she asked. She was excited, eager to press on.

Cormac shifted in his seat, kept his eyes on the road. What they needed now was a warrant, and he could do nothing at all about that.

"You'll need to go to Moira with the theory and the information, press for her to get a warrant for Loughnane's phone records."

Deirdre was quiet for a moment. "She'll never approve that," she said. "I told you, she's out to get Peter. She wants to prove that Kelly *wasn't* involved. She'll hardly get a warrant that might prove the opposite."

"If you make a strong argument as to why the warrant is necessary, she'll have no choice," Cormac said firmly. "Look.

Moira doesn't like Peter much, that's true. And I think it's likely that she was given a push to see this case in a particular light. But she's not dishonest, and she's not stupid. She's going to have to cover her bases. Just make sure you document your theory about Loughnane on the permanent file before you take it to her."

Cormac was fairly sure that Moira would approve the warrant application, if only because she wouldn't expect to find anything. Loughnane would hardly have been stupid enough to call Kelly from his personal phone.

"Okay, will do," Deirdre said, and Cormac felt another pang of guilt. Should he be doing this? Was he leading another young officer down a path that led to suspension or worse?

"Deirdre, look. You need to be careful. I don't want you crossing any lines here. It was fine that you came to me last night, and fine that you called me today, but after this, you need to work within the confines of the team, all right? Look around. You'll see that you have some allies there, too. Talk to Dave McCarthy. He likes to act like he doesn't care but he'll have your back."

"Right," she said.

"And stay away from the drug squad, right? From Healy and Trevor Murphy in particular."

"That won't be too difficult," Deirdre said. "They left this morning for Dublin. Not due back 'til next week, as far as I know."

That got his attention. "Dublin? What are they doing there?"

"I don't know. But I could find out if you like?"

"No. No, that's fine, Deirdre. Better to stay away from all that, okay?"

They hung up and Cormac was left wondering if he should have encouraged her or shut her down from the off. He had every intention of doing whatever was necessary to pull Peter

Fisher out of the hole he was in, but that could be done most effectively when he was back inside the fold, doing the work he was made to do. Playing games like this, drawing junior officers out and sending them on errands in direct defiance of their superior officer, this was . . . not him. Deirdre Russell needed to have faith in the system. He should be encouraging her to do good work within the rules, not to ignore them when it didn't suit her.

Cormac pushed the thought away and focused his mind on other things for the rest of the drive. He had just pulled into the underground car park of his hotel when his phone buzzed again, this time a text from Deirdre.

> H and M in Dublin for scheduled destruction of seized drugs, Tullamore incinerator, Sunday 2pm. Let me know if you need anything else!

The address Matt had provided for the meeting with Internal Affairs led Cormac to a derelict Georgian terrace on Moss Street. The ground and first-floor windows of the house were boarded up, the front door had been replaced by something secure and functional and the walls displayed aging graffiti. Cormac stopped on the doorstep, looked around, and took out his phone to double-check the address. Yes: 31 Moss Street. He examined the door more closely, tried the handle, and found that it was open.

Christ. The place smelled foul. Damp and rotting with an overlay of what might have been rat urine. It was dark too. There was light coming from a doorway at the end of the corridor, and Cormac, stepping carefully on crumbling floorboards, made his way toward it. He pushed open the door and found Matt and two strangers waiting inside.

"Cormac," Matt greeted him with a nod. They shook hands.

"This is Rebecca Murray," Matt said, indicating with another nod the only woman in the room. She was in her forties, blonde hair, tough looking. "And Aidan Kennedy. Aidan and Rebecca are both Garda Internal Affairs. We've been in communication about this issue for some time." Kennedy was tall and very thin. Murray was wearing jeans, boots, and a bomber jacket, but Kennedy was wearing a suit and highly polished leather shoes, no coat. There were nods all around. Cormac tried to read the room. There was an atmosphere, as if he had walked into the middle of an argument.

"This is . . . picturesque," Cormac said, gesturing to their surroundings. "Is it strictly necessary?"

"Where did you think we'd meet?" Murray asked. "Phoenix Park?"

"Bec . . ." said Kennedy, in a placating manner.

"Rebecca and Aidan felt it best to meet away from headquarters," Matt put in. "There's a good chance you would be recognized, Cormac, and they don't have any reason for meeting with you. It would draw questions."

"Look, I still don't know what we're doing here," Murray said. "No offense to you, Reilly, but you're sticking your nose into places you have no business being. This is our operation."

Matt opened his mouth to speak, to intervene, but Cormac cut across him.

"What is?" he asked.

She looked back at him, not following, but clearly pissed off.

Cormac spread his hands wide. "I'm asking, what is your operation? Because as far as I can see you've known for nearly two years that Anthony Healy and Trevor Murphy are on the take and you've done nothing. Murphy was promoted last year. Right now, they have more resources and more power than they've ever had. So what exactly is this operation you're talking about *doing*?"

Murray shook her head. "It's very fucking easy to come in here with eagle-eyed hindsight, knowing absolutely nothing about what's been going on, and point the finger at us. You have no idea how many times we've tried to go after those guys and failed. And before you jump to another conclusion and assume that me and Aidan are useless fuckers, we're not. They're just very well informed, and very well protected."

Matt lifted a hand in a pacifying gesture. "Can we just all take a breath here? We're on the same side."

"You don't know that, Matt," Murray said. "You and Reilly here might be good mates from back in the day, but that means precisely nothing to me."

"You think I'm on the take?" Cormac said mildly.

She looked at him, her expression flat. "You could be. This whole thing about your suspension—it's all very visible, isn't it? Could be that was all arranged just to put you in this room, with us. And even if it wasn't, let's say that the suspension is genuine, what good are you to us if you're about to get the boot?"

Cormac laughed, shook his head. "Looks like I can't win, right, Murray?"

"We met you out of courtesy to Matt," she said. "But I'm not sharing a word of what we know with you, Reilly. Not a word. I don't know you."

"Rebecca . . ." said Aidan.

"No, Aidan. No way," she said.

Cormac made eye contact, tried to convey the seriousness and sincerity of his intent.

"I'm not here to ask for information, or to wheedle my way inside your operation. I'm here to bring information to you, and to help you do something with it."

She held his gaze.

"Did you know that Trevor Murphy and Anthony Healy are personally supervising the destruction of drugs at Tullamore incinerator the day after tomorrow? The incineration is scheduled for two o'clock on Sunday, and Healy and Murphy have made changes to their schedules so that they can be there."

Murray exchanged a glance with Aidan Kennedy.

"How do you know that?" Kennedy asked.

"Did you know it?" Cormac asked.

Two blank faces looked back at him. They clearly hadn't known. Rebecca Murray had been all Jack-Russell-terrier in-your-face energy from the moment he'd arrived, and now her body language told him she was suddenly much less certain.

"There's only one reason Murphy and Healy have made those arrangements. They're not burning drugs. They've already switched them out and they're going to supervise the burning of whatever they've switched them out with to make sure that nothing goes wrong."

"How do you know about the incineration, Cormac?" Matt asked.

Cormac thought about how much to tell them. This lack of trust went both ways, but he supposed they had to start somewhere.

"Someone I work with tipped me off, and I made a phone call to confirm it."

"Jesus, Reilly," Murray said. "You might as well have taken out an ad. Who did you talk to?"

"I spoke to someone I've known for twenty years. Someone I trust," he said. "This is why you've been stuck for the past year. If you trust absolutely no one, you're never going to make any progress."

They stood there without speaking for a long moment. It was Kennedy who broke the silence.

"Rebecca?" he said.

Rebecca Murray took a breath, let it out. "All right," she said. "All right. Let's talk. But if we're bringing you in on this, then you have to do something for us."

"Okay," Cormac said. "What is it?"

It was Kennedy's turn to talk. "We want you to try to find someone."

Cormac looked at Matt, who shrugged. He didn't know where they were going with this.

"There's been a crackdown on CHIS. I don't know if you're aware . . .?" said Kennedy.

"I am," said Cormac dryly. It wasn't exactly a secret. The old garda system of informants had been investigated and found wanting over the past number of years. The Covert Human Intelligence Sources system was the new garda system for managing and formalizing the use of informants and it required gardaí to register their informants on the system, as well as the flow of information and money.

"Well, all of the successful raids the task force has been involved in—and there have been a lot of those over the past three years—have been the result of tip-offs from informants. Trevor Murphy has registered a number of informants on the system since he joined the task force, all of whom have received substantial payouts. Most of them were one-offs but there is one name that comes up again and again as *the* source for pivotal information that has led to major seizures."

"Trevor registered the informants? Trevor Murphy, not Healy?"

Kennedy nodded.

"Okay." Cormac was slightly thrown. Not so much by

Trevor's involvement—he'd been front and center with Healy since he'd joined the task force—but because he'd registered a name. The CHIS was controversial because the paperwork and processes involved were a colossal pain in the arse. If you could find a way around the system, most would. Many did. And if Trevor Murphy was working for the McGrath gang, they would be the source of his information. He would hardly register an informant that would lead right back to them.

"And this informant's tip-offs led to the raids against the Killeens?" Cormac asked.

"Yes," said Murray.

"Right," he said. "Okay." He was thinking, thinking.

"The informant's name is Niall Collins," said Kennedy. "We have an address for him, from the system, but I can't tell you if it's current."

"And he's been paid?"

"According to the register, close to fifty thousand over the last three years."

Which might explain why Trevor had registered him on CHIS. He'd have had to have gone through the formal approval process to get his hands on that amount of money.

"If you have his name, and you have an address, why do you need me?" Cormac asked. Kennedy and Murray exchanged a long look and for a moment he thought they weren't going to answer.

"We've been ordered not to speak to him," Murray finally said.

"Ordered? By whom?"

"By our boss. By our boss's boss," Kennedy said. "The official word is that Niall Collins is a high-level informant. His life would supposedly be at risk if we approach him, so officially there's a do not approach order against him."

"So you're asking me to do it?"

"You're suspended already," Murray said. "Unless we pull something out of the fire in the next couple of weeks, you're gone anyway. And officially at least, you don't know anything about the order. What do you have to lose?"

There was an eagerness, an intensity about them that was off-putting. They were facing into him like they wanted to back him into a corner.

"There's something you're not telling me," Cormac said. They wanted this too much. Cormac didn't believe that Niall Collins was a genuine source. If he was, Trevor Murphy would never have given his name.

"We've heard a few things," Murray said. "We think he's got something that could take down Trevor Murphy, and if we take Murphy down then the whole house of cards will come down with him."

"What something?" asked Cormac. "What has he got?"

Murray shook her head. "We don't know. We don't have any details. But a source we trust told us there's definitely something there."

Cormac was the first to leave the derelict old house that afternoon. They'd agreed to leave separately, but Matt caught up with him before he'd gone halfway down Moss Street.

"Well?" he said, over Cormac's shoulder.

Cormac threw him a sideways glance. "Well, what?"

"Are you happy?"

"It sounds like it's going to be a skeleton crew for the raid on the incinerator."

"We won't need an army," Matt said. "We just need the right people. And the more we bring in the bigger the risk that something will get back to them."

"And what about you, Matt?" Cormac asked. "What's your role?"

Matt grinned at him. "I don't have a role. I'm just your friendly Interpol observer."

"Okay."

"You were right about Healy and the money, by the way," Matt said. "The house Healy's wife is living in—the one in Spain? It's worth five and a half million."

"Sorry, what?"

"I'm serious. Five and a half million. And I'll say this for her. She's got good taste. A traditional Spanish villa, up in the hills with a view down to the sea. Six bedrooms, seven bathrooms. Beautiful gardens, swimming pool, wine cellar. You name it."

"It's not in Healy's name." He wouldn't be that stupid. That arrogant.

"Well, here's where it gets interesting. Seven years ago the wife filed for divorce. Six months after filing, she withdrew her application. Two months after that the house in Spain was transferred, mortgage-free, into her name. Now, before the transfer, it was owned by a company established in Panama. But for at least three years before the transfer, she lived in the house and according her tax returns, she wasn't paying rent."

"Meaning what, exactly?"

"We don't know. Well, my guess is that the company is owned by Healy, and the transferring of the house was part of a deal he made with her for her to withdraw the divorce petition."

"Christ," Cormac ran a hand through his hair. "Five and a half million euros."

"That's not all," Matt said. "We've got her bank statements. She's getting twelve hundred euros a month, transferred directly from Healy's bank account to hers."

"Okay," Cormac said. That sounded like reasonable

alimony for a garda sergeant to pay. Healy would be bringing home about three and a half grand, net.

"She gets a second transfer, this one for twenty-two thousand euros a month, from . . . you guessed it, that friendly little company in Panama."

Cormac shook his head. This was unbelievable. Healy was making virtually no attempt to hide things. He might as well be dancing about in the streets, waving bags of cocaine and cash about.

"What about the house in Ireland?"

"Well, he's a bit more discreet there. The house is worth a packet now, but it wasn't when he bought it back in 1990. Would have cost him about two hundred and fifty grand, give or take."

1990. Healy couldn't have been with the gardaí for more than a couple of years at most at that stage. Cormac tried to remember what sort of money he'd made as a new garda in the early nineties. It couldn't have been much more than a grand a month, could it? How could Healy have managed a mortgage on a quarter-of-a-million property by himself at that stage? Cormac thought about the studio he'd rented as a young cop, the beans on toast that were a regular meal toward the end of each month when things got tighter.

"What about Murphy?" Cormac asked.

"What about him?"

"Anything in his financials that raises questions?"

"I haven't looked yet," Matt said. "The priority was Healy, and honestly, there was so much there that as soon as I started looking there was no time for anything else."

"Right," Cormac said. "Of course." He needed more. The fact that Healy had access to significant wealth and that wealth was being funneled through shell companies should have been enough to at least kick off an inquiry, but it wasn't. He needed something simple, something that couldn't be explained away, and ideally, something that would also catch Trevor Murphy in the trap.

"You were right about the numbers, too," Matt said. "They don't look right."

"Prices?" Cormac said.

"Yes. All of it. Of course, it's not an exact science. No one can say for sure how much is getting into the country. But our people tell me that with the amount of stuff that's been seized over the past twelve months, we should have seen a spike in Dublin heroin and amphetamine prices. And that's just not happening. Drugs are cheaper today than they ever have been."

"The sooner we stop this, the better," Cormac said. "I can't believe they've been standing over this for two years. What the hell were they thinking?"

"It's more complicated than you think, Cormac. It's hard to know where the lines of this thing are drawn, who's involved, who isn't. And then there are those who don't want to know. Murray and Kennedy have been handed this thing to solve, but at the same time they're heavily constrained."

"Constrained in what way?"

"Come on. You know the way this works. If you were the Commissioner or the Minister for Justice, and you're told there's a chance that there's a large-scale criminal conspiracy at the heart of An Garda Síochána, are you going to be the one to try to root it out? Or do you just assign the investigation to someone and then do what you can to make sure they can't make any headway?"

Cormac stopped walking, turned to his friend. "Are you serious?"

"The Commissioner's been in his job for five years. This

thing happened on his watch. If it's exposed, then he's exposed too. As incompetent, or worse."

"You're not telling me that the Commissioner is in on it, too?" Cormac asked.

"No, I'm not saying that. But I'm saying that he must know about Murray and Kennedy's investigation, and yet it doesn't seem to be a priority, does it? They've had as much obstruction as they've had assistance through this thing. That's where the frustration and the lack of trust comes from, you know. You have to give them a break, Cormac. They've been doing a thankless job, and they've been doing it alone."

CHAPTER TWENTY-FIVE

Roundstone, Ireland

Given the bad news about Maggie, the newspaper article, and general loneliness, Peter had expected to sleep badly. But he built up the fire so his living room was actually warm, and in the end he slept solidly, waking only once as the fire burned low. He piled on the last of his firewood, and slept again until morning, then woke later than usual. The room was still warm, though the fire had burned to embers. It had snowed overnight, and looking out the window he saw that the snow was beginning to stick. Bloody hell.

Peter dressed and ate another bacon sandwich for breakfast. He went outside and the cold caught his breath. He got the car engine running, went back inside to fill the kettle, waited for it to warm up so that he could defrost his windscreen enough to see where he was going. That done, he set off, swinging by Horan's on the way to the station. The lights were on inside— he saw Sharon behind the till. Peter parked the car, looked around for the sacks of wood and turf that were usually stockpiled by the front door. Nothing. The bell above the door chimed as he went inside, and Sharon looked up.

"It's bloody freezing, isn't it?" she said. "The radio says it's going to get way worse, too. It's going to snow all weekend, and it's due to drop to minus twelve on Sunday. I'm warning you now, if it gets that cold, I'm not getting out of bed."

"I was just looking for firewood," Peter said.

She looked toward the door. "There's none out there?"

He shook his head.

"Jesus Christ, that lazy bastard. He was supposed to bring it around last night." She heaved a sigh. "Hang on. I'll get some for you. What were you after?"

"If you point me in the right direction, I'll bring it around," Peter said.

Sharon smiled. "I'm not going to say no to that."

She brought him around the back of the shop, to a small parking lot and a fenced-in storage area, where sacks of turf and logs were piled high.

"I only need a couple of bags of turf," he said. "But . . . do you need me to bring a bit more of it around? Get you set up?" He was early for the station. He might as well help her out for ten minutes.

"Well . . . thanks," she said. She glanced at him over her shoulder as she unlocked the padlock on the gate to the storage area. "That would make life a bit easier."

He took the time to lug bags of turf and logs around to the front and stacked them by the door where he'd seen them before. He kept going until there was no more room at the front, until he was sweating a little under his layers. She came out to watch him bring the last bags up.

"Thanks," she said. "Are you terminally bored, or just extremely nice?"

Peter laughed. "Neither," he said. He followed her inside to pay. She took his card, ran it through the machine.

"That's it?" she said. "Just the firewood? No microwave dinner today?"

"I might risk the pub this evening," he said. He'd have to chance running into Des. "I need a break from nuked mashed potato."

She wrinkled her nose. Hesitated before handing him back his card.

"I heard you were asking about the Lynches at the pub the other night," she said. He gave her a look, and she half-smiled, let her eyes slide away from his. "My cousin Mike works behind the bar."

"Right."

It was Peter's turn to hesitate. Clearly, anything he asked her would be around the village by lunchtime. On the other hand, she was obviously connected enough that she might have some useful information.

"Did you know them at all?" he asked.

"Who, the Lynches?" She sat back on her stool, shook her head. "They came in here for their bits and pieces, same as everyone else, but they weren't exactly chatty."

"Did you ever hear anything about Miles Lynch selling his farm?" Peter asked.

She widened her eyes. "No," she said. "Who was he selling it to? Someone local?"

"Can you think of any likely candidates?" Peter asked.

She shook her head. "I can't think of anyone who would have had the money. Or who would have wanted it. The land out that way isn't great for farming. Maybe a neighbor?"

Peter nodded. "Thanks," he said. He raised a hand in farewell, headed toward the door.

"You could try the lawyer," she said. "If anyone knows, I suppose it would have to be him."

"Which lawyer?" Peter asked.

Sharon rolled her eyes. "There's only one. But you'll have to drive if you want to see him. He's in Clifden. Stuart Connolly. Everyone goes to him."

Peter was growing used to having the station to himself in the morning, and he wasn't disappointed. The place was dark when he arrived. He unlocked the doors and let himself in. It was warm inside—the heat was obviously set to come on automatically—and he took off his outer layers gratefully and made himself a cup of coffee. There were cookies—chocolate Hobnobs—and he helped himself to two before making his way to his desk. He felt . . . better. He was worried about Maggie, yes, and he couldn't quite shake the fear that the investigation into his shooting of Jason Kelly would be reopened, but right now, in this moment, he felt better.

He took out the Lynch file again, started working his way through it, double-checking to make sure he hadn't missed anything about the sale of the farm. There was no mention of it. He started making notes of his conversations with Stephen Kielty and Naoise O'Gorman. It was possible that Naoise's information about the sale of the farm might be a complete red herring, but he would follow the path as far as it took him. He was comfortable with that decision. It felt like good police work. Peter paused. This was Reilly's approach to investigation. Follow every path, every trail. Dot every i and cross every t because you don't know what you don't know. It had been days since he'd spoken to Reilly. He'd promised to do what he could to clear Peter's name, but maybe he'd moved on. Maybe he was busy building his own landing pad.

For once, Des arrived before Jim Brennan.

"Peter. How are you?" he said, as he hung up his coat. "Cold out there. The forecast for the weekend isn't good."

They'd last seen each other after the trip to the Lynch farm.

Peter didn't know what he had expected—a bit of a cold shoulder, maybe. But Des, it seemed, was determined to be affable.

"How did the interview go?" Peter asked. It was the wrong question. Des scowled.

"He's a smooth little bastard, I'll give him that. He had an answer for everything."

"The worst ones always do," Peter said.

Des settled himself into his chair. "Jane's father called yesterday evening. He wants to come in to see us, with Jane, this afternoon."

"That doesn't sound too good," Peter said.

Des looked grim. "Let's see how it goes," he said. He turned on his computer, and Peter turned his attention back to his work. He thought about telling Des about his conversation with Naoise O'Gorman, rejected the idea.

"I went by Maggie's yesterday evening," he said instead.

Des looked up.

"The doctor was with her. She had a fall. Or fainted. She seemed confused. Very tired."

"Anna wasn't with her?" Des asked.

"She was at work. She got back just before I arrived."

"Right." Des's brow was furrowed.

"The thing is, the doctor seems to be thinking that Maggie needs to go into a home. He says she has problems with her blood pressure, and that she's forgetting too much. Not eating."

Des frowned. "I suppose it was bound to happen, though she seemed fine not so long ago." He paused. "Anna could always stay on in the cottage, if Maggie does go. She probably couldn't pay much in the way of rent, is the only thing."

It irritated Peter, that Des seemed more concerned about Anna than he was about Maggie.

"Where did you find her, anyway?" Peter asked. "Anna, I mean."

Des put his pen down. "She got the bus out from Galway, arrived in the evening, and landed at the pub." He laughed. "She'd arranged to rent the same shitty little flat you've ended up in. All she could afford, I suppose. I couldn't have that. She had the little girl, no car to get her about. So I thought of Maggie."

"Anna told me her daughter doesn't like cops," Peter said.

Des leaned back in his chair, a sardonic look in his eye. "What are you suggesting, Peter?" He stared Peter down, daring him to take it further.

"Nothing. It's just unusual, that's all. There must be a story there."

"Maybe there is, and maybe there isn't," Des said. "But you know what? Some stories are best left alone. Give people their privacy. Give them a chance to make a fresh start."

Peter made a noncommittal noise, looked back down at his file, and started working again. He didn't want to be drawn into an argument.

"You need to finish up with that thing," Des said. "It's a dead case, stinks like a week-old fish. I want it put away by the end of the day." He looked toward the window. Snow had started to fall again. "And this afternoon I want you out on speed patrol. It's dangerous weather. Let's see if we can get them to slow down."

Peter didn't object. No one would be speeding with snow on the ground and with the temperature plummeting, and he'd be frozen solid if he stood out on the side of the road with a speed gun in hand. But he nodded anyway. He had plans of his own for the afternoon, and if Des thought he was otherwise occupied, so much the better.

CHAPTER TWENTY-SIX

After lunch, Peter packed up and left the station. It was still freezing outside—he had to let the engine and heat run for a while to clear the windscreen. Clouds had gathered overhead, and more snow was obviously on its way. It was a half-hour drive to Clifden in good weather. Peter gave himself an hour and chose the coast road. He would have to crawl along, keep an eye out for black ice. Snow started to fall gently again as he passed the turn-off for Dog's Bay. He checked his watch, slowed his pace again. The snow was sticking. The drive back could be more of a challenge.

Peter got in to Clifden at ten minutes to two. Stuart Connolly's office was on Market Hill, a narrow little street in the middle of the town with no views of the water. The building was obviously old but looked like it had been recently renovated. The plaster that had covered its cut-stone facade, unlike that of the neighboring buildings, had been sandblasted away to reveal the original sandstone. Peter pushed open the outer door. There was a receptionist, headphones on, fingers busy on the keyboard. She saw him and slid her headphones off one ear, tilted her head in his direction.

"Can I help you?" she asked.

"I have an appointment," Peter said. "Garda Peter Fisher for Stuart Connolly."

She pointed him the direction of a small waiting area.

"Garda Fisher?" Connolly appeared in the doorway, offered his hand. He was in his thirties, dressed in navy slacks and an open-necked blue shirt. "Come on through."

Peter followed Connolly into his office, took the seat that was offered to him.

"Good to meet you," Connolly said. "You're new to Roundstone?" He had a slight Dublin accent.

"I'm on a short-term reassignment from Galway," Peter said. "Helping out with a few things."

Connolly nodded. "I don't do that much criminal work," he said. "But I thought I'd met all the gardaí in the local districts. How can I help you?"

"I was hoping to talk to you about Miles and Carl Lynch?"

Connolly raised an eyebrow. "Oh?"

"Did you know them?"

"Who, Miles and Carl?"

Peter nodded.

"Miles was a client." Connolly gestured behind him to a filing cabinet full of manila folders, some of them aging. "I bought this practice from a solicitor who'd worked here for fifty years. Miles was one of his. I only met him a couple of times. He came in once to change his will . . . I suppose it must have been six or seven years ago. And then once, maybe a year later, to arrange a lease for some farmland adjoining his own. I didn't see him again after that, I don't think, and I've never met his nephew."

"I've been told that Carl Lynch believed that his uncle would leave the farm to him in his will." Peter chose his words carefully. Miles Lynch had died. Stuart Connolly couldn't owe him a duty of confidentiality, but some lawyers were sticky about these things, wanted to call the next of kin before they'd have a conversation.

"That's true," Connolly said. "That was the point of making the will, actually. He wanted to leave the place to his nephew."

Connolly was curious, Peter could see it in his eyes. That was good. If he was curious, he was more likely to want to keep the conversation going. "And he didn't change it? Miles never changed his mind about that?" Peter asked.

Connolly shook his head. "No. In fact, I'm doing the probate of that will at the moment. Miles's second cousin lives in Yorkshire. Carl was the primary beneficiary, but as he died at the same time as Miles, everything went to this other man. I'd be happy to give you his name, but I should ask his permission first."

It seemed Connolly's openness had its limits.

"That's fine," Peter said. He paused. "I've been told that Miles and Carl fell out, in the last few months. That Miles had agreed to sell the farm to someone else. Not the farmhouse—he was keen to stay living in it, it seems. But the land was to go."

Connolly's eyebrows shot up. "That seems unlikely," he said.

"Miles didn't come to you? Talk to you about a sale?"

"No. Not at all."

"Is there anyone else Miles might have gone to?"

"Maybe," Connolly said. "But there's only one other solicitor within easy driving distance and he's all but retired. And . . . I don't know why Miles would bother."

"Well." Peter took in the room. The decor was clean and spare, very modern. "Don't take this the wrong way, but Miles was in his late seventies. I get the impression he was very much . . . of that generation?"

"Whereas I'm young and groovy and could have put him off by my progressiveness?"

Peter shrugged. Connolly looked amused.

"People around here can be slow to accept newcomers," Peter said.

Connolly laughed. "Jesus. You're telling me." He held up one hand. "No, I get it. Believe me. My ex—who has since decamped to West Cork by the way—is Swedish. She was the one who dragged me down here. She didn't like Dublin, wanted to get out of the rat race to somewhere quiet, by the water. Somewhere with a close-knit community. By the time she decided that Clifden was a tad too close-knit for her, I'd already bought the practice and signed a ten-year lease for this place." Connolly looked about the room with a dispassionate eye. "Not every client was happy when the old fella sold his practice to a blow-in from Dublin, particularly as I'm the wrong side of forty for some of them."

"But Miles was okay with it?" Peter found himself warming to Stuart Connolly. He was very comfortable in his own skin, was not at all defensive, and seemed to welcome the conversation with Peter as an interesting diversion from an otherwise routine day.

Connolly shifted his position on his seat. "Look, it's like this," he said. "This practice is mostly probate, with a bit of conveyancing and a small bit of criminal defense work. That's it. But probate is my bread and butter. The wills my predecessor spent fifty years building up, and the wills he bought from the man before him. The testators from the oldest wills are passing away; their wills are here, in the safe, so nine times out of ten the executors of those estates come in to see the will, then they ask me to do the legal work. The fees are good and I get to pay my bills. So the will bank is a valuable asset for me. And I want to keep it that way. One day, I'm going to want to sell this place myself, retire somewhere sunny, and the more wills I have in my safe, the better the price I'll get." Connolly shrugged. "It sounds a bit mercenary, but that's business. What I'm trying to say, I suppose, is that I've had to . . . adjust, a bit, to how people do things around here."

"Okay," Peter said.

"I get farming people in here all the time. I had a couple in just this morning. Nice people, in their sixties. Three grown-up children. They want to get their affairs in order, make a will. Great. I ask them about their kids. They have one boy, two girls. Very proud of them all. Boy is working in London in the City. He's some kind of math genius, works for one of the merchant banks. One of the girls is a nurse, married and living in Dublin. The other lives in Galway, has her own business. But their instructions are very clear. They want to leave the farm—which is a good one, worth about half a million—just to the son. That's it." Connolly sighed. "Now, that kid is never going to come back to Clifden to farm. Not a chance. And they love their girls, you can see it. But they will still leave everything they have to their boy, because *they will not split up the land*. Even though he will sell it six months after their death and bank the proceeds, while the girls get nothing."

Connolly sat back in his chair, picked up his pen. "Now you may think, and I may think, that decision is madness, but probably more than eight out of ten couples that come in here want exactly the same thing."

"So, what do you do?" Peter asked, drawn in despite himself.

Connolly shook his head. "I gently point out the unfairness and impracticality of what they are proposing, and then I do exactly what they want. It's their money, their farm, and they can leave it to whoever they like. Whatever I may think about their mindset, it's not my place to change it for them. So, you see, Miles Lynch had no reason to go elsewhere for his legal work. I wrote his will for him. And when he wanted a backup beneficiary who wasn't a woman, I helped him track down his next male relative, who is, by the way and just between us, the principal of a private school. Quite well to do. Very pleased to inherit, of course, but has already instructed me to put the farm on the market as soon as probate clears."

"Right," Peter said. He felt deflated. His original instinct in the Lynch case was to follow the money. The only thing Miles and Carl Lynch appeared to own of any value was the farm. He'd jumped on the trail of the inheritance straight away. Des had told him he was on the wrong track and he'd ignored him. Naoise O'Gorman's comments about the deterioration in the relationship between the two men, and the cause of it, had given him fresh impetus. But it felt like he was hitting the end of the road. A private school principal in Yorkshire seemed no more likely a candidate for murder for inheritance than Naoise O'Gorman had been.

"What's the farm worth, do you think?" he asked Connolly.

"I've had it valued," Connolly said. "For probate purposes. Including the farmhouse, just over six hundred thousand. It has great views over the water, and there's still a market for that kind of thing. But just the farm by itself? It's about sixty acres, I think. Poor quality land. About five thousand an acre, very best-case scenario. So about three hundred thousand."

Peter was surprised. "That's more than I was expecting."

"Back in the boom, he could have sold it for a million, maybe. With views like that, over the sea? Not that you'd ever get planning permission to build there, but people were buying speculatively, you know, for crazy money, in the hope that land would be rezoned."

"Right," Peter said. Three hundred thousand wasn't a million, but it was a lot of money for the right person. Maybe it would be worth looking into the Yorkshire principal a bit further. Just to make sure he wasn't a bit less well to do than he appeared.

Connolly looked thoughtful. "There were rumors, you know, that land to the west of the village was going to be rezoned for a mix of amenity and residential. That was, I don't know . . . a year ago? Maybe less? But it was all talk. Came to nothing."

"Land to the west of the village—that would include the Lynch farm?"

"Probably," Connolly said. "But as I said, it was all talk. There was no formal proposal that I ever heard of, which means no map and no boundaries. Look, it was probably someone's hopeful notion that got people talking."

"But if the land *was* rezoned, that would make it more valuable, wouldn't it? Maybe that's why Miles came to you. Maybe he thought he was going to sell for big money."

"It's possible," Connolly said. "But if he did, the notion would have come crashing down pretty quickly. You can't sell for big money unless you have a buyer willing to pay it. And no one's going to pay top-dollar on the possibility of a future rezoning. That sort of madness ended with the Celtic Tiger."

They heard voices from the waiting room, and Connolly gave Peter an apologetic smile. "Sorry," he said. "I have an appointment, more's the pity."

Peter stood. "Thanks for your time," he said.

"Well, I'm sorry that I couldn't be more help."

"Not at all. If you could give your client a call in Yorkshire, ask him if he'd be happy to have a chat, that would be great."

Connolly agreed, walked him out.

"Thanks again," Peter said, and he shook Connolly's hand.

"Jesus," Connolly said, turning to look out of the window. "Look at that weather. You'd better go if you're going to make it back to Roundstone. If it keeps going like this, we'll be snowed in."

CHAPTER TWENTY-SEVEN

Peter made it back to Roundstone in one piece, but the drive was challenging. The temperature had dropped again. Snow was sticking on the surface of roads that were already frozen. The roads around Clifden had been gritted, but a half mile out of town they were very slippery. He passed more than one car abandoned in the ditches by their drivers. It helped that the roads were very quiet, at least, so that when he did skid, and it was impossible to avoid it entirely, he had a bit of room to correct his course without careening into someone coming the other way. The hill up to Maggie's cottage, however, proved impossible. Peter parked the car in the village and trudged up the hill on foot. Doctor Barrett's car was parked outside when he arrived. No sign of the bicycles.

Peter knocked on the front door, and Anna answered it. She stood back to let him in.

"Doctor Barrett's upstairs with Maggie," she said. "Do you want to wait?"

He followed her inside. The living room was warmly welcoming—everything was clean and tidy and there was a good fire burning in the grate. It was a charming picture of a lovely family home, and he wondered if it was for his benefit or if things were always like this. The little girl—Tilly—was sitting on the floor by the coffee table, coloring. She looked up at Peter with cautious eyes.

"Hello," he said. He sat down quickly, made himself a bit smaller. "What are you drawing?" She seemed to be making a comic. She'd divided her page into six squares, had already filled in four of them with images and speech bubbles. He could make out a dragon and what might have been an archer but when he leaned in for a closer look she spread her hand over the pictures. He would have put it down to timidity, but she was trembling slightly, in a way that went beyond the normal shyness of a young child for an adult who was a stranger.

"Oh, sorry, it's private, is it?" He smiled at her, but she wouldn't look at him.

"Why don't you go upstairs for a little while, Tilly?" Anna said. "You can read, if you like. Finish that later."

Tilly hesitated, then gathered up her pages and left the room, with a worried backward glance for her mother.

"Is she all right?" Peter asked. "She seems bothered about something."

Anna compressed her lips. "She's gotten very close to Maggie since we've been living here. The last couple of days have upset her."

"Right," Peter said. "Of course."

"Before Maggie got sick Tilly was very happy. The school is great. She's got good friends. Everything's been going great."

"That's good," Peter said. She was so obviously defensive that he wanted to know more. There was a mystery here, and he wanted to solve it.

Anna had her arms tightly folded. She looked at him, her eyes measuring. "You think it's my fault, don't you?"

"Sorry?"

"Maggie. You think it's my fault that she's sick. You think I haven't been making sure she's eating."

He thought about lying, brushing off her queries until he'd found out more of what had been going on here, but the look in her eye said she wouldn't be easily put off.

"I've wondered," he said. "I'm not suggesting . . . look, I'm not suggesting that you've been neglectful or anything like that. I'm just saying . . . well, you don't have a carer's qualification, do you?" He sounded like an idiot. It wasn't like him, to stumble over his words like this, but something about her was throwing him off his stride.

Anna snorted. "A carer's qualification? What's that? You need a qualification now to feed someone? To bath them, dress them?"

Peter said nothing for a moment.

"*Has* she been eating?"

It was Anna's turn to pause. "Not much," she said eventually. "And less and less, lately."

"Well," Peter said.

They fell silent. There was a noise from upstairs.

"No school for Tilly today?" Peter asked. He glanced out the window, where the snow was still falling.

"Not in this weather," Anna said, and she was irritated again. "I didn't want to risk walking her down the hill. There's no footpath. If someone lost control of their car, we'd have nowhere to go."

"It's really coming down, isn't it?" He'd meant to move the conversation on, not give her reason to feel more defensive. But he was curious about the little girl.

"It's supposed to get down to minus twelve over the weekend," Anna said.

"If it keeps going like this, we'll be snowed in," Peter said. "I couldn't get my car up the hill."

Anna nodded, and the conversation sputtered to a stop. She stood up abruptly.

"I'm going to get dinner started," she said. She paused awkwardly for a moment. "The doctor should be down in a minute." She disappeared into the kitchen. Peter looked at the door she'd closed behind her. Something was very wrong here. They seemed, both of them, to be afraid of him. Anna's was better hidden, under all that spikiness, but it was there. And it wasn't just fear that he might push Maggie into a home and throw them out on the street. She was *afraid*-afraid. As if he might hurt them. It was unsettling. Maybe Anna had been a victim of domestic violence? It would make sense. Her showing up here with very little money, needing somewhere to live. And maybe he looked like her ex or something? Or the ex could have been a garda, which would explain Tilly's fear. God, that was an awful thought. Better to leave her alone, give her a bit of space. Peter stayed by the fire, let the heat of it ease out his tiredness and his worry. Just being there, in Maggie's house, was such a comfort. He let his eyes wander around the room, cataloging what made this place a home, compared with his shitty flat, which felt like subsistence. There was a blanket neatly folded over the back of the couch. There were books on the bookshelves, a few more on an end table. Tilly's coloring pencils lay where she had left them. The decor was Maggie's. It wasn't necessarily what he would have chosen, but the fact was that it had been chosen, every bit of it, with the love of a place in mind, and with the desire to make that place a source of comfort and of safety.

Peter closed his eyes. He could hear Anna moving about the kitchen. He could smell onions frying. For a second he was transported back to his childhood. He opened his eyes quickly. It was all too close to home. Except this time, instead of his mother, it was Maggie in a bed upstairs, slowly dying. He stood up, paced the room. How much longer would Barrett take? Peter's eyes fell on some small plastic jars of medication, lined up on the mantelpiece. He went over, read the labels one by one. They were all prescribed for Maggie. *Prinivil. Norvasc (Amlodipine Besylate).* The brand names of the various drugs meant nothing to him.

A door opened behind him, and Peter turned.

"Doctor Barrett," he said. "How are you?"

Barrett looked tired, like he'd aged a few years since Peter had last seen him.

"Good," Barrett said. "Busy. The weather makes it harder, you know yourself."

They shook hands in greeting, sat by the fire.

"Where's Anna?" Barrett asked.

Peter nodded toward the kitchen. "Would you like me to get her?"

The doctor shook his head. "Why don't I bring you up to date about Maggie's condition, and you can talk to Anna afterward? I'll let you decide how much you should tell her."

Peter felt his heart sink.

Doctor Barrett sat back, his face grave, eyes sympathetic. "I'm very sorry, Peter, but Maggie is no better today. If anything, I would have to say that her condition has deteriorated."

Peter sat with his arms resting on his legs, hands clasped together.

"I don't understand," he said. "Is it her heart?"

"Maggie suffers from hypotension," Barrett said. "Low blood pressure. Hypotension can be difficult to treat in the elderly. It often requires more than one drug to keep it under control, and it's very important that patients take the correct dose at exactly the right time."

"Are you saying that Maggie hasn't been taking her medication?"

"I don't want you to leap to any conclusions like that. It's possible that Maggie has been taking her medication exactly as I've prescribed it, and her condition has just progressed."

"Or . . .?" Peter asked.

"She may have missed some doses or taken too much. It's difficult for me to know for sure. But her condition has certainly worsened rapidly over the past few weeks. Poorly controlled hypotension can lead to kidney problems, and in elderly people that leads quickly on to other issues. I see symptoms of kidney problems in Maggie." Barrett paused. "And I think she may have had a small stroke."

"Christ," Peter said. "We need to get her to a hospital. Get her blood tested, and get her medication sorted out. Right?" He wanted to stand up, put Maggie in the car, and set off straight away. There was a small hospital in Clifden, but he wouldn't bring her there. He'd drive straight to Galway. Back to civilization. Aoife was there. She'd fix her.

"Maggie is eighty-two years old," Barrett said, very gently. "What's wrong with her . . . well, there's no cure for it. We can look at her medication, certainly, but at this point that can only have so much impact. Peter, I understand that this is very hard to accept. I know this may feel very sudden for you. Can I just urge you to take some time before you consider treatment that might be very uncomfortable for Maggie?"

Peter felt tears thicken his throat. "Are you . . . you're telling me that she's dying?"

"I'm so sorry," Barrett said. "It's never easy news to deliver."

"How long does she have?"

Barrett sighed. "It's impossible to be exact about these things. I would say weeks, but it might be less."

Peter couldn't talk. He swallowed back more tears and tried to pull himself together.

"I'd urge you, if you can, to keep Maggie at home. She's happy and comfortable here. I'll come every day to check on her. I think you'll find that she'll sleep more and more over the coming days." Barrett's voice was very quiet, very steady. "And then the day will come when she won't wake up, and she'll slip away from us."

Peter tried, but he couldn't find words to respond. Barrett sat with him in silence for a minute, then stood and put a comforting hand on Peter's shoulder.

"There are worse ways, Peter. She'll be home, comfortable and happy, surrounded by the people she loves."

Peter thought about his mother's pain in her last days of life and could only nod his head.

He found Anna in the kitchen. She had something baking in the oven, shepherd's pie maybe.

"That smells good," he said.

"Maggie taught me," she said, without turning around. Her hands were busy in the sink, washing up. "I wasn't much of a cook, before."

"Well, it smells good," he said again, lamely. He put his hands in his pockets, didn't know where to start.

"What did the doctor say?" she asked.

He didn't know if he wanted to tell her. Didn't know if he trusted her. What Barrett had said about the medication—could that be Anna's fault? But no. If anyone was to blame, it was him. He should have been here. Should have looked after his grandmother so that she hadn't had to rely on a twenty-something-year-old stranger to cook her meals and make sure she took her pills.

"Do you want to sit down, or something?"

"I'd rather if you just told me." There was fear in her eyes, and he could tell it wasn't for herself.

"Anna," he said. "Please. Just take a minute."

She took up a tea towel and slowly dried her hands, then joined him at the kitchen table, taking the seat at the other end so that they were sitting as if at an interview.

"Well?" she said.

It was hard, suddenly, to find the words. "Doctor Barrett thinks that Maggie is getting worse. He says . . . he thinks she won't recover from this."

She was staring back at him, expectant. She hadn't understood.

"He says that she may only have a couple of weeks left. Maybe less."

It took another moment, a long moment. And then she shook her head rapidly, once, twice, then she put her hands to her face and clenched her eyes closed, like a little girl trying to shut something out. He wanted to reach out and hold her, but he couldn't do that, so he sat there, helpless, feeling her pain and his own until finally he cried a few hard and painful tears. There was no relief in it.

Anna stood in a sudden rush of energy. She wiped away tears with the back of her hand, found a tissue box on the counter, blew her nose, and mopped her face. When she spoke again, her face was dry but she looked brittle, as if she had been hollowed out.

"It's impossible," she said.

"I know."

"I mean, it's impossible. She was fine only a few weeks ago. You don't know. You haven't been here. We were here, every day, and everything was fine. Everything was lovely."

Peter took in a deep breath. Let it out. "I know," he said. He almost crumbled then but caught himself. "I know."

His acknowledgment seemed to suck all the fight out of her. She raised a shaking hand to her mouth and gnawed at the corner of her thumbnail.

"I'm sorry," he said. "It seems like you're very close to her. Maggie can be very kind."

She flinched.

"Maggie's not *kind*." Anna spat the word out as if it were an insult. "Kind means you're doing something to make yourself feel good. It's handing someone on the street a tenner and congratulating yourself all the way home. I don't want *kind*."

Peter was utterly drained. He felt battered by the day, by the terrible news. His weekend in Galway was disappearing fast—he couldn't leave Maggie like this. Anna was all hard edges and resentment and he didn't want to deal with it.

"What *do* you want, Anna?" He didn't really expect her to answer. She was so private, so closed off. But she was upset too and her barriers were down.

She took two quick breaths.

"I want a place of my own. I want my own money in the bank, my own food on the table. A job that pays me better than a living wage. I want Tilly safe and smiling. And Maggie understands that because she was in exactly the same boat herself when she was my age." Anna drew in a shaky breath. "Maggie's been helping me, yes, but I was helping her just as much. And it wasn't kindness. It was better than that."

"What was it, then?"

She searched for the words.

"Friendship," she said simply, in the end. Her eyes flooded with tears, and she wiped them away with the back of a hand. "What happens next?" she asked.

"Doctor Barrett's suggested that we keep her at home. Keep her comfortable. It's where she'd want to be."

Anna nodded. She turned back to the salad she was preparing. "I'm so stupid. I don't know why I've made all this. Maggie's not going to eat it. Tilly just wants pasta. I'll end up throwing it all in the bin."

Peter stood up and bent down to look into the oven. "Well," he said. "I don't know about you, but I'm absolutely starving. If you'll have me, I'd love to share it with you."

She didn't smile. Neither of them was capable of it in that moment. But after a moment she nodded, and some small thing changed between them. They finished the work of making the food together. Tilly had her dinner while Peter sat with a sleeping Maggie, and then, with Tilly in bed, Peter and Anna sat down together in front of the fire, their dinner plates on their laps.

"Wait a minute," Peter said. He stood up, went to rummage in the bottom of a cupboard in the kitchen, and emerged a moment later brandishing a bottle of wine and two glasses. "Maggie isn't much of a drinker, but she always has one stashed somewhere."

He poured for both of them.

"Thanks," Anna said.

"Do you like wine? Sorry, I should have asked."

"It's good," she said. "I like it."

They ate in silence for a few moments. She'd been quiet all evening. When the food was finished, he took the plates to the kitchen, came back to the living room, and poured them both a second glass. They sat in front of the fire and drank.

"It's getting heavier," Anna said, looking out at the snow. It was dark outside now, but the snow was thick and constant, great flurries of it blowing up against the window.

"Yes."

"You should stay," Anna said. "It's too late and too cold to be walking around out there. You could sleep on the couch here if you don't mind a couch . . .?"

He smiled a small smile. "A couch is brilliant. This couch, in particular, would be brilliant. Thanks, Anna."

She looked away. "You don't have to thank me. This isn't my house."

The words hung in the air.

"Anna," he said. He waited for her to look at him. "I don't know what decisions Maggie has made about this house, or anything else. But I just wanted to say to you, if I have any say in it, you don't need to worry about finding somewhere new to live. I'm sure Maggie would want you and Tilly to stay as long as you need to."

Why had he said that? Was it the wine? The tiredness or the bad news? Or the fact that for the first time since he'd pulled that trigger, he didn't feel alone?

Anna's brow furrowed. "I wasn't . . . I didn't mean. . . Look, I can work. I've been saving. Tilly and I will be fine."

"That's good," Peter said. "But I just wanted you to know that you have a home here, all the same. As long as I have a say in it, I mean."

"Well, it's all right," she said. "You don't need to worry about us."

They fell silent again for a while. The room was so warm and so quiet with the snow drifting down outside. There was something very calming about it. It soothed away rough edges.

"Maggie and Tilly get on?" he asked. There was no edge to the question.

Anna smiled. "They do now. You know Maggie. She's no-nonsense, but she can be kind." Her eyes shot to his as soon as she said the word, and she flushed. "You know what I mean."

"I do," he said. He didn't smile but it was there in his voice.

"They went for walks together, in the beginning, before Maggie stopped going out. And they did a bit of gardening together."

"Jesus," Peter said. He raised his eyebrows. "That's not exactly Maggie's thing."

Anna laughed. "She did it to please Tilly. They'd clear a bit of ground, plant a few seeds. Nothing ever grew, as far as I could see. Or not for long anyway. But they had fun with it."

Peter smiled properly this time. "That's nice," he said.

"Maggie didn't do that with you?" Anna asked.

"Ah, no. But times were different then. Maggie was working, you know? And she was nursing my mother, most of the time we lived with her."

The curtains were drawn now. Only the corner lamp was lit, and the fire had died down. Shadow played across Anna's face as she spoke.

"What happened to your mother?" she asked.

The question took Peter by surprise. "Maggie didn't tell you?"

Anna shook her head.

"She died," he said. "She had cancer."

"I'm sorry," Anna said.

"I was eight," Peter said. "It was hard." He'd never really spoken to anyone about his mother. Only to Aoife, and then only once, when they were kids. It must be the shock of the news. Or maybe it was Anna's stillness.

She was nodding. "I was six when my mother died. She was hit by a car. My brother ran out into the street and she ran after him. He was fine, but she died."

"Jesus. Anna, I'm sorry."

"Our father hadn't been around for years, so after that we went to live with my grandmother."

"Just like me and Maggie," he said.

"Not like you and Maggie," she said. "Not at all." She was twisting her wine glass around in her hand, her eyes far away.

"You weren't close to your granny?" Peter asked carefully.

"I think she blamed us for our mother's death. Or maybe that was just the excuse. She was always angry. She kicked us out the day Niall turned eighteen."

"What age were you?" Peter asked.

Her eyes were dark, very calm, unreadable. "Fifteen. Niall looked after me. It was better, for a while."

"I'm sorry, Anna," Peter said.

She looked into the fire. "It's all in the past now," she said. "I don't ever think about it."

"Still," he said.

"Still, what?" She'd looked up at him, a softness in her face.

"Just. Still," he said.

CHAPTER TWENTY-EIGHT

Dublin, Ireland

Rebecca Murray and Aiden Kennedy had been ordered not to approach Niall Collins on the grounds that he was an informant whose life would be put at risk by any garda contact. In Cormac's experience, there were two methods of initiating contact in such sensitive circumstances—either very, very quietly or very, very loudly. Given that he had no access to a surveillance team and very little information about Collins to go on, Cormac thought that the best approach would be the latter. He would make little or no effort to disguise the fact that he was a garda looking to speak with Collins. If Collins really was an informant—and the chances of that must surely be slim—it would be easier for him to explain away an overt garda approach than a botched covert one.

The search for Collins took Cormac out of the city, toward the Liberties. The address Murray and Kennedy had provided was a flat in an area he knew well from his early days as a uniformed garda, and he found it easily enough. A fourth-floor flat in a block of social-housing apartments, paid for by the government, and occupied by people who needed a bit of support to get by. Single mothers mostly, a few old-age pensioners. It was a relatively new building. The building it had replaced had been an eyesore and a no-go area colonized for years by drug dealers and their customers. The kind of place gardaí didn't visit without stab vests and plenty of company. Out of old habit, Cormac avoided the lifts—back in the day they had never worked, had functioned instead as an informal toilet. This building was different though, everything seemed well maintained, clean, and tidy. He didn't miss the security cameras on every floor and at every stairwell.

Cormac knocked on the door of the apartment. It was opened after a minute by a young woman in her mid-twenties. Her hair was pulled back into a ponytail. She wore elaborate make-up on one side of her face—heavy eyeliner that flicked out from the outer corner of her left eye in a perfect curve, a lipsticked mouth, a perfectly groomed dark eyebrow. The other side of her face was entirely bare. It was very disconcerting.

"Yeah?" she said.

"I'm looking for Niall Collins," Cormac said. "Is he about?"

She gave him a powerfully withering *are you stupid* look. "He doesn't live here anymore. He's moved on."

"Any idea where?"

She shrugged. Glanced back over her shoulder into the flat. Making it clear that she had better things to do than talk to him.

Cormac made a gesture toward the make-up on her face. "That looks great," he said. "Are you a professional?"

She looked at him with suspicion, but the hostility faded when she found only honest interest in his expression. "I did a course out of school, but it was shite," she said. "I taught meself most of it."

"Why only half?" Cormac said.

"I'm making a video," she said, then rolled her eyes at his look of confusion. "For YouTube? I have my own channel. I do make-up. Hair. The lot. Tutorials, you know? I've got two hundred and fifty thousand subscribers."

Cormac didn't have to feign his surprise. "Jesus, that's great," he said. "Good on you."

"I'm only at it six months," she said, her chin coming up. "Zoella has twelve million. But give me a year, like."

Cormac laughed. "Can you make any money out of it?" he asked. They were chatting now. She was leaning against the doorjamb, a bit more relaxed.

She made a face. "You can, but you need to be at it all the time. A new video every day. Have to come up with something different. And you need loads of energy, to keep it interesting. But I made three grand out of my last video." She shrugged at his start of surprise, but a smile lurked at the corners of her half-painted mouth. "Don't tell the welfare office."

They both laughed. Cormac leaned back against the wall opposite her door, giving her a bit of space.

"What's your name?" he asked.

"Shauna."

"Cormac," he said. "Look, Shauna, I know you've stuff to be getting on with, but anything you can tell me about Collins would be a real help."

"You're a guard," she said, with a hard look.

"Got me," he said. "But look, I'm not looking to arrest him or anything, and not trying to make trouble for anyone. I just want to have a chat."

She rolled her eyes again, like she'd heard it all before, and knew exactly what a *chat* entailed. "Look, I don't know him. This wasn't even his place. It was his sister's. She got it because she had a little one. He was just living with her and her little girl. Then she bailed, and he stayed on until welfare found out and kicked him out."

"Right. Any idea where he might have gone after that? Maybe he followed his sister? He could be living with her again."

Shauna made a face. "Don't think so. She hasn't been around."

"But he has?"

Cormac could tell that she was beginning to lose interest in the conversation.

"All I know is he's a junkie. You should have seen the state of this place when I got it. They send in the cleaners, but they only ever do half the job. Me ma came to help but it still took us two days to get the place straight."

"And you haven't heard anything about him since?"

"No." Her hand was on the door.

"All right, Shauna." Cormac reached into his back pocket, pulled out a card, and gave it to her. "If you ever do hear anything, you give me a call or drop me a text. And hold on to the card. I don't forget a favor. If you ever need something in return you can give me a shout and I'll do what I can."

She examined the card, then looked up at him. "Try the drop-in center on Liffey Street. My cousin said he goes there sometimes."

"I'll do that," Cormac said.

He was walking away when she called after him.

"That counts, right? For the favor?"

He turned back. "It does if I find him."

She sniffed. "Ye're all the bleeding same," she said, and she closed the door.

The drop-in center was only a fifteen-minute drive from Shauna's flat. Cormac flashed his badge at the man sitting behind the reception desk.

"I'm looking for Niall Collins," he said.

The man behind the desk—a clean-cut twenty-something with a hipster beard—had looked up with a friendly smile, but his expression darkened as soon as the badge came out.

"I haven't seen him for a few days," he said.

"Right," Cormac said. "But he does come here?"

The receptionist flushed a little. "Sorry. I'm not supposed to share any information about our clients. Not without a warrant. I'm not trying to be difficult. It's about respecting people's privacy."

Cormac nodded. "I get that." He drummed his fingers on the reception desk, thinking. He looked around. The place was all bright colors and openness. It must have been a recent refit, and whoever had funded it had had money to spend. Cormac found it difficult not to be cynical about drug rehabilitation. He'd seen too many serial failures, people who sucked up their family's resources to pay for expensive rehab, only to return to the needle or the pills again and again. Still there was the occasional success, and people needed hope. And this place had a sense of hope about it. He could see past reception into a canteen area. There were clients sitting around, playing cards, and drinking coffee. A couple of people were engaged in private conversations that looked like they might have a counseling aspect to them. Cormac made a gesture in their direction. "Do you think there's anyone else here who might know Niall? Might be able to point me in his direction? I'm guessing your other clients don't have the same confidentiality obligations."

The receptionist gave him the dirtiest of looks, then picked up his phone and dialed a number, muttering a quick description of the problem before hanging up. "Someone will be with you in a minute," he said.

The someone in question was a young woman, attractive, with dark hair to her shoulders, blue eyes, and very clear skin. She held out a hand to him. "Karen Allen, Director of Services. Would you like to come this way, Detective?" she said.

He followed her into an office. She sat and picked up a pen like she was about to take notes, gesturing to the seat opposite her. "Please do sit. I understand that you would like to speak with Niall Collins. We can't help you with that because Niall isn't here. He hasn't been here for a few days and he may not come again."

"I'm not trying to invade Mr. Collins's privacy unnecessarily. But I would like to talk to him. I understand he was living with his sister until recently. Do you know where he's living at the moment?"

"I think he's homeless, so it could be anywhere."

Cormac didn't quite manage to hide his surprise at that. The woman saw it and nodded.

"Niall had been doing very well in his recovery. He was one of our volunteers on our peer-support program for many months. But things went downhill for him five or six months ago and he hasn't been part of the program for some time. Niall does sometimes drop in for a chat or something to eat, but he's been coming in less lately. Beyond that, there's really nothing I can tell you. I'm not his counselor, and if I were, I wouldn't be able to share anything Niall has spoken about in confidence anyway."

"Understood." Cormac hesitated. He wanted to ask her more, ask for her impression of the man, but he'd spent enough time here. It was a drug treatment center. If there were six degrees of separation in most of the world, as a general rule there were no more than four in Ireland. And surely here no separation at all between the drug users who came here to seek treatment and the drug gangs who fed their habits. It was one thing to be open about his approach, but he didn't want to be so open that Collins bolted before he got to him.

Cormac stood up. "Thanks for your time," he said.

"Do you want to leave a card? I can let Niall know you were looking for him."

"Thank you, but no. I'll keep looking."

He spent much of the early hours of Friday night walking the streets of inner-city Dublin, talking to the homeless. There were far too many of them, men and women, young and old. Some obvious addicts, and some who were tidy and put-together and seemed at first glance to be in good shape, until you saw the look of despair in their eyes. He found a few who were happy to have a chat, two who professed to knowing the Niall Collins he was talking about. One young fella agreed to ask around, see what he could learn about Collins's location by the following night, in exchange for appropriate compensation. And that was it. At one a.m. Cormac retreated to his hotel for some sleep, intent on getting some rest and trying again the following day.

He checked his phone before he went to sleep. At some point in the night, he'd missed another call from Emma. Shite. She would assume he was avoiding her, and maybe he was. There was only one way they could be together, and that was if he walked away from his job, rolled the dice on a new life. It seemed impossible. He'd been a garda for more than twenty years, and false modesty aside, he knew he was bloody good at it. Walking away from all of that didn't feel like a step toward a new life, it felt like taking a step off a cliff. What else could he do? There was only one possibility. If Matt Staunton could introduce him to the right people, there might be an opportunity for him at Interpol. The chances were slim, and it was hard to imagine leaving Ireland, leaving the gardaí, but losing Emma felt like an impossibility. Lyon wasn't Brussels, but Emma could undoubtedly find a lab in France, if it came to it. He needed to talk to her, tell her what he was thinking, but it would have to wait until things were a bit more certain.

Cormac sent her a text message, a simple good night, and a promise to talk the following day, then he rolled over and fell asleep.

Tuesday, September 1, 2015

ANNA

Outside Dublin, Ireland

By the time they were an hour out of Dublin, Tilly had her head buried in a library book, which would now never be returned, and Anna was taking advantage of the free Wi-Fi on the bus to search for flats. Anna knew she would qualify for rent allowance, but even if she applied first thing in the morning it would take two months for the money to come through. Besides, putting in an application for rent allowance meant formally forgoing the flat to the next person on the housing list, which meant that Niall would be evicted all the sooner. She couldn't quite bring herself to pull that trigger. Not yet, though she couldn't afford to delay for very long. In the meantime, she and Tilly needed somewhere to stay. Anna flicked through the images on a real-estate website, sorted them so that the cheapest came up first. She'd started by searching for single rooms, but there were only two single rooms to rent, both in houses already occupied by university students. They wouldn't want the likes of her. And even those single rooms were asking for four hundred euros a month. The next cheapest place on the list was a shitty one-room for five-fifty. Jesus. They'd want a month's rent in advance, which would leave her a hundred euros in her savings, and then she'd be back to living week to week on her welfare payments. There had to be a better solution.

Anna widened the search field to the entire county, set the maximum rent at three hundred euros a month, and came up with nothing. Not a single hit. She moved the cap up to four hundred euros and got three results. Two student accommodation places, and a lovely little cottage in a place called Kilmore. But as far as she could see from the map, the cottage was miles from the nearest village, so what chance would she have to find work there, and how would she get Tilly to school? Anna felt tears threatening. Tilly tugged on her arm, looked up at her anxiously, and Anna forced a smile.

"Are you hungry, Tils?"

Tilly nodded, smiling tentatively back at her. This was all a big adventure. Anna handed her a sandwich and a bottle of water. Tilly tucked the water at her side, then, balancing sandwich and book, continued to read. Anna returned to her search. She couldn't eat until she'd figured something out.

She pushed the cap up to four hundred and fifty, and one other place popped up. A one-bedroom flat in a seaside village called Roundstone. Anna flicked through the pictures. They looked blurry, but it might be all right. It wasn't right in the village, but walking distance, surely. She looked up the village online and it was very pretty. There was a primary school. There were a couple of pubs, a small hotel. Surely there'd be a bit of work available? But could she afford it? Four hundred and fifty upfront. Anna bit her lip. She looked at the flat again. Tried to zoom in on the photographs. It was listed for rent by the owner, not an agency. All right. Well, she'd said she was going to be tough, to fight for her daughter, and this was the place to start. The ad included a mobile number.

> Looking for a place to rent for me and my little girl. I'm a great cleaner. Would you take three hundred and fifty and I'll give the place a great clean for you?

Anna closed her eyes and let her head rest against the seat. Please. Please please please. Her phone buzzed a moment later.

When would you want it?

Anna stared down at the message, her fingers were clumsy in her haste to respond.

Today, if that's all right.

The wait for a return message felt like forever.

I'll let you have it if you paint it. Flat comes as is.

Comes as is? What did that mean? Anna glanced uncertainly at Tilly. But how bad could it be? They'd have a roof over their heads. An oven. A fridge. And she could fix it up. On her phone she flicked back to the photographs of the village, the painted terrace houses, the gleaming water of the bay, and the little fishing boats. It was a million miles from the Liberties, a million miles from the world they were leaving behind. She suddenly wanted it very badly. But she couldn't afford to be stupid.

I'll paint it no problem. But you'll need to supply the paint, and I'll need a discount off the rent.

A long, long pause.

Two fifty for the first month.

Anna nearly dropped her phone in her haste to type in her acceptance. She pressed *send*, then clutched the phone in excitement. She was doing it. She was going to make this work. She picked up Tilly's hand and gave it a squeeze, returned Tilly's smile, this time sincerely, then searched in the bag for her own sandwich. She was absolutely starving.

They arrived in Galway at five forty-five p.m., exactly on time, which left them only twenty-two minutes to gather their bags and make their way to the departure point for the Clifden bus. The Clifden bus was the only one to stop in Roundstone, there was only one departure per day, and Anna had already decided that they couldn't afford to stop in Galway for the night. She was going to make every penny she had work as hard as possible. They hurried, made it with only a couple of minutes to spare, and Anna was too hurried and too distracted to notice the man who followed them off the Galway bus, and who continued to watch as they boarded the bus to Clifden, his mobile phone pressed to his ear.

Tilly was caught up at first by all the activity in the bus station but as the bus pulled out, she went looking in the bag for more food. Anna handed her the muffin, felt her own stomach grumble. Oh well. It was only an hour and a half. They could pick up a bit of food when they got there.

The bus was only half full when they left Galway, and they lost passengers steadily. For the last leg of the journey, Anna and Tilly were the only passengers on board. The roads were terrible, narrow and potholed, uneven and full of sudden sharp turns. But the landscape was beautiful. The road met the coast as they approached Roundstone and a dazzling view of the ocean opened up before them. The sun was setting, the last of its light brightening and warming the headland. In the shadow the water was the color of a bruised blueberry. It made Anna catch her breath.

The bus dropped them on the main street. Anna took Tilly by the hand, caught up their bags and baggage, and crossed the road into Gilmartin's pub, where she'd arranged to meet her new landlord. The hum of noisy talk, the warmth of a busy pub, and the smell of good food reached out and grabbed her. She paused at the threshold for a moment—it was a lot after the near-silence of the bus journey—then made her way to the bar, Tilly following close behind. The barman was tall and blond, looked more Swedish than Irish, and had his hands full. All the bar stools were occupied, men in conversation. One of them, older, overweight, and with the reddened nose and cheeks of a regular drinker, turned to look at her.

"Do you want to sit?" he asked, moving as if to vacate the stool. His eyes flicked to Tilly behind her.

"No, you're grand," Anna said. "We're not staying."

He nodded. "Looking for someone?"

Anna shrugged. She wasn't going to get into it with a stranger. He seemed to get the message after a minute, turned back to his pint. At least he hadn't taken offense. You never knew with older men. She had to wait another couple of minutes before the barman made his way back down to them. That was all right. They served food here, too. Anna counted the tables . . . twelve tables in the front bar where people were eating their dinner. If they served lunch as well, she might be able to get a few shifts waitressing.

When the barman approached, she gave him her biggest and brightest smile.

"Howr'ya," she said. "I'm looking for Dieter Blume. I'm Anna. He said he'd meet me here."

The barman didn't get a chance to answer. The man who'd offered the barstool cut in instead.

"Dieter's not here," he said. "He's not been in yet this

evening." He offered his hand. "Sorry for butting in. My name's Des Fisher. I'm the local garda sergeant. Can't seem to mind my own business. Isn't that right, Mike?" The last was said with a friendly nod to the barman, who laughed lightly. "Can I get you a drink while you're waiting? Would the little one like a mineral?"

Anna's sense that she was in control of her situation dropped away. She wanted to retreat to the farthest corner of the room, but she knew it would only draw more attention. She forced herself to smile again.

"Ah, no," she said. "You're all right."

"Don't be silly." He turned to the barman. "Mike, we'll have a mineral for the little one, and . . . what'll you have yourself?"

"Just water would be great. Thanks." Anna felt her face flush. Tilly was standing very close, crowding her. Anna looked for her phone. "I'll just send him a message."

She looked up in time to see the look that passed between Des Fisher and Mike the barman. Des turned to her.

"Anna. Is that what you said your name is? I hope you don't mind me asking, but are you planning on renting Dieter's flat? Is that why you're meeting him?"

"I . . ." Anna looked back and forth between Des and the barman. But there was no point in lying. It was a small village. The garda sergeant would figure out quickly enough that she hadn't told the truth and he would wonder why. And there was no reason to lie anyway. She wasn't doing anything wrong or illegal. It was taking her far too long to answer. They were both staring at her now. "Yes," she said, and felt the flush deepen in her cheeks.

"Just for a night or two, is it? You're here on holiday?"

She shook her head. "I'm not sure yet, but I'm hoping a bit longer."

Des dropped his eyes, tutted. “I’m not sure that’s such a good idea,” he said.

“Why?” Anna asked.

“It’s not in great shape, his flat. The heat doesn’t work, and he won’t get it fixed. He keeps trying to rent it to tourists and it causes all sorts of trouble.”

Anna’s heart sank. “Well,” she said. “I’ll talk to him about that.” She could figure that out. Maybe she could get it fixed herself, get another discount.

But Des’s eyes flicked again to Tilly. “That’s not the only reason,” he said. “Dieter has a bit of a history with . . . well, it might not be a suitable place for you. He lives in the downstairs flat you see. He likes a drink and when he has drink taken he goes looking for company.” He was watching his words, obviously conscious of Tilly standing there, taking it all in. Still, his meaning was clear enough. “When he’s the worse for wear, he doesn’t like to take no for an answer.”

Oh Christ. All of Anna’s energy and confidence fell away. Only the fact of Tilly’s presence beside her kept her from melting into tears. Des saw it.

“Traveled a long way, have you?” Des asked. And his voice was so sympathetic, so unexpectedly gentle, that the tears did come, no matter how hard she tried to blink them away.

“Don’t worry,” he said. “Come on, now. Let’s get you a bit to eat, and we can have a chat.”

Anna let him lead them to a table, let him buy dinner, and before she knew it she had told him everything. Or almost everything.

“Right then,” he said. “You need work and a place to stay. A place that suits your little girl. I might just have a solution that will work for you.”

PART THREE

Saturday, November 7, 2015

CHAPTER TWENTY-NINE

Roundstone, Ireland

On Saturday morning, Peter woke to the sound of cartoons playing on the television. He opened his eyes to see Tilly, well wrapped in pajamas, a dressing gown, and thick socks, curled up on the armchair opposite him. He blinked himself awake, sat up a little.

"Hello," he said.

"Hi," she said. Her voice was very soft, and she didn't look directly at him, but she didn't seem all that surprised to find him sleeping fully clothed on the couch, and if she wasn't bouncing around the place with welcome, at least she seemed to have lost some of her fear of him.

He watched the cartoon blindly for a minute, then sat up.

"Are you hungry?" he asked. "Can I make you some breakfast?"

She looked surprised. "I can make it myself," she said. "Come on." She led the way to the kitchen, showed him where to find the Honey Nut Loops and milk and they had settled companionably enough into cereal chomping and more cartoons when Peter's phone buzzed. A text message from Des.

Meet me at the station, ASAP.

Peter sighed.

It actually wasn't too bad, walking into the village. There was no one else about, for a start. It was very still, there was little to no wind, and though the clouds were gathering again, it wasn't snowing. Yes, it was cold, but the air was fresh and clean and the crunch of the snow underfoot felt good. He'd been worried that the snow might have kept coming overnight, that it would be piled in drifts and make the roads impassable, but it seemed like they'd had only another inch or two. The only problem was that under the few inches of fresher snow, the roads were frozen. He slipped more than once on icy patches. He passed a road gritter on his way down the hill. It had a snowplow fitted to the front, was doing decent job pushing the snow to the sides of the road and spreading grit in its wake. After that the going was easier. Peter made his way into the village and found his car. He let the engine run for ten minutes or so, until the windscreen was fully defrosted, then drove on to the station. He got there just after nine and considered it good going. Des was there before him.

"Have you seen the forecast?" Des asked, as Peter hung his coat and hat on the hooks near the door.

"Not today," Peter said.

"They're saying that we've another blast of snow coming our way this evening, and the temperature is due to drop again overnight. The county council has put out a warning. They're running low on grit and salt, and they won't get a delivery until Tuesday. So after today they're not going to grit secondary roads."

Peter groaned inwardly. "That's going to make it harder to get around."

"We need to get out and about today. Do a round of the older residents and a couple of people with a disability who aren't best placed to look after themselves in this weather. Check that they've got the heat on or firewood in and enough food for at least a few days. If we get snow on top of ice and then another freeze, people won't go out. A lot of people won't be prepared."

"What about the social workers?" Peter asked.

"What about them?" Des said. "Do you think they're going to drive out from Clifden in this weather? What's the matter, Peter? Do you think you're too good for the work?"

Peter held up two hands in a pacifying gesture. "Jesus. I wasn't objecting. I'm happy to do it. I was just planning on spending some time with Maggie today."

"You can see Maggie any time," Des said.

"Actually, I can't."

Des looked at him blankly for a moment.

"I told you about her fall," Peter said.

"Yes. Right."

Peter felt a surge of anger. Des had the headspace to worry about other older residents of Roundstone, just not Maggie. Anger made him blunt.

"She's very sick. Doctor Barrett thinks that she's not going to get better. She may only have weeks left."

"What?" Des shook his head. "That doesn't make any sense. You must have misunderstood, Peter."

Jesus. "That's not something you misunderstand. Barrett was very clear. He was very sympathetic."

"But . . ." Des shook his head again.

"She's eighty-two years old. She has hypotension. Kidney problems. She's been losing weight."

"She's not going to die because she lost a few pounds. For god's sake, Peter, use your head."

Peter gritted his teeth. "Obviously there's more than that going on."

"What, then?" Des said.

"Barrett said she might have had a small stroke. But it's

not any one thing. I think it's a combination of everything. Her body's just breaking down."

"All right. Well, what are the options?" Des spoke with a forced patience that was utterly infuriating.

"There are no options. Barrett said she could have treatment to prolong her life, but it would be uncomfortable and difficult. He recommends that she stays at home."

Des was silent for a moment. He looked at his hands. "That's very bad news," he said, eventually.

Peter's anger at his father drained away. "Yes," he said.

Des stood up. "I'll make tea," he said.

Des made the tea, added sugar without asking, handed a cup to Peter along with an open packet of cookies.

"I thought she had years more before we'd get to this stage," Des said.

"Barrett said it can happen quickly, sometimes."

"I suppose so," Des said. "You just never think it will to one of yours."

For the first time in years, Peter felt a surge of fellow feeling toward his father.

Des pushed the remains of a biscuit into his mouth, washed it down with a sip of tea. "I suppose we'll need to talk about what happens later?"

"Later?"

"After she passes. It would be better if Anna and her daughter could stay on in the cottage. You might think you'd like it for yourself. But then you're set up where you are, or you could still move into my place. There's plenty of room. You needn't think I'd be in on top of you." He said the last gruffly.

"It's way too soon to think about that," Peter said.

"Well, I just think we should make sure that Anna and Tilly stay on."

It was hard to know what to say to that. This was not the time to tackle his father's assumption that Peter was in Roundstone for the long term. He was a long way from making that commitment. But it was good that Des cared about Anna and Tilly. And it wasn't due to any kind of romantic interest. Anna was very definitely not the type. Maybe Des had changed over the years. A little part of Peter whispered that he may have misjudged his father. His view of Des had formed when he was a lonely and angry child. Maybe he'd seen only what he wanted to see.

"What happened with the interview?" Peter asked.

"Hmm?"

"The interview with Jane Cummins's father. Did he want to meet you yesterday afternoon?"

Des's expression darkened. "He did."

"It didn't go well, I take it?"

"He dragged his daughter in here. She was pale as a ghost. With her father standing over her, Jane told me that she might have misinterpreted things. Maybe her Uncle Séan was just being affectionate. They want to drop the charges."

"Shite," Peter said. "Where was the mother?"

Des shrugged. "She's gone very quiet all of a sudden. The family is closing ranks."

"You're not going to leave it there, are you?"

Des looked at him steadily. "I'm not," he said. "I'm going to make damn sure he doesn't hurt her again."

Peter looked away. It was clear from Des's manner that whatever he was planning to do next, it wasn't going to be strictly by the book. And maybe that was okay. Maybe it was necessary.

Des stood up. He went to the coffee station, dumped his cup, then found a piece of paper and scribbled a short list. He handed it to Peter.

"Here's what you need," he said. "Names and addresses of the people you need to check on." He took a roll of fifties from his back pocket, handed it to Peter. "Go to Horan's first and buy a few bags of coal, some basics like milk and bread. Stock up."

Peter was looking at the money in his hand.

"Keep the receipts," Des said. "I'll want to claim it back on expenses."

Sharon was just unlocking the doors at Horan's when Peter arrived. She jumped a little when she opened the door and saw him, put a hand to her chest.

"Jesus. You put the heart across me."

He half-smiled. "You sound like an old woman."

"I am an old woman. In spirit if not in body." She gestured for him to come in, closed the door swiftly after him. She was still in her coat and hat. The shop was still chilly, but it was warmer than outside. "Old women are the best. They know everything about everyone, so you can't get one up on them. They don't care what you think about what they're wearing or how they look. And they've outlived all the men they grew up with who gave them shit along the way." She gave him a look that said, *There, what do you think of that?* He just smiled again. It was the only sensible reaction.

"What do you need?" she asked.

He told her the story, and she led the way through the back of the shop and the storeroom and out to the locked storage shed at the back. Hessian sacks of coal, machine-sewn closed, were stacked along the fence. Peter brought the car around, managed to get five bags of coal into the trunk, a few bales of briquettes on the floor of the back seat, then with Sharon's help made up seven bags of basic groceries: he bought tea, sugar, milk, bread, beans, biscuits, sausages, and a couple of microwavable meals per bag.

It took three hours of driving, knocking, chatting, and unloading to deal with the first three names on the list of seven. The first of them, seventy-eight-year-old Rachel Doran, opened the door in response to his knock. She had a book in one hand and was immaculately dressed in neatly pressed slacks, a soft gray cashmere sweater, and an expensive-looking silk scarf.

"Can I help you?"

Peter tried to explain the purpose of his visit, and she seemed surprised and a little confused by his presence. She invited him in, but it was very clear that she didn't need his help. The house was warm and tidy, the smell of baking wafting from the kitchen. All in all, Rachel Doran was doing far better than he was. A little embarrassed, Peter extricated himself as gracefully as possible and drove on. He wondered briefly if Des had sent him on some sort of a fool's errand for reasons only known to himself, but he found the next person on Des's list—a man named Tom Mulligan—in a very different situation.

Tom was confused and belligerent, kept repeating again and again that he'd done nothing wrong and that no garda was going to walk into his house without so much as a by your leave. Peter spent ten minutes trying to talk him around, then gave up trying to *plámás* him, walked into the house, and got on with things. Mulligan wasn't managing anywhere near as well as Rachel Doran. His heat was turned off—which could have been due to confusion or a need to save the money—and his cupboards and fridge held only out-of-date condiments and half-empty jars that should have been binned weeks back. The draining board beside the kitchen sink was laden with dishes that had been half washed and left to dry.

Peter looked around, feeling a bit helpless, then set to work. Still talking, talking all the while, to an agitated Tom, Peter unloaded firewood and food from the car. He put on a big fire and filled the coal bucket at the right of the fireplace. The lighting of the fire settled Tom down. He folded himself into the armchair closest to the fireplace, found his remote control, and turned the television on. He settled there happily enough while Peter packed the fridge and the cupboard, gave the few dishes a proper wash and dry with a clean tea towel he found neatly folded in a drawer. Then he made sausages and beans on toast for Tom and delivered the plate to him beside the fire with a glass of milk.

"Will that do you, Tom?" he asked.

Tom took a bite of toast. "It's grand," he said, around the food in his mouth, his eyes still on the TV.

Peter smiled to himself and quietly let himself out.

CHAPTER THIRTY

With the weather, everything took ten times longer, and some of the people Peter visited weren't in a rush for him to leave. As a result, it was getting dark and snow had started to drift down again as Peter pulled into the driveway of the house that was last on his list. He sat and watched it fall for a moment. This kind of heavy, sticking snow was dangerous, particularly when they were so woefully underprepared for it, but it was so beautiful to look at. His phone rang, shattering the peace of the moment. He looked at the screen, didn't recognize the number.

"Peter Fisher," he said, by way of answer.

"Detective, it's Stuart Connolly here. We met yesterday?"

"Yes?"

"I had a look at the deeds' safe after you left yesterday," Connolly said. "I suppose I'd reassured you so thoroughly that we still had Miles Lynch's title deeds, and then I suddenly panicked that I'd misled you. I had a look, and we do have all the original deeds still on file, but the records show that Miles Lynch came to the office a year ago and asked for a photocopy of his Land Registry folio."

Peter frowned. "I'm sorry, Mr. Connolly, I don't know what that is."

"Call me Stuart, please. A folio is just a written record—it's the record held by the Land Registry of ownership of land. It lists the owner, any mortgages or other charges, and any rights of way. Then there's a map showing the relevant land."

"Okay," said Peter. "So maybe Miles Lynch was selling after all?"

"He might have been thinking of selling," Connolly said. "But he still couldn't have completed the sale without coming to my office. A copy of a folio just won't cut it. We have original deeds showing rights of way, all of that sort of thing."

"Right," said Peter. He watched the snow fall as he mulled it over. It didn't seem like much.

"I don't know if that's any help to you, but I wanted to let you know."

Peter thanked him and ended the call. The mystery of whether or not Miles Lynch had been planning to sell the land and to whom was interesting, and it was worth trying to get to the bottom of, for completeness sake at least. But the sale of the land could not have been the motive for the murder. The only person who was angry about a possible sale had been murdered alongside him.

Peter got out of the car and lugged a bag of coal to the front door, then went back for a bag of food supplies. He knocked on the door and waited. He tried again a minute later, but there was still nothing. He was at the point of going around the back when a voice called from next door.

"Can I help you?"

The voice belonged to a young woman who was waving over from the porch of a new build next door. She pulled on a puffer jacket over what looked like gray cotton tracksuit bottoms and a pair of slippers and waved at him again.

Peter took a couple of steps in her direction "I'm Garda

Peter Fisher," he called. "I have a delivery for James Madden, but there's no answer."

"Just a minute," she said. She disappeared back into her home, reappeared a minute later, this time with a pair of boots on her feet and a set of keys in her hand. She climbed the fence between the two houses and approached him. "Can you believe the snow?" she said. "I can't remember it ever being this bad before. Except in 2010. Was it 2010? Whichever it was, anyway, I think we were snowed in for a week. Will it be the same, do you think?" She reached him and offered a hand and a smile.

"Alisha," she said. "I'm James's daughter-in-law. We live just next door. And you're Peter Fisher? I heard you were back." Her eyes drifted to the firewood and coal Peter'd left at the front door, the bag of food still in his hands. "What's all this?"

Peter explained, and she looked dubious. "Well, that's really kind," she said. "You're welcome to bring everything in, but you can let Des know that we'll be looking after James, of course, as we always do. He likes to stay on top of things, doesn't he, your father?" The words were friendly enough, but Peter didn't miss the irritation beneath them. She clearly considered Des's gesture to be unnecessary interference.

She walked past him to the front door, talking all the way.

"I don't know why anyone would think James is in any danger. We just live next door. We look after him. I drop his dinner over to him every day and he comes to us every Sunday. I'd like him to come more often but he can't be persuaded. Ever since Sheila died, but that's lots of years ago now, and you'd think he'd be better at seeing other people. That's not a judgment, now, just for his own sake, you know?"

She unlocked the front door. "He must have fallen asleep," she said. "But I have a key to the place. I'd have to, really, to keep a proper eye on him. Did you know his wife? You must have met her. Sheila was a great friend of your granny's. They used to spend a lot of time together. You know, since James withdrew into himself a bit, Maggie was the only one who would go to the trouble of calling over and spending time with him. He had lots of visitors in the beginning, but they all fell away. Fairweather friends. Not Maggie. She comes at least once a month, gets a little group together to play a few hands of cards. She's a good woman."

Alisha finally stopped talking, stepped into the hallway, stood waiting for an answer.

"Yes, I remember Sheila," Peter said. "She and Maggie were very close." Sheila had been a talker too, to the best of his memory. Maggie had always said you'd have had to put a hand over her mouth to get a word in edgeways. Maybe James Madden kept to himself because he was grateful for the quiet.

Alisha closed the door behind them. "James?" she called. The house was warm, and Peter was grateful for it. It was seriously cold outside now.

"James?" Alisha called again. Then, to Peter, "He must be really out. That's not like him, not in the middle of the day." Peter felt the first stirrings of foreboding. He put the food down on the hall table. Alisha opened a door off the hall, and led the way into the living room. James Madden was seated there, in an armchair pulled in close to the fireplace, where a fire burned low in the grate. He had a blanket folded neatly across his lap, an empty cup of tea, and a large-print paperback on a table at his knee. His eyes were closed.

"James?" Alisha said again, and her voice was uncertain. James looked . . . odd. His face was slack, his mouth open. His head lolled back against the chair, almost, but not quite, as if he was sleeping. Peter put his fingertips gently on the old man's neck. There was no pulse, and his skin was cool to the touch.

"I think . . . I think he's passed," Peter said.

Alisha looked at him, eyes wide. "But he was fine this morning. I came over after breakfast. We had a chat about the weather, about what he should get the children for Christmas. He was absolutely fine." She was very pale, but there were no tears in her eyes. She was in shock.

"I don't know," Peter said. "I'm so sorry. Maybe it was a heart attack. Or a stroke. We should call Doctor Barrett. He said he would be in Roundstone today. Maybe he came, despite the weather."

Alisha nodded. She sank down onto the couch. "Poor James," she said weakly. "He died all alone. He couldn't have wanted that."

"Had he been in pain, at all?" Peter asked.

"He was as healthy as a horse. Well, he might have been a bit depressed. It wasn't normal, to want to spend so much time alone."

Peter looked around the room, but there were no empty pill packets. Nothing to suggest that this had been anything but an entirely natural death. So why did he have the strongest feeling that something wasn't right?

"Is there someone I can call for you?" he asked Alisha, as gently as he could. "Or, I can wait for the doctor if you'd like to go back to the house."

She stood up. "Yes. I think I need to go. The girls are at home. John is on his way." Her face crumbled. "He's going to be devastated. Sorry. Sorry . . . I need to go."

She all but ran from the room and Peter heard the front door close behind her. He took out his phone and called Richard Barrett's surgery. Spoke to a nurse who confirmed that he was already in Roundstone, making house calls, and she would redirect him to the house. The doctor's red Nissan Patrol pulled into the drive five minutes later. Peter went to meet him and they shook hands at the door.

"Are you all right?" Barrett asked.

"I'm fine," said Peter.

"The timing of this could be better for you," Doctor Barrett said.

Meaning that he thought it could be Maggie next, for a call like this. Peter felt the blow of that, then shook it off. Barrett examined James gently and efficiently.

"It was almost certainly a stroke," the doctor said. He straightened up. "It's very sad. James was a good man, but I suppose it isn't a great surprise. He'd been unwell for some time."

"Had he?" Peter asked, surprised. "I spoke to his daughter-in-law. She said he was healthy. As strong as a horse, I think she said."

Barrett shook his head as he packed away his stethoscope. "He didn't want them to know. Didn't want the fuss. But he wasn't afraid of dying. He was quite a religious man. He believed that he was going to see his deceased wife in heaven." Barrett looked up at Peter. "That's not something I understand myself, that sort of belief, but I suppose there's no arguing that it's a comfort for those who have it."

"I'd better call the coroner's office," Peter said. "Though I don't know if they'll be able to get anyone out in this weather."

"You can if you like," Doctor Barrett said. "But there's no need. There won't be an autopsy in this case. As I was treating James, I'll be signing the death certificate. This isn't a case for the coroner."

"All right," said Peter. "I suppose I'd better call the morgue."

"I'd better go," Barrett said. "The weather's getting worse, and I want to call in on Maggie before I go back to Clifden. I've got a four-wheel drive, but another few hours of this and I think we'll all be snowed in."

"I'll just let the family know," Peter said. "It'll be tomorrow before they can send someone out from the morgue to get him, I'm sure. They might want some help laying him out at home."

"That would be good of you," Barrett said.

Barrett took his leave. Despite the cold, Peter stood in the doorway and watched him go.

After a few minutes, Peter went back inside and sat on the couch that Alisha had so recently vacated. James looked smaller, somehow, than he had when they had first come into the room. Diminished already by death.

"You poor man," Peter said quietly.

He stood up and let himself out of the house, pulling the door closed behind him. Alisha had left her keys behind; they were still hanging in the door. He followed her footprints across the snow-covered lawn, over the fence to next door. His boots sank into the snow, which was now well above his ankles. She opened the door to him with puffy eyes, and a bundle of tissues clutched in one hand.

"Come in," she said. "Sorry, I shouldn't have run away. I'll make you a cup of tea. John's inside with the girls."

In the kitchen he found John Madden, sitting on a kitchen chair. He was a big man, all muscle, with a wiry beard. The girls, both blonde like their mother, were hugging their father as tightly as they could, and he had his arms wrapped around them, holding on. It took them a minute to realize that Peter had joined them. John drew a shaky breath, untangled himself, and stood up. He offered his hand, and his thanks for Peter's visit.

"I don't want to intrude," Peter said. He held out the keys.

"Alisha left these in the door, and I wanted to drop them off." He put them on the kitchen counter. "Also . . ." His eyes dropped to the girls, and he lowered his voice. "I wanted to see if you needed any help with him."

It took John a moment to understand, then his face blanched as the reality of the situation struck him. "Right," he said. "Right." He looked at his wife for guidance. For a moment she could only look helplessly back at him, then seemed to gather herself.

"I think it would be best if we move James to his bedroom for now," she said.

"I can do that," Peter said. "If that would help." He wanted to spare them the memory. He took up the keys from the counter again. John Madden cleared his throat and nodded.

"Thank you," he said. "I'll come with you."

John lingered in the hall while Peter checked upstairs and found the right bedroom. It was unbearably neat and tidy, everything just so with a pair of navy striped pajamas folded at the end of the bed. Peter pulled the covers back and went downstairs. James Madden wasn't heavy. Peter lifted him easily and carried him upstairs, laid him gently on the bed, and tucked the covers over him. He thought about carrying Maggie up to bed just a couple of nights before, and his heart ached. He was grateful that rigor mortis hadn't set in. At least now, if the family wanted to visit James, to sit with him overnight, it wouldn't be a horror.

John shook his hand again when he went downstairs. "Thank you," he said.

"I'm very sorry for your loss," said Peter.

"What happens now?"

"I'm not sure anyone will be able to make it out this evening, with the weather. Maybe tomorrow you'll be able to have someone come and collect him. Doctor Barrett's already been. He'll arrange for the death certificate."

"Barrett's a good man. To think he was here only this morning. If he'd come an hour later, maybe Dad would still be with us. Or if I hadn't gone out to fucking work. Today of all days. I could have stayed home."

"Who was here only this morning?" Peter asked.

"Doctor Barrett. Allie said he called in on his rounds. He was great like that. Dad could always talk to him. He wasn't much of a talker—Dad was slow to trust people, you see. He liked your Maggie, though. I think he had a bit of a soft spot for her, to tell you the truth."

Peter could tell that John was talking just to prevent himself from crying.

"I'll go," Peter said. "I'll leave you to get back to your family."

John offered his hand again. "Thank you," he said. "We're very grateful."

CHAPTER THIRTY-ONE

Dublin, Ireland

Cormac had planned to try to track Niall Collins down on Saturday evening, but before that, he had something else he needed to do. He made his way over to the south side of Dublin, to a rugby pitch, where an enthusiastic game of tag rugby was being played. Tag rugby had been a thing long before he left Dublin. It was rugby with no tackling, no rucks, and no lineouts. Players wore special shorts with colored flags on each hip, attached by velcro. Players were deemed tackled when a flag was removed. Teams were mixed, and a try scored by a woman was worth three points to the single point that could be scored by a man. Essentially, it was speed dating on a rugby pitch for Dublin's young professionals and it attracted every skill level from off-season near-professionals to rank beginners. The woman he was here to see—Orna Cox—was a fine player and her team appeared to have structured their gameplay around the very basic strategy of getting the ball to Orna as often as possible. It kept her busy and she didn't notice Cormac watching from the sideline until a couple of minutes before the whistle blew. Afterward, Orna shook hands with the opposing team, chatted briefly with her teammates, collected her jacket from the sidelines, and wandered in his direction.

"Cormac," she said. "This is a surprise."

"That was a good game," he said. "What was the score in the end? I missed the beginning."

"Twelve–seven, I think, or something close to it. We won, anyway."

"Well done."

Orna pulled on her jacket and undid her ponytail, retied it. She was pink-faced and warm from exercise, but it was bloody cold. The sun had gone down and floodlights were on. Without a jacket, she'd be shivering in minutes.

"I thought tag was a summer sport," Cormac said. "For the off-season."

"It is, mostly. Just a few of the more serious teams have set up a kind of minileague. We play year-round, when we can get space on the pitch."

Cormac nodded.

"So . . . have you spoken to Tara lately?" she asked. "She's married now. They have one little one, another due in March."

Tara was Cormac's ex-girlfriend, had been Orna's best friend. Still was, as far as he knew. "I knew about the first, not the second," Cormac said. "That's great news." He cast his eyes skyward, where black clouds were gathering. "Listen, Orna, I was hoping to have a chat with you about something. Can I buy you a drink?"

"In the bar?" She glanced toward the clubhouse.

"Might be a bit busy. Would you mind if we went somewhere quieter?"

She glanced over her shoulder to the other side of the pitch, where another player was gathering up markers and rugby balls, and taking his time about it. "I'd like to, but I have . . . I suppose I have a date." She looked pleased and slightly embarrassed at the same time.

Cormac nodded. "Right, I won't keep you."

"You need a favor, don't you?" she asked.

He shrugged and gave a half-smile.

"If I said it's a data kind of favor, would I be right?" Orna zipped up her jacket, pushed her hands into its pockets. "Can't do that anymore, Cormac. You know. Everything is tracked on the system. Every time I run a search it's tagged, and I have to have a formal garda request and warrant to reconcile every search to or I'll get myself fired."

"Yes," Cormac said. "I get that. And I wouldn't ask you to break the rules. There should be a warrant for this in the system already, or there will be shortly. I'm just asking you to add a little more to the picture."

"I don't understand. If there's a warrant, then why can't you just add the request to the official channels?"

Cormac grimaced. "It's complicated."

Orna crossed her arms. It was clear that she wasn't going to give him anything unless she heard more.

"It's not my warrant request, that's the first problem. And the team who did submit it, well, my concern is that they aren't that motivated to get to the truth. They'll do the bare minimum, tick the boxes, but they won't go the extra mile."

Orna made a face. "Is this some kind of internal politics drama? Because, honestly, Cormac . . ."

"No," Cormac said. He didn't want to lie to her. "There are politics, but it's bigger than that, too. Look, I can't tell you any details, but this is about a little girl, at the end of the day. And the safety of other little girls in the future."

Orna's eyes searched his. She wasn't stupid. She knew he wasn't telling her everything. But she would be better off if he didn't.

"Orna, you know I wouldn't lie to you."

She nodded reluctantly. "Tell me what you need."

"I'm looking for a data filter. There should be a warrant on your desk for the call records of a man called Francis Loughnane. Address on Headford Road, Galway. You'll be asked for a record of all calls and texts made, sent, and received over a period of time. We think he called someone, tipped them off. The only thing is, I doubt that the warrant will show anything. He would have been careful. I think he would have used a burner. Can you run a data filter for the same period? Pick up any phones that were in close proximity to Loughnane's phone for whatever period the warrant covers?"

She thought about it. "I can do it. But I'm going to give the information to the team that sent in the warrant."

"That's fine," Cormac said.

Orna hesitated. "You're not going to ask me for a copy?" she asked.

Cormac shrugged. "I'd love a copy," he said. "But as long as the information gets to the team it should be okay."

"Okay," she said. Then paused. "How dodgy is this, Cormac?"

"I'm not going to pretend that it's all above board, Orna," he said. "But if anything went astray with what I'm doing, none of this would land at your door. Check to make sure that you have the warrant. Just respond to it and add on the data filter. If you need to, if anyone ever asks you about this, just tell them straight that I asked for it and you thought it would be okay."

She gave him a look. "Come on, Cormac. That wouldn't wash and you know it. You've come here to have a quiet chat with me, off the record. How did you even know I was here, by the way?"

He smiled at her. "I Googled you," he said. "The first hit that came up was a site with tag rugby results and fixtures. I thought I'd come by, have a good chance of finding you here."

She shook her head. "Just as well I don't have a stalker then, isn't it?" She made eye contact and held it, and he thought then that it would be all right. She hadn't had a stalker, exactly, just an obnoxious ex-boyfriend who hadn't been happy about their break-up and was intent on making sure Orna knew it. Cormac had stepped in with a little show of garda interest, some light intimidation, and the ex had fucked off.

"It really is important, Orna. You know I wouldn't ask . . ."

She nodded, glanced over her shoulder again. "I do. Look, I won't make any promises. But I'll keep an eye out for the request. If I get the chance to run a copy, I will. But no guarantees, and you have to promise me that you tell no one you got it from me, all right?"

After he left Orna, Cormac made his way back into the city center. He'd made arrangements to meet his homeless connection from the day before at the same location, in the hopes that he'd manage to pick up a few hints of Niall Collins's location during the day. And he struck gold. In exchange for a hundred euros, he was pointed toward a flophouse in Clontarf. Clontarf was one of Dublin's up-market suburbs, but Cormac's new friend explained that the place in question had been boarded up, maybe for a renovation, and for reasons unknown the work never happened. Eventually someone in need of a place to sleep found their way in, presumably with the help of a crowbar.

"Those places get completely disgusting after a while, you know? People come in to shoot up or sleep for a few days and they leave their shit everywhere and then the rats come and it's just manky. I'd rather be on the streets." He was only in his early twenties, this young fella bundled in a sleeping bag and sitting on the steps of the Central Bank, but he had sunken cheeks and the eyes of a much older man. "But I've heard this one is all right. There's a woman there—Bess or Beth or something. She lays down the law."

Cormac thanked him, paid up, and set out. He didn't have a lot of hope that the information would lead to anything but it was worth a shot. He stopped just long enough to buy a flashlight, then drove out of the city. He tried Emma's phone on the way. She didn't answer.

The house was on Victoria Road, right in the heart of Clontarf and less than twenty minutes' drive from the city center, even in heavy traffic. Two streets back from the seafront. A prime location. The house itself was impressive at first glance. It was a period red brick, the front garden neatly kept with a box hedge and lawn, both recently trimmed. If it wasn't for the boarded-up front windows, you would assume that the house was occupied by some upper-middle-class family or professional couple, just like every other house on the street. Cormac opened the front gate and followed the side path down and around to the back of the house. It was a dark night and overcast, but there was enough ambient light from neighboring houses to see that the back garden was very overgrown. He switched on his flashlight as he approached the back door, tried the handle, and it opened. Cormac made his way inside, into a kitchen that had seen better days. Some of the terra-cotta tiles remained but most of them were gone, leaving bare and battered concrete in their wake. There was an old stove, but it was clear it wasn't working any parts that could be removed had been. The walls showed rising damp. There was no sign of any occupants. Cormac made his way farther into the house and up a staircase.

He passed a bedroom on the first floor. The door was open, and he shone the torch inside. There was a woman sleeping there, curled up on a mattress in a sleeping bag. She didn't react to the light, seemed deeply asleep. He moved on.

The next bedroom was also occupied, this time by a man. Another mattress, another sleeping bag. Cormac approached, floorboards creaking under his feet, scanning the room as he went. It was reasonably clean, just a couple of fast-food wrappings in the corner, a few water bottles. There was no sign of any drug paraphernalia, but unless this man, who he hoped to god was Niall Collins, was the world's deepest sleeper, he was on something. Cormac checked for any hidden weapons, then shook the man awake. It took a minute.

"Niall? Niall, wake up. I need to have a chat with you."

Eventually the man came around enough to sit up a little, blinking his eyes slowly. He was having trouble focusing on Cormac and looked like he might drop off again at any minute.

"You're Niall, aren't you? Niall Collins? I just need to have a bit of a chat with you, Niall, and then I'll leave you to go back to sleep."

The other man looked at him blankly. Cormac was aiming the beam of the flashlight off to the side so that he could see Collins's face but avoid blinding him with the direct glare of the beam. There was a camping lantern sitting to the left of Collins's mattress. "Can you turn on your light there, Niall, so we can see each other a bit better?"

It took Collins a long moment to process what Cormac wanted, another to fumble with the lantern and turn it on, but the action seemed to bring him back to himself a little bit more.

"What the fuck?" he asked. "What are you . . . why are you in my room? I don't want you here."

"You are Niall, aren't you? I was at your old flat today. Your sister's old place in the Liberties."

Cormac was just making conversation, trying to lead off with something innocuous, but Collins's reaction was immediate and entirely unexpected. He shuffled backward in his sleeping bag until he was up against the wall. "I didn't do anything," he said.

Cormac kept his tone relaxed and neutral. "No one's suggesting you have, Niall. I just wanted to have a chat with you because I'm told you've been very helpful to the police in the past. I have a little problem with a drug dealer—nothing major, nothing very high level—but I thought you might be able to confirm a bit of information for me."

"I'm not a dealer," Niall said, shaking his head. "I'm just the fucking eejit who buys from them. I can't help you."

"Ah Niall, there's no need to run yourself down. I know you've been a big help to us in the past. You've come very highly recommended. And I'm just looking for anything you can give me about James Arnott," Cormac said, naming a man who he knew to be a minor dealer in the Killeen network. "I want to have a chat with him. It would be very helpful if you could let me know where I might find him. If there's a pub he likes in particular, or a girlfriend you know of."

Niall shook his head. "I don't know anything. I don't know him. I can't help you."

Cormac gave him a hard look and Collins flinched as if Cormac had threatened him. It was very difficult to believe that the man in front of him was some kind of super-informant. Maybe he was just that good at playing a part, but he seemed like a man near the end of his road.

"All right, Niall," Cormac said softly. "Maybe there's been some kind of mix-up. Maybe you can't help me. But just so I know I'm speaking to the right man, you did live in the apartment in the Liberties? That was your sister's place before she moved out?"

Cormac had intended to settle the man down with a series of unchallenging questions, but if anything Collins looked more frightened than ever. His eyes flicked from Cormac to the door and back and his hands clutched at his sleeping back. Cormac felt a sudden concern for the missing sister.

"That's a very simple question, Niall," Cormac said. "I know you can answer this one. Did you live with your sister at the flat?"

He got a single stiff nod in return.

"Grand," Cormac said. "And where is she now?"

Collins shook his head. "I don't know. She went away. She just . . . I was asleep, and when I woke up, she was gone."

"And you haven't seen her since?"

Another head shake.

"You haven't called her? Heard from her at all?" Cormac asked. He could see the answer in Collins's wretched expression. "Why haven't you reported her missing? Aren't you worried about her?"

"Nothing happened to Anna," Niall said. "She'd just had enough. All her stuff was gone. I told you, when I woke up she'd packed everything up and just left. I think she found somewhere better. That's Anna. She's a survivor." He said it with admiration, not bitterness.

"Right," Cormac said. There was a ring of truth to Collins's words. But the other man was clearly hiding something. Cormac bit back his irritation. He didn't have time to get sucked into any side alleys. And he was tired now, and bloody cold.

"All right," Cormac said. He'd been leaning against the wall opposite Collins. Now he stood up. "Thanks for your time." He looked around the room. There was a fireplace, but it was black and empty, and the room was freezing cold. "Will you be all right here?" he asked. "You know the forecast is bad for the weekend. It's going down another five degrees at least. You're going to have to get somewhere a bit warmer than here."

Collins shrugged. "It's not my first winter sleeping rough," he said.

"It's going to be too cold, Niall," Cormac said. "You should find a hostel tomorrow." His words were met with another shrug. Collins wasn't interested in a lecture. He was waiting for Cormac to go. Cormac pulled out his wallet. He only had a tenner. He handed it over. "Get something to eat, will you?" he said.

Collins looked at the money, then he reached out and took it without a word or a look in Cormac's direction. That was okay.

Back in his car, heater on, Cormac looked up at the dark house and phoned the drop-in center. It was well after midnight, but the phone was answered almost immediately.

"Karen Allen." The Director of Services he'd met earlier that day.

Cormac looked at his watch. It was coming up on one a.m. "You don't sleep, Ms. Allen?" he said.

She gave a polite laugh. "I work night shift, from time to time."

Cormac explained the problem, the setup in the house, the fact that he was worried about the cold.

Karen Allen sighed. "We have so many people on the streets, and they'll all be trying to get a place in the next twenty-four hours. It won't be easy."

"If there's anything you can do," Cormac said.

"We have an outreach team," she said. "This wouldn't be strictly kosher, given that they are squatting, as you say. But we might be able to arrange for a firewood delivery, if there are working fireplaces in the house. And bring a bit of food and keep in touch with whoever's there."

"That would be great. Thank you," Cormac said. He started the car.

"No. Thank you," she said, and it sounded like she meant it.

CHAPTER THIRTY-TWO

Roundstone, Ireland

Peter went to the pub after the Madden house, ordered dinner and a pint, enjoyed his second decent meal in as many days. Afterward, he walked up the hill to Maggie's to check in on her. Barrett had already been and gone. She had rallied briefly in the earlier part of the day, but was sleeping by the time he got there. He sat with her for a few minutes, talked briefly with Anna and Tilly, then set off. He walked back down to the village, picked up his car, and drove back to the flat. The roads outside the village limits were much worse now and he nearly ended up in the ditch twice.

Peter was exhausted when he finally reached the flat. He laid the fire automatically, lit it, and ate a couple of slices of toast standing up. Then he took off his boots, lay down on the couch fully clothed, pulled the covers over himself, and fell into a deep and dreamless sleep. He was woken by a hammering on the door. Disoriented and only half awake, Peter stumbled to the door and opened it to a blast of freezing air and his father.

"I need you," said Des. "Right now."

"What?"

"Now," Des insisted. "Get your shoes. For god's sake, hurry up."

Peter shoved his feet into his boots, grabbed his jacket, and followed Des out the door. Instead of a squad car, there was a battered-looking LandCruiser parked outside, engine still running, snow chains on the tires. Borrowed, probably. Or maybe it was Des's own. Des took the driver's side, and then they were off, careening down the drive at a pace that struck Peter as insane, snow chains or no snow chains. He braced himself against the side of the car and leaned down to tie his bootlaces.

"Where are we going?" he asked.

"Jim needs us," Des said tersely.

"Where? For what?"

Visibility was horrendous. Des cursed and leaned forward, trying to see where he was going through the heavy snow.

"For Christ's sake. Let me concentrate on what I'm doing," he said.

Peter shut up, kept his eyes on the road. Des was driving far too fast for the conditions. His hands gripped the steering wheel tightly, and he changed gear like a rally driver. Ten minutes later he turned off the road, pulling into the driveway of a small, unremarkable-looking bungalow. There were two cars already in the driveway, a squad car, and a standard saloon. The door to the house was wide open. Des jerked on the handbrake, then was out of the car and running for the house. The adrenaline was catching, and Peter was right on his heels.

Then they were in the house, and Jim Brennan was there. He was standing over the body of a man who was lying face down and there was blood on his clenched fists. Jim looked up as they entered, and smiled his friendly, wide-open smile.

"You started without us, I see," said Des.

"You know me, Des. I don't like to dillydally," Jim said. And he drew back one booted foot and kicked the unconscious man in the head as hard as he could. The head snapped back from the force of the kick and Peter heard something crack, but there was no voluntary movement from the body, no signs of life.

"Jesus," Peter said. He recoiled.

"Careful, Jim," Des said. He leaned down toward the body, listened for a moment, then made a regretful sound. "We'll have to leave it at that, I think," he said. "He's breathing, but just about."

"Ah, sorry about that, Des," Jim said. "You probably wanted to get a few in yourself."

"I did tell you to wait," Des said.

Jim shrugged eloquently, as if to say that Des should have known better.

Peter was freaked out, speechless. It was like he had stumbled onto the set of a bad gangster movie, and all the while Jim Brennan was smiling away at him as if he was about to offer him a cup of tea.

Des nudged the unconscious man with his foot. "Peter, meet Séan Cummins."

"For Christ's sake, leave him alone," Peter said. He pushed Des back from the body, leaned down, and turned the man over. His nose was obviously broken, his lip split. Blood was seeping from his nostrils and the corner of his mouth. Peter had a flashback to that cold lakeside and another body covered in blood.

"I wouldn't have rolled him over, if I were you, Peter. He might choke on the blood," Des said, conversationally.

"Fuck." Peter rolled Cummins into the recovery position, supporting his neck. He felt for a pulse, found it. "What have you done?"

"What needed to be done," Des said.

Peter had his hand on Cummins's shoulder. It was freezing in the house.

"We need to get him to a doctor," Peter said.

"That man you're so caring for so thoughtfully is a child molester. A rapist. You haven't forgotten that, have you?"

"I haven't forgotten anything," Peter said. He stood up, suddenly feeling vulnerable crouching on the floor with Des and Jim looking down at him. "But what are you going to do, kill him?"

Des smiled. "Not this time," he said. "You needn't worry, Peter. You're not going to end up in prison."

Jim laughed, like it was all a very good joke.

"No, but when Cummins here wakes up in the morning, he's going to get in his car and drive a very long way from here. And he's never going to come back."

"And then what?" Peter said, very quietly. He felt like all the breath had been sucked out of his lungs. "What happens after that?"

"He'll never touch Jane or any other little girl in this village again," Des said. "That's the point."

"And what about all the other little girls?" Peter said. "All you'll have done is moved him on to the next place. It's our job to put him in prison. To get him on the register. To stop him forever, not just for now."

Jim's smile finally dropped away. He shook his head, as if Peter's naivety had disappointed him.

"This is the world we live in, Peter," Des said. "If we could have put Cummins away, we would have, you know that. But Jane's family wanted the charges dropped and Cummins was just going about his business. I wasn't going to tolerate that. Not in my village."

It sounded so reasonable. Understandable.

"And what happens when he reports this?" Peter said. "He knows who you are, Jim."

"He's not going to report anything," Jim said.

"Cummins knows how this works," Des said. "It would be his word against ours, and there isn't a garda in the country who would take him seriously."

Peter stood there in silence. There was a ringing in his ears. All he could hear was his own breathing. Des and Jim were waiting expectantly, as if they wanted something from him.

"This is bullshit," Peter said. "This isn't policing."

Des and Jim exchanged a glance, and both men turned to go.

"You're just going to leave him here?" Peter said. They were at the door. "We can't just leave him here, Des. He could die."

"Give him the keys, Jim," Des said. Jim took the keys to the squad car from his pocket, threw them to Peter. "And grow the fuck up."

They left. Drove away in the LandCruiser and left him there with the unconscious body of a pedophile. Fuck. *Fuck*. He paced the room. What the hell was he going to do now? He wanted to call Aoife, went so far as to take out his phone and find her number, then stopped himself. If this all came out—and surely to god it would—then he didn't want Aoife tangled up in it. He crouched down, checked Cummins's pulse again, examined him. He was still shallow breathing, didn't seem any worse, and the flow of blood was slowing, but he was still unconscious. He could have a bleed on the brain. He could be dying right there on the floor, while Peter did nothing. The fucking bravado and bullshit of Des and Jim, to walk away as if they were in control of everything, as if they knew for sure what was going to happen. They weren't doctors. But maybe they weren't worried about Cummins dying. Maybe if he did, they'd find a nice convenient bog hole to dispose of the body, and then they'd run a tidy little investigation into his disappearance and that would be that. Jesus. Maybe they'd done it before.

Peter had a sudden headache, like a vice was tightening around his forehead and the back of his skull. He couldn't be part of this. He wasn't going to be responsible for another man's death, whatever he might have done. He was a garda, not judge, jury, and executioner in one lethal package.

He went out into the snow, opened the back door of the squad car, then went back in and lifted Cummins, carried him to the car, and laid him down in the back seat. He did what he could to put the body in the recovery position and fastened a seatbelt around him. Then he set off. Doctor Barrett lived on the outskirts of the village. He was Cummins's best chance. There was no way an ambulance would be able to make it out in this weather.

The car slipped and slid its way down the drive. Peter cursed and tried to turn into the skid, maintained control of the car but only just. How had Jim managed to get it here? Visibility was still brutal. He drove on grimly, trying not to think about the body in the back seat and what it might mean. There were no other cars on the road, though he passed one abandoned in the ditch. Still, Peter turned on his flashing lights, just in case. He slowed the car to a crawl. If he came off the road, it would be so much worse. Who could he call for help? How could he keep Cummins warm and alive here until the morning?

Peter kept driving, resisted the urge to look behind him and check on Cummins. And he made it to the house. Barrett's house was a handsome two-story with a cut-stone facade and a gravel drive. The driveway was buried under snow, but at least there was no hill to tackle. His headlights illuminated the doctor's Nissan Patrol in the drive, a heavy coating of snow on the roof and hood. Peter parked the car, turned off the engine with a sense of profound relief, and ran for the front door. He rang the doorbell once, twice, then a third time. It occurred to him that he didn't know if Barrett was married or had children. He could be waking an entire household. The least of his worries right now. Barrett was slow coming, and Peter hammered on the door with his fist.

"Doctor Barrett? It's Peter Fisher. I need you to open the door."

Through the glass panel to the side of the door, Peter saw a shadow approaching from inside the house. Barrett opened the door and for a moment, just a fraction of a second, Peter saw a look of fear in Barrett's eyes.

"What's the problem, Peter?" Barrett said. "Is it Maggie?"

"I need your help, doctor," Peter said. And he didn't miss the fact that relief had replaced the fear in Barrett's expression. "I have a body . . . a person . . . he's unconscious. He's been beaten up."

Barrett helped Peter carry Cummins into the house. They brought him into a downstairs bedroom where they put him on the bed. Barrett examined him, talking all the time.

"The risk is skull fracture or hematoma. He needs a CT scan, but we're not going to be able to get him to the hospital tonight." He took a little torch out of his medical bag, lifted each of Cummins's eyelids in turn, checked for pupil reaction. "How did this happen?" Barrett asked, turning to Peter.

Peter opened his mouth to answer and couldn't find the words. What could he say? What did he want to say?

Understanding crept into Barrett's eyes and he turned back to the patient. "This is Séan Cummins, isn't it?" he said.

"Yes," Peter said.

Barrett sat back. "Well," he said. "There's no way to know without a CT scan, but my best guess is that he'll come out of this. His eyes are reactive and I don't see any leakage of brain fluid. It's concerning that he's still unconscious." He paused. "What do you want me to do?"

"I want you to . . . look after him," Peter said.

Barrett shrugged. "I can do that. I can keep him here overnight. Observe him. Tomorrow, depending on how he's doing, I can call the helicopter out for him. If that's what you want. If you're sure."

Peter felt like he was sinking into tar. Nothing made sense.

"I don't understand," he said. "What are the alternatives?"

Barrett spoke very slowly and deliberately. "Well. I can be discreet," he said. "You know. For a complicated situation like this. If that's what you want."

"I want . . . I just want you to take care of him, all right?"

"Of course," Barrett said.

Peter moved toward the door. "I'll call in the morning. See how he's doing."

Barrett looked at his watch. "Morning is only a few hours away now," he said. "You're welcome to stay if you want. There's coffee."

"No, thank you," Peter said. "I'll go. I'll speak to you in the morning."

He left, made for the squad car, and slowly made his way to the flat, a white-knuckle drive that had him swearing that it was the very last time he would drive in this weather. He made it inside, freezing, hungry, and freaked out. He stripped off his outer jacket, fell onto the couch, and slept.

Sunday, November 8, 2015

CHAPTER THIRTY-THREE

Dublin, Ireland

Cormac woke early on Sunday morning. He hadn't slept particularly well, but then he never slept well the night before a big operation. He thought about calling Emma and decided against it. He wanted the whole thing behind him before he spoke to her again. He took a slow shower instead, thinking through the plans for the day ahead, hoping that Matt would be able to come through. He dressed and called Matt before he left the hotel room.

"Well?" he said.

"We're a go."

"Excellent." Cormac felt a welcome rush of adrenaline. Finally, things were moving in the right direction.

"We're very low on bodies," Matt said. "I'm going to be there as an observer only. Same goes for you, given you're on suspension. But it's a skeleton crew, so be prepared to jump in if it looks like you're needed. That's the unofficial word from Murray and Kennedy."

"If it goes down the way we want it to, we can tidy up the formalities in the wash afterward anyway," Cormac said. Damnit. He wanted to be running this operation. To have the logistics and the team and the timing of the thing in his hands.

"Exactly," Matt said. "Are you armed?"

"No. I handed my gun in."

"Maybe it's just as well," Matt said. He explained the details, the location, and the timing. "I'll see you there," he said, and he hung up.

Cormac dressed quickly, made his way downstairs, and went to the front desk to check out. He wasn't the first there, was obliged to wait in line for a few minutes for his turn. When he reached the desk, the woman seated behind it gave him a professional smile.

"No breakfast this morning, sir?"

"Not today," he said. "I need to get back."

She nodded, her eyes on her computer screen as she went through the motions. She took his card, swiped it, and they waited.

"Heading back to Galway this morning?" she asked.

He nodded. She would have read his address on his check-in details. She handed him back his card and receipt.

"Some of the roads are closed this morning. The weather, you know."

"Thanks." Cormac gave her a nod of thanks and turned to leave.

"I heard on the radio this morning that they've run out of grit," he heard the woman behind him in the line say as he walked away. "And there's more snow coming tonight. The whole country is going to come to an absolute standstill."

By the time Cormac had retrieved his car from the underground garage and was navigating his way through Dublin traffic, he'd listened to five minutes of radio coverage and he was having second thoughts. The streets in Dublin were clear of snow and ice, but if the radio presenters weren't exaggerating, the midlands and the entire west coast were close to shutting down, and likely to stay that way for the best part of a week. Shite. He needed to get to Tullamore. Cormac did a U-turn and pointed the car in the direction of Dublin airport. He phoned every car rental place he could think of on the way. There were plenty of cars available—the weather had resulted in lots of cancellations apparently—but most of them were not much more suitable for snow and ice than his own ancient but beloved BMW 3 Series, with its rear-wheel drive and fat tires. He was getting close to the bottom of the list when he got lucky.

"We've got one Range Rover. Just got a cancellation for it. Expensive, but I'd grab it quickly if you want it."

Cormac did want it. The rental cost for three days was enough to make him wince, but so be it. He pulled into the side of the road for long enough to give the guy his credit card number, then drove on to the airport. He would leave his own car in long-term parking. If he was going to fly out to see Emma again next weekend, he could pick it up then.

Cormac got back on the road. With the detour to the airport and the car-rental paperwork, he had lost time, but he had hours yet until the raid kicked off. He pulled in to a roadside café, grabbed a table at the back, and ordered some breakfast. He called Emma again, but it rang out. He left a message asking her to call him back. They really needed to talk. Ten minutes later, as he was starting on an omelet, his phone rang. It was Deirdre Russell.

"We got it," she said.

"Got what?"

"The phone calls, all the phone calls. The information came back on the warrant, but we got all this extra stuff with it. Whoever ran our warrant at the phone company, they must really like to use their initiative." Deirdre was excited, half-laughing. "There was nothing useful on Loughnane's phone. He didn't call anyone except on the day of Peggah's disappearance, so if it wasn't for this additional data, the warrant would have been a dead end."

"And it isn't?"

"No. They ran a data filter. I didn't even know it could be done. I had to get one of the tech guys to explain it to me. Basically, they map the location of the phone you're interested in, and then they run some sort of filter through the system to try to identify any other phones that were consistently in the same locations at the same times. That way they can find out if someone was using a second phone. Did you know they could do that?"

"I'd heard something about it," Cormac said.

"Well anyway, they turned up a second phone. Loughnane must have had a burner. And now they've sent through all the calls and messages to and from that phone. But get this—it was used to call and message only one other number. We don't know who owns that one yet, but I'd bet you anything that the mystery phone will turn out to be Kelly's. On the day of the abduction, Peter spoke to Loughnane at around two o'clock. At ten minutes past two, there's a call from Loughnane's burner to the mystery number. That must have been the call to Kelly to tip him off that we were looking for him."

"That's fantastic news, Deirdre. Great work."

"How lucky can we get, right? What are the chances? I didn't request this data filter and you should have seen Moira's face when it came through. She looked like she was chewing glass. But what could she do? She couldn't exactly complain about it."

"No," Cormac said. He thought about Orna and smiled to himself.

Deirdre's voice lost some of its ebullience. "She still doesn't seem to be running with it, though. She says she's going to talk to Murphy about it on Monday, before she takes it any further."

"Don't worry about it, Deirdre. Hang in there. A few more days, all right?"

If everything went well he'd soon be in a position to run the case himself, and with this to work with he'd have Loughnane in a jail cell and Peter Fisher's reputation restored by the end of the week.

Cormac gave himself two hours to drive what would usually be a sixty-minute trip to Tullamore, and he needed every minute of it. All he felt after the first twenty minutes was relief that he'd rented the Range Rover. The weather was terrible. It wasn't like they hadn't had the cold and the snow to deal with in Dublin, but at least the roads were well gritted, and the snowplows were out every day. The motorway would have been gritted in the morning but the snow was still coming down and traffic had slowed to a crawl. Once he turned off the M6 and took the N52 toward Tullamore he found no traffic, but for good reason. The snow was six inches deep, and there were drifts piled up against the hedgerows.

He kept going. He still had time—he was due to meet Matt and the Internal Affairs team at the rendezvous point in fifteen minutes. Cormac had slowed to a stop, trying to figure out which of the un-signposted country roads would get him to his destination, a task made more challenging when the signal dropped out and the GPS on his phone stopped working, when he got a text message from Matt. *It's kicking off. They're going in. Get here if you can.*

Shit. Cormac oriented himself, hit the accelerator, and went into a skid. He recovered, took a couple more turns, drove a few minutes more, and found the road that led to the incinerator. He took the turn, driving too quickly. There were no houses here, just farmland, and a narrowing lane. There had been no gritting or snow clearance here, and the lane must have had a good eight inches of snow covering. There were tire tracks—multiple vehicles had passed this way—but it was very quiet now. Cormac turned the corner and had to hit his brakes. The way ahead was blocked by two police cars, parked end to end and blocking a gated entry into a small industrial premises. There was nowhere to discreetly park this monster car, no way to make an unobtrusive approach, no way to approach other than in the open. Cormac thought about just staying in the car—he didn't even have a garda vest he could pull on to keep himself from being shot by a jumpy member of Matt's crew—but in the end couldn't do it. He got out of the car.

It was eerily quiet. The police cars were empty, and there was no one to be seen in either direction. Cormac turned, looked for vantage points where someone could be watching, but there was dense forest on the other side of the road. If someone was positioned in there, Cormac couldn't see them. He must be too late; Matt's crew must be inside the incinerator complex.

Cormac reached the gate, noted the hazardous chemical warning signs either side of it, and kept going. Something about the scene wasn't right. There were too many cars, too many police vehicles. There was a white unmarked van parked right by the facility—probably used to transport the drugs. Two unmarked cars were parked to the right of the van and four more took up every inch of the small car park beyond that, parked haphazardly as if the crew had driven in at speed, dumped them, and run for the building. Six cars here, four at the gate, the van. As many as forty-two officers then, if every vehicle came in fully loaded. Too many. Way too many. Even at two officers per vehicle it still came out at twenty-two. Matt had made it clear that they would operate a skeleton crew only, a handful of hand-picked officers who could be trusted. Cormac found himself reaching for a gun that wasn't there. He was about fifty feet from the door of the building when it opened.

Matt came out first, his face grim. He saw Cormac almost immediately, locked eyes with him, shook his head. Other officers came out in Matt's wake, first plainclothes like him, then uniforms. Matt came to Cormac, walking fast. He put an arm over his shoulder, turned him, and guided him away from the building at speed, talking urgently all the while.

"You need to go. Fast. Christ, Cormac, it's bad enough but you don't want him to see you here, too."

"What is it? Matt, what's going on?"

Matt kept up his forced march, and Cormac stayed with him. A glance over his shoulder saw a press of bodies still spilling out of the building. Lots of uniforms, no one he recognized. Three plainclothes officers were in step with Matt and Cormac, a few paces behind. The grim disappointment on their faces matched Matt's. Cormac stopped abruptly, Matt tried to drag him onward. Cormac held his ground.

"Matt, what the fuck is going on? Did we get it wrong? Were the drugs here?"

Matt took a step back toward Cormac, lowered his voice to a hiss. "We didn't get it wrong. We were just too bloody late."

They heard a scuffle and muffled cursing behind them and both men turned on time to see Anthony Healy being led from the building in handcuffs. Healy was bleeding from a cut to his mouth. He was pale-faced and wild-eyed, like a panicked animal. He made a clumsy, flailing break for freedom as the uniforms moved him toward the squad car, but that was dealt with swiftly. He was lifted and stuffed unceremoniously into the back seat, the door closed on him.

Cormac looked at Matt, waiting for the explanation, but Matt's eyes hadn't left the scene behind them. Cormac looked in time to watch the last man leave the building. It was Brian Murphy, impeccably dressed in a navy suit, stripping off a garda vest and handing it to a subordinate. He was talking to a chastened-looking Rebecca Murray and Aidan Kennedy and looked very much the man in charge.

"We got here early," Matt said. "Set up back in the trees, with two guys on the radio, ready to come in with the cars at the right time. Healy and Trevor Murphy arrived with the drugs, started unloading them. We were watching, recording. We would have gone in within another minute, but before we could, he got here." Matt nodded toward Brian Murphy. "He had a full team with him, even forensics to do the drug testing right here on the spot." Matt's gaze switched to a woman in a white suit carrying a test kit to a marked car.

"What are you telling me, Matt?" But witnessing Brian Murphy marshal his troops with cool confidence, Cormac had the horrible feeling that he already knew.

"Brian Murphy took Healy down before we could. They ripped half the packs open right there in the building. The test kits weren't even needed. The arrogance of the fuckers. They'd stuffed the drug packs with newspaper, hadn't even bothered to get a bit of flour for the weight of it."

"Where's Trevor?" Cormac asked.

Matt was shaking his head. "He's still inside, getting his pats on the back. They're claiming he was working undercover the whole time. Jesus, who knows? Maybe he was. Or maybe Brian Murphy realized that you were getting close and stepped in before you could get there. Either way, we are never going to know because after this he will be fucking untouchable."

Brian Murphy had seen Cormac. He walked toward him with deliberation.

"Detective Reilly," Murphy said.

Afterward, Cormac would wonder what would have happened if he'd had the presence of mind to come up with some excuse. To pretend that he'd driven to Tullamore at the tail end of an active op just to have a word with his commanding officer. It would have changed nothing. Murphy had executed this little plan perfectly, and had always intended for Cormac to be caught up in it.

"Ah," said Murphy, stepping closer. "I see. You were the instigator of this little side drama, were you? But you didn't come to me, as your superior officer. And you didn't go to the Commissioner's office, and you didn't go to the office of the garda ombudsman." Murphy smiled, and it was like watching a minnow turn into a shark. "You went to your friend here, at Interpol, who seems to have called another friend, who called a friend. That's an interesting chain of command. I wasn't aware that Interpol had the authority to run operations on Irish soil."

"Sorry, Detective Inspector, that isn't what we . . ." Matt started to say. A look from Murphy quelled him.

Murphy drew Cormac aside. "You're finished," Murphy said, and his tone was matter-of-fact. "There'll be an investigation into all your off-the-book activities, but you should know that that will be a mere formality. After today, your career in the Garda Síochána is over. You will never run an investigation again." He gave Cormac one last, vicious smile. "Pity," he said. And he walked away.

Cormac left the incinerator without another word to anyone. When he glanced back, Matt was deep in conversation with Brian Murphy, no doubt trying to work out a deal where they could take joint credit for the successful raid and where Interpol could emerge smelling of roses. Best of luck to him. He might have a chance, too, now that Murphy had achieved his goals. He'd extracted his son from a messy situation, had probably secured a promotion for both of them while he was at it. And as an added bonus, he was now rid of Cormac. Murphy was absolutely right about that. There could be no coming back from this for him.

Cormac drove aimlessly. He had nowhere to go. How fucking stupid he had been? How could he have so completely underestimated Brian Murphy? Hadn't he known, from their very first meeting, that that gormlessness had to be an act? And yet he'd somehow assimilated it, made it part of his picture of the other man. And had been utterly, utterly misled. Cormac called Emma's number. No answer. That was probably as well. Christ. What could he say to her? His career in the gardaí was over. Europe would be closed to him after this too. Cormac let out a shaky laugh. Of course. Why wouldn't Murphy put the boot in while he was at it? He would happily do a deal with Matt to let Interpol off the hook for breaking virtually every procedural rule there was, if they would just do one small thing for him.

Cormac's phone rang. It was Emma, calling him back. He pulled into someone's driveway, answered the call.

"Emma," he said.

"Corm, I'm sorry I missed you." Her voice sounded hoarse, tired.

"No, look. I should have called earlier. I know you tried to get me. This week has been . . ." He let his voice trail off. He didn't have the energy to catalog the disasters.

"You called last night, and you called this morning," she said. "I'm sorry I didn't answer. I just . . . I wasn't ready for this conversation."

Cormac blinked. The silence went on too long and Emma was the one who broke it.

"It's all right," she said, eventually. "I was angry when you left. Angry and upset. It felt like you were giving up on us. But I've been thinking about it all week. Being a garda, that's who you are. It's who I fell in love with." Her voice cracked a little. She was crying. "I still love you, Corm. I think part of me will always love you. And it breaks my heart to let you go. But I know that being a garda is part of who you are. You wouldn't be happy being anything else, and I don't think I could be happy watching you try. I wish I could say that I'll come back."

"Emma . . ."

"No," she said. "I know it's selfish. And I think maybe I'll regret it, in years to come. But I just can't come back, Corm. I can't do it."

Cormac's hand tightened around the phone. "I wasn't avoiding you because I wanted to break up," he said. Whatever happened between them, he couldn't let a stupid misunderstanding be the reason that they didn't work it out. "I was trying to find a solution. For both of us."

He waited for her to ask what the solution could be and searched for words with which he could answer her. But she didn't ask. She just fell silent again, and that was when he realized that it didn't matter. She'd already let him go.

"It's all right, Emma," he said. "It's all right."

"I'm sorry," she said, one last time, and then she hung up.

Cormac closed his eyes and leaned forward, his head rested on his steering wheel. He'd lost her. He'd lost everything. Christ. He felt utterly hollow, unmoored. Emma had walked away and he had let her do it. She'd gone because he didn't make her happy, the life he'd had to offer her didn't make her happy. And now he didn't even have that life. He had nothing. Nothing at all. Cormac raised his head from the steering wheel, stared blankly ahead. The world blurred around him.

After a few minutes, a woman emerged from the house he'd

pulled up at. She stood looking at him but came no closer. He was worrying her, probably, a stranger sitting in his car in her driveway. Cormac wiped his eyes and started the engine.

He kept driving. But he had nowhere to go, really. He thought of Galway, had no urge at all to return to the little house on the canal. What a house of ashes that was. He could go to his parents' place, his sister's, but he wasn't ready to explain things to them.

Oh Christ. Peter Fisher. Cormac rubbed his hand over his head. Peter was alone now, hanging out there, and there was nothing Cormac could do for him. Would Murphy leave him alone, now that he'd taken Cormac down? Maybe, maybe not. Peter needed to know what had happened, and sooner rather than later. Cormac plugged "Roundstone" into his GPS, which immediately came back with a warning about poor conditions and serious traffic delays. It was roughly a sixty-mile drive he had ahead of him, in weather. If he headed straight there now, he'd make it before nightfall if he was lucky. With more resignation than resolution, Cormac turned the car north and west, and drove on.

CHAPTER THIRTY-FOUR

Roundstone, Ireland

Peter woke far later than he should have on Sunday morning. He was disoriented, thick with sleep, and confused by dreams and snatches of nightmare that were slow to let go of him. It took a moment before the events of the night before came back to him. When they did, he reached for his phone and called Doctor Barrett.

"He's conscious," Barrett said. "In a lot of pain, some memory issues, but I think he's out of the woods. I'll keep him here under observation for another day or so, and then if the weather shows any signs of improvement, he should to go the hospital and get properly checked out."

"That's good," Peter said. He breathed out a sigh of intense relief. "Thank you."

"You're welcome," Barrett said. There was still no suggestion of outrage or concern about what had been done to Cummins, no anger on his part. It was strange, coming from a doctor. But even the very best of people took extreme positions when it came to pedophiles. They weren't exactly a sympathetic group.

"I'll do my very best to call in to see Maggie today on my rounds," Barrett said then. "With the weather the way it is, I can't guarantee anything. I may need to borrow a set of chains from somewhere if the snow doesn't let up."

"That would be great, thank you," Peter said automatically.

They hung up, and Peter was left wondering if Barrett had cleaned up messes made by Des and Jim before. He told himself that he was being paranoid, but something about the doctor had been off the night before. That look of fear in his eyes, as though Peter was there for something other than help. What did he have to be afraid of?

Peter threw some coal on the last embers of his dying fire. He waited for the room to warm up, then braved the cold shower. The water was icy. He was lucky the pipes hadn't frozen, but it didn't feel like much to be thankful for as he stood under the spray for just long enough to get the soap out of his hair. He got dressed quickly, made tea and toast with the heel of the loaf, and took it to the fireplace. Something was nagging at the back of his brain, something about Barrett that he'd heard or read that hadn't sat quite right with him. It finally came to him. Barrett had discovered the bodies of Carl and Miles Lynch when making a house call. According to his statement, Barrett had entered the Lynch house to check the bodies, to confirm that they were dead. Except that Miles and Carl had been dead for a week by the time Barrett was making his house call. Dead for a week, in the warmth of an Indian summer, and in a cottage where the front door was open. Peter had seen the photographs of the bodies. The flies had been at work for days. It would have been clear from the doorway that they were dead. Why then had Barrett entered the crime scene? It couldn't have been to confirm death, as per his statement. He must surely have known it at first glance. Peter thought again about the unidentified fingerprints found in the Lynch house. Had Barrett's prints been taken, as they should have been, to rule them out? He couldn't recall for sure, but he didn't think so. And something else nagged at him, too. A connection. Peter stalked up and down the living room, thinking things through, trying to make sense of his burgeoning theory. He had the beginnings of something, maybe, but he couldn't figure out a motive.

Peter picked up his phone and called the Madden house. John answered the phone. Peter made polite inquiries as to how they were doing. John said that the morgue in Clifden had promised to do their best to get out to the house on Monday.

"John, this may seem like an odd question, but can you tell me, did your father own any land or other property?"

There was silence for a long moment and Peter could almost hear John's leap of suspicion.

"He had a farm," John said. "He's been retired for years, though, so the land was leased. Why are you asking?"

"Do you know if James had any plans to sell?"

"If he did, he didn't tell me," John said.

"And earlier this year, your dad didn't come into any money at any stage, did he?" Peter was thinking about the new roof on the Lynch farmhouse. The new kitchen. Where had the money come from to pay for all of that?

"I don't understand . . ."

"I know. I'm sorry, John. I'm sure this is all nothing, but if you could answer the question . . ."

"He sent us on holiday," John said. "Me, Alisha, and the girls. In June. He paid for us to go to France for a few weeks. We were delighted, but we were surprised too. Dad didn't have a lot of cash sitting in a bank somewhere. He had the bit of rental income from the farm, and a small pension."

"And he didn't tell you where the money came from?"

"He wouldn't get into it, just said we'd know all about it by the end of the year."

"Where's the farm, John?" Peter asked. "Who's the tenant?"

"It's just off Coogla Road," John said. "Miles Lynch was the tenant until he died, that is. Dad's farm was right beside the Lynch farm, you see. Down by the sea. Look, Peter, what's all this about?"

"I'm not sure," Peter said. "Really, it's probably nothing. Can you leave it with me? I need to make a few more inquiries, but I'll call you as soon as I know anything."

John let him go, reluctantly, and Peter made a second phone call, this one to the lawyer, Stuart Connolly. The phone rang out. Peter left a message, waited an impatient forty minutes, then tried again. This time Connolly answered.

"Peter, how can I help you this fine snowy day?" he asked. His tone was upbeat. He obviously didn't mind a Sunday interruption.

"I have a few questions." Peter wasn't exactly sure where to start. "Look, you mentioned that Miles Lynch had been in to pick up a copy of the record of his ownership of the farm—his folio, I think you called it?"

"That's right."

"If Miles had been planning on selling the farm . . . you said that he couldn't have done so without all the original documents you have in your office?"

"That's right," Stuart said. "He would need all the paperwork to complete a sale."

"Okay, but could he have *agreed* to sell the farm, using just the folio to identify the land in question? You mentioned the folio includes a map?"

"Well, yes. Depending on the buyer. But a verbal agreement wouldn't hold up. You can't form a binding contract for the sale of land in Ireland without a written contract. The law doesn't allow it."

"Right," Peter said. His original idea had been that the killer was someone who wanted to get their hands on Miles Lynch's land. Now he wondered if maybe the situation was almost exactly the opposite.

"Stuart, Miles came into some money in June. It was enough to pay for a new roof and a new kitchen for the farmhouse. And Carl Lynch called his sister a couple of weeks later. He was angry, upset because Miles was going to sell the land. I'm thinking he may have been paid a deposit of some kind."

"That's possible," Stuart said. "The standard Law Society contract provides for a ten percent deposit to be paid on signing, the balance on closing after the title has been fully examined."

"Do you think there's any chance Miles would enter into a contract like that, something so serious, without talking to a solicitor? Without talking to you?"

Stuart was quiet for a moment, thinking. "He might. If he was persuaded to. If he trusted the person he was dealing with. And if the money was right."

"I've been thinking about what you said about the rezoning rumors. What if someone signed the contract to buy the land thinking it was about to be rezoned, and then found out it wasn't? Could they pull out of the contract?" Peter asked.

"Not if the contract was unconditional. It would really depend on how the contract was drafted. I couldn't tell you without reading it."

"But it's possible?"

"Yes. In fact, if you're right about the deposit money, then it would have to have been an unconditional contract. The money doesn't get released otherwise. It would have been held in escrow by the solicitor involved . . . assuming there was one, of course."

Pieces of the puzzle were clicking into place in Peter's brain. It made sense. In many ways, it made sense. Barrett might have believed that the land was about to be rezoned which would have doubled land values. He'd had access to Miles Lynch—and to James Madden—that others didn't. They trusted him. He was their doctor. He saw them alone. He could have convinced them to sell their land to him—maybe he'd even offered a bit above the going rate to sweeten the deal. And then the rezoning had fallen through, and Barrett had wanted out. He wouldn't just have lost his deposit. If the contracts were unconditional, he would have been on the hook for the entire overvalued price of both plots of land. Peter could see the scene in his mind's eye. Barrett visiting the Lynch farm late one evening, sure that he could talk his way out of the contract as easily as he'd talked his way into it. And Miles Lynch—stubborn, unyielding, refusing to let him go. Barrett could have lashed out in a rage. Hit Miles with the poker, and from that point there was no going back. He'd killed one man in a temper, the other to cover it up. He hadn't been able to risk a similar scene with James Madden, so decided to make the problem go away before it even surfaced. Peter racked his brain for other loose ends the doctor would have had to tie up—loose ends which could be evidence if Peter could track them down. The realization hit him like a blow to the head.

Oh god.

"Stuart, I have to go," Peter said. He hung up, grabbed his jacket and keys, and made for the door. He found the car covered in snow, the windscreen frozen.

Shit. Shit shit shit.

He turned it on, got the engine running, put the heat on full blast. He couldn't see a thing through the ice. He dialed Maggie's number and Anna answered the phone.

"Anna, is Barrett there?" Peter said.

"What? No, he's not here."

"He said he's going to go and see Maggie today. If he comes

to the house, don't let him in, okay. Just keep the doors locked and *do not* let him in to see Maggie, under any circumstances. I'll be there as soon as I can, all right?"

Moving as fast as he could on the ice and snow, Peter went back inside to grab a kettle of water. He defrosted most of the front and rear windscreens, then set off for the village. He had to drive at a crawl, couldn't risk ending up in the ditch, but the delay was sending his blood pressure through the roof. He couldn't get the car up the hill to Maggie's house. He tried three times, and on the last he ended up sliding ten yards backward and into a wall. Peter abandoned the car, started to run up the hill, his feet slipping but making progress all the same. It took him minutes, but it felt like days. When he got to Maggie's house, the driveway was empty, but he could see tire tracks in the freshly fallen snow. Peter ran for the house. The front door opened before he could knock. Anna stood there, face tight, stepping from foot to foot with pent-up anxiety.

"I wouldn't let him in. He didn't like it. He tried to make me open the door, but I said no. I thought he was going to break the window, for a second. And then he just left."

The relief hit Peter so hard that he wanted to sink to his knees. "Thank god. Oh thank god. Thank you, Anna." He wanted to hug her and then suddenly, without any conscious movement, he found himself with his arms wrapped tightly around her, bending down so that his cheek was against the top of her head. "Thank you," he said again. Her slight body stiffened and he let her go immediately.

"Sorry," he said.

"It's all right," she said.

"I . . . uh . . . I should see Maggie."

Anna stepped back to let him go through, then followed him up the stairs. Maggie was sleeping when they went in.

"She's been waking and sleeping all day," Anna said, quietly. "Last time she woke up she ate a bit of lunch. She seemed to me to be a little better. She wanted to see Tilly. They had a cuddle, Tilly read one of her stories, and Mags went off to sleep again."

Peter nodded. Maggie did look a little better, to him at least. Her face had more color, maybe, than the day before. He went over and touched her forehead. She felt warm, human. He kissed her cheek, and she murmured and moved a little.

Tilly was watching television when they went downstairs. Peter smiled at her and she gave him a small wave but didn't move as Anna led the way into the kitchen, and closed the door behind them. Anna folded her arms and leaned back against the kitchen counter.

"What's going on?"

"I have to make a phone call," Peter said. "After that, I promise I'll tell you everything I know."

She didn't like that and didn't particularly try to hide it.

"Just one thing, Anna. When did Maggie start seeing Barrett?"

"I . . . hasn't he been her doctor for years?"

"But when did he start coming to the house?"

"I don't know. He came to visit about two weeks after Tilly and I moved in at the start of September. Tilly . . . well, she wasn't talking at the time. The doctor had come to see Maggie, but he had a look at Tilly, too." She frowned.

"What?" Peter asked, confused.

She shrugged. Her expression was unreadable. "I didn't like him much. And we've had enough of doctors, Tilly and me."

"Okay," Peter said. "But he had been coming to see Maggie for a while then, at that stage?"

"I don't think it had been that long. I said something about Dublin doctors not doing house calls, and Maggie said it was a new thing, but that Barrett was very good to his older patients. She said he looked after all her friends the same way."

"How did she seem to you, before and after he came to see her?"

Anna raised her hands helplessly. "She has been getting worse over the last few weeks, but she always seemed in good form when she knew he was due to visit. I never noticed anything that made me think he might be hurting her, if that's what you're asking."

Peter nodded. "Okay," he said. "I'm going to make a few calls now. I'll be back as soon as I can."

With Anna in the kitchen and Tilly in the living room, there was nowhere left in the little cottage where Peter could make a private call. He thought about going back outside and sitting in his car, and then remembered that it was crashed at the bottom of the hill. So he sat on the stairs and dialed Des's number. It rang a few times before Des answered.

"Peter? Where are you?" From the noise in the background, it sounded as if Des had chosen to ride out the weather in a pub.

"I'm at Maggie's. Can you find somewhere quiet? I need to talk to you."

The background noise got louder for a minute, then there was the sound of a door closing and the noise died away.

"I'm here," Des said.

"James Madden is dead," he said. "I never got a chance to tell you yesterday. He was on my old folks list, but he was dead when I got to the house."

"I'm sorry to hear that," Des said. "He wasn't a bad sort."

"Yes," Peter said. "But that's not the point. Look, I called Doctor Barrett. He came and examined the body and said it was likely a stroke. What he didn't say is that he had visited

James that morning, that he was probably the last person to see him alive."

"So what?"

"The family say that James had shown no signs of illness over the last while. He was in excellent health."

"That's how strokes happen, Peter," Des said, with exaggerated patience. "They do tend to come out of the blue."

"If James Madden was in excellent health, why was Richard Barrett paying him a visit?"

"I have no idea. But I suspect Madden wanted a private consultation. His daughter-in-law is the biggest talker in the village. Maybe he didn't want whatever was wrong with him talked about by every idle eejit in the place."

"Listen to me, Des. Maggie was in great health until just a few weeks ago. Then Barrett started to pay her house calls at home, and suddenly her health deteriorates to near the point of death, within months. And Barrett was also Miles Lynch's doctor. He found the bodies, for god's sake. They'd been dead a week, and the weather was warm. He would have had to have known they were dead. So why did he enter the crime scene to confirm it?"

"He was in shock," Des said. "It happens."

"Miles Lynch had plans to sell his land," Peter said. "Carl was furious with him about it. They fought for at least a month about it—I have that from two separate witnesses. But I went to see Miles Lynch's lawyer, and he said Miles had never discussed a sale with him."

"So? Maybe he changed his mind. Where are you going with this?" Des sounded more irritated than interested.

"Don't you think it's worth looking into, that James Madden and Miles Lynch, both lonely, isolated patients of Richard Barrett, have died in suspicious circumstances?"

"They fucking haven't," Des said. "Miles Lynch was

murdered by a gurrier from Dublin and James Madden died of a stroke. The rest of it is pure bloody fantasy. Do you think I wouldn't know, Peter, if someone in this village was a murderer? You think I wouldn't have seen that coming from miles away?"

"I just think . . . Listen, you weren't there when Barrett came to examine James Madden. There was something off about him. Particularly when he talked about signing the death certificate."

"Something *off* about him?" Des repeated.

"Look . . ."

"No, *you* look," Des said. "You've got some half-baked notion of a motive for the murder of Miles Lynch. Some sort of land deal gone bad, is that it? Well, what about James Madden? Was he selling his land?"

"I don't know yet," Peter said. "But he did come into money. He sent his family on holiday." Peter was deeply regretting the call. He should have done more legwork before bringing Des into things, but he hadn't expected this degree of hostility. He should have known better.

"You don't know. Well, how about doing a bit of bloody legwork before you go off and brand one of the most respected men in this county a murderer? A doctor who has been living here looking after this community for at least twenty years, I'd like to point out."

"I'll talk to the Maddens," Peter said. "Maybe there'll be something in James's house, in his papers, about a sale." Peter had his head in his hands, phone pressed to his ear.

"You will in your shite," Des erupted, suddenly roaring down the phone. "You will shut your mouth and stop your stupid questioning before you spread rumors the length and breadth of Galway. If you have your way, we'll be defending a defamation suit by next week."

Peter pushed his right hand through his hair in frustration.

It occurred to him that Des might be drunk. How long had he been in the pub?

"I've explained this poorly," he said. "I know there's a lot more work to do, to substantiate all of this."

"Substantiate what?" Des said. "You've gone on a flight of fancy." Des took a deep breath, lowered his voice. "Is this about Maggie?"

"In what way?" Peter said.

"I don't know. Is this your way of denying what's happening with her?"

"Jesus, Des. That's not it."

"You know what, Peter? Enough of that shite too. You can call me Sergeant Fisher in the station, and Dad at home. That's the end of this 'Des' business. And let me make one thing very clear. You are not going to make up for your fuck-up in Galway by coming to my town and trying to be a hero with a bunch of bullshit." Des hissed the words, almost spitting them out in another sudden rage. "You come to the station tomorrow, prepared to do the work that *I* assign to you and nothing else, or you can fuck off back to Galway and see how long they keep you. I'd give it a week before you get notice that you're under criminal investigation. And if I hear one word, if you so much as make a single phone call about this bullshit again, I'll fire you myself. Have you got that?" He hung up without another word.

Peter pushed the palms of his hands into his forehead, eyes screwed shut in frustration and anger.

"Christ," he said.

"He didn't believe you."

Peter turned to see Anna, hidden in the shadow of the staircase. "How long have you been there?" he said.

"Long enough. Why didn't he believe you?"

"It's my fault. I hadn't done the groundwork. And he might be right. Maybe I've got it all wrong."

"I don't think you're wrong," Anna said, her small face grim. "I never liked Barrett. I was always surprised that Maggie didn't see what I saw."

"Maggie has a pathological need to see the best in people. The only person in the world she hates—or hated—is my father. She looks at everyone else through rose-tinted glasses."

"What will you do now?" she asked.

"I don't know," he said.

"If we could get a different doctor to visit Maggie, to . . . I don't know, check her blood or something? Maybe we could prove then if he's been messing with her."

He stared at her. "That's a bloody brilliant idea."

Anna gestured helplessly toward the window. "But we can't. The weather."

"I've got a friend," Peter said. "She might be able to help." He dialed Aoife's number, felt a great surge of relief when she answered. He quickly filled her in on James Madden's sudden death and his suspicions about Maggie's drastic decline. Aoife listened in silence, and didn't tell him he was mad or paranoid, in denial, or trying to save his own skin.

"Have you got all the medicine she's been taking?" Aoife asked. "I'm in A&E. I can't stay on the phone. But put all the meds together, and I'll call you back as soon as I can."

Peter filled Anna in, and she gathered Maggie's various jars of pills and brought them all into the kitchen. Peter and Anna waited, and, half an hour later, Aoife called back.

"Hi," he said. "I'm here and Anna's beside me. We've got all the medicine here."

"Sorry," she said. "I got caught up with a patient." She lowered her voice. "Okay, first, this man you mentioned, the one who supposedly died of a stroke. It is possible to kill someone and make it look like a stroke, but you would need access to certain medication, and you would also have to ensure that there's no autopsy. Doctors in small villages like Roundstone are generally dispensing doctors, so I'm going to assume Barrett is too. That means he would have access to, say, a massive dose of insulin, enough to kill an elderly man. And if Barrett treated James Madden within the last month, he can legally sign the death certificate without an autopsy. Which would mean no one would ever look too closely at the body."

"That's exactly what he is doing," Peter said. "What about Maggie?"

"Read out her medications to me."

Anna was sitting across from him, four little jars of tablets in her hands. She handed them across one by one, and Peter read out the names.

"I don't know," Aoife said. "Those are all fairly standard drugs for an elderly person. What about dosages?"

Peter looked at the bottles. "There are dosages for all of them written on the labels, except for one. Do you want me to call them out?"

"Which one doesn't have a dose?" Aoife asked.

"Uh . . . Digoxin," Peter said. "Ten milligrams."

"Put me on speaker," Aoife said. She waited for a moment, then continued. "Anna, can you hear me?"

"Yes," Anna said, nodding.

"Did you help Maggie with her meds? Give her her tablets every day?"

"Yes," Anna said again. "I didn't, in the beginning. And then Doctor Barrett asked me to start putting them out for her. He said that he was worried she would forget."

"How many of the Digoxin do you give her?"

"Four tablets," Anna said promptly. "One tablet, four times a day, always with food."

"Okay, thanks," Aoife said. Then, "Peter, can you take me off speaker again?"

Anna locked eyes with Peter, alarmed, as he picked up the phone.

"Okay, Aoife. It's just me."

"Peter, that is probably more than double what Maggie should be getting. That sort of dose, it would make her confused and nauseous, she would lose her appetite, and she would probably suffer from heart arrhythmia. Basically, every symptom Maggie has could be explained by Digoxin toxicity."

Peter felt sick. Anna was watching him anxiously.

"Okay. What does that mean? Do I need to try to get her to the hospital?"

"Ideally, yes," Aoife said hurriedly. "If she were my patient I'd want her on an IV. But given the weather . . . look, if she's resting comfortably now then it should be safe to keep her at home until the weather clears a bit. But you need to stop all Digoxin and keep a close eye on her. And you should get her in at the first opportunity. She needs to have her potassium checked."

"Okay. We can do that," Peter said.

"I'm so sorry, Peter, but I have to go," Aoife said. "There's an emergency here. I'll call you when I can." She hung up, and Peter put down the phone.

Anna sank slowly into a chair. "I've been poisoning her. That's what she said, isn't it?"

Peter nodded. "Yes."

"But that's what Doctor Barrett told me to give her. I'm absolutely sure. I would never make a mistake like that."

"Did he ever write it down for you anywhere?"

She shook her head and her face was very pale.

"That absolute bastard," Peter said. "You almost have to admire it. He manages to get rid of Maggie, and he knows the chances are that no one will look too closely, because everyone trusts him. But even if they do . . . say if Maggie were to die and I were to insist on an autopsy, and maybe the autopsy shows she had too much of that stuff in her blood. Well, it's very easy to lay the blame for that at your door, isn't it?"

Anna's lips were bloodless. "He set me up."

Peter turned to her. "He *tried* to set you up. He hasn't succeeded."

She turned to the stairs. "Maggie . . ."

"Aoife thinks she'll be all right," Peter said hurriedly. "We'll get her to the hospital as soon as the weather clears. But she should be okay."

Anna lowered her head and pressed the heels of her hands into her closed eyes. "I could have killed her," she said. "I could have killed her."

"You didn't do anything wrong, Anna. There's no possible way you could have known what he was doing." He reached out and gently pulled her hands away from her face. She let him.

"What are we going to do?"

"We keep him away from Maggie," Peter said, thinking out loud. "Keep him out of the house. And I'll . . . I'll call the Maddens. Ask them to search the house for anything that would show that James was planning on selling his land."

The Maddens would start asking questions, of course, and those questions would set Des off if he heard about them. It looked like his time as a garda in Roundstone was drawing to a close, without the help of Cormac Reilly. Peter picked up his phone to make the call, was interrupted by the sound of the doorbell. He glanced at his watch. It was six-thirty p.m. already and they were all but snowed in. Maybe a neighbor? Or Des coming to shout at him in person.

"Are you expecting anyone?" he asked Anna.

She shook her head.

Peter went to the door, opened it. Cormac Reilly was standing on the doorstep, as if Peter had summoned him by the thought. Reilly looked more tired than Peter had ever seen him. There was a snow-covered Range Rover parked in the driveway.

"How did you get here?"

Cormac nodded toward the vehicle. "I paid an extortionate amount of money for snow chains," he said. "Can I come in?"

Peter led him inside. Anna was still in the kitchen. Tilly was sitting at the kitchen table. She had a slice of bread and an open jar of Nutella—from the look of her face she'd given up on the idea of making a sandwich and had taken to eating the Nutella straight from the jar.

"This is Anna Collins. And her daughter, Tilly. Anna, this is my old boss, Detective Sergeant Cormac Reilly."

"Not for much longer, I'm afraid," Cormac said. He offered his hand to Anna, gave her a tired smile. "Hi Tilly," he said softly to the small girl, who looked back at him gravely, chocolate all around her mouth. Then to Peter, "I have a lot to tell you, and I'm afraid very little of it is good."

Peter nodded. "Sit down," he said. "I'll get you a cup of tea."

Anna left the room taking Tilly with her when it was clear that Cormac wanted to speak with Peter alone, closing the door gently behind her.

They sat at the kitchen table and Cormac started to talk. He talked about the task force, about garda corruption and drug running, about Brian Murphy, and the disastrous outcome of the raid. And while he talked, Peter thought about Des, about what he had said about Cormac's paranoia, his burning of bridges. After a while, Peter got up and searched in the fridge. Maggie, he knew, liked the occasional beer. He found a couple of bottles buried at the back of the bottom shelf, handed one to Cormac.

"I like this house," Cormac said. "It reminds me a bit of my parents' place."

He seemed different. Very tired, yes, but something else. Not defeated, exactly. More like someone who had been fighting something for a long time and had chosen to let it go.

"So where does all this leave you?" Peter asked.

"I'll be fired," Cormac said. "Just as soon as they get around to it. I broke all the rules when I took the thing to Matt. I've also been sticking my nose into a few other things that weren't strictly my business. I think I'm about to pay the price for it all." Cormac shook his head. "I won't be able to help you, Peter. I'm very sorry."

Peter shrugged and smiled. He'd never really believed that Cormac could pull him out of this fire, had he?

Cormac took a breath. "Look, it might be better for you when I'm gone. Give it a bit of time. With a bit of distance from me and some good work under your belt, there's every chance you'll be brought back into the fold."

Peter started to laugh. He picked up his beer bottle and took a long drink. "I think it's a bit late for that," he said. "I've been busy burning a few bridges at this end, too."

Cormac raised an inquiring eyebrow.

"There was a double murder a few months back, here in Roundstone," Peter said. "I was supposed to tidy up the paperwork—the investigation was done and dusted and the murders attributed to a Dublin gang on a rural raid, though there were no arrests. But it didn't make any sense. I asked some questions and . . . look, to tell you the truth, I stumbled across some of it. I think now that the local GP did it. I think he had agreed to buy land from the victims. He thought the land was about to be rezoned and skyrocket in value and when he found out that that wasn't going to happen, he wanted out of the deal."

Peter still wasn't exactly sure how and why Barrett had been led to believe the rezoning had been about to happen. Maybe he'd listened too closely to a rumor and had allowed a bit of gold-rush madness to sweep him up. Or maybe he'd been more involved than that. Maybe he'd had a corrupt pal in the planning department who'd let him down at the last minute. It would be something to question him about, if Peter ever got the chance.

"I think Miles Lynch, one of the victims, wasn't willing to let the good doctor off the hook, and so this GP—Barrett is his name—I think he lashed out in a fury and killed Miles and his nephew Carl. Then murdered another man who was in on the same deal, but this time he planned it, covered it up as a stroke. And . . . this might sound crazy . . . but I'm pretty sure that he's been slowly poisoning my grandmother." Peter quickly explained what they had learned about Maggie's medication and her rapid descent into ill-health.

Cormac was listening carefully, his expression intent, his eyes very dark. "And your arrest of this man has lost you some friends?" he asked.

Peter laughed. "There's been no arrest. It's just my theory, and not a very popular one. My father has made it very clear to me that I either shut my mouth and do as I'm told, or there'll be no room in the gardaí for me, either."

"Christ," Cormac said. "Is your grandmother all right?"

"I hope that she will be. She's asleep upstairs," Peter said. "We're going to get her to the hospital, as soon as the weather clears."

"What's the connection?" Cormac asked. "Between your grandmother and these other victims, I mean? Was she in on the land deal you're talking about?"

Peter shook his head. "No, but she was their friend. She talked about playing cards with Miles Lynch the first time I spoke with her. I think James Madden was part of that little group. I think maybe Miles told James and Maggie about the deal."

"And your father doesn't want this investigated? That makes no sense."

"If you knew him, it would," Peter said.

Cormac opened his mouth to say something and then some of the animation went out of his face. "I'm sorry," he said flatly.

A shrug. "I'm going to leave the force," Peter said. "It was only a matter of time, once I came here. I knew that."

"I'd hoped to get you back."

Peter took a breath. "I blamed you for it all, you know? I laid it at your door. I knew Murphy had it in for you, and I told myself that he took a hard line with me because it was a way of getting to you."

Cormac laughed. "He did."

"But that's all crap, isn't it? Because I got myself into this mess. I dealt with the whole situation badly. I should have waited for backup. Should have done something other than pull out my gun and shoot that man three times in the chest. They were right about me. I was trigger happy."

"Jason Kelly abducted Peggah Abbassi. There's no doubt in my mind about that. If I'd had a little more time, I would have been able to prove it. And who could you have brought with you? When you left the station that day, you didn't know if you were going on a wild-goose chase or not. The only officer left was Deirdre Russell, and you couldn't empty the station entirely."

Peter thought about it. "The way I see it now, it's not so

much that I did the wrong thing as it is that I did it for the wrong reasons. I was so sure I was right, and I didn't have the patience to wait."

"There was a little girl out there whose life was at risk. As far as you knew, she was running out of time. I probably would have done the same thing."

Peter shook his head. "Maybe." He paused. "I wanted to be the man. The truth is, inside my head, it was more about me than it was about Peggah. I wanted to be the one everyone was talking about, the one on the fast track. So when everything went to shit, when Murphy hauled me over the coals, I didn't have the words to defend myself. Because I knew I couldn't justify it. A man is dead because I wanted to show off how smart I was."

"Kelly isn't worth your regrets," Cormac said. "What would he have done to that girl if we hadn't scared him off? We would never have found her body."

Peter drank again, finished his beer, wished there were another in the fridge. "I'd like to think I've learned a lot . . . There's so much I'd do differently. But I suppose it doesn't matter now. I've got to figure out something else entirely."

Cormac drained his bottle in one long swallow. "Any thoughts on what that might be?"

"Not a fucking clue. You?"

Cormac shook his head slowly, smiled a slow and rueful smile.

"I thought you'd go to Europe for sure. With Emma already there, and your background."

"That's not for me," Cormac said. "It's not real police work. And I think it's safe to say that the raid closed that door pretty firmly."

"We're screwed, basically," Fisher said. He didn't ask where that left Cormac with Emma. Something about the look on the other man's face made him think that the situation there wasn't good.

Cormac laughed. "I think I'm going to have to start thinking about something completely new. But you've got options, Peter, if you want to stay in policing. You should look overseas. I heard the Australians are back over, looking for recruits. You could start again, in the sunshine. Learn to surf."

It was Peter's turn to laugh. He shook his head. "What kills me is that they'll get away with it. Healy's going down—and, by god, I'd love to know how they're planning on keeping him from talking—but all of the rest of them. The Murphys and everyone who worked with them. You're convinced that Brian Murphy was in on it?"

"As much as I can be. But I've no evidence and nothing to work with."

"Was he in on it from the beginning, or did he just step in when he found out that Trevor was knee-deep in it, do you think?"

"I think he knew enough. Up until the raid, I wasn't sure, but now, whether he's in on it or not, he's willing to protect those who are. And now he'll head up the investigation—he'll be the one questioning Anthony Healy and any other fall guys they come up with. Trevor Murphy will continue on, the whole thing will be downplayed, and other than Healy and whoever else they throw under the bus, everyone involved will just stay in place. How long before they have something similar up and running again?"

They sat in silence for a long moment.

"I don't suppose you have anything stronger," Cormac said, waggling the empty beer bottle in Peter's direction. "Also, I don't suppose you have a couch I can commandeer until the morning?"

Peter laughed again. Everything was in the shit, and yet he felt oddly cheerful. "I'll have a look for the something stronger. As for the couch, we might be fighting for it." He went to the corner cupboard. Maggie nearly always had a bottle of whiskey tucked away somewhere. He talked as he moved things about, looking for it.

"I don't know who does more damage. Trevor Murphy, because he's corrupt as fuck, or my father, because he's lazy. You know, they settled on that Dublin crime gang theory for the Lynch murders purely on the basis of a few tire tracks. Barrett's driving a brand-new Nissan Patrol now. But I'll bet you a tenner his last car was a LandCruiser, and I'll bet you a hundred he got rid of it right after the murders."

"A brand-new Nissan Patrol," Cormac repeated slowly. He looked up. "It wouldn't be red by any chance, would it?"

Peter turned and stared at him.

"The roads are empty," Cormac said. "I didn't pass anyone for the last forty minutes or so, except for a few cars abandoned in ditches. Including one red Nissan Patrol, about fifteen minutes' drive from here, on Galway Road."

"Jesus," Peter said. "Barrett must have made a run for it. He came to see Maggie earlier today. I'd told Anna not to let him in. That must have spooked him." He thought. "Do you think he's still there?"

"The car looked abandoned when I passed it, or I would have stopped," Cormac said. "But as far as I can remember there were no homes nearby. If I were him, I'd be tempted to try to ride it out until morning, set off again then. If he thinks you're after him, he wouldn't go home." Cormac gave Peter a slow smile. "The weather's getting worse," he said. "Should we be good Samaritans and go and give him a lift, do you think?"

CHAPTER THIRTY-FIVE

Cormac drove very slowly down the hill. Peter sat in the passenger seat, his right knee bouncing with pent-up energy. He wanted Barrett. Wanted him in a cell.

"I can't believe you came all the way to Roundstone," Peter said. "In this weather."

"It wasn't exactly the kind of news I could share over the phone," Cormac said. He gave Peter a glance. "And I was kind of at a loose end."

"How far, do you think?" Peter asked.

"To where I saw the car? About six miles, give or take."

It was getting dark, the roads were utterly deserted, and the snow was still falling. It took nearly forty minutes of slow and careful driving before they turned a corner and Cormac said, "We should be coming up to it soon."

And there it was, Barrett's red Nissan Patrol, driven into a ditch and sunk into deep snow. The car was on, the engine running. Cormac pulled the Range Rover in, though he was careful to stay on the road. Barrett had obviously tried to dig the car out. Signs of his efforts were evident around the back of the vehicle. Some of the snow had been pushed away and he'd tried to jam the floor mats from inside the car behind the back wheels, presumably in an attempt to gain traction. It had obviously failed, and Peter wasn't surprised. The car was in too deep. It would have been all but impossible to get the car out without a tow.

Cormac and Peter got out of the car.

"Do you want to lead?" Peter asked.

"You do it," Cormac said.

The driver door of the Nissan Patrol opened before they reached it. Barrett climbed out. He saw Cormac first.

"Thank god you stopped," he said. "I didn't know if I had enough fuel to keep the engine running all night." His eyes moved to Peter, he did an obvious double take and stopped in his tracks.

"Hello, Doctor Barrett," Peter said. "Having car trouble?"

"Peter," he said, uncertain. His eyes went to Cormac, then back. "Yes, I lost control and slid into the ditch. I can't get it out, and I have to get to Galway. A family thing."

"Oh yes?" Peter said. "Something last minute? It must be important to get you out in weather like this."

"I got a phone call. A family member, my uncle, is very unwell. I'm hoping to see him before he passes." Barrett's eyes flicked to Cormac. "And you needn't worry about Séan Cummins. He went home."

Peter nodded. They were right up in Barrett's face now. There was nowhere he could go. "I'm very sorry to hear about your family member," Peter said. "We seem to be having quite an epidemic, don't we? Of older people, passing suddenly."

Barrett clearly didn't know if he was expected to answer. His eyes were darting back and forth, back and forth. "It's the time of year," he said, in the end. "The weather. It's very hard on older people."

"Yes," Peter said. "And if the weather doesn't quite do them in, you can always give them a little push, can't you?"

"I don't know what you mean," Barrett said.

"I think you do."

They stood like that, in a stalemate, for a few seconds. Peter felt a great roaring of satisfaction that he kept hidden behind an impassive face. Maybe it was the fact that he had been sitting trapped in a snowstorm for the past hour, or maybe it was the simple fact of being questioned, but Barrett was shaken and he was afraid. An hour of questioning, maybe two, and he would fall like a bowling pin. Career criminals said little to nothing in an interview. Amateurs could, on occasion, be gifted liars. Most ordinary people could lie reasonably well, at least for a little while, until the wheels started to come off. And then, every once in a while, you'd come across someone like Richard Barrett. Just a half a minute standing there in silence, with Cormac Reilly's hulking, unexplained presence to his right, and that answer, Peter's accusation hanging in the air, and Barrett was terrified.

"You murdered Miles and Carl Lynch in a dispute over land," Peter said.

"I did not." Barrett shook his head, took a step back. His foot sank deep into the snow and he stumbled. The wind started to pick up, and Peter had to raise his voice to be heard.

"We're going to take you back to Roundstone, where I will interview you with the assistance of my colleague here, Detective Sergeant Cormac Reilly." Peter took great satisfaction in using the title, in enunciating each word carefully, and watching its impact on Barrett's face. Cormac might be suspended, but he was still a Detective Sergeant until he wasn't. They might as well get the benefit of it on what would probably be their last day on the job.

"This is ridiculous," Barrett said, his voice shaking. "Of course I haven't killed anyone."

Peter stepped forward, put a hand on Barrett's shoulder, and moved him firmly out and around. "Hands behind your back, please." He wasn't going to put Barrett in a car with no safety barrier without handcuffs. Barrett moaned as the cuffs went on, as Peter cautioned him and gave him the formal notification of arrest.

"I'll be searching your vehicle now, Doctor Barrett," said Cormac. He opened the driver's door and bent to look inside as Peter walked Barrett to the car.

"You didn't just kill Miles and Carl," Peter said. "You killed James Madden, too. You tried to make it look like a natural death, but there'll be an autopsy now. The pathologist will know what to look for, I suppose. What do you think the chances are that they'll figure out the real cause of death?" He put Barrett into the back seat, put a seatbelt around him, and pulled it taut. He closed the door. In the few minutes they had been there, Cormac's car had begun to sink a little into the snow, the residual heat from the vehicle melting the compacted snow and ice on the road. It would freeze again soon. They should get moving.

"Ready?" he called to Cormac.

"Just a second," Cormac called back.

Peter climbed into the passenger seat, turned to speak conversationally to Barrett who looked utterly shell-shocked.

"Oh, and along the way, you poisoned Maggie Robinson. I haven't quite figured out your motive for that. My best guess is that you were worried that James Madden had told her something you didn't want known. She was his friend, wasn't she? His confidante. And you couldn't have that."

Barrett's eyes were wild and terrified. "I absolutely did not kill anyone," he said. "I don't know where this is coming from, but I'm not talking to you until I've seen my lawyer."

Cormac got to the car, climbed into the driver's seat. He had a computer bag and a medical bag with him, and some papers, taken from Barrett's car. He handed them to Peter before putting on his belt and slowly turning the car back toward the village.

"What's this?" Peter said.

"I thought you'd find it interesting," Cormac said. "I found it on Doctor Barrett's passenger seat."

Peter started to read. It was a contract, for the sale of land, signed by James Madden. The purchaser was a company, Wired Land Management Limited. Peter lifted the document, showed it to Barrett. He pointed to the company name.

"Is this you, Barrett? If we trace this company back, will we find you at the other end of it?"

Barrett started to weep, silent tears filling his eyes and slipping down his cheeks. It was all self-pity, and Peter felt a wrenching disgust.

"You took this from James Madden's house yesterday, didn't you?" Peter asked. "After you killed him? You should have destroyed it straight away, you know. Sloppy, sloppy." Peter tapped the contract in his hand. "What happened, Doctor?" he said. "Did you run out of money?"

Barrett was still crying. He just kept shaking his head. "No," he said. "No."

"It was buyer's remorse, wasn't it, Doctor Barrett?" Cormac said, his eyes still on the road. "You convinced them both to sell their land to you, but after they'd signed the contracts you decided you didn't want the land after all. Only, they didn't want you to walk away. They wanted to sell. A deal's a deal, after all."

"No," Barrett said again. "It wasn't like that."

"What was it like, Doctor Barrett?" Cormac asked, and his voice was low and gentle. The voice of a good friend. The voice of a confessor.

Barrett clenched his eyes shut and closed his mouth.

Peter called Des before they reached Roundstone. He answered, the noise of the pub still there in the background.

"What, Peter?" he said.

"Meet me at the station in ten minutes," he said. "I've got your suspect for you." He hung up before Des could respond.

Cormac gave Peter a look.

"Well, I'm not babysitting him at the station overnight," Peter said, nodding to a still sniveling Barrett.

The heat was still on in the little station, and it was warm. They locked Barrett in the small holding cell at the back of the station, then at Peter's request, Cormac went to sit in the car. Peter sat on his desk, legs swinging, and waited for his father to show up. He didn't have to wait long.

"What's this about?" Des said. He was evidently drunk, not quite at the slurred-speech stage, but not far off it.

"Did you drive, or did you walk?" Peter asked.

"None of your fucking business," Des said. He stripped off his hat and coat. He'd lost his gloves somewhere. The knuckles on his right hand were bruised. "I asked you what all of this is about?"

"Richard Barrett is in the cell," Peter said.

"What did you say?" Des's voice was slow and dangerous.

"I arrested him on suspicion of murdering Miles and Carl Lynch, James Madden, and for the attempted murder of Maggie Robinson."

Des took a step forward, getting in Peter's face. Peter kept talking.

"He did it. We found him in a ditch on the side of the Galway Road. He was making a run for it. We found a copy of a contract that he'd taken from James Madden's house, after he killed him. James had agreed to sell his land to a company that I believe is controlled by Barrett. The deal went sour. That's why Barrett killed him. Everything's in the station. The documents, his medical bag, his computer."

Des glanced toward the cell, doubt creeping into his face.

"Didn't you ever wonder?" Peter asked. "Didn't you think, even for a second, that it was strange that Barrett entered the crime scene and touched the bodies?"

"I told you, I thought it was shock," Des said. "It happens. How sure are you of all of this?"

"I'm very sure," said Peter, standing up. "Now it's your turn to do some work." He dropped the keys to the cell on the desk. "You can babysit him today and overnight. I'll be back in the morning. I'll help you wrap this case up, because I want Barrett in jail. But after that, I'm finished. I can't work here anymore."

He was almost at the door when Des spoke again.

"Don't be too hasty, Peter," he said, quietly. "Let's talk tomorrow."

Anna was waiting for them when Cormac and Peter got back to the cottage. She laughed and cried when they told her the news, then she produced Maggie's bottle of whiskey and toasted them both. They ate warmed-up beef stew and crusty bread in front of the fire, washed it down with a few drinks, staying up well into the night talking. Anna didn't say much. She ate with Peter and Cormac, then she'd left them alone while she went upstairs to check on Maggie and Tilly. When she came back, she settled into the corner of the couch, listening rather than contributing to the conversation but seemingly happy to be there. It was well into the early hours of the morning when she finally stood up.

"I've moved Tilly into Maggie's room," she said. "We'll both sleep in there tonight. I'll be able to keep a closer eye on Maggie that way, anyway. You take my room."

Peter was drunk, and he was tired, and he was happy. "Thanks, Anna," he said. "I owe you one."

She shook her head, smiled, and disappeared.

Peter refilled Cormac's glass, then his own, clinked the glasses in a toast.

"Thanks, Cormac," he said.

"For what?"

"For everything."

"Ah, Peter. I didn't do a thing. I just provided the right kind of vehicle."

"Well, thanks for the snow chains then."

"You're welcome."

Monday, November 9, 2015

CHAPTER THIRTY-SIX

Cormac woke early the following morning. That wasn't so much a matter of choice, as it was that he was sleeping on the couch, and Tilly arrived well before first light to watch cartoons. It was obviously a regular part of her routine. She curled up on the armchair in her dressing gown and a pair of socks, and turned on the TV. Cormac woke to the sound of *Teen Titans*' Beast Boy and Raven arguing loudly about something. He sat up, feeling all the effects of the previous night's drinking. He looked around for the empty bottle and glasses, didn't see them. Peter must have cleared up before he went upstairs.

Tilly flicked her eyes in his direction but didn't say anything. They watched together comfortably for a while, Cormac laughing out loud at all the best bits.

"Beast Boy is my favorite," Tilly said.

"Which one is he? My nephew loves *Teen Titans*, but I always forget the names." Cormac asked.

"The green one. With the horns. He's totally crazy. But he really likes Starfire, and she doesn't notice at all."

"Which one is Starfire?"

"The one with pink hair."

"Oh right."

By the time the program ended, dawn was breaking and light

was creeping through the curtains. Tilly went to the window and pulled back the curtain halfway. “Look at all the snow. There’s loads of it. Great big heaps of it. I bet you could make a snowman out of that. Loads of snowmen.”

“Have you ever made a snowman?”

“My friend Ruth said she made five snowmen last year. Ruth’s really, really good at making snowmen. She’s easily the best in our whole class.”

She was so full of enthusiasm and excitement that Cormac couldn’t help but smile at her. “Do you want to build one now?” Christ. He could almost hear the *Frozen* song playing in his head.

She looked down at her slippers and back up at him.

“Why don’t you run upstairs and get dressed into something very warm. Tell your mum too, make sure she’s okay with it. When you come back down, I’ll show you how to make a snowman. Deal?”

She smiled at him like he was Santa Claus. “Deal.”

She took the stairs two at a time and was down again before he’d finished lacing his boots. They found hers along with her winter coat in the hall. Her gloves and hat were stuffed in the pockets so that solved that problem.

“Your mum said it was okay?”

She nodded. “She said she’ll be down in a few minutes.”

“Grand.”

They went out into the snow. And there was such a pure and simple pleasure in it. In playing out there, with a happy, healthy child. Showing her how to roll a fat snowball across the garden as it gathered snow to it, to compress it into shape, and roll it again until the snow underneath crunched with the weight. When it was big enough, they found a good spot for it, right in front of the living room window. Then they gathered handfuls of snow and packed it on to make it fatter and taller. By then the snow had soaked through Tilly's gloves and she had peeled them off, abandoned them in the snow. Anna had come to the window, watched them for a while, then disappeared. Tilly was satisfied to leave the rolling of the head to him, but she ran into the house to request a carrot and the three lumps of coal with great enthusiasm. The carrot was the nose, of course, and the coal worked well for three buttons down the tummy. They found stones for eyes, and Cormac sacrificed his own scarf. Then they stood back to admire him.

"He needs a hat," she said. "You can't have a snowman without a hat."

"True enough," Cormac nodded. He made a show of feeling around on the top of his head. "I don't have one for him," he said. "Should we ask Peter? Maybe he'll give us his garda hat, and we can make him a police-snowman."

All the excitement and pleasure of the moment drained out of Tilly's face. Just fell away from her as if it had been shot and had fallen to earth at her feet. She looked . . . numb. As frozen as the icy creature they had built together.

"Are you all right?" he asked.

She nodded stiffly.

"Did something I said frighten you?" he asked. "I didn't mean to say anything that would upset you."

She shook her head. "It's not your fault," she said, and he could see the effort it cost her. "I didn't used to like policemen. But Peter's a policeman, and I like him. Mam says that he's different from the others." She flicked her eyes in his direction, just like she had at the beginning of the day. "Are you like Peter too?"

"I am, I think," Cormac said, very carefully. "At least, I'm a garda, like him. My job is to look after people, to keep them safe. You don't need to be afraid of me, or Peter either."

She nodded, but it was the nod of a child trying to please

an adult. There was no conviction behind it. The joy had gone out of the activity and her hands were red and cold-looking. "Should we go in and have a bit of breakfast?" he asked. "We can ask your mum and Peter to help us finish our snowman later."

She ran off like she'd been released from a trap, and Cormac followed more slowly behind.

Cormac told himself that he would have figured it out much faster if he hadn't been wrecked from the drive, and if he hadn't arrived right in the middle of the Richard Barrett drama. Anna Collins and her daughter, Tilly—or Matilda—had arrived in Roundstone a couple of months ago. At exactly the same time that Niall Collins's sister and niece had disappeared from Dublin. What an outrageous coincidence, that he should stumble across them here. Over breakfast, he watched Anna, looked for facial similarities to Niall Collins, and found very little. Where Niall was pinch-faced and too thin, Anna was rounded and healthy. Where Niall was haunted and afraid to the point of paranoia, Anna seemed confident and comfortable in her own skin, if a little quiet. Though he suspected that there was a reason for that. Now that he was paying closer attention, he noticed how watchful she was. She hid it well, but she was hyper-aware of him, of Peter, of the flow of conversation. Anna may not be as obviously terrified as Niall Collins, but she was frightened all the same. And he needed to know why.

"I've been in with Maggie," Peter said, as he arrived down late for breakfast. "She seems much better this morning." He cast a look at Tilly, but she seemed to be off in a dreamworld of her own, paying little attention to the conversation. "I haven't said anything yet, and she hasn't asked me anything Have you spoken to her about it all yet, Anna?"

"Not yet," Anna shook her head. "Maybe we should wait a few days, until she feels better."

Peter sat and poured himself a cup of tea, buttered some toast.

"Jesus," he said. "My head is splitting."

"No sympathy for the self-induced," Anna said.

Peter laughed. "Fair enough," he said.

Before breakfast was finished, Tilly, who had clearly had enough of adult conversation, stood and disappeared into the living room. She found a coloring book on the coffee table and set to work in front of the television. Once Cormac was sure she was settled in, he stood to close the door between kitchen and living room, then returned to the table. Anna looked up straight away and her whole body stilled, as if she knew what was coming.

"So, Anna," Cormac said. "What brought you to Galway?"

She shrugged. "We needed a fresh start. Dublin wasn't the right place for us."

Cormac glanced toward the living room door. "Tilly seems like a very happy child," he said.

"She wasn't always," Anna said. Her hand tightened around her cup.

"No?" Cormac asked.

Peter looked at him, eyes narrowing. He'd picked up on the shift in the tone of the conversation.

Anna shook her head. "No," she said. She straightened up in her chair. "But all that's behind us now. And we're never going back. We'll stay here, if that's what Maggie wants. Or I'll find another place close by, but we're not going back to Dublin."

"I understand," Cormac said. "I met your brother, you know. Just a couple of days ago. He's doing all right. He's living in a squat in Clontarf, with a friend. I just thought you'd like to know."

Terror bloomed in Anna's eyes. She pushed her chair back and stood up, almost falling over in her haste to put distance between them.

Cormac reached a hand out to her. "It's all right, Anna," he said. "This isn't what you think it is."

"What does she think it is?" Peter asked, his face a picture of confusion. He was half-standing too. He'd moved instinctively, turning his body so that it was between Cormac and Anna, sheltering her.

Cormac chose his words very carefully. "I think Anna and Tilly had a very frightening encounter with some very bad people, in Dublin. People who know Anna's brother, Niall. People who maybe use her brother." Cormac was watching her face, reading her as best he could, looking for confirmation that he had it right. "At least one of those people was a garda. Anna's given me the benefit of the doubt, up until just a minute ago. But now she's wondering if I'm one of them. If by mentioning her brother, Niall, I was actually threatening her. Isn't that right, Anna?"

Anna nodded slowly. She was still standing, but Peter sank back into his chair.

"You don't know me, Anna," Cormac said. "You've no reason to trust me. But I think you trust Peter. And Peter has known me for a long time, he'll vouch for me. I know that there are corrupt gardaí in this country. I've been working to try to take them down, to try to send them to prison for what they've done. If you can trust me enough to tell me your story, I'll do everything I can to help you and to help your brother."

He could see her thinking about it, weighing his words, and what she'd seen of him the evening before, trying to decide. She would be afraid for her daughter, for Niall.

"Please, Anna," Peter said.

She closed her eyes.

"I wasn't there," she said, eventually.

"You weren't where?" Peter asked.

"I wasn't there when it happened." She opened her eyes again. "But Tilly was."

She told them her story. The premature death of their mother. Her grandmother's decision to take them in, and then, a few years later and just as abruptly, to reject them. Niall's slow descent into drug addiction. His entanglement with the gang. The little favors that started small and built and built.

"Niall got clean." Anna was very tense but her voice was clear and strong and her eyes were dry. "It was so hard. But he loved Tilly very much and he got clean for her. He pulled back from the gang. He didn't outright refuse them, he's not stupid, he just stayed inside as much as he could, stayed out of sight. We were going to try to get away together, all of us. I was just working, putting the money away so we'd have enough."

"What happened?" Cormac asked.

Anna swallowed. "One night, at the very beginning of summer, I was at work. Some men came by while I was out. Two of them were . . . people Niall used to know. Used to work for."

"And one of them was a garda," Cormac said.

Anna nodded. "They brought someone with them. A man like Niall. An addict. Someone they weren't very happy with. They brought him there to show Niall. To show him what happens when you make them angry."

"They killed him, didn't they?" Cormac asked quietly.

"They shot him. He did it. The garda. Right there in the living room. Tilly saw it. She was in her room, but I think she came running when she heard the shot. She saw the body, saw them roll it up in my rug and carry it away. Niall told me later that they buried it in the back of an industrial estate, just around the corner. When I got home, Niall was in a state, there was blood everywhere, all over the carpet. He'd put Tilly to bed, but he was in shock. He wasn't able to comfort her. And then he took off. They'd left him a little packet of heroin, as a welcome back gift. He took that with him."

Silence hung between them for a long moment.

"Jesus, Anna," Peter said. He couldn't seem to find the words.

"They taught us a lesson, all right," she said. "You don't cross the McGraths."

"Do you know the name of the garda? The one who did the shooting?"

"Yes," Anna said. Her hands were trembling now. What a risk she was taking, in telling them all this.

"I think I know who it was," Cormac said. "But I need you to tell me."

And then, just as he'd known she would, Anna opened her mouth and said the name.

"Trevor Murphy."

"Jesus Christ," Peter said. He stood up, paced the room.

"You knew him," Cormac said.

Anna nodded. "Niall knew him, so I knew him. I'd seen him before."

"There are cameras all over your building," Cormac said. "They would have been recorded, entering and leaving your flat. Carrying the body."

She shrugged. "They didn't seem worried about it."

"They have to have switched them off," Peter said. "They must have control of them."

Of course they did. The cameras would be run by a private

security firm. The McGraths probably owned the fucking thing. Cormac rubbed his hand across his jaw. This. This was exactly what he had been afraid of. With gardaí as part of their own private army, the McGraths would be unstoppable. And he'd screwed it up so badly that he'd not only managed to lose his job, but all credibility along with it.

"I'll go to Dublin," Cormac said. "I still have friends, contacts. I'll see if there's anything I can track down." He wasn't going to ask Anna to give a statement. The way things were, it would be a death sentence, for her and her daughter. He would need other evidence. There were options. An anonymous tip to the right person might get them out digging at that industrial estate, for starters.

"Anna, what is it?" Peter said, like he thought she had something left to tell.

She was looking at her hands, her face very still.

"I love my brother," she said. "And I trust him. Really, I do." She lifted her head. "But when you're an addict, you're not always the one making the decisions. Sometimes, you let the drugs do that for you."

Anna stood up. She went over to the kitchen counter, where her handbag had been sitting. She reached inside and took something out, put it on the table in front of them. It was a memory card.

"I had to leave Tilly with Niall every night when I went to work. I was worried. He was doing well, but what if he went back on the drugs? I mightn't have realized straight away."

"You got a camera," Cormac said. He couldn't stop staring at the little square of plastic on the table.

"They call them nanny cams. You just plug it into the wall, like an air freshener. When someone moves, it starts recording."

"Have you looked at it?" Cormac asked.

She nodded.

"And?"

"It's all there."

Half an hour later, Cormac was ready to go. The snow had finally stopped, though the roads were still horrendous, but he couldn't wait with this. He needed to get to Dublin now, today. This time there would be no messing around. He was going straight to the Commissioner. He'd loaded the memory card onto his own phone and watched the video. All the evidence he needed was on that little card. He said goodbye to Anna and Tilly inside and shook Peter's hand on the doorstep.

"You'll need to stay here," he said. "Once I get to Dublin, things will kick off. Keep them safe. No one knows they're here, so I'm sure everything will be fine, but just in case."

Peter looked troubled, but he nodded.

"You'll keep me posted?" he asked now, as Cormac took his leave.

Cormac nodded. "As soon as I can, though I'll have to stay off the phone for the time being. This may move very quickly."

"It might be a long road," Peter said. "Unpicking the threads, figuring out who was involved and who wasn't."

"Yes," Cormac said. "But we'll get them all, Peter. Every last one of them." He was absolutely sure of it. Cormac looked back at the house once more. Meeting Anna had been a stroke of good luck that he hadn't deserved. He wasn't going to let her down. "Thank her for me again, will you? She was the key to everything in the end."

CHAPTER THIRTY-SEVEN

After Cormac left, Peter returned to the kitchen. He cleaned up after breakfast, thinking all the time. Anna brought some breakfast up to Maggie, came back downstairs in a lighter mood.

"She's eating her toast," Anna said. "She said she wants a cake for afternoon tea."

Peter smiled at her. "That's brilliant. Are you any good at baking?"

"I'm terrible," she said. "The worst."

"Ah well, you can't be good at everything."

She gave him a crooked smile. "What about you?"

He closed one eye, screwed up his face in an exaggerated effort of thought. "I can make a pretty solid chocolate sponge cake thing. Particularly if it's from a box."

She laughed at him. "Well, you'd better go shopping then."

"I will," he said. "I'll walk down into the village, see if I can get my car moving. Worst case, I'll pick up a few bits from Horan's, be back in an hour."

Peter took his time walking into the village. He wasn't the only one out and about. A man with a shovel helped him dig his car out. The damage to the front was worse than he'd thought, but it was driveable at least. He went on to Horan's. Sharon was dealing with a line at the till, and the shelves were already half empty. He filled his basket with whatever he thought would be useful, including one Decadent Chocolate Cake boxed mix—"Just add one egg." He paid for his shopping and walked outside. He thought about Anna waiting back at the house, hesitated, then pressed on, very carefully, to the station.

Des was still there, at his desk, drinking coffee. He looked like he was feeling every pint he'd sunk the night before.

"About bloody time," he said.

Peter leaned against the doorjamb and looked at his father. "No Jim today?" he asked.

"He'll be here," Des growled. "In the meantime, I haven't had a bite to eat all morning, except a few bloody biscuits. You took your time."

Peter nodded. "You know," he said. "It occurs to me that you never told me the full story about how you came to meet Anna."

Des looked up sharply. "I told you."

"No," Peter said. "You didn't." And he stared his father down.

Des held his gaze for a long time, and then his face flushed and his chin rose in anger.

"What is your problem?"

"It never really made sense to me. You aren't the kind of man who does something out of the kindness of your heart. For you it's all about tallying it up. All your little favors."

Des shook his head. "You know, Peter, you talk some amount of shite."

"She was followed, wasn't she? From Dublin. And you got a phone call. Someone asked you to keep an eye on her, to report back and you did exactly what you were told. You packed Anna and Tilly off to Maggie's and you watched them, and it never occurred to you to ask why. You never wondered, Des, who you were working for, when you did that good turn?"

Des's eyes were opaque now, all expression wiped from his face.

"A bunch of murderous fucking drug dealers, and their corrupt friends. That's who."

Des shook his head, an instinctive rejection.

"Oh yes," Peter said. "Yes, indeed."

"That's rubbish. I kept an eye on them, yes, for a friend. The same friend I called when I needed to get you out of trouble."

"Brian Murphy," Peter said. "Who is as corrupt as it gets and a puppet for the McGraths. But you knew that, didn't you, Des?"

Des was rocked by that, by the McGrath name, and maybe by Peter's confidence. Peter felt like a different person today. In control.

"You didn't care," Peter said. "You should be very grateful that the McGraths were happy with what they heard when you made your little reports. If they hadn't been, they would have sent a man down to kill Anna and Tilly, and probably Maggie too while they were at it. And what would you have done then?"

"You're making this up," Des said. He waved a hand. "All this shit about the McGraths. That's all bullshit. Just one of your fantasies."

Peter jerked his head toward the cell at the back of the station. "Just like that was one of my fantasies?"

Des fell silent.

"Did you talk to Barrett last night?" Peter asked.

Des hesitated. "I did," he said eventually.

"What did he tell you?

"Enough." Des blinked, looked down at his hands, his half-empty coffee cup. "He claims Miles set him up. That Miles spread the rumor about the rezoning to entice him into the deal, all the while playing the naive country farmer. It might be true. Once the contracts were signed and the deposits paid, the truth came out. The rezoning was never going to happen. Barrett was in trouble. He'd overextended, planned on borrowing at least half the money to complete the deals, and the bank wouldn't have a bar of it once the land value tanked. He would have had to sell his house to honor the deal on the farms. And everyone would know that he'd tried to take advantage of Miles and instead he'd been played. He was humiliated and he was furious. Afraid that he was about to lose his home and his reputation. He lashed out."

"If it's true, the con only worked because he was greedy. He thought he was the one fooling them."

Des nodded. He was silent for a long moment. Then, eventually, he said, "About Anna. I didn't know. I didn't know about the McGraths. At least, I didn't know everything."

Peter nodded. He could almost feel sorry for his father, if it weren't for the fact that he was the thin edge of the wedge.

"Go home," Peter said. "Go home and sleep it off."

Des stood up, very slowly. "What are you going to do?" he asked.

"I'm going to clean it all up," Peter said. "Every last bit."

CHAPTER THIRTY-EIGHT

Galway, Ireland

Deirdre Russell sat at her desk in the squad room of Mill Street Station, a sinking sensation in her stomach. To her left was Rory Mulcair. He was leaning forward, filling her in on all the gossip. "They took Healy in yesterday," Rory was saying, his voice pitched low. What he was telling her might be a secret, officially, but a glance around the squad room told them that they ran a very little risk of being overheard. Every other garda present was also deep in conversation with someone, almost certainly about the same topic. "He's in the cells now. And the super's leading the interview."

"I don't understand," Deirdre said. "You said Sergeant Reilly was there. At the incinerator?"

"Yeah, but he wasn't supposed to be," Rory said. "Moira says he's deep in the shit now. Apparently he had some side op going on, off the books, while he was on suspension. Some cobbled-together thing with a few old cronies."

She shot him a look and Rory held up a hand. "Her words, not mine."

"So what happened then?" Deirdre asked.

"The super had words with him, Moira said. She says Reilly's definitely screwed now. There's no way he's coming back from suspension after this."

"Oh Jesus." Deirdre felt like she might be sick.

"What?" Rory said, leaning in closer. "What's wrong?"

It was her fault. She'd told Reilly about Anthony Healy and Trevor Murphy's plans for the incinerator. It was because of her that Reilly had been there. Deirdre thought back to Thursday morning. The information about the planned drug destruction had come to her from the superintendent's office. Brian Murphy's aide had come to her desk and asked that she make herself available to provide additional support to the task force, if required, during Anthony Healy and Trevor Murphy's absence from the station. The aide then made a point of telling her the reason for the absence. But there'd never been any need for any additional assistance, had there . . . and no reason in the world for the aide to explain why Healy and Murphy would be in Dublin for a few days.

"It was a setup," she said.

"Yeah," said Rory, looking puzzled. "That's what I said."

"You don't get it," Deirdre said. She felt like she might cry. Reilly gone, never coming back. The black mark against Peter Fisher's name never to be lifted. And that wasn't even the worst of it. There was no one now to carry forward the investigation into Jason Kelly and Francis Loughnane. Loughnane had known about the abduction, she was sure of that. Whatever fate they'd had planned for Peggah Abbassi, Loughnane had been part of it. And what would he do now? Lay low for a while, certainly. But as the months passed and no one knocked on his door, would he look around for a new target? Maybe not. It was possible that his involvement had been peripheral. Maybe he'd never have done anything without Jason Kelly to talk to, to bond with. Maybe even with Kelly he'd only been a bystander. But deep down she didn't believe it, and she couldn't rely on it.

"Where's Moira?" she asked.

"Moira Hanley?" Rory asked. He looked around. "I don't know. She was here earlier."

Deirdre stood up. She couldn't live with this.

She felt a bit shaky, but she was determined not to show it. She took her jacket from the back of her chair. "I've an interview to do," she said, as casually as she could manage. "Moira asked me to follow up on a loose end. Do you want to come along and give me a hand? I could do with someone to take notes."

Rory looked pleased. He stood up quickly. "I've got some time," he said.

They took a squad car from the basement. Deirdre let Rory drive, directing as they went. It would be better if he was distracted. She made sure of it by keeping him on the topic of Anthony Healy's arrest, encouraging him to speculate on who else might be involved. The roads were well gritted and traffic was light. The conversation continued right up to the moment that they pulled in outside Jason Kelly's house. They got out of the car. Rory started up the path toward Kelly's front door, where blue and white garda tape had come loose and was fluttering in the wind.

"Not that one," Deirdre said. She walked up Loughnane's drive and Rory followed.

"A neighbor?" Rory said. "A witness?"

She pressed the doorbell. "Something like that," she said.

The door was opened by a man in his late fifties. He had curly gray hair at his temples, a nose that was too small for his face, and lips so thin they'd almost disappeared.

"Can I help you?" he said.

Deirdre flashed her ID at him. "Garda Deirdre Russell," she said. "And this is my colleague, Garda Rory Mulcair. Do you have a few minutes, Mr. Loughnane? We've just a few loose ends we need to tidy up?" She smiled at him as sweetly as she could manage and he relaxed a little.

"About Jason?" he asked. "I don't know if there's anything more I can tell you, but whatever I can do to help."

Deirdre shivered, glanced toward the sky. "If we could talk inside, that would be brilliant."

He stepped back, held the door for them, then led the way into a neat living room. The furniture was blandly matching and everything was very clean and tidy. There was a fire burning in the grate and a movie paused on the TV.

"Not working today?" Deirdre asked.

"No, well, the weather's too bad for it," Loughnane said chattily. "I'm doing a bit of roofing work at the moment, for a developer out on Clybaun Road. We haven't worked all week. Can't say I'm sorry." He took a seat on the couch and gestured toward the armchairs. "Can I get you a drink or anything?"

Deirdre took a seat in one of the armchairs and Rory took the other. "We won't be with you long, Mr. Loughnane. As I said, we're just following up a few loose ends from the investigation into the abduction of Peggah Abbassi."

"Right, right. Well. Anything I can do to help." Loughnane spread his hands, the picture of relaxed cooperation.

Suddenly, Deirdre felt panicked. She should have given this a few minutes' thought, at least. She wasn't sure where to start, was conscious of Rory sitting in the other chair. He'd taken out a notebook, but he was obviously relaxed, not expecting anything more than a few softball questions and a quick departure. Deirdre took a breath.

"How well did you know Jason Kelly?" she asked.

"Not well at all, I'm afraid."

"You lived next door to him for the last few years. Is that correct?"

Loughnane shrugged. "Longer. I bought this place back in 1992, before the boom went bananas. Kelly moved in a couple of years later, I think, but I don't remember the exact date. He was renting."

"Did you spend time together? Maybe head to the pub for a drink every now and again? Call over to watch a match?"

Loughnane wrinkled his nose. "It wasn't like that. We'd nod hello if we were bringing out the bins. We had a chat once because one of the neighbors—number four—rented their house out to a bunch of students and after the third party we'd all had enough. Someone called you lot, actually, to the last one, to break it up. Jason and I had a chat about that, about whether or not the students had moved out. Other than that one conversation I don't think we ever exchanged more than a few words."

Loughnane was all confidence. He was bouncy with it.

Deirdre allowed a look of confusion to cross her face. She retrieved her own notebook from her jacket pocket, leafed through a few pages, looked back at Loughnane. "You didn't phone each other? Didn't exchange text messages?"

"No," Loughnane said. He was a good liar. His only tell was that his facial expression, which had been very animated, stilled.

"And you never worked together?"

"No."

"And just to confirm, Mr. Loughnane, am I right in thinking that you live here alone? You're not married, are you? No girlfriend? Boyfriend?"

"No. I mean, that's right. I live alone. I'm not in a relationship."

Deirdre smiled at him, a small bit of reassurance. "That's what I thought," she said. "So any phone calls or messages sent from this house to Jason Kelly. If they were sent from this house, they'd have to have been sent by you, wouldn't they?"

Loughnane's whole body had stilled now. He was being careful . . . trying to think ahead and consider which of the possible answers would help him and which would box him into a corner. He was wondering what Deirdre could possibly know, trying to figure out if she was bluffing. But while all those thoughts ran through his head, while he tried to be clever, his body gave him away. The silence had gone on a little too long now. Deirdre raised an eyebrow, and Loughnane felt the pressure.

"I . . . I'm not sure what you mean."

Rory was sitting forward now, paying much closer attention.

Speaking slowly and carefully, Deirdre asked the question again.

"I'm just asking you to confirm that if calls or text messages were sent from this house, no one else could have sent them? You haven't had any regular guests, or anyone to stay for a few nights in the last six months, for example?"

"Well, I've had the odd guest. I mean, six months is a long time. I don't remember everyone I've had to stay off the top of my head."

Loughnane's eyes were fixed to Deirdre's face, trying very hard to read her, to figure out what she knew.

Deirdre wanted him off balance. She smiled at him warmly.

"You don't know who you've had to stay?" she asked. "Jesus, I could count on one hand the number of people I would invite into my home, to stay overnight. My sisters, sure. A couple of old friends from college. That's about it. But you're different, are you, Mr. Loughnane? You like a lot of company?"

Loughnane was flushing a little now. "Well, I wouldn't go that far. But I do have guests from time to time."

"But not strangers," Deirdre said. "You wouldn't let a stranger stay in your house."

Loughnane hesitated, but Deirdre's obvious incredulity drove him to an answer. "No," he said.

Deirdre nodded. "That's good," she said. "So, give me a few names. The dates don't have to be exact, just approximates will do. I can call everyone to check. Probably some people keep diaries. Or they'll be able to check back over their text messages, see when you made arrangements. Phones are so handy like that. All that information, at our fingertips."

"I'm not sure . . . I can't recall . . . my sister might have been down. With my mother, at Easter."

Deirdre nodded again, made a show of noting the information down in her notebook. She took the sister's name, the mother's, both phone numbers. "Great," she said. She allowed her brow to furrow. "But I'm really thinking about someone who might have been here a lot. Regularly. Day in, day out type thing. You can't think of anyone who fits that bill?"

Loughnane shook his head slowly. The confidence with which he'd started the conversation had slowly deserted him.

"Right," Deirdre said. "So it's just you then." She turned a page in her notebook. "Talk to me about the gym. How was it that you came to be working there?"

"I'm sorry?"

"The gym. Sorry, let me just . . ." Deirdre flicked back a page, read out loud. "Rocket Gymnastics, on the Ballymoneen Road. Am I right in thinking you've done a bit of work there?" She raised her head, wrinkled her forehead as if she was unsure of herself. She was fishing, actually. They knew Jason Kelly had worked at Rocket Gymnastics—Cormac Reilly had found that out at the very beginning. The gym owner had since admitted that Kelly had brought another man on the job with him on at least one occasion. It would be a deeply stupid move on Loughnane's part to confirm that he had spent time at the gym, but she had him scrambling now, certain that she knew something, but not sure how much. Assuming the second man had been Loughnane, he would be thinking about the times he visited the gym, wondering who could have seen him, realizing that it was possible that he had been seen. With the number of cameras around these days—all those private security cameras that people could buy for half nothing—he could even be on film. He would decide it would be too risky to deny it. He would need a plausible explanation.

"No. I . . . uh, I didn't work there, in the end, but I did swing by. Do you know, I had forgotten all about it? I'm sure you hear that a lot." He gave a nervous laugh. "But in my case, it's the truth, of course. I bumped into Jason outside one day." He gave a nod toward the front window that looked out on the street. "He asked me if I was interested in helping him finish a bit of work he was doing at the gym. I dropped by one afternoon and had a look."

Deirdre nodded, as if that made sense, and slowly, slowly, took notes. "Right. And what date was that?"

"I'm not sure. I'm sorry, but I can't remember."

"That's all right," Deirdre said. "Could it have been in August? Late August?"

Loughnane grimaced. "That could be right. I'm sorry, I wish I could be sure, but I'd almost forgotten about it entirely."

"What went wrong?" Rory asked. He was staring fixedly at Loughnane. Deirdre wanted to stand up and pat him on the back. He was listening, and he was on her side.

"Sorry?" Loughnane said.

"With the work. Why didn't you do the work?"

"Uh . . . the best I can remember is that it was some carpentry work, and I think I felt the quote wasn't high enough. You know, Jason was a bit of an odd-job man. He did a bit of everything. But I'm a qualified carpenter and I can earn more working for developers. Doing bigger jobs."

Deirdre nodded. "It's a pity he didn't tell you that before he dragged you over there."

"Right, well, I suppose I might have been passing. I don't remember it as a big deal."

"Sure," Deirdre said, finally allowing her skepticism to show.

Loughnane gathered himself, clearly deciding that umbrage might be a better tack to take. "Look, this is all very odd. Jason Kelly was my neighbor, that's it. I don't understand all these questions. Should I . . . I mean, I don't know, this all sounds ridiculous. But I feel like I should be calling my lawyer."

"Do you have a lawyer, Mr. Loughnane?" Deirdre asked.

"I'm sure I can find one."

Deirdre looked at Rory Mulcair, then back at Loughnane. "That's a decision at your absolute discretion, Mr. Loughnane. But while you're having a think about that, and just to ensure that everything is covered, Garda Mulcair here will caution you."

Loughnane reacted like Deirdre had slapped him. His expression was of mortal offense. "I . . . but this is all totally unnecessary. I don't understand what it is you're trying to say."

Rory spoke in a monotone. "You are not obliged to say anything unless you wish to do so, whatever you say will be taken down in writing and may be given in evidence."

"Look, there's no need to get formal. I'm happy to answer your questions. I just don't know what it is you're hoping to achieve. Jason is dead, isn't he? The girl he took is at home safe with her family. And I had nothing to do with any of it. If I could help you, I would. Of course I would."

"Do you have a second phone, Mr. Loughnane?" Deirdre asked.

Loughnane shifted in his seat. "What?"

"It's a simple question. I've asked if you have a second mobile phone. I know you have a mobile phone registered to your name." She read out the number. "Do you also own a second phone, a pay-as-you-go phone, that you used to communicate with Jason Kelly?"

"I . . . I don't know what you're talking about."

"You didn't send a text message to Jason Kelly on any of the following dates?" Deirdre called out a list of dates taken from the data filter.

Loughnane shook his head. "No. No. That wasn't me."

"On all of the dates I've mentioned, messages were sent to Kelly from a mobile phone that was in this house."

"You're lying," Loughnane said. "You can't tell that. You can't tell exactly where a mobile phone is located. I mean, the general area, maybe, but not the house. Those messages could have been sent by anyone around here."

"Ah, that's not going to work, Mr. Loughnane." Deirdre shook her head, all regret, as if she had been rooting for him all along and hated to give him the bad news. "The trouble is, you made a bit of a mistake. Did you carry both phones around with you all the time? Your normal phone and your secret phone?" She waited. "I can see from your face that you did. Both phones left an electronic trail, you see. We can track the historic movement of your registered phone as it moves about the city, as you go to work, to the pub, to the cinema. As you go home. The thing is, the mystery phone leaves the exact same electronic trail. Exactly. Down to a couple of feet. Down to the second. Isn't that interesting?"

"That doesn't mean anything," Loughnane said. He looked like he was going to be sick.

"I've tried to think of another explanation," Deirdre said. She shrugged. "Couldn't come up with anything. Do you have any ideas?"

"Maybe . . . maybe someone followed me."

Deirdre frowned, looked down at his notebook, flicked

through the pages. "Followed you. To work every day. And home. For months?"

Loughnane said nothing.

Deirdre lowered her voice, spoke gently. "We've sent in a request for the text messages. That'll take a week or two. The phone companies are bloody slow, you know. It's not like on TV, where coppers get everything the minute they ask for them. It'll take a while. But we'll get them in the end. And when we do, what do you think we'll find? I'm sure you were careful, but it's hard to be careful for weeks, months, when you're discussing something you both feel . . . strongly about."

Rory was staring at Loughnane, couldn't keep the disgust off his face, and Loughnane caught it. "I didn't do anything," he said. "I didn't take her. That was all Jason."

"But you called him that day, didn't you, Mr. Loughnane? You called him to let him know the police were looking for him?"

"I . . . no, I didn't."

"Are you sure about that? It's better to tell the truth, you know. Better if you cooperate now, when it counts, rather than later, when all the evidence is in and there's nowhere left to go."

Loughnane just sat there, looking back and forth between Deirdre and Rory, as if searching for a way out. Deirdre offered him one.

"Kelly was very charismatic," she said. "The kind of man who could lead you down a path you'd never go down yourself. It might have been easy to think that he didn't mean what he said. That it was all a fantasy. You might not have realized that he meant it all until he actually took her. Was that how it was?"

Loughnane's eyes locked on Deirdre's. He opened his mouth to speak, was teetering on the edge of a confession. "I didn't think he was serious," he said. "I swear. I thought it was all just fantasy. Until he took her."

Deirdre kept her expression as neutral as she could, suppressing the blazing surge of triumph that she felt. She clenched one fist until her knuckles tightened, down by her side where he couldn't see it.

"Why don't you tell me all about it, Mr. Loughnane? And we'll see what we can do for you."

"I'm telling you, it was all just fantasy, as far as I was concerned. I never for a second thought he was serious. And I thought she was older, too. Sixteen, at least. I'd never be interested in a child in that way. I'm not a pervert."

After that, the floodgates opened. Loughnane confessed to a prolonged conversation with Jason Kelly leading right up to the abduction. It was Kelly who had seen Peggah first. He'd described her in detail to Loughnane. He'd talked about taking her. Loughnane claimed again that he'd thought it was just talk. But he confessed to calling Kelly immediately after speaking with Peter on the day of the abduction, tipping him off. Reilly had been right all along. It was that call that prompted Kelly to dump Peggah on the side of the road, to drive on to the lake. He'd been planning on sinking his car into the water, to get rid of it and destroy any forensic evidence at the same time.

Deirdre stood up.

"Mr. Loughnane, I'd like you to come in to the station now," she said. "We'll take an official statement, in a little more detail, and we'll compare it to the evidence from the phone records. And we'll see where we go from there."

Loughnane nodded reluctantly. Where they would go from there was directly to a charge of conspiracy to kidnap. Some part of him must surely know that. Deirdre felt giddy with success and terrified that something could still go wrong. But Rory was there, taking his notes, his face flushed with anger and revulsion. Once they brought Loughnane in, Moira Hanley would have to follow the case through to its natural conclusion, and maybe Peter, at least, would be saved. Maybe that would make up in some way for what she had done when she had all but sent Reilly into a trap.

She walked Loughnane to the squad car, one hand on his shoulder, Rory following in her wake. Even if he never came back, she would track Cormac Reilly down and tell him about this. He deserved to know.

CHAPTER THIRTY-NINE

Dublin, Ireland

The house was on Erne Street in the south inner city of Dublin. Another Georgian terrace, but this one far from derelict. Cormac parked on the street outside the house and took a breath. He half-expected someone to come knocking on the window. Did Matheson have protection? During the Troubles, every garda commissioner had had a protection detail. Since the permanent ceasefire, the question of a protective detail had become a more flexible one, dependant on ongoing risk assessment and, to some degree, a commissioner's personal preference.

Kevin Matheson had been commissioner of An Garda Síochána for a little over a year. He had taken over when the previous incumbent had been discreetly bumped into early retirement due to some political scandal. Matheson was a career cop. He was an uncontroversial choice for the acting role, considered a safe pair of hands during the lengthy recruitment process that was required for a permanent appointment. There had been some surprise when Matheson had won the permanent role, though Cormac had seen it coming. He knew Matheson, if only slightly, and the man was a sharp operator.

Cormac clenched his fists for a moment, then gathered himself and got out of the car. It was near midnight and the street was empty. The house was in darkness. Cormac thought again about checking into a hotel, coming back in the early morning, but he had a real sense of urgency, as if delaying even an hour longer would cause disaster to unfold. He climbed the well-worn stone steps to the front door and pressed the bell. He waited with his back to the door, keeping his eyes on the street, checking both directions. He pressed the bell again. A minute later, he heard footsteps and a hall light went on. The door opened and Kevin Matheson was standing there. He was barefoot, wearing jeans and a T-shirt, and looked seriously pissed off.

"Commissioner, I'm sorry to wake you," Cormac said. "You may not recall but we worked together on a case a few years back. I'm—"

"I know who you are, Reilly," Matheson said. "The better part of my day was spent trying to resolve a mess you seem to have been knee-deep in. What are you doing on my front porch?"

Cormac held up the laptop. "There's something I need to show you, sir."

Matheson didn't look at the computer. He kept his eyes on Cormac's face. "I've been told, by people I should trust, that you've been running off-the-book operations fueled by paranoia and self-importance, that you've pulled others into your mess. You seem to be particularly good at getting officers to ignore their chain of command, getting them to do what you want them to. A cult of personality. That's not what policing is about."

"Sir, I don't think—"

"It's been recommended to me that you should be prosecuted for obstruction of a garda investigation, among other things. What are your thoughts on that?"

"Well, obviously, I don't agree," Cormac said, abandoning all attempts at careful civility. "And if you're half the cop I think you are, then you already know that those *people you should trust*, as you call them, are the last people who should have your ear."

There was a beat, a moment, where Cormac felt it could go either way, then Matheson stepped back and let him into the house. Matheson closed the door behind them and led the way into a small living room off the hall. It was sparsely but beautifully furnished, with polished hardwood floors, a wood-burning stove, a small couch, and a single armchair. Matheson sat and gestured to the other chair.

"I'll give you ten minutes," he said. "Use them wisely."

Cormac said nothing. The laptop was ready to go. He opened it, turned it so it faced Matheson, and pressed play.

"Yesterday there was a raid on the incinerator in Tullamore. You'll have been told it was the culmination of an undercover operation into corrupt garda activities by Sergeant Trevor Murphy. That is not true. This is a video of Trevor Murphy shooting and killing a man by the name of Cahir Dempsey. Dempsey was a low-level drug dealer for the McGrath crime family. He wanted to get out of that world. Murphy killed him to send a message to everyone involved that getting out wasn't an option. That talking would be punished."

Matheson was leaning forward, looking closely at the video, focused and taking it all in.

"Sir, I believe that there has been corruption of the Garda Síochána on a large scale, and that Trevor Murphy and Superintendent Brian Murphy have been at the center of that corruption for some years. I believe that they, and others, have been working hand in hand with the McGrath family to seize and resell drugs brought into the country by rival drug dealers. The story that Trevor Murphy was undercover is a convenient lie."

The video came to an end, and Matheson looked up at Cormac. "I know," he said.

There was a pause. "Sorry," Cormac said. "I don't understand."

"I know," Matheson said again. "Or . . . let me be clear. I've *suspected* for some time. But suspicion is easy. Proof, less so. This conspiracy, this corruption. It is more deeply rooted and more widely spread than I think you realize, Reilly." He put his head to one side. "Speaking of which, how did you know you could trust me? Or did you take steps, to put this video into other hands, in case I should make it magically disappear?"

Cormac smiled grimly. "I thought about the kind of person who could be induced or blackmailed into joining a drug gang," he said slowly. "And then I thought about you. And I decided you're just not that fucking stupid. Sir."

Matheson laughed briefly, a little huffed-out breath, quickly swallowed, and Cormac felt a knot of tension unravel.

"Well, the question remains, Reilly, what do we do about this? The challenges haven't gone away. If they've corrupted even Internal Affairs, and I believe that they have, how are we to police this?"

Cormac tapped the laptop. "Trevor Murphy is as venal and self-centered as they come. And we have him—lock, stock, and barrel—for murder. We need to find where the bodies are buried, literally. Bring him in, offer him something. Once the McGraths know we have him for murder, they're going to see him as a risk and they're going to want rid of him. General population in any prison in the country would be a death sentence for him. Offer him protection and he'll give us what we want. Christ, he'll be *motivated* to give us what we want. He'll be as keen as we are to expose every corrupt officer in the force because everyone who remains will be a threat to him."

"You think he'll turn on his father?"

"I don't think he'd even blink," Cormac said.

Matheson sat back in his chair. "This won't be easy," he said. "It's going to be a long, difficult haul, and afterward, a longer haul building up the force again."

"Yes," Cormac said.

"There were rumors that you might be contemplating an overseas move, before all of this went down."

"No."

"No?" Matheson said.

Cormac said nothing.

"That's good, then, if you're sure," Matheson said. "I need you here. There's work to be done."

EPILOGUE

Galway, Ireland

One month later, almost to the day, Cormac Reilly entered Mill Street Garda Station for the first time since Brian Murphy had suspended him. He wasn't alone. He had officers with him, officers handpicked by Kevin Matheson, men and women he'd grown to trust over the past weeks of quiet, focused work. Peter Fisher was with him too, quietly reclaimed weeks ago from his Roundstone assignment. Officially, Peter was on leave. Cormac could have done the work without him. He just hadn't wanted to. They climbed the stairs, then made their way through the squad room to the offices beyond. Heads turned as they walked. Dave McCarthy was there, Deirdre Russell. They exchanged a nod. Moira Hanley stood and watched them progress, a look of consternation on her face. Cormac didn't knock when they reached the office of the superintendent. Just opened the door.

"Brian Murphy, you are under arrest for conspiracy to pervert the course of justice. You are not obliged to say anything unless you wish to do so, but whatever you say will be taken down in writing and may be given in evidence."

Brian Murphy pushed his chair back from his desk, half-stood. "You're on suspension," he said. "Under investigation. Get out of my office."

"Fisher," Cormac said. He handed a set of handcuffs to the younger man. Peter took Brian Murphy by the arm, turned him forcefully, cuffed him, and patted him down all before Murphy could utter another word. Murphy bucked suddenly, kicking out.

"Get your fucking hands off me. You can't touch me. I'm going to have you put in the darkest hole of a cell that can be found in this country, do you hear me? You'll never be heard from again."

"Shut up," Cormac said. "Don't embarrass yourself."

Murphy seemed almost more shocked by that, by Cormac's confidence, than he was by the handcuffs.

"Don't tell me you never saw this day coming," Cormac said. "You never thought that you'd be caught? Come on, Brian. That someday you'd have to pay a price for it all?"

They'd done the work right. Had quietly exhumed the body of Trevor Murphy's victim from the industrial estate Anna had mentioned, found it still wrapped in the carpet from her apartment. Then, over the course of two short, sleepless days and nights, they'd made targeted arrests. One after another the dominoes fell, until they took Trevor Murphy from his apartment at two in the morning, brought him to a cell, and presented him with the watertight case they'd built against him. When he'd realized that there was no way out for him, he'd opened his mouth and spilled everything, in exchange for a guarantee to keep him safe in prison.

Cormac was still unclear on Brian's motivation. Anthony Healy had been the instigator, it seemed. He'd had a long and sordid arrangement with the McGraths, had been taking smaller bribes for years to look the other way at the right times. But Trevor Murphy had taken that petty corruption and had seen the potential. Over the past three years, he had recruited a police force within the police force, including his own father, all on the payroll of the biggest drug gang in the country. Cormac still wondered if Brian had gotten involved out of some sort of misplaced loyalty to his son or if he'd done it out of good old-fashioned greed. In the end, maybe the motivation didn't matter.

"You didn't wonder why Trevor's been so quiet over the past few days? He hasn't been quiet really, Brian. He hasn't been quiet at all."

Cormac walked Brian Murphy out through the squad room, his hand firmly on the older man's shoulder while Peter held Murphy's other arm. He was panicked and wild-eyed, unable to process what was happening to him and ready to make a bolt for it. Cormac half-expected to be challenged, that at least one officer would step forward and ask what the hell they were doing, handcuffing and marching the superintendent through the station. But nobody did. They stood back and watched. Cormac thought about what Matheson had said about the cult of personality and shuddered inwardly. He stopped at the door.

"Dave," he said.

Dave McCarthy stepped forward. Cormac showed him the warrant. "We're taking him to Salthill station," Cormac said. "He'll be questioned there. Special custody arrangements have been made."

"Right," Dave said. He was trying to avoid looking directly at Murphy, who had started to make small involuntary noises, like a trapped rat.

Cormac and Peter led Murphy downstairs, put him in the back of a squad car. Cormac was driving. Peter turned to look behind them as they drove away.

"Don't worry, Peter," Cormac said. "We'll be back."

AUTHOR'S NOTE

Beware! This note contains spoilers.

Roundstone is a real place. It's very pretty, with excellent pubs, fantastic food, and friendly people. I recommend a visit. The Roundstone in this book is not a real place. It's a hodgepodge of memories and made-up places, and it is populated with made-up people. I'm absolutely certain that the local doctors do not go around murdering their elderly patients, nor are the local gardaí corrupt or inept. I hope they will forgive the liberties I've taken in pursuit of a good story.

ACKNOWLEDGMENTS

Writing an acknowledgments section for a book is an incredible privilege. This is the third time I've had a chance to sit down and think about a book and think about all the people who helped me to make it. I have to admit, though, the last eighteen months flew by in a blur of children, life, writing, editing, promoting, and traveling, and I am at the end of it, looking back, and wondering if I can remember a single specific day of the whole process. Still, even if the writing of the book has become a blur, the thanking part is easy. Because the people you want to thank are always there, minding your back and propping you up and laughing and encouraging and living the blurred life right there with you.

So! Thank you to the readers. Thanks for loving a good story the same way I do. Thanks for your heart and your imagination and your generosity.

Thank you to my husband, Kenny. My best mate and my partner through thick and thin. Love you, K.

Thank you to my children, Freya and Oisín. For the funnies, the hugs, the drawings, the encouragement, and the love. Also for the introduction to the *Teen Titans*.

Thank you to my besties, Claire, Libby, and Sara, for being child-rearing experts, and just generally brilliant, generous, and interesting women who work so hard and still know how to have fun. Also for the introduction to the *Teen Titans*.

Thank you to my other bestie, Sara Foster, for always being willing to talk books, publishing, kids, and everything in between, and for having a sense of humor about it all, even on our grumpy days.

Thank you to my editor, Anna Valdinger, who is always there with a wise word or a joke and with immaculate timing, knows which is needed. Thank you to Rachel Dennis and Emma Rafferty, too, for all your hard work on *The Good Turn*.

Thank you to Alice Wood. Alice, you are a campaign manager extraordinaire. Thank you for all your hard work, your insight and your generosity of spirit. It's a privilege to work with you.

Thank you to the entire HarperCollins team, including James Kellow and Brigitta Doyle for your support, Darren Holt for your fantastic covers, and Tom Wilson, Darren Kelly and the entire sales team for everything that you do.

Thank you to all the booksellers and librarians I've met over the past couple of years, and to those I've yet to meet. I'm so grateful for all of your extraordinary support. Thank you for being the backbone of our industry.

And a deep and heartfelt thank you to my agent, Shane Salerno. Shane, I don't know what I did to deserve you (nothing, probably) but I feel extraordinarily lucky to have you as my agent. Thank you for your limitless support and for all the things you do, every day, that no one ever knows about but that make the difference between a book and a career. Also, for the jokes.